DEADLY DARKNESS

DEADLY DARKNESS

TSUNAMI PLOT TO DESTROY THE WEST COAST OF NORTH AMERICA

WILLIAM W. BENNETT

Auctorem House
276 5th Ave, Ste 704-2591
New York, NY 10001
www.auctoremhouse.com
Phone: 1 888-332-7718

Published by Auctorem House: 12/02/2025

ISBN: 978-1-968059-12-5(sc)
ISBN: 978-1-968059-13-2(e)

Library of Congress Control Number: 2025920934

To my children: Jeremy, Jeff, and Serena

Special thanks to my beloved wife, Cathy.

[7]But whatever things were gain to me, those things I have counted as loss for the sake of Christ. [8]More than that, I count all things to be loss in view of the surpassing value of knowing Christ Jesus my Lord, for whom I have suffered the loss of all things, and count them but rubbish so that I may gain Christ, [9]and may be found in Him, not having a righteousness of my own derived from the Law, but that which is through faith in Christ, the righteousness which comes from God on the basis of faith, [10]that I may know Him and the power of His resurrection and [11]the fellowship of His sufferings, being conformed to His death; in order that I may attain to the resurrection from the dead.

–Philippians 3:7-11 *NASB*

PROLOGUE

Junio, 1598

It was a typical June morning in the South Pacific as Captain Tabiendo watched the towering cumulonimbus clouds with a critical eye. It was raining again. In this part of the world it rained far too often for his taste. He wrinkled his nose at the smell of his armor, and the musty smell of his uniform, mingling together as a sour unpleasant odor of rust and sweat. Familiar odors, even if unpleasant were bearable. Once more he glanced back at the English ships. Smaller and lighter they were moving faster putting on more canvas, now that the wind had calmed.

His was one of the huge galleons boasting two decks of cannon numbering one hundred and twelve in all. But the ship was heavy, even without her cargo of precious gold and stone from the temples of the Inca and Mayan days of glory. Two thousand three hundred tons empty, she ran low in the water now, her cargo slowing her even more. Of the three English ships giving chase none equaled her in size or firepower, but they did not know that he carried little in the way of powder and shot and only a third of the cannon. At least he hoped they did not know or guess that fact. Yet he could not explain their boldness otherwise.

To make up for the weight of her cargo he had unloaded two-thirds of his cannon, shot, and most of his powder. Few dared to challenge the great Spanish warships on the open sea. The English must know what cargo he carried. Grunting in disgust as warm rainwater poured from his helmet and ran down his back and into his trunk hose he turned to look forward.

Steam seemed to rise from the ocean and it seethed, even as the two English ships in the lead came alongside, and suddenly the heat was unbearable. Men opened their mouths to scream and died as the heat seared their lungs. Fire burst from the sea all around them. Behind them, Captain Dodd stared in horror as the ships disappeared in a wall of fire.

"Ready about!" He screamed. "Keep to your posts you louts or we join them! Hard alee!" He ordered.

Men ran to their posts, pulled on the sheets, as the ship ponderously turned into the wind. The roar behind them filled their ears and a hot blast of wind seemed to hurl the ship forward. For a moment Dodd thought the masts would be uprooted and swore the deck buckled beneath his feet. Then they were running swiftly before the wind. Wind! It was hurricane strength! From the expressions on the faces of his men he knew the horror that lay behind and prayed that his ship would outrun death this day.

It was the island that saved them. Tacking around the eastern end of the island a smoking volcano parted the heat wave that washed over them. In seconds his throat was parched but he continued to bark orders. At last the roaring and heat passed over them and died down.

"Set a course south!" He ordered. "Hug the coast of the Americas when we reach them. At the first sign of fresh water we send the longboats to shore!" He turned then and looked up at the sky behind them, wondering at the huge gray cloud that seemed to rise forever. He had never witnessed a volcano at sea before, and hoped he never saw another. The sheer power of nature was frightening!

Months passed as they sailed south, hugging the coast of what would one day be known as South America. Each day Dodd returned to his log to read the account of that fiery disaster off the tropical islands. Soon the days grew colder, and the sea rougher as they approached Drake's Passage.

Dodd realized that they were far off course and in the midst of a wild storm that left the pilot blind in snow and ice, and it drove the ship sideways more than forwards so he knew that his ship might well be lost. After his final look at the log he wrote the following words, not knowing into what deadly darkness he would plunge future seafaring men and women.

Are we being punished for our greed? Was the cargo of that galleon cursed because it belonged to the Devil's own? I am packing this log in an oilcloth, a leather valise, and a well-oiled leather sack, and sealing it in a tar coated box. I do not think we will survive the savage storm that has thrown us so far off course. Perhaps in time this will come to light and men will know how God punished us for our greed, and how the El Dorado Espanola, Merryweather, and Guided Star perished in a fiery sea. May God have mercy on our souls and the souls of all who perished in that fiery portal to hell. Amen.

Dodd squinted into the driving snow, shivering with cold as the savage winds pushed his ship further south. More and more ice flows appeared and the solid thunk of wood against ice made him wince. Two of his men dropped, frozen to death, but they were at the bow, and he could not see them. Suddenly the ship seemed to rise up, and the sound of shrieking and breaking wood reached Dodd. He fell, sliding into the railing as the ship stopped and began to heel over, striking his head hard enough to keep him down.

Huge waves broke over the stern, seeming to freeze even as they landed on the deck. Dodd lay stunned, grew tired, became so warm he vainly tried to shed his cloak, and eventually drowned and then froze solid as more and more ice piled upon and around the ship.

Three hundred and fourteen years would pass before anyone discovered the ship, frozen in the ice of Antarctica. Almost fourteen years would pass again before the unopened tar-covered box would be offered up for sale at an auction. Though none could explain why, no one opened it to see what lay inside. In those days, boxes covered in tar usually contained clothing or paper goods that one wanted to keep dry. Almost every part of the ship had been recovered and most of the artifacts sold or donated to maritime museums. The box was one of the few things that went last, a treasure undiscovered.

Andrea Orvieto had a feeling about that box. He smiled at his beautiful wife Rosa, and he lowered his number card with a sense of anticipation. The box now belonged to him, for a surprisingly low price of three hundred and twenty-seven dollars. Fitting price, he later thought to himself, for that was the number of years that passed while it remained sealed. His had been the only bid over three hundred and twenty-five dollars. Even he did not know what adventures it would bring, but he was a collector of pieces of maritime disasters. Once his good friend Alistair Gregg opened the box they would see if his instincts were right. Even as he thought it, he knew, deep inside, that he had something valuable. Rosa sensed his excitement and squeezed his hand.

Present Day

Merlin Bahdijn waited patiently for the secure phone connection to be made. Moments later the voice of Abu Kareem al-Jameel ibn Nidh'aai answered.

"Greetings revered one." Bahdijn said respectfully. "I am assured a place on the President's Cabinet. He loves my ideas on making FEMA more efficient. The President elect sends his sincere regards and thanks for your contributions to his campaign. This is the one we've been waiting for, a man completely corrupt, who will do anything for money and power."

"He is to know nothing of our plans." Kareem said quietly.

"To be sure. Admiral Jacks also knows only the small part he is to play. Now especially, revered one, we must be silent and careful, for patience is finally rewarded! Our day arrives!" Bahdijn could not keep the excitement out of his voice.

"Patience, friend. Only three of us know the full plan. All must be in place or the plan fails, and we begin again. Let us pray to Allah that it will be our hand that strikes the death blow to the heart of the Great Satan." The phone clicked off.

Bahdijn smiled. Forty years of patience, careful manipulation, bribery, blackmail, and murder finally put him in the position he had been aiming for. Looking at his face in the mirror behind his desk he realized that he looked quite normal despite the thoughts of death and destruction that were going on in his mind. It made him laugh. His American secretary knocked on the door and entered his office. She was quite beautiful and had already provided him great pleasure on his huge mahogany desk. Thoughts of success made him feel the need to demonstrate his power.

She caught the look in his eye and smiled coyly. Her boss was generous and always gave her a bonus when he asked for sexual favors. Although he was sixty, he looked younger, was still handsome, and a very generous lover. He always did things to make sure when she left his office her muscles were pleasantly sore, and her body satiated and spent. With rising excitement, she quietly closed the door behind her as he stood and beckoned for her to join him behind the desk. To Bahdijn she represented the typical American, interested in pleasure and money. When she talked about her escapades to her office mates it only added to his reputation.

Americans were so shallow. *How did they ever become the greatest military nation in the world?* He lifted the secretary up onto the desk and slid her dress up with one hand, caressing her breasts as she began to moan and breathe irregularly. She wiggled her bottom to help him get her panties down and pointed her toes to make it easier to remove them over her shoes. To him, women were items of pleasure, nothing more, and he more than satisfied his own lust, making sure she was more than satiated. Unsteady on her feet and covered in a slick sheen of sweat she slid off his desk, picked up her underwear, and moved into his private bathroom to tidy up. She thought he must have had very good news and smiled at the thought of her bonus. Smiling at her reflection she noted the satiated look in her eyes.

CHAPTER 1

A s a young Fortune 500 company *Bring It Up SAR* surpassed everyone's expectations. Jim stood proudly on the bridge of their newest purchase, a research ship designed and built for the company. Built by Halter Marine of Pascagoula, Mississippi, it was designed along the lines of the *R/V Atlantis* owned by the U.S. Navy and operated by Woods Hole Oceanographic Institution.

Calvin Beardsley, Bill Kline, Wade Adams, Master Chief Warner, and Zeke Kline all had a hand in the design and modifications. Dr. Penny and his wife worked with the Wozniacs to create the perfect medical facility on the sea. James Earl James had command of the galley and dining area. Even Cecilia got in on planning the master cabin where she and Jim would enjoy luxurious comfort at sea. All of the cabins on this ship were worthy of any cruise ship.

Painted in the company colors she lay opposite the Fleet Ocean Tug that served them so well. The Powhatan class tug had been renamed *Coral* and the new vessel christened *Pearl*. John now had command of the *Coral* with a crew of 31. Twelve of them served in a non-military capacity. Nineteen served as part of the paramilitary anti-terrorist special force *Omega*.

That was new too. As omega was the last letter in the Greek alphabet, so Jim's paramilitary unit was the last word on the new breed of terrorism. Jim commanded a crew of 48, fourteen serving in a non-military capacity, along with a science team of eighteen, filling the ship to capacity with bodies.

No one imagined that in a few short years a team of twenty would become eighty-two. Jim was pleased that his military unit now numbered thirty-six specially trained men. Penelope made the number thirty-seven, though she still served more in an advisory capacity. Her connections to MI6 were as strong as ever, but she was now on permanent loan to *Omega Force*. It was a formidable force of the finest men anywhere in the world, and MI6 felt her talents and training were best used working closely with that group.

Pay rates and partnerships in the company lured the very best minds away from the Navy and academic research world as well. Somehow, the company had managed to add a host of beautiful women among the science team, a fact that had many of the military unit and crewmembers quite happy. Yet each addition was carefully screened, serving the science team, knowing they were among the best of the best in their given fields. Everyone knew of the clandestine mission behind the totally credible and real service to oceanography and search and rescue. Each and every one approved of and agreed to the need of *Omega Force* and its mission. It was, Jim decided, a tight crew of dedicated men and women, and he sighed happily.

As the two ships moved in tandem with the light swells of the Pacific Ocean Jim listened to the chatter on the radio and looked over his new ship with proprietary pride. Few men his age had accomplished what he and his partners enjoyed. They had the best ships for the work and the very best men and women for the jobs they had to tackle.

Dr. Iris Copeland, a young marine biologist hardly looked the part as she glided into Jim's vision. She had light-brown hair, intelligent blue eyes, and an innocent almost tentative smile that dazzled. Her bubbly personality didn't seem to fit her status, yet she was acclaimed in her field, holding the Mary Sears Woman Pioneer in Oceanography award, the Henry Melson Stommel Medal, and the Henry Bryant Bigelow Medal in Oceanography. Her students at the University of Washington were certainly sad to see her go. She was one of the more popular professors on the campus.

Dr. John and Alice Dinsmore, also marine biologists, were on loan from the British Oceanographic Institute. Alice was the recipient of the BH Ketchum Award, the Henry Bryant Bigelow Medal in Oceanography, Henry Melson Stommel Medal and Mary Sears Woman Pioneer in Oceanography Award. Her genius was behind the experimental hybrid remotely operated vehicle (HROV) units that the crew would be testing soon. These hybrid remote operation vehicles were so designated because the single vehicle performs two different, but related, missions. It can do research while tethered to the ship, and while swimming freely

Jim's company happened to have the funds to develop the program and the oceanographic study centers had welcomed them into the fold with delight. Zeke and Sparks surpassed themselves, and even Wade and TRT surprised the scientists with their ability to overcome design problems and program glitches. Working together the team had tackled each problem and overcome it. Now that they were about to make their maiden voyage the vehicles were ready for their final tests.

Dr. Dinsmore and her husband were inseparable and to Jim it was obvious they loved each other and their work. At the moment they were saying goodbye to Rosa, who had to fly back to Italy to oversee the wine harvest. Andrea held her tightly, and Dr. Alistair Gregg and Gwyneth, his wife, stood close together with the pair. Jim sighed. He would miss Rosa's influence on his uncle, and he knew the man would miss is wife. Wondering what it would be like when Andrea actually retired made Jim quickly change the direction of his thinking. He needed to stay positive.

Mary Ann Lewis and Barbara Stafford stood on either side of the Gregg couple, capable administrative assistants to the great archaeologist. They were going to have their hands full keeping the young women who served as lab technicians out of trouble with the crew. Jim smiled. They would enjoy that assignment, making it fun for everyone. So far there had been no issues.

Dr. Carol Lowe and Dr. Lisle Mirelle walked by one deck below, both with thick dark hair, one pale, one already deeply tanned, both lovely. Dr. Lowe was a Marine Biologist, and Dr. Mirelle was a marine archaeologist, both rising to the top of their respective fields of study and both already published. They were of similar age and were already inseparable friends. Loving their research above all they had avoided romantic entanglements, and both were still single. To Jim this said volumes, because they were truly lovely women.

Dr. Angela Rysdale and Dr. Heidi Van Haaten walked on either side of the handsome Dr. Michael Putnam, a Marine Biologist and Botanist. Dr. Rysdale was a Paleontologist, and Heidi was an Archaeologist.

Putnam could easily pass for one of Jim's soldiers, an avid weightlifter he was solidly built and quick. His tanned body was sculptured, and he was handsome in a rugged way. Standing five-feet six-inches he seemed larger because of his strength and vitality. He seemed, because of his broad shoulders, almost as wide as he was tall.

Dr. Rysdale was seven inches shorter with dark hair and vivid blue eyes. Dr. Van Haaten was of the same height as Putnam with light brown hair, light brown eyes and a sparkling personality. The men called Dr. Rysdale Dr. Angel and Dr. Van Haaten "Sparkles." Both nicknames fit the women perfectly.

Elizabeth Minor was working on her Master's degree in paleontology, and serving as a lab technician on the boat. She was just about five feet four inches tall, with wide set green eyes and a lovely smile. The men had dubbed her "Cup Cake" and she seemed to be settling in nicely.

Rachel Hague and Stephanie Morris stood to either side of her as the three girls talked. Rachael had a face that was both mysterious and mischievous, with the slight hint of a dimple on her chin, and big green eyes that had that "knowing something" look in them. Stephanie was a buxom beauty, slender, small, with wide set blue eyes and a smile that would melt any heart. Because of her last name she had been given the nickname SOS, and Rachael had been dubbed Miss Chief, pronounced mischief. He smiled at the women, knowing they would live up to their names. They tended to flirt with the men of the crew, but in a wholesome way.

Jim looked down under the deck and caught the Millstein sisters, René and Tiffany with Lynn Ross. Those three were going to be a handful. They were experienced lab technicians and good at their jobs, but all three looked like they could easily grace the silver screen. The twins were opposite Stephanie, who was small, delicately boned, looking like she should be gracing the cover of a fashion magazine rather than serving on a science ship. René and Tiffany had silky red hair and were both well-endowed with full figures, and when men looked at the three of them, they tended to purse lips in appreciation.

As for Lynn, she was simply the life of the party, often dancing and singing her way about the ship and pretty enough to turn every head on a male body. The Millstein sisters were known as Hot Lips and Tiffer, and Lynn was Little Miss Sunshine. The nicknames certainly fit in this case.

"I have something for you to see." Andrea said at his elbow. Jim looked up and realized that Rosa was gone, and the gangplank was retracting, and they were about to head out to sea. His musings usually didn't distract him, however, studying his crew had certainly taken more attention that it usually did. Looking intently at his crew he realized he'd been weighing the science crew and decided they would do very well. He sighed with pleasure as he looked at his uncle.

"You got something at the auction?" Jim asked, curious.

"Yes, Nephew! I got something!" Andrea said, laughing suddenly. The two walked up to the bridge together and as Andrea took the wheel Jim spoke. Andrea pulled away from the dock with care.

"I hope we aren't going to have to search Antarctica!" Patting Andrea's shoulder gently he watched as the ship headed into the Pacific. Andrea glanced away from the steerage of the ship and his eyes sparkled with anticipation. The Island of Hawaii slipped away behind them.

"Papa, this is the engine room." The voice was that of Zeke Good, Master Chief Petty Officer and head mechanic on the ship.

"Go Goody." Andrea replied.

"Take her up to 12 knots, please." Zeke was a polite officer.

"Roger that, throttles to full." Andrea replied.

"I said 12 knots, not full throttle!" Goody said immediately.

"I thought 12 knots was full throttle!" Andrea grinned as he pressed the "talk" button.

"Not anymore." Goody replied. I'm pretty sure we can get fifteen knots out of this baby.

"Roger that Goody. Going to twelve knots." Andrea pushed the throttles forward until Smitty confirmed twelve knots on Forbes Log. There was room for the throttles to go forward. Looking at Jim with shining eyes Andrea laughed with glee.

"*Bring It Up Pearl!*" Jim smiled as the crew shouted their delight together.

"You're still a bunch of slow-pokes!" A voice spoke over the radio.

"What are you doing on this channel?" Jim replied, smiling despite the comment.

"Is this the wrong frequency?" JR said in mock amazement. "I'm so sorry! I had no idea I was thinking out loud!"

"Marines, boss. What ya gonna do?" FM said in his usual lackadaisical voice, the sounds of the engine room loud behind his voice. Everyone chuckled at the interchange.

"Seriously though, Jim. News says Zeke has us all linked." JR said, referring to Ned Vintner, the CIC specialist on the *Coral*. According to Zeke, News was almost as good with computers as the great Uncle Zeke. That was high praise.

"Roger that JR." Jim said, and then added, "Why wasn't I informed first?"

"Hey! You don't see I'm working here?" Zeke said in mock irritation. "Sorry Shep. News got the scoop on me that time!"

The nicknames were an important part of their lives, Jim knew. Some of the names were made up as a joke, some because they just fit the individual. Matt Banks, for instance was nicknamed Bond, not because he was like James Bond, but because of bank bonds and his last name. He never complained about being called Bond. The men always teased him.

"My name is Bond, Banks Bond!"

He would reply with a ready quip. "You're just jealous because your balance is double O naught!"

Steve Coleman, a muscular six foot-four two hundred-and twenty-five pound ex-Marine was called Santa, not because he resembled the legendary Christmas character, but because his initials were S.C. And so it went. Jim didn't mind and had the nicknames memorized already, even with his new crew. Understanding the bonding element of nicknames was elementary.

For a moment he allowed his mind to linger on his new soldiers. *Omega Force* was now indeed the last word on terrorism, and Jim was proud to command a unit of thirty-six men, the finest ever in his career. SAS lost four more good men to his unit. Norm Geissler, Lee Ainsworth, Lloyd Brookstone and Earl Duncan were already riding the crest of the wave of perfection all soldiers sought. And they had counter-terrorist training and experience.

Four new Marines joined, much to the joy of JR, Wade, C.G., and Vince. Terrance Red Claw led them, a full-blooded Blackfoot Indian. Gene Hardesty, Neil Meyers and Mel Pierson came highly recommended. And the Navy suffered the loss of four more of its best. Tom Izbicki, Steve Coleman, Bernie Finlay and Richard Kagan were excited to be back with their former SEAL commander Jim Shepherd. Nor were they sorry to leave behind the now almost incomprehensible management paradigm of the American Military.

Everyone had processed through the bonding period as the two ships moved toward Hawaii. Those who were new to *Omega Force* were working hard to narrow the gap in skills between them and the men Jim had already trained. They were aware that this was something new, a higher level of training, and exulted in the challenge and the skills they were developing. That they contributed to the training by sharing things they'd learned along the way was gravy.

It wasn't all wine and roses. Living together on a ship in close quarters and going through the daily routines and disciplines took its toll, as did the usual gambit of emotions involved in becoming a part of something entirely new and foreign. Having the luxuries afforded this venture helped a little, and carefully orchestrated evening activities afforded opportunities to let off steam without exploding.

Jim soon discovered that his science team lacked some of the discipline he wanted to see, and for a few weeks he'd ridden them hard, earning a few comments about "Captain Bligh" and less complimentary comments spoken when people thought he couldn't hear. However, in the past few days the science team members had finally settled into the routine and disciplines necessary to the proper maintenance and operations of the ship.

His greatest challenge had been getting all of them involved in daily physical and martial arts training. Especially the girls resisted at first, but after three weeks of constant training they were fitting into the discipline without complaining. After much explaining he thought they finally understood the need to know how to defend themselves against any and all enemies, especially if the military team was TDY somewhere away from the ships. He hadn't had to discipline any for having a berth in total disorder for several days either.

Cecilia had been a whirlwind during the past three weeks, soothing ruffled feathers, teaching young women how to maintain a ship, and explaining over and over again the absolute necessity of everything they found so tedious and unfair. Gwyneth had been less tactful but equally helpful in keeping the young women in check. Mary Anne and Barbara, however, with their wit and comedic approach to life, had saved the hour and managed to get every single science team member towing the line. One major storm at sea had also contributed to the understanding of a clean berth.

Those two also kept the girls from forming romantic attachments to any of the male crewmembers. Somehow, they'd convinced the girls to enjoy a taste, but nothing more when it came to the men. Will and Donna Penny spent an hour every night for the first two weeks teaching about healthy relationships on board a ship. So impressed with their curriculum and skill in teaching was Jim, that he insisted they teach the same seminar on the *Coral*. John and Wade had been equally impressed and aware that the information was more than valuable.

Now, in their sixth week at sea, it looked very much to him that the men and women of both ships had learned not only to live in close proximity to each other, but also how to get along with even those who irritated them the most. Part of that was due, Jim knew, to a class Abe, Sturdy, and Windy taught on personality styles and social styles. Abe taught the five Biblical secrets to getting along with everyone, and Sturdy finished the course with an in-depth look at coming to God on His terms and living life on His terms.

Since Jim had insisted that every new crewmember be a professing follower of Christ, Abe and Sturdy's lessons were received with the proper respect and appreciation. No one thought denominational ties were as important as the knowledge that they all belonged to one body under one God. Daily morning and evening prayer, optional morning devotions and mandatory evening Bible study seemed to be helping keep things together as well. Knowing that the lively discussions at Bible study was one of the key factors Jim approved of that challenge, especially since he benefited. Jim sighed and turned his thoughts back to the challenges he was still facing.

CHAPTER 2

Dark winds of change swept over America as President Royce was preparing to leave office, and Congress became less and less connected to mainstream America. Jim knew that the new President, a puppet president at best and newly elected, would never know about the labyrinth beneath his feet, or the union of Intelligence organizations that would continue to meet there. *Omega Force* was virtually unknown outside of that circle, though Jim knew it was only a matter of time before someone connected all the dots. However, as long as there was never any evidence implicating his crew, he knew he was safe.

Admiral Runion knew his time was limited; and preparing to retire maneuvered a much younger man with all the right qualifications into his old office as director of NCIS. Vice Admiral Donald "Duck" Ashley was introduced to the group and sworn in as a life member of *Omega Chapter*. Ashley was already respected as an intelligence officer and very comfortable with a paramilitary unit working outside usual oversight paradigms. The fact that he was friend to both Admiral Runion, and the Shepherds was a side benefit. He was now the Director of Operations for NCIS under the Secretary of the Navy.

Getting his fourth star was a lifelong dream for Admiral Ashley and he did not take the promotion lightly. Admiral Jacks, on the other hand, was furious. The promotion before his party took the presidency, and his friend became the president, effectively blocked him from the promotion he desired. Learning that the newest four-star Admiral knew of his duplicity didn't help matters.

Even though he would be protected by the powers of government, the knowledge of that duplicity could hurt him badly. Jacks felt stifled and struggled to give himself more room to operate, a way to regain his footing, to once again pursue his dream of political office and the power that represented.

Donald Ashley, having been approved by congress for his new position, was already putting into place a network to keep tabs on Jacks and all his friends. They represented a real threat to American security, and with the continued rise of the new sinister power in the world he wasn't about to give Jacks any freedom to operate. With Admiral Rook out of the picture Jacks and the Secretary of the Navy represented the only ones left in Military command with old Communist ties, and new terrorist ties. Yet both politicians were canny operators and stayed beneath the radar.

The new sinister power in the world was not just the old Islam and Jihad with a new twist. Few understood the real threat terrorist cells posed and fewer still the fact that this war had been going on for decades and was not limited to religious influence. Oliver North warned congress of the most-evil man he had ever met, Osama bin Laden. But bin Laden had been no more than one arm of the new threat to the world. He, like many others, had been used as a means to an end. America was simply unprepared to meet this new threat from within.

Bin Laden had been dealt with, a blow to many in the new network. Yet he was merely one small part of the whole. This sinister power readily adapted, America and her military did not. As a result, the world was constantly playing catch-up and forced into being reactive instead of being proactive. Every change that came from this new threat was too late and too little.

With *Omega Force* in place Duck Ashley felt that he had an ace in the hole. Jim knew his team was up to the challenge. When it came to covert missions his highly motivated and talented deadly force was unrivaled. They were versatile. He could divide them into nine teams of four, six teams of six, and three teams of twelve. And they were driven to be the very best. Though they were by far the most outstanding military force in the world, they also knew that mortality made every soldier vulnerable. Yet they accepted the risks gladly to protect America.

None knew the threats that faced their beloved country better. Jim knew his men all felt very much the same way he felt. Dying for his country was an honor, and if it came to that, every one of his men would willingly lay down his life for her. But he reminded himself that death was the easiest burden. Heaviest of all the burdens carried by the men was duty. Duty meant that with honor one did the right thing, regardless of circumstances. Often like trying to lift a mountain, duty remained the highest challenge.

Such patriotism was scoffed at in what Jim called Neo-America. Sacrifice, diligence, hard work, and high standards seemed a thing of the past. Evil was now masked as political correctness. Narcissism marked a society that had once been marked by purity and strength of character. Yet the world was always like this. Rarely exposed or discussed, the darkness of the human heart always left its mark in every generation.

Jim and his team were not fools. They understood the underlying evil in every human being, and the thin line between order and chaos, law and anarchy. As any nation moved away from goodness, self-sacrifice, hard work, and purity it suffered incalculable loss. Yet among those who lived in this once great nation there were still many who held to what was good, just, and right. They were the ones who offered what little protection could be offered in such a time. Inevitably it would be they who would preserve what was good. Yet the cost for them would be high. Jim sighed again.

He broke out of his reverie and got back to work as the two ships made their way toward the Loihi site. It was there they would complete the grant research and establish a bolder and more aggressive approach to understanding vulcanology, further establishing his bona fides. What scientific mysteries they would unlock remained hidden, but he was sure his team would find many.

"Dr. Gregg is going to begin studying the log today. What that ship was doing so far off course is a mystery; and our new relative is bursting at the seams to discover the answers. I am convinced he will find much more than an answer to why the ship was so far off course. What do you think?" Andrea said.

"Nobody unlocks historical information better than Alistair." Jim nodded, checking the calm seas around them. Just off to the left a school of dolphins leaped and played in the water, keeping pace with his ship for a few minutes and chattering to each other as if excited about the discovery. An atoll appeared on the horizon.

CHAPTER 3

Onboard labs and the computer room hummed with the kind of activity that reminded Mrs. Gregg of an impending storm. Gwyneth Gregg was pleased to share this new home with her new husband. He seemed staggered by the size and opulence of his cabin and position in the company. Jim, she knew, was aware that Alistair was deeply in love with her, and she shared the same feelings. Both boys were glad to see her happy and knew their father would approve of this man as a second mate to his beloved wife.

Thrilled to be part of the grand scheme of things the Greggs enjoyed sailing with their sons in the upcoming adventure. Gwyneth knew her staff would keep up the mansion, knowing she would miss them. They were friends. Yet she also knew she could contribute to her husband's work, and that thrilled her most of all. To be part of something this amazing continued to fill her with awe and expectation. The short trip home, and the long journey to Hawaiian waters seemed almost unreal. Admitting that she liked routine helped her understand her love of being on board this ship.

Though the men of *Omega Force* appeared to be relaxed work continued as usual. Beneath the decks their training went on as they crested the wave of military perfection, working at keeping that fine-tuned edge, focused and dedicated. Even the new men were quickly approaching the crest of that wave, already close in military training, they now exulted in a very different and much more difficult training. Seeing that excellence excited Gwyneth, and she was proud to be traveling with such men, and to see her sons as respected leaders of such men.

In the computer lab, Dr. Heidi Van Haaten sat at a table studying the ancient document under a huge magnifying light. Stephanie Morris sat beside her at a laptop entering the text as Dr. Van Haaten deciphered it. Barbara Stafford and Mary Ann Lewis looked over her shoulder, helping her with various difficult symbols. Since it was written in fifteenth century English deciphering it moved at a good pace. Everyone was being careful to read the manuscript with the utmost care.

Fortunately for them Captain Dobbs penmanship was that of an educated man of his time. The archaic expressions and odd strokes of the pen pleased Dr. Van Haaten as she read, becoming more and more familiar with the style until she could easily decipher what was on the written page. It was sad, she thought, that schools no longer taught this type of cursive penmanship. Each letter was formed with exacting care, every stroke of the quill clear and concise. It was as if the writer knew and appreciated the art of calligraphy.

Mary Ann looked over at the laptop and raised an eyebrow. What was happening there was quite extraordinary, and unexpected. On a split screen Stephanie was entering the information while the other screen translated it into modern English text.

"I didn't know you could do that!" She exclaimed, moving to stand behind Stephanie.

"It's a program I wrote. Based on random sections of the text it translates the original into something a little easier to read." Stephanie said this without looking up, but her smile said she appreciated the compliment. "It also corrects any longitudinal and latitudinal errors based on older maps and sextant readings."

"You *wrote* the program?" Heidi asked, looking up from her reading.

"I couldn't find one." Stephanie said her fingers busy on the keyboard.

"You're that good with a computer and you want to be an archaeologist?" Barbara asked with a laugh.

"Computer science was my second major. I have a doctorate degree in that because it was easier." Stephanie said, sitting back with her delicate fingers resting on the keyboard. "Don't get me wrong, I love computers, but not like I love archaeology."

Frank Miller walked in at that moment with Zeke Kline. Stephanie looked at the two with a mischievous twinkle in her beautiful blue eyes. Lithe and strong she had a few salient features that drew men to her. One, she was very attractive, with a pretty smile, wide set vivid blue eyes, and a straight nose, all set in a heart-shaped face that with her smile made her alluring. Second, she had an amazing full figure, and third, she was intelligent and a good conversationalist. The men and women of the ship adored her, though she did not know that.

"I wanted the easier text for our soldier boys, since I know most of them only read comic books." She quipped.

"You stay out of my comic book collection!" FM said without missing a beat. "And while you're at it, college girl, answer a question."

"What's the question?" Stephanie asked as FM sat in a chair close to her. She liked the way FM joked with everybody. He was handsome and rugged looking, his arms filling his sleeves without flexing his powerful muscles, his mobile face usually lit by a smile that absolutely required one in return. Funny and nice she liked his company.

"Why is 'abbreviated' such a long word?" FM asked.

"Wow! A five-syllable word and you were able to pronounce it!" Heidi beamed at him as she made the statement. "I didn't know that ship's mechanics possessed such a grasp of vocabulary.

"I read it in one of the engine manuals and looked it up. Hey, and while you're at it, tell me why sheep don't shrink when it rains." FM added. Everyone burst out laughing at that.

"They do!" Zeke answered with a straight face. "They call them poodles then." Zeke always had a shadow of a beard and mustache with his dark hair and pale skin. He smiled at everyone as he spoke.

That brought more good-natured laughter. Zeke was invited to look at the program Stephanie developed. For several long minutes he studied the program, line by line, strangely silent. At last he looked at the pretty woman who wrote the program.

"Anything you want from the mainframe is yours. I'll give you the passwords. Also, I'm going to have Smitty look this over and make some suggestions. When it comes to navigation, he's the best there is. That split screen also tells me you know your way around a Mac computer. Bright Eyes can fill you in on how to use the Crays to access just about any information in the world. You're in the club!"

"Computer geek's pet!" FM said when Stephanie looked at him. She smiled and stuck her tongue out at him. FM, of course, didn't miss the opportunity. "Not on the first date." He quipped. Everyone laughed again.

On the following day the Inauguration of the new president took place. Most of the group on both ships watched it on television, unimpressed with the handsome figure that had swept the election. His political views were well known, not at all in keeping with traditional American values, and there was something about the man that made the hairs stand up on the back of necks of most of the *Omega Force*. The fact that he was anti-military might have something to do with that.

Admiral Jacks gave his best imitation of the Cheshire cat artists drew for the loved cartoon movie Alice In Wonderland. His time had come at last. This president was a friend and owed some big favors to other friends who shared Jacks' political views. Within a week he and his friend Rear Admiral Hogg had what they wanted. Both were positive it would take back control. That the new president would help them was expected.

President Stephens didn't mind being a pawn. As a pawn he'd taken the highest office in the country, and he knew what he owed those who put him here. Whatever these men and women in power wanted, he willingly gave. It paid to be obedient. His account in

Belize was mute testimony of that. Once he was out of office the money would keep coming in! Signing the request quickly he handed it to his new Secretary of the Navy, Rear Admiral Hogg. He neither read it nor asked what was in it.

Hogg, not looking at all what his name suggested, neatly stacked the signed documents and tapped them on the desk to straighten them. Thin, almost emaciated, he nodded at the President, then put the papers in a file, stuck the file under his left arm, and saluted the President. A soldier always showed the utmost respect to the office of Commander and Chief.

Hogg wasn't in his office yet. Admiral Runion had two days left in his current position. He passed the office without looking into the open door. Had he done so he would have been disconcerted to see the Admiral watching with a critical look in his eyes. Admiral Runion, a fact that would have had Hogg backpedaling quickly, knew the contents of every document that was just signed. More than that, Admiral Runion and Admiral Ashley knew the current plans of both men. That too, would have been a shock. Not all Naval leaders were skilled in espionage, and Hogg's only skill seemed to be politics.

Runion picked up the phone and speed dialed Jim Shepherd's secure phone. Jim picked up on the second ring.

"Are we still on for lunch tomorrow?' Runion asked brusquely. Jim did not hesitate, even though they had no appointment for tomorrow, knowing that the Admiral needed him and wanted to know if he could be there by then.

"And hello to you too!" Jim grinned. "Yes. See you at noon." After he hung up the phone, he made plans for he and some of the men to fly to Washington. Whatever was going down, he knew he needed a full team to deal with the situation. Duty called, and that meant he was now in danger, as were his men.

Later that same day Admiral Jacks attended a meeting of his own, assured that his meeting with Leone Camiri was a well-kept secret. Camiri was head enforcer of one of the most powerful families on the west coast, a man with vast amounts of money and a reputation of being quick to kill. Very few people enjoyed a meeting with Leone, even those who knew they had nothing to fear. No one outside his organization knew of his trip to Washington, or so he thought.

Camiri never noticed the FBI agent that tailed him from the train to his meeting with Admiral Jacks. Jacks never noticed the operative that followed him from his office to the meeting with Camiri. By the time both were seated Admiral Runion knew about the meeting and he had the ability to record every word spoken at the table, even if the men spoke in whispers. He had Jim and John Shepherd to thank for that little secret.

"I need some help with something." Admiral Jacks said quietly to his friend. "I'm going to take down an enemy and get back some files he has on me." He added.

"My uncle said to give you whatever you needed." Camiri said, sipping his coffee almost as he spoke. Washington was not a safe place, and he hid his lips so that none could read them when he talked. Having this meeting here in public had been a mistake. He couldn't change it. Jacks had been the one to set it up and Camiri was committed.

"I need two hitters." Admiral Jacks said, looking around the room carefully and keeping his voice down.

"Tell me where and when." Camiri said.

"My office, tomorrow night after seven." Admiral Jacks provided the information quickly.

"They're coming in from Vegas. They'll keep a low profile because I'm working someone else's territory. This way no one can tie it to an East Coast organization." Camiri said. Without further comment he rose from the table and left the restaurant. The FBI agent who tailed him to the restaurant remained, his backup taking over outside. He, in turn, would be replaced by others of a team of twelve; all assigned to watch this most dangerous criminal.

"Those buttons Sparks and Zeke designed have paid handsome dividends." Admiral Runion said, sitting down at the table where Jim, John, and Wade were waiting. "It appears that I'm about to be hit by two pros from Vegas." He added, taking a menu from a waiter.

His three friends digested that information calmly. Admiral Runion studied them while he pretended to look at his menu.

"You want we should take out the Jackster?" John said, mimicking a New York accent as he grinned at the Admiral. "My buddies Vinny and Al can take care of this for you!" He added as the Admiral laughed. John sounded very much like a New York tough, but the offer was real. Vinny and Al wouldn't hesitate, he knew, to step in where needed.

"Let's not kill the goose that's laying all the eggs." He said, closing his menu. They all ordered and after a few minutes of getting each other up to date Jim leaned forward.

"I have a marker I can call in with the top enforcer on the East Coast." Jim said. "They don't like it when somebody operates in their territory without paying their respects. This individual is especially effective, and he won't kill anyone unless he's defending himself. He helped me with something once a while back and made a promise."

"The Mace?" Admiral Runion asked quietly, raising his eyebrows.

"The one and only." Jim replied with a nod.

"What did you do to earn a favor this big?" Charles asked, leaning back as the waiter put a platter with a one-pound cut of rare prime rib, baked potato, and steamed vegetables in front of him.

"My third mission, the one in Venice, Italy, do you remember?" Jim asked.

"Oh! His sister was the one you rescued!" Admiral Runion nodded as he put a tender slice of meat into his mouth. "This is always so tender!" He added, enjoying the taste of the meat. He chewed with pleasure and looked at the men at his table. In a rare moment of reflection, he realized he would miss the chase.

At the moment no one was assigned to follow him. He was already past it in the eyes of the Navy, not worthy of much consideration. Tomorrow would be his last day in office and then he was through. But the work would go on. From their home in Greece he and his two partners would provide much needed intelligence work behind the scenes as part of *Omega Force*.

The last two years, working through Jim and his special force of soldiers, had been exciting, harrowing, and rewarding. Now he would be considered no threat, on the outside, retired, no longer kept in the loop, and worse, considered not viable for intelligence work. Nothing could be further from the truth. Certainly, the Shepherds did not see him that way, but the Navy and his government would. He sighed and enjoyed his beef, knowing the chase would continue, if in a different manner.

John was working on a Porterhouse steak, and Wade was cutting crab legs with a scissors. Jim had the same cut of meat as the Admiral on his plate and nodded as he masticated his own mouthful. To a soldier, meat like this was a special treat, and he loved red meat. This particular restaurant served the very best.

"His mother was part of that too." Jim added after swallowing a little of his wine.

"Will his boss play?" Charles asked.

"Camiri's nephew stuck a knife in his son a few years ago. He had to fly into New York to apologize personally. The two families don't like each other very much. The Nephew didn't die, but they roughed him up some. The nephew did die a few weeks later when he shot a police officer after he returned to Las Vegas. The other officers on the scene took him down." Jim said with sadness.

They passed the rest of the luncheon talking about the new ship, the new *Omega Force* additions, and the science team. Admiral Runion was very interested and listened as John and Wade described things in detail while Jim sat quietly. Extending an invitation to eat dinner at the mansion the Shepherds and Wade took their leave of the Admiral.

Jim called 'The Mace' from his secure line at the house and explained what was happening, respectfully asking for help. After the conversation Jim thought about the enforcer. Lee was the result of a drunken coupling between a crooked cop and a hooker in the back seat of an old squad vehicle. In North Carolina he had grown up on the other side of the tracks, learning to fend for himself, growing hard.

He killed his first man when he was only sixteen, a favor for the crooked cop, and fled the state. In New York he went to work at a meat packing plant and worked his way up the ladder into the organization. At six feet seven inches in height, and two hundred and seventy pounds of hard worked muscle, he developed into a skilled enforcer. A stint of five years in the state penitentiary refined his talents.

Jim knew him only slightly, but the man would have given his right arm to the SEAL who saved his sister and mother. The Mace did some checking of his own and learned just how deadly Jim Shepherd was. His boss was a firm believer that American soldiers were the best in the world, and Lee knew that. Having seen Jim in action he also knew firsthand that this information was absolutely true. Nor was he foolish enough to want to tangle with a soldier just to see who was the better man. Testosterone driven urges like that could get a man killed.

Jim knew a great deal about the enforcer too. The Mace had respect for innocent people, women and children. Twice he'd been asked by his boss to make a point with a family man. Both times he'd made sure that his boss would look after the wife and children while the men recovered from the lesson. The Mace dealt mostly with criminal figures that stepped out of line. Jim thought that in different circumstances the man might have made a good soldier.

With a sigh he went in search of Tom Izbicki, leader of Team Nightfall. Tom's team had flown back to Washington with him when he got the Admiral's call. He found him in the shooting range below ground with the other members of his team, honing targeting skills, a constant practice for soldiers.

CHAPTER 4

Izbicki was a few inches shorter than Jim, topping out at six foot even, weighing in at two hundred and five pounds. Every ounce of that was hard Marine muscle. Tom was firing one of the new Sig Sauer P-226 Para pistols, putting several rounds in the space of a quarter, his stance perfectly balanced.

Steve Coleman was in the next bay, four inches taller, twenty-pounds heavier, demonstrating the same skill with the pistol. Jim grinned at the taller man as Steve turned to see who entered the room. Coleman nodded and went back to shooting. He too was relaxed in his stance, his shots grouped very closely.

Bernie Finlay, whom the men jokingly called "Fingers" was watching Coleman shoot. Bernie was average in height and in a suit looked like a CPA. The look was deceptive because Bernie was a dangerous man. Beside him, two inches shorter, was Richard Kagan, nicknamed Fagan after the wily character in Charles Dickens' classic *Oliver Twist*. The fact that he looked the part was amusing. Jim knew that Fagan might very well have been such a man if not for the military. He was quite glad the military had taken hold of Kagan, because he was a fine soldier.

Jim waved the men over. He watched with interest and respect as they first safed their weapons and put them down with care. These were good soldiers, the best the SEALs had to offer, and now they were his to command. It had him feeling exceptionally proud.

"We're going on a mission together. It goes down tomorrow night." He said as the men gathered around.

"Really? Here in the States? Who we taking down?" Bernie asked. He was eager and Jim grinned.

"An admiral." He replied.

"You're serious, aren't you?" Tom asked.

"Yes. He's bringing in two hitters from Vegas to lean on Admiral Runion. His name is Admiral Barlow Jacks and he's about as deep in slime as a man can go and still be human." Jim said, his voice hard. "I don't want him dead, but I want to make a point. The hitters will fight back. To make it all righteous, the top enforcer for the east coast families is going to lend a hand. He's about as good as they get in his field, and he's returning a favor."

"And what are we supposed to do?" Tom asked, his eyebrows climbing his forehead.

"Jacks will have some unsuspecting navy muscle to help him, probably first year's crop, still wet behind the ears but excited to help an Admiral. Your job is to neutralize them. Try not to frighten them silly." Jim added with a wry grin.

"And the hitters from Vegas who are going to fight back?" Fagan asked.

"The Mace will deal with them. I'll lend a hand if necessary." Jim replied.

"He's that good?" Coleman asked.

"I don't know." Jim answered honestly. "The hitters won't be stupid. They'll be ready for anything. But I will be in the room with them, so I'll help if I must." Jim grinned.

"Okay. We're in." Tom said nodding his head. "Where does this all go down?"

"In Admiral Runion's old office on the base." Jim replied.

"You want us to take out the whole base? Hmm! I'm reviewing the situation!" Fagan said rubbing his hands with his most wicked smile, repeating a favorite line from the musical hit *Oliver.* Jim actually laughed at the man's antics.

"We'll give them a pass on this one." He replied. "However, after we're done, I want everything in Runion's office removed, photographed, and destroyed. Then I want his office flash burned."

"Holy Pelican Spit!" Steve Coleman said in a whisper. It was a strange expression he'd picked up as a boy, but it brought a hard smile to Jim's face. He looked around at the faces of these dedicated men and smiled.

"Couldn't say it better myself." He replied. "Let's go up to the ready room and lay out our plans." The men followed him up into the library and through the bookshelf doors into the hidden room behind.

After nine, the following night, Admiral Jacks entered the U.S. Naval Station Washington from the heliport pad with the two hitters from Vegas in badly fitting suits and a dozen seamen excited to be doing extra duty for an Admiral. Jacks told them the two men were CIA, and they swallowed his line without question, as Jacks suspected they would. As Jim suspected, no one on the base paid them the slightest heed, probably because Admiral Runion ordered them to stand down, regardless of what happened.

His own team climbed from the borrowed Rigid Raider on the waters of the Anacostia River, deeper shadows among the shadows. Even the guards who were looking the other way for Admiral Jacks and his goons didn't see the seven men slip from the shore onto the base. It made Jim proud to lead men this skilled and he enjoyed slipping past the guards unnoticed.

Admiral Runion looked up from his desk as his door burst open and the two big men from Vegas shouldered their way in. Both had guns out, silenced, pointing at the Admiral. The seamen looked nervously as they entered the office, but Jacks calmed them.

"This man is a traitor!" He said. "He has evidence somewhere in this office and we're going to tear it apart until we find it!"

Runion smiled at the men as they nervously began opening files. Those that were locked he unlocked without demure when asked, and even allowed them into his inner sanctuary. It was, after all, completely cleaned out, the elevator shut off until Duck Ashley moved in. Jacks became more and more impatient as the men found nothing out of the ordinary. Finally, he ordered the seamen out to put up a perimeter around the building. He could see they were beginning to doubt him. For this part of the operation he didn't want witnesses. He knew they would obey his orders, even if they didn't like what they were being told to do. No personnel were ever punished for obeying the orders of a higher ranking officer.

As they filed out of the office Jacks kicked the door closed and so did not see the seamen raise their hands as they faced five armed commandoes. Coleman disarmed them as Fagan sprayed each one in the face, rendering them unconscious immediately. It was almost comical to watch them. So confused by what was happening only one of them offered a question.

"Were we on the right side tonight?" He asked.

"You obeyed the orders of a higher-ranking officer." Jim replied kindly. "No one gets busted for that." The man nodded and inhaled the spray, sinking to the floor as Finlay eased him down. Jim felt bad for those men, because they would struggle with what happened on the base tonight. Jacks had a lot to answer for. As the last man sank to the floor the enforcer from the east coast families put a hand on Jim's shoulder.

"These were good kids, huh?" He asked. Jim nodded.

"Duped, but good kids." He answered. "They will learn from this, I hope, to question when ordered to do something that isn't by the book.

They slipped into the alcove of the door undetected and heard Jacks shouting at Admiral Runion. He wanted the files Runion had on him and if Runion didn't cooperate he was going to let the hitters have him. As Runion replied that the files were in the keeping of the Shepherds he saw Jim and his team slide in through the broken door.

Sensing something out of place the two hitters turned, and hesitated when they saw The Mace. Hesitating saved their lives.

"People call me the Mace." He said tersely. "Our families don't do this sort of thing anymore. The FBI will be all over the two of you and the Camiri family like flies on horse shit! How dare you come into my territory without talking to my boss!" Both men swallowed, their weapons slowly lowering as his did not waver. The Mace put a bullet in each one's thigh, bringing them down with painful moans. Like a huge cat he was over them, kicking their weapons away. His voice was deadly as he spoke.

"You don't go back to Camiri. He never knows what happened here and he never hears from you again. There's a cruise ship in New York Harbor heading for Australia. It leaves day after tomorrow. You'll be on it, crutches and all. Either of you have any idea about putting up a fight?" He asked as he frisked them. He was thorough and removed knives, brass knuckles and spare guns. Both men nodded in the negative. The Mace rolled them over and tied their hands with plastic restraint ties, then rose to his feet. "Either of you talks to Camiri I finish this. Do you understand me?" He asked dangerously. Their hurried nods told Jim they understood and would comply, at least for now. The Mace's reputation was one well known in criminal circles.

"You'd best be leaving, Admiral." Jim said. His gun was trained on Jacks and the latter stood shaking, his face pale. Admiral Runion nodded once and eased around the outside of the room and out. He passed the unconscious bodies, went out to his car, and ordered his driver to the Whitehouse. In the office of Secretary of Navy, he would spend his last hours, and answer the questions he knew would come. For that he was more than prepared.

"I have a message for this Admiral." The Mace said, looking at Jim. "From my boss." He added unnecessarily. "He don't like corruption like this scum in the military, so he asked me to express his disappointment."

Jim lowered his pistol and motioned for Team Nightfall to do the same. The Mace stepped in front of Admiral Jacks.

"My boss don't like the fact that you brought Leone Camiri to this city, or that you asked for his help in a matter none of the families would condone. He wants I should give you this message personally."

Unceremoniously the Mace pushed the Admiral to the floor, lifted a leg, extended and twisted it, and snapped the femur, fibula, and tibia of the right leg with a powerful blow. Because of the pressure and extension, the bones snapped and exploded from the skin and the Admiral screamed once and then passed out. Some of the men watching winced at the spraying blood and loud snaps.

"My boss says you got a message to give this heap of garbage too." The Mace said, stepping away. "He'll come around in a few seconds."

Steve Coleman looked at Jim and then knelt over the Admiral. When his eyes opened, clouded with pain, he focused on the huge Marine and SEAL. Steve smiled.

"I'm Santa, and I've got a message from all the good little boys and girls in this country. You've been very naughty and for Christmas this year you're not getting toys but a lump of coal. My elves will be watching you, Mr. Jacks, and if you step wrong, I'll know. Mr. Shepherd here is going to wrap it up for you." He added, stepping away.

Jim did the same thing the Mace had done, and the Admiral screamed as the bones burst from his other leg. Pain of this kind doesn't allow a human to pass out long, and the Admiral lay, breathing fast, panting literally from the excessive pain, barely able to think. A blackened blade of a Recon Tanto Knife filled his vision, the sharp edge gleaming as the point came to rest on his eyelid.

"The next time you raise your hand against Admiral Runion, I take your eye." Jim said in a flat voice. Admiral Jacks wet himself and whimpered, weakly trying to protect himself. Jim slapped away his hands. "Do you understand me?" He asked. His eyes were hard as agate and glared into those of Admiral Jacks with such intensity that the Admiral knew the words were spoken with conviction and truth. Feeling craven he stopped breathing for a moment.

Admiral Jacks could only nod his head and continue to blubber and whimper. Jim stood up and put his knife back in its sheath and for a moment he and The Mace locked eyes. They read each other correctly and The Mace nodded once, as Jim did the same. Fagan and Fingers were shaking their heads as the hitters looked on with horror. Tom grinned. He'd learned something about his boss tonight. This man was serious about what he did, and that meant this team would be the same, in every situation. That, he thought, was a very pleasant change.

"A pleasure doing business with you." The Mace said, putting out a hand to shake. Jim griped that hard hand and smiled. The Mace continued. "I may not owe you any favors, but you need anything, anytime, I'm there." He added. "My organization may operate outside of the law at times, but we do believe in what this country stands for."

"Thanks. Same here, Lee! Let's finish what we came to do." Jim replied.

Thirty minutes later the fire alarms sounded in Admiral Runion's office. There wasn't much to save. Izbicki used a chemical compound designed to burn at almost a thousand degrees Kelvin, lasting only a few seconds, but destroying everything within its reach. Firemen who responded to the call recognized the use of a military explosive and reported it. With security heightened on the base it wasn't long before Admiral Jacks was discovered outside, some distance from Admiral Runion's office with the unconscious Navy personnel. Jacks was out cold, having been administered morphine to take away the pain.

Jim dropped The Mace and the two hitters off at a pier on the other side of the river before slipping away in the darkness. The Mace, he knew, would provide a doctor to clean up the leg wounds and send those two on their way to Australia. Smiling in the night he thought of Admiral Runion, sitting in his office, prepared to meet the barrage of questions. Admiral Jacks' discomfort didn't weigh on his conscience at all. He'd get good medical care at Bethesda hospital, which was more than he deserved. His own bona fide reason for being at the Live Oaks Retreat was concrete and no one had seen any vehicles leave the property that day or night.

Back at the mansion the men were cleaned up and in bed before the military police arrived. The papers from Admiral Runion's office were gone, but the photographs were safe in the secret room behind the bookshelves.

An NCIS Commander introduced himself nervously. "Commander

Iverson. Sorry about this, Mr. Shepherd, but Admiral Hogg has requested we search this premises and test you and your men for residue of a specific type. I understand that you are now a civilian and this is highly unusual." Iverson was very nervous, because he was doing something illegal.

Jim gave permission for the grounds and mansion to be searched thoroughly and stood yawning in the hall beside Much as the men went about their business.

"Do you know an Admiral Jacks?" One of the investigators asked as the search was going on.

"Only by reputation." Jim replied, not bothering to hide his yawn.

"What does that mean?" The investigator asked, catching the note in Jim's voice.

"He's a slimy politician, not a suitable man to hold the rank he holds." Jim replied, looking bored. "A few years ago, I gave evidence against him." He knew the investigator knew this already but offered it freely. "I was honored to expose him for what he really is."

"May we take samples from your hands and under your fingernails?" The inspector asked. Jim knew he was looking for any kind of evidence that would tie him to the event, but he wasn't worried. All of them had worn gloves and used a special agent to wash afterwards. There would be no trace evidence to link him to the crime.

"Sure!" Jim said with another yawn, holding out his hands. The inspector's shoulders drooped in defeat. He was sure there was nothing to find here. Nor did his swabs of the Captain's hands show any evidence he'd participated in the crime. He had suspected that would be the case in any event. Jim Shepherd knew enough to remove any such evidence if it did indeed exist. Investigations of this nature went against his grain and he liked and respected Jim Shepherd. But he had a job to do.

"Did Jacks order this search?" Jim asked as the men began to file out. The inspector owed him at least an explanation.

"No sir. He claimed you broke one of his legs, and that an enforcer for the Mafia broke the other leg and shot two hit men from Las

Vegas in Admiral Runion's inner office. Admiral Hogg ordered the search after he heard Admiral Jack's story. Hogg is the new SEC-NAV replacing Admiral Runion. The new SEC-NAV ordered the investigation." Watching Jim carefully the man realized that he was not going to get anything here.

"Nice." Was all Jim said, turning away and waving the man out. Then he turned back. "Was Admiral Runion hurt?" He asked. For a moment the man believed in Jim's total innocence.

"No sir. Admiral Runion is at his office in the White House. He sends his regards." The inspector said.

"That's good then. He's a good man." Jim answered, turning back to rejoin Much and walking up the steps to the bedroom as the latter locked the door.

"What do you think, sir?" Another MP asked his boss as they walked down the front steps. He was still very impressed with the opulence of the house he'd just helped search. The search, as they suspected, had turned up nothing.

"We have a dozen recruits not even dry behind the ears yet that claimed five commandoes took them out at gunpoint. They all claim that Admiral Jacks ordered them to take apart Admiral Runion's office because according to him Runion was a traitor. We have an admiral with two broken legs claiming the Mafia and Captain Shepherd are in cahoots together. That alone is so outrageous I don't know what to believe! I'd say the man is loony." The inspector said.

"Either way, I'll be sorry to see Admiral Runion go. He's one of the few who mattered in the upper ranks." The other MP offered.

"Indeed. I have to give my report to Admiral Ashley." The investigator said. "He's going to love this one!"

CHAPTER 5

At eleven Admiral Runion was finishing his last report when a bevy of Secret Service and Military Police appeared outside his open door. He looked up, stacked his papers and stuck them in his safe, then turned and put his hands on his desk to signify that they could enter. This was standard procedure and the men respected his office and the need to keep some things from prying eyes. There were those in the group who had watched each move with deep suspicion.

"It's eleven o'clock, gentlemen. Make it fast." He said.

"Sir, how long have you been in your office?" One of the Secret Service operatives asked.

"I came in after nine thirty, I think. If you checked the duty roster I did have to sign in and the time was noted by the guard." He answered honestly.

"And where were you before that?" An investigator from Navy Intelligence asked.

"Dinner." The Admiral said, raising his eyebrows. "What's going on here?"

"I'm sorry to say that your office was broken into and ransacked at the base, sir." That was the Navy Intelligence officer.

"What!" Admiral Runion shouted, rising to his feet, his pale blue eyes suddenly hard.

"It appears that Admiral Jacks was involved somehow." The Navy Intelligence officer said nervously.

"He wouldn't dare!" Admiral Runion spat.

"Well, we found him outside your office with two broken legs!" The officer replied, licking his lips. It may be his last day in office, but Admiral Runion was a force to be reckoned with.

"Spineless little nerd!" Admiral Runion said, sitting back down. "He thinks the new political changes are in his favor. Never would he have tried something like this when Jack was President! Did he say for whom he was acting? A man like that doesn't act alone! Did you say he had two broken legs?"

"Yes sir." The officer replied. "Both legs badly broken, compound fractures, he claims were the work of the Mafia and Captain James Shepherd of *Bring It Up*."

Admiral Runion sat back and began to laugh. He laughed for a long time, wiping tears away as the men watched him. Some watched with wary eyes, but most were resigned to the futility of this investigation. Finally, he sighed.

"The Mafia and Jim Shepherd! Now that's one for the books!" He said, chuckling again. "Jacks probably owed some money to somebody and they made an example and he concocted this whole story to cover his sorry ass!"

"Sir, with all due respect, can you verify where you were between the hours of eight and nine-thirty?" The officer asked. He hated asking the question and actually knew that the Admiral had a solid alibi.

"Pete's Crab House in Baltimore." The Admiral said quietly. "Didn't you already question my driver? I stopped at my office for just a moment on the base and came here." He knew they had. He and Admiral Ashley had put the whole plan together to cover their tracks. Duck had been eating in his car to give him the alibi, so that empty food containers would be in evidence.

"Yes sir, we did." The man replied. "We also found the bags from the restaurant in the car, and a receipt for the purchases timed at 20:05 hours with your credit card and signature."

"If you knew where I was why did you ask?" Admiral Runion said slowly.

"Admiral Ashley asked us to cover all the bases, sir. This is strictly for the record, and there is no suspicion that you have done anything wrong, sir." The officer responded quickly.

"Damn right!" A deep voice said from the hall as Admiral Ashley shouldered his way into the office. He'd been poised outside, listening and schooling his face to show no emotion but anger as he moved into the room.

"Hey Duck!" Admiral Runion said, rising and shaking hands.

"Heard tonight that you were shipping out." Admiral Ashley said, looking the people in the hallway over.

"Greece. Bill and Roger invited me to share in the purchase of a modest house overlooking Athens Bay." Admiral Runion replied.

"You're leaving the country?" The Secret Service operative asked, suddenly suspicious. Admiral Ashley rolled his eyes and grinned at Charles.

"No, you idiot!" Admiral Runion replied, irritated. "I bought a house in Greece so I could sit around in a nursing home and look at pictures! He took control of his feelings with obvious effort at the stupid question. Bill and Roger and I have talked a long time about retiring there. We'll travel back and forth, of course, as much as we can afford, anyway. Our families still live here, and our loyalties lie here. The house is a quiet and permanent getaway."

"When will you be leaving?" Admiral Ashley asked.

"Sometime in the next three months. I'm going to California to visit my daughter and her family for a few weeks, and then up to Oregon to visit my son and his family. After that I'll probably put my house up for sale and leave when it clears escrow." Admiral Runion replied.

The suspicion went out of the Secret Service operative's face immediately. A guilty man didn't hang around for a couple of months to get caught. He smiled lopsidedly. President Stephens had been adamant about checking everything. At no time had he really suspected Admiral Runion, but he had to be sure.

"Sorry for doubting you, sir." He said. "It's been an odd night."

"You should be, son." Admiral Runion said abruptly. "Now get out of my way so I can go home." He added. Everything he needed was already packed in his briefcase and he was more than ready to leave his old office at the White House.

Admiral Ashley walked out with him and invited him for a drink before he went home. The two took a cab to a nearby club, drank and talked of old times, and then left. Operatives following them reported that nothing in their conversation was suspicious in any way and the new Secretary of the Navy frowned. Surely they had mentioned something, gloated, given some sign!

"What did they talk about?" He asked.

"Admiral Runion talked about how much the house cost in Greece, and how he planned to manage his pension. Admiral Ashley talked about administrative duties and hating paperwork. They both talked about old days. Most of the talk involved reminiscences of their distinguished service." The operative replied, reading it out of a notebook.

"That's it?" Hogg asked in irritation.

"Yes sir." The man replied without inflection.

"And the Shepherds?" He asked the Navy Intelligence investigator.

"Nothing to report, sir. We searched the house and the grounds, took swabs from Captain Shepherd's hands, and counted heads. Captain James and John Shepherd, Wade Adams, and four new crewmembers flew back from Hawaii yesterday and are returning tomorrow. They met with an attorney about business, I believe. The rest of the crew is on the ships in Hawaii." Hogg grunted at the report. The operative looked speculatively at Admiral Hogg.

"You have a question?" The Admiral asked.

"You've had a private citizen's house searched by Naval personnel, and a retiring Admiral grilled about his whereabouts when we had clear evidence he was where he said he was. We even tested the food to be sure it was fresh. It was. Just exactly what do you suspect, sir?" The man replied after a moment of thought.

"Leave no stone unturned." Admiral Hogg said dismissively. "That's my motto."

Liar! The Intelligence officer stood and saluted and left with his thought unspoken. In the back of his mind he put the new Secretary of the Navy on his list of people who could not be trusted. His list was getting longer by the day. That always happened with the arrival of a new President.

The next morning, he appeared in Admiral Ashley's office. Duck invited him in with a wave and the officer sat down and sighed.

"Do we have a problem with Admiral Runion and Captain Shepherd?" He asked without preamble.

"Now why would you think that?" Admiral Ashley said, expressing surprise at the question.

"I know Captain Shepherd, sir, and his reputation. And I've known Admiral Runion most of my career. They are good men, sir, and I've felt that Admiral Hogg might want to hurt both of them." The man replied honestly. His honesty impressed Don Ashley.

"Oh, he does!" Admiral Ashley candidly replied. "Never doubt that for a moment. Just remember that Admiral Runion is the wiliest pirate that ever walked these halls, and it'll take a much smarter man than Hogg to ever pin anything on him! As for Captain Shepherd, he too can take very good care of himself! Personally, I think Hogg is a fool for making an enemy of Jim Shepherd."

"I don't think Admiral Runion's the only pirate that's walked these halls, sir." Captain Neilson smiled as he said it.

"I'll take that as a compliment." Duck replied with a laugh. "Keep Jacks and Hogg under close scrutiny, son." He added.

"With pleasure, sir." Neilson said, standing up and saluting. *It used to be we watched foreign nationals and spies. Now we watch our own as much as we watch the other threats to our country.* He sighed heavily.

CHAPTER 6

"Imagine the artifacts!" Alistair Gregg said, waving his arms dramatically as he looked at the group gathered around the conference table.

"Imagine the gold, mate!" Lee Roy Brown smiled as he said it, and several of the men laughed at the Australian's quip.

"It will be melted." Gregg said, waving the comment away, then smiling. "But we can still gather it up as well!" He added.

"We're supposed to drop some seafloor nodes around the Pele Pit and the vents." Jim said. "We'll be right on top of the site!"

"Where do you think she lies?" Wade asked.

"If the new pit didn't destroy everything, I think she lies just north of the Forbidden Vents. There are lava caves there and I suspect they will lie somewhere embedded in the ash in the cave system." Alistair replied. On the display in front of them a multi-colored diagram of the Loihi new summit pit crater appeared, each color designating a depth. The men and women studied it in silence for a few moments.

"So, we locate the site of this disaster and excavate the gold and artifacts and sail away happily ever after?" Terrance Red Claw said sarcastically.

"How, Chief?" Norm Geissler was the one who spoke. Because

Terrance Red Claw was a full-blooded Blackfoot Indian the men called him Chief.

"They don't talk like that anymore." Gene Hardesty said with a straight face.

"Like what?" Geissler asked, stymied for a moment

"How, pale face!" Red Claw replied, mimicking the Hollywood stereotype. Everyone laughed and Geissler joined them.

"We'll use the HROVs to monitor heavy gold deposits. That gold should have melted into one large puddle." Heidi said.

"We need a Geologist." Inchworm offered. Inchworm was Walter Fitzhugh Rule, second to Master Chief Warner on the *Coral*. Although a deck machinist he was also blessed with a keen and humorous mind.

"Great! Now we get somebody with rocks on the head!" John laughed.

"It is a sound theory geologically." Bob Neff replied. He was a geologist.

"Speak of the devil!" FM retorted as Neff spoke.

The good-natured bantering went on for some time, but the plan came together, piece by piece, while Jim listened and took notes. He made his own contributions from time to time, and he missed nothing in the conversation. After two hours of discussion he slid his notes to Zeke, and Zeke very quickly entered the plan.

Conversation grew quiet as the plan appeared on the computer monitors in front of each crewmember. Printers began to hum as the plans were printed so everyone could study them carefully. Half an hour later they broke for a well-deserved lunch after which Jim gave them all a free afternoon. He noted that all the men seemed easy with each other, continuing to tease and joke. Work would begin in the morning.

At dinner that evening Jim sat down next to Andrea. His uncle had been on the phone that afternoon to his wife, Rosa. Jim tried to imagine being away from Cecilia for months at a time and decided his uncle needed a friendly face and a kind word.

"How's the harvest coming?" Jim asked, after hugging his uncle.

"Rosa says it will be a fine year and our label will grow in popularity as a result. She claims we are going to be very wealthy wine merchants." Andrea was grinning as he spoke.

"Then she's probably correct. You're also going to be very wealthy partners in another venture. You already know your hunch paid off and we have a likely cache of gold and Mayan and Inca artifacts of untold value." Jim replied, picking up his plate and heading for the buffet as he spoke.

"I must phone my Rosa and tell her the news!" Andrea beamed as he contemplated this news. "When do we begin operations?"

"Tomorrow morning." Jim replied, returning with a full plate and slapping Andrea on the back. "You might want to save that as a second reason for calling her." He added. "Now let me tell you a very funny little story!" He recounted to Andrea what he'd done to Jacks.

It was three in the morning, during his first night in the hospital, when two very pretty female agents in Duck Ashley's NCIS office lured the guards away from Admiral Jacks' hospital room. Jim slipped through the door quietly and stood beside the bed until the Admiral opened his eyes. Just seeing Jim Shepherd made him gasp and shiver. Jim leaned over his bed.

"Boo!" He said. That was all, but it frightened the poor man into peeing himself once more.

He left as silently as he'd come. Though the Admiral swore he was visited by Captain Shepherd, insisting over and over his story was true. The hospital security tape, when consulted, showed nothing. Zeke took care of that, showing his amazing skills even though several thousand miles away. Both of the guards wisely kept quiet about being lured away from the door, as Zeke suspected they would. They learned quickly that the monitors on the hall showed them there the entire time.

In the morning two days later Jim stood on the bridge looking out to the ocean, knowing with a sense of accomplishment he'd left a very badly shaken Admiral Jacks behind. *Pearl* took the lead, setting the pace, and they headed toward the islands.

In the science labs everyone was busy getting the nodes ready, preparing for taking samples, and recording their discoveries. It would be their second trip to the islands for research. On the deck the crew kept the ship in pristine condition and Jim looked with pride at the gleaming ship. True, the purchase of the ship had dipped deeply into the company treasury, but no one regretted the expense. With this ship, and its technology, they could only increase their success in their maritime endeavors.

Although he did not require it, Jim was not surprised to see the entire Science Team in their new uniforms. The crew wore work uniforms, a usual practice after their first day out to sea. Jim suspected as long as they hugged the coastline of the United States his science team would resist wearing the coveralls that were normal for working outdoors in the brisk autumn weather. Eventually they would realize the benefits.

Jim walked toward the bow on level two and found Dr. Putnam sitting in a deck chair, shirtless, his hard-muscled torso already turning a darker brown. The crew nicknamed him Dr. Dundee for reasons that were still a mystery to Jim. Mike grinned at the Captain as Jim walked by, sketching an informal wave. Jim stopped and sat down on the edge of another deck chair.

"I heard about your work with nanobot technology, Mike. What's the new project?" He asked.

Mike looked at the Captain and smiled. He liked working for this man, liked the easy manner the Captain employed with his crewmembers, and the fact that he worked as hard as any of the other men on jobs few leaders would undertake. Captain Shepherd was smart too, a willing and able student. Putting down his notebook, which Jim noted was full of mathematical equations, the young scientist spoke.

"I'm working on a theory that would employ nanobot technology in heavy concentrations of red algae." He said with some excitement.

"Will you need storage facilities for the nanobots?" Jim asked.

"Until we figure out how to design them so they don't need freezing to keep them inactive, I'll need a freezer unit of some kind." Mike replied. "So far that seems to be the best way to keep them still."

"If you figure out how to make this work, let me know." Jim said, standing up. "When it comes to red algae, we need all the help we can get. And it won't hurt the company if you are awarded another BH Ketchum award or Henry Bryant Bigelow Medal." Jim smiled. "You make an admirable addition to our Science Team. I'm proud to have you on board."

"The patents alone would set us up for years of research to come!" Mike said, laughing.

"That too." Jim replied. His willingness to allow his scientists to think outside the box, and to excel, set him apart as a leader, and Dr. Putnam smiled with satisfaction. With this company he could move forward much more swiftly than in a traditional setting.

Moving down the steps Jim encountered Wrench working on the portable HIAB deck crane. Romentowski had shaved his head and face and with the cleft in his chin looked ruggedly handsome. When he paused Romentowski did not hesitate to ask for an extra hand.

"Hey Shep. Can you check the valve on the other side and let me know when it settles on zero?" He asked, barely looking up from the adjustments he was making. Jim nodded, went to the side and watched the valve in question until the needle settled on zero.

"That's it, Wrench." He said when the gauge hovered at zero.

"Thanks, Shep. I think the heavier air and humidity throws the air pressure sensors off a little." Wrench said, critically looking at his adjustments. He depressed the talk button on his headset.

"The gauges are set, Goody." He reported to his immediate supervisor. "The Captain was good enough to stop by and lend me a hand. We could use a second set of gauges."

"Roger that, Wrench. Well done on using the Captain of our vessel to undertake a simple job that should have been handled by one man!" Zeke Good's voice came over the set, heavy with sarcasm. "Captain, stop interrupting my men from their work, please!" He added with a grin. "Hammer needs a hand in the DSOG Electrical Shop." He added. "Wrench, be careful! Don't let that ham-handed walking short electrocute you."

"I heard that!" Hammer's voice came over the headset. "Blast!" There was the sound of sparking through the headset and Jim laughed with Wrench. Hammer was a laugh a minute, and so experienced with electricity he could do all kinds of things that made it look very hazardous, just for show. Sam just loved making people laugh and had discovered a clever way of holding his own comedy show whenever anyone was around.

Every day Jim saw his crew improving, checking, and double-checking everything on the ship and he always paused to lend a hand when he could. At other times he took the job upon himself. When he crawled from beneath a sink in the wet lab, he found Rachael Hague and Lynn Ross standing over him with incredulous looks on their faces. Obviously, they hadn't expected the Captain to make the repairs.

"Do you always double as a plumber?" Rachael asked, that mischievous smile playing on her lips.

"Everything else is too complicated for me." Jim said with a smile, as he pulled himself up. "With plumbing all one really has to know is water flows downhill and turns to the right tighten, and to the left loosen!" He laughed.

"We didn't know you'd have to fix this." Lynn said, tossing her head in a habitual manner of moving her blonde locks from in front of her eyes.

Jim wiped the pipe wrenches he'd been using carefully and put them in the toolbox attached to the floor and wall. "I was closest when you reported the leak." He said.

"Let me guess! You weren't doing anything important?" Rachael asked with an impish smile.

"Not until I fixed the leak, anyway." Jim replied. His manner was easy as he moved toward a closet and his smile engaging. To their surprise he pulled a mop out of a closet and wiped up the water under the sink.

"I'm a little disappointed though." Rachael said, her nose twitching in amusement.

"Why's that?" Jim asked.

"I didn't see any plumber's crack!" She said, laughing. Jim blushed. Beautiful women still were able to unnerve him, it seemed.

"I fixed it. That's what was leaking." He answered with a straight face. Both girls burst out laughing. Jim smiled as he continued mopping the floor, being careful to do the job well. Again, when he was finished, he put away the tools he'd used, grinning as the two girls continued to chuckle.

"What's going on in here?" Mary Ann Lewis was in the door, having heard the laughter. "Are you distracting my lab technicians?" She said with a smile and wink at the Captain.

"I'll get right back to work, ma'am!" He said, giving her a mock salute. He patted her shoulder as he moved through the door.

"He's an unusual Captain." Lynn said when Jim was out of earshot.

"You have no idea!" Mary Ann said, shaking her head. "I thought there was a leak in here." She added.

"The Captain fixed it." Rachael said.

"I'm not at all surprised." Mary Ann said. "What did I miss?" She asked.

The girls told her, and she laughed with them as they began to work in the wet lab together. From beneath them the sound of water rushing past the hull seemed somehow appropriate for a wet lab and the girls enjoyed their time there. Dr. Alice Dinsmore joined them before long and they turned their attention to the HROV and its delicate instrumentation.

Everyone called Dr. Alice Dr. Wonderland, not just because of the name Alice, but also because her HROV design was the first to film the very depths of the ocean. It was a veritable wonderland of discovery. Dr. Dinsmore didn't seem to mind her nickname, nor did her husband, whom they lovingly called Dr. Flush. John was big teddy bear of a man with a humorous way about him, always ready to share a laugh.

What they were checking today included the propulsion unit nestled between the two towers that housed all the sensing equipment and computer boards. Incredibly strong Plexiglas outer shells had been painted with the design of *Bring It Up*, aqua blue, pearl white, and burgundy, and were marked with the logo of the company. *Bring*

It Up funded the building of the units and spared no expense and for the first time in the experience of Dr. Wonderland she had carte blanche when it came to her equipment.

Working together the four women were surprised when the supper bell rang over the intercom. They looked at each other with excitement and anticipation. In the morning the hybrid HROVs would be in the water and operating. It was a crowning moment in her career and Dr. Dinsmore knew she owed much of it to her staff, technicians, and the crew of *Bring It Up*. They cleaned up quietly together, eyes straying from time to time to the amazing HROV units. Alice sighed with contentment, for she was on the ocean, her favorite place in the world, and doing what she loved.

"Let's go see what JimJim has for us tonight!" She said with a delighted smile when everyone was ready.

CHAPTER 7

"**H**awaii Pearl Harbor, this is *Bring It Up Pearl, Pearl One* speaking, over." Jim said into the ship to shore radio.

"*Bring It Up Pearl* we read you five-by-five." The voice on the radio sounded clear, no static to interfere. "This is Pearl Harbor Control, Ensign Michaels speaking. Over."

"Roger that Ensign Michaels. We are preparing to launch submersibles to deploy Multidisciplinary Instrumentation in Support of Oceanography nodes. Sonar and radar codes are registered with your department. Please be advised we will have multiple units in the water. Over." Jim said.

"We have you anchored at 18° 52' north and 155° 16' west." Ensign Michaels indicated. "You are cleared to launch submersibles at your discretion, and we will inform you as soon as the nodes are on-line. Over."

"Thank you, Command. Over." Jim put the microphone back on the hook and pushed the talk button on his headset.

"Launch *Sea Bullet* and *Steel Crab*." *Steel Crab*, the salvage bathyscaphe designed by Kockums in Sweden, was so named because with its mechanical arms it looked very much like a crab on the ocean floor. *Sea Bullet* was new, developed and constructed in 2006 by the Applied Sciences Division of Litton Industries. Both 18-ton submersibles were capable of diving at depths of 30,000 ft. In this case they would be diving in about 3,500 meters or 11,375 feet of water.

Frank Miller would be piloting the newer craft, and Driver would be piloting *Steel Crab*. Sparks was going down with Driver and Mark Drumheiser would be the third crewmember in the "fishbowl" as they referred to the command center of the sub. FM would have Hammer and Fagan accompanying him.

Because *Pearl* was designed and specially outfitted for launching the *Sea Bullet*, they had the submersible in the water first. *Steel Crab* wasn't far behind. Both submersibles were operating on battery power rather than being attached to their mother ships. The HROVs would also be operating, and they would be attached to the ship. As the two crafts sank beneath the surface Jim and John entered the CIC on their vessels to observe the operation.

Piloting the submersibles FM and Driver kept their eyes on the instruments and the bottom as it seemed to rise up to meet them. Their powerful dive lights penetrated the darkness and illuminated the bubbles from the hydrothermal chimneys. Temperatures rose as they settled closer to the volcano, taxing the cooling systems to their limits. Here the water was murky, disturbed by the escaping gasses and magma.

"First MISO released." Fagan reported from *Sea Bullet*.

"Second MISO released." Mark Drumheiser's voice followed Fagan. "We have some activity here. One of the vertical spires just went down on the west side of the pit and we can feel vibrations."

"Roger that, *Steel Crab*." John said, watching the picture on the computer monitor. "Hydrothermal activity is nominal according to our sensors."

"Third MISO released." Fagan reported.

"*Steel Crab*, this is Dr. Dinsmore." Alice said into her headset. "Set the fourth node two degrees west of original position, please."

"Fourth MISO released, two degrees west of original position." Mark reported.

It went on as they dropped the nodes around Pele Pit and worked toward the summit region. Mark was the first to spot HUGO, the

Hawaii Undersea Geo-Observatory, a permanent University of Hawaii un-manned research "station" on the seamount.

"Hey Dr. Wonderland?" Mark spoke.

"Yes, Lieutenant?" Dr. Dinsmore replied.

"You can tell Dr. Duennebier that HUGO looks like an engine block stuck in the seamount." Mark said.

"That's a rather cavalier way to speak of a multi-million-dollar titanium structure that has changed the history of undersea geological, geochemical, geophysical, biological and oceanographic study." Dr. Dinsmore said. "Pay attention to what you're supposed to be doing Lieutenant." Alice added with a smile.

"All those geo-whatzits on-line now?" Mark posed the question with a grin, winking at Driver. The two shared a grin as FM quipped, having listened to the conversation on his own headset. They waited impatiently for the response of Dr. Dinsmore, who tended to be quite colorful.

"Geo-whatzits is a term from a book he's been reading." FM said. "It's entitled HUGO facts for Idiots.

"Oh! You can read, Mr. Drumheiser?" Dr. Dinsmore said dryly.

"It has lots of pictures." FM said casually. "Captain, I have an unusual reading!" The change in FM's voice was obvious.

"Copy your reading, FM. You are clear to come home." Zeke said.

"Heading for the surface." Both pilots reported.

"Shep!" Zeke looked over his shoulder at the Captain.

"Give me the facts." Jim said soberly, leaning over Zeke. They were talking off-line and quietly.

"It's a diesel submarine, using the bottom to confuse sonar readings, running silent at the moment." Zeke said, his fingers flying over the keyboard. FM read it from the side. We're not seeing it from up here. It's Russian!"

"What do we have on the surface?" Jim asked.

"A container ship reportedly from Bandar-e Bushehr, an Iranian port city in the Persian Gulf. Also, there's a research ship from Jiddah in Saudi Arabia, a port on the Red Sea. I smell a rat!" Zeke said. "Checking them now." He added as his fingers flew over the keyboards.

"JR, I'm on my way over." Jim said, switching to a frequency only the *Omega Force* could hear. Anyone listening in on that particular frequency would hear static without the proper code. On both ships the change was instantaneous, and crewmembers and science team felt the difference. Something changed, that quickly, and for the first time the new partners realized the true nature of *Omega Force*. Many of the women shivered involuntarily.

"Roger that Jim. Ready to receive." JR replied calmly.

"Rock 'n Roll, get Miss Morris up here now. I want both of you monitoring everything. We have more sensitive equipment on this ship and should be able to keep track of the sub and those two ships out there." Zeke ordered as he pulled off his headphones and rose to follow Jim out of the CIC.

Richard Nelson nodded and pushed his talk button. "SOS, report to the CIC now, please!" He said quietly. Stephanie was used to being called SOS, the old Morse code signal for help. She hurried up the steps to the CIC while she replied to her summons. Her thoughts were on the changes she'd felt, more than seen, in the crew.

FM and Fagan hurried to the Rigid Raider that was waiting to ferry them to the *Coral* with the other fourteen *Omega Force* team members. Hammer, Goody and Wrench secured the submersible and washed it down. It felt strange to FM and Fagan not to help, but they were needed elsewhere.

Scrambling to the deck of the *Coral* the men trotted to the bulkhead and hurried through the hatch and down the steps to the conference room. The conference table was designed for thirty-eight people, each seat with a laptop. Zeke sat down in his place, plugged his laptop into the network and connected them all to the CIC on *Pearl*. Quickly taking their seats the men sat quietly and waited.

"We have a diesel submarine, Russian make, probably sold to Iran or Iraq in the last three years on the bottom, playing hide and seek." Jim said as the computer monitors came to life. "On the surface we have a research ship from Saudi Arabia and a container ship from

Iran. They are recent arrivals, here less than two weeks. How do you read it?" He asked.

"Stinks to high heavens!" Sam Colt said quietly.

"These blokes are up to no good, filthy pelicans!" Sean Oxton added. "With Pearl Harbor this close they're taking some kind of risk!"

"Zeke, can you get me a secure line to Pearl Harbor Command?" Jim asked.

Without saying anything Zeke punched some keys and nodded at the phone beside Jim. Jim picked it up.

"To whom am I speaking and is this line secure?" He asked.

"This is Rear Admiral Komentowski, Captain Shepherd. This line is secure." Jim looked at Zeke with new admiration. Not only had he made a connection, but he had reached the desk of the base commander! He smiled and nodded at Zeke to let him know he noticed this expertise.

"We have detected a diesel submarine hiding on the bottom, sir." Jim said. "With a research ship from Jiddah and a container ship from Bandar-e Bushehr I think there is some cause for alarm." Jim could almost feel the admiral thinking quickly.

"I know your reputation, Captain Shepherd, so I won't waste time asking if you're sure. We have been getting some odd readings, but each time we try to nail whatever is out there it disappears. Since you are already on location, and you have a valid and credible reason for being there, I'm going to ask you to do us the favor of nailing this down. I understand you have very sophisticated equipment that can help with that. I would appreciate it deeply. Keep me informed and thank you." Admiral Komentowski hung up the receiver.

"We're scheduled to go down tomorrow to activate the MISO equipment. FM and Driver, I want your teams to keep your range very narrow until I give the order. Passive detection only! I don't want them to know we're on to them." Jim said.

"Uh, boss?" Driver said.

"Wait! Let me guess!" Jim held up a hand, smiling at Driver, and the rest of the team waited to see what was coming next. "You want a Navy nuclear sub near enough to come to your aid in case they decide you're a hindrance to whatever plans they have?" Jim asked with a grin.

"Well, if you're going to read my mind, go right ahead!" Driver said, shaking his head. "But that's a thought." He added. "We do have some defense down there, but not enough to make me comfortable!"

"That might give us away, but a sub operating just beyond us might make them think twice before making an attack. Don't forget, our submersibles are equipped with the new detection and defense system DWTD." Jim said thoughtfully.

"We haven't even tested those yet!" FM shook his head. "I'm sure they work just fine, but I'll be down there, if you catch my drift!"

"If we have a nuclear sub down there, they won't show themselves. Plus our heat signature system should be able to tell us how big a crew they have." Jim answered. "You can use the acoustics if they get aggressive. My guess is they won't even know we're reading them as long as we stay away from sonar and radar. I don't think they know what we have in the way of detection gear."

"I hate being the bait!" FM said. He grabbed Driver's arm. "Come on fellow bait. Let's see if the whale will try to bite us."

"Ain't nothing down there would even think about eatin' anything this disgusting!" Driver said, waving his hand in front of his face and waving at FM.

"I'll have ye know I smell like this on purpose, laddie." FM said, mimicking an Irish accent.

"Doctor! Is there a doctor on this ship?" Driver said as Dr. Wozniac looked over from his seat at the side of the room.

"What's up Driver?" He asked, playing along.

"This man thinks he's bait, and he smells like bait!" Driver said, pointing at FM. "He's trying to pull me into his delusion and I'm starting to feel like a worm on a hook!"

"I'm sorry, Driver. The psych ward is filled to capacity. We even had so many we had to add a second ship, just to carry them all." Doc said, grinning. "I'm sure there's a discussion group starting any time."

"I'm gonna go have myself examined to see how crazy the rest of you are!" Driver said, shaking his head.

"Meanwhile, let's be bait buddies!" FM quipped.

Driver threw up his hands and followed FM out of the conference room. Everyone else rose from their seats and followed, while Jim took the opportunity of being aboard the *Coral* to inspect the ship and commend John for running a tight ship.

"Hey JR!" He said, ducking through the hatch into the bridge. "This baby bad boy still looks like he just rolled out of the shipyard. Looking good. Your crew is exemplary in keeping him looking great and running as he should! I didn't expect anything less, but I wanted you to know I noticed. Good Captain's do that I've been told, and I've always believed it." Jim smiled at his brother. Both knew they were equal in more than just rank and John grinned at his brother.

"Just because your ship is forty-eight feet longer than mine doesn't mean you can call this a baby!" JR retorted. "This is actually a ship, compared to that floating tub you're commanding."

"Is this a 'mine is bigger than yours' thing?" Pippi said, sliding past Jim to give JR a kiss.

"I regret to inform the crew of both vessels that I just witnessed Captain JR Shepherd kissing a lieutenant." Jim said into his headset.

"'Good for you JR!" Cecilia's voice came back quickly. "There's an ensign over here who really wants to plant a passionate kiss on her Captain! And stop blushing!" Cecilia added. "Get over here pronto so I can bestow that kiss upon your virgin cheek!"

Jim was indeed crimson with embarrassment. Penelope merely laughed and told him to see to that ensign's needs, and JR stuck his tongue out at his brother.

FM's voice came over the radio. "Hey Shep, if you're done blushing, the raider is about to depart from the stern. That's the back of the ship, just incase that ensign put you in a state of confusion." FM said into his headset.

"Hey man! He's from Massachusetts, not confusion!" Fagan said over the headsets. Everyone laughed.

"You boys better behave or ensign in question, who has many

girlfriends on this ship will make you regret picking on her captain!" Cecilia said into her headset.

"Sure boss! Hide behind a woman's skirts." FM said as Jim climbed on board.

"She's wearing her coveralls today." Jim said, and then seemed to stumble and suddenly FM was in the water. That, of course, set off a free-for-all 'king of the boat' contest that went on for about twenty minutes with the crew of the *Coral* crowding the stern rail to watch and cheer. It took four of them to get Jim in the water, but they finally managed to dump him over the side, three of them taking their fourth dunking with him.

Soaking wet and laughing the men climbed aboard the raider and headed back to the *Pearl*. Once the raider was mounted all of them worked companionably to wash it down before they headed in a happy group to their cabins to change. Jim was just entering the shower when Cecilia came in.

"Oooh! Naked Captain!" She said, pretending to press her talk button. Her grin was huge as he blushed crimson, his eyes going wide.

"Honey!" Jim whispered loudly, gesturing for her to cut the communication connection. She laughed and took off her headset to kiss her husband. One thing led to another and it was nearly an hour later when Jim stepped out of his cabin, with Cecilia glowing and flushed following.

CHAPTER 8

On the *Pearl* the Science Team prepared to activate the very latest and best technological breakthrough in oceanographic sensing and imagery systems. The complex system was designed in a cooperative effort with doctors Copeland, Dinsmore, and Lowe to design the parameters and Zeke Kline and Ned Vintner to write the programs and algorithms.

Using advanced very high resolution underwater thermal imaging (AVHRUTI) and moderate resolution imaging spectroradiometer (MODIS) technology, and employing databases with synthetic sequences, real sequences, and *in situ* measurements, and several differential algorithms to interpret data sent back by four HROVs the program promised precise measurements and information on anything below the surface, living or inanimate.

The HROV package included acoustic recording packages (ARP), beam transmissometers measuring the fraction of light from a collimated light source, and thermal imaging cameras made by Fluke. Designed to measure currents, thermal changes beneath the ocean floor and determine the exact formation of the ocean floor itself this equipment used 36 spectral bands and thousands of frequencies and was perfect for its assignment. It was, Dr. Dinsmore thought, her crowning achievement.

With the system on-line the four HROVs could precisely segment the oceanographic structures as well as tracking any motion using additional modules (initialization, preprocessing, and postprocessing) to increase effectiveness. Information provided by the segmentation step reduces computing times, initializes the motion estimation parameters with appropriate values, and increases the overall performance of the system. All in all the science team was very proud of this accomplishment.

Enhancing the system was their connection to two Geostationary Operational Environmental Satellites (GOES). GOES observations could be acquired up to 48 times a day as compared to the twice per day sampling provided by other orbital satellites. With the information from all these systems exact data could be computed to determine exactly what was going on near, on, or beneath the ocean floor.

Captain Shepherd climbed to Level 5, the observation platform over the pilothouse. Here one of the main differences between his vessel and the *RV Atlantis* could be easily detected. *Pearl's* pilothouse extended to cover what was an open deck in front of the pilothouse on the *Atlantis*. Level 5 had that extra space added to the observation platform.

He walked slowly around the deck, looking out over the surface of the water, and down at his lower decks with pleasure. The aqua railing gleamed in the sunlight and the non-slip coating on the deck held his feet securely as he walked.

Bring It Up Pearl was larger than *Atlantis* by design. She stretched 322 feet in length; her draft was twenty feet, with a displacement of 4,122 LT. The ship had a range of 21,000 nautical miles and could cruise at 15 knots. Her beam was 61.75 feet and she weighed 3,757.75 tons. *Atlantis* had a length of 274 feet and a beam of 52.5 feet, yet her hull allowed a cruising speed of only 11 knots. Jim was proud of his ship.

Pearl could complement 48 people. The crew made up 14, and there were 18 scientists aboard. Technically, the 16 Omega Force men on board were also part of the crew, but they were divided separately because of their dual role on board.

Pearl and *Coral* could stay at sea for 60 days at a time. This was called the endurance of a ship and indicated how long food and other supplies could last. *Pearl's* fuel capacity was 378,000 gallons to power her diesel-electric, azimuthing stern thrusters, azimuthing jet 1,180 HSP bow thruster and three 715 kw 600 VAC ship service generators. She could also accommodate six 20-foot portable vans.

Jim's ship boasted both traction and hydro winches. The traction winches utilized 36,000' of .68" EM or 9/16" wire, and the hydro winches 36,000' of 3-cond. EM or ¼" wire. She also had two HIAB cranes at 42,000 pounds capacity, and a midships hydro boom. Her sewage system was the Envirovac flushing system.

Other features included a dynamic positioning system, ROV, HROV and submersible hangars, a fully equipped machine shop, and two rigid-hull inflatable rescue/work boats. *Bring It Up SAR* owned the ship exclusively. Instead of borrowing the funds to purchase the ship the crew had voted unanimously to purchase it outright and Jim agreed this was the wisest course of action.

Jim walked down to Level 4 and entered the pilothouse. Inside was the Command Intelligence Center (CIC), the brain of the ship. Andrea was at the wheel and Jim stepped up to stand beside him, looking over the display that showed the ship's operating system at work. Computers in a horseshoe configuration showed every aspect of the ship systems.

At anchor Andrea used the bow thrusters to keep the ship as stationary as possible. Gentle swells lifted and lowered the ship, but her heading remained the same. Most of the work was done by autopilot but Andrea was there to oversee it all and to make sure everything was working properly. He nodded to Jim, but his eyes were constantly roving over the display.

Jim clapped him on the shoulder without saying anything and strolled back through the radio and chart room to the computer center. Smitty waved from the chart room. He was monitoring the radio. Captain Shepherd waved back, nodding his head. His steps took him into the cool temperatures of the computer room.

Zeke, Cecilia, and Stephanie sat at stations in a horseshoe configuration of computer equipment. Jim smiled at Cecilia and leaned down to kiss her. He nodded and smiled at Zeke and Stephanie and the latter stuck out her lower lip in a pretty pout.

"I didn't get a kiss." She said in mock sadness. "Captain's pet!" She added, sticking out her tongue at Cecilia making the two of them giggle at each other.

"I didn't either!" Zeke said, raising his eyebrows at Stephanie.

Jim bent down as though to kiss Zeke's head, paused, and did something that was way out of character for him. He waved his hand over his nose. "Whew!" He exclaimed. "Time to change that oil!"

"Uncle Zeke remembers!" Zeke said, shaking a finger at Shep with a big grin. "I don't get even, I get ahead. Never forget that!"

Laughing Jim left and walked down to Level 3. Two luxurious cabins occupied the forward section of this level, and a third the port side. One belonged to Jim and Cecilia, the other to Alistair and Gwyneth Gregg, and the portside cabin to John and Alice Dinsmore. Jim's office and that of his executive officer, Tom Ives occupied the starboard side.

Tom watched the captain check the lifeboat on that side of the ship before hearing him enter the door. A moment later the captain appeared at his door.

"Hi Tom. I'm taking a tour of the ship. I'll be back in a bit." Jim said easily. He liked Ives far better than Finn, though the latter had come far. Ives settled in much quicker than Finn, made no enemies among the rest of the crew, and accepted the "rank signifies responsibility" motto of the leadership.

Tom didn't salute or stand, merely waved, and went back to work on his computer. Smiling to himself Jim checked his in box on his desk and decided he could do a thorough inspection of his ship.

He walked down the portside steps to Level 2 and checked the telescoping boom crane. Behind it, toward the stern was the ROV hydro boom, but it was invisible at the moment, retracted behind the

ROV and HROV hanger. Jim turned to starboard and checked the CTD hydro boom and the hydrographic winches behind that, and then looked in the aft control station.

FM was overseeing the loading of the fourth HROV on the crane to deploy it. The man's powerful arms and hands manipulated the controls with the expertise and gentleness of a gifted machinist.

"Hey Shep!" He said when he noticed the captain. Then he pressed his voice button on his headset. "Be aware that the Captain is looking over my shoulder people!" He said laconically. "Let's try to look like we're actually doin' somethin'!" His grin was infectious.

"Your acting has improved!" Jim said into his microphone, playing along with FM. Everyone laughed.

The final HROV was loaded and the boom stretched out over the water. FM lowered it gently to the surface where three divers removed the Crosby sling saver web hooks releasing the HROV. Jim moved to the port railing to watch the release and waved at the three divers. All three waved back as the boom web line was lifted.

Walking toward the bow he entered the crew quarters and hospital section of the ship. There were three cabins on the portside, the forward most a luxury cabin to house Dr. Will Penny and his wife Donna. Opposite their quarters was the examination room, and the hospital section forward of those two areas.

Jim stepped into the examination room and saw the Doctor and his wife examining Earl Duncan's leg. Duncan was inevitably nicknamed "Donut" after the famous Duncan Donut chain of stores. Duncan was two inches shy of six feet with true black hair, green eyes. Powerfully built, as were all the soldiers on the crew, he watched with a critical eye as a cut on his leg was cleaned, stapled and bandaged. Like every soldier the sight of his own blood did not necessarily distress him, especially since the wound was not too painful.

"What happened?" Jim asked when Duncan looked up.

"One of the HROV fins caught me in the hanger, Shep. Nothing serious." Duncan replied.

"Three staples equal scrious!" Dr. Penny huffed as he finished his work. "You're on the light duty list until I say otherwise!" He was smiling as he said the last, though his voice was still gruff.

"What does a cowboy know about serious?" Duncan asked with a laugh. Cowboy was the nickname Dr. Penny carried, because of the famous book character Will Penny. "All they do is ride a horse and jingle their spurs."

"Be careful you lout, or this cowboy will put the spurs to you!" Dr. Penny replied with a laugh. "Now get back to work and try to keep that clean. Come back at sixteen hundred hours so I can check it." Dr. Penny added. He smiled at the soldier as he sketched a wave and limped away

Jim left them and walked back along the starboard side past the two cabins there and back out to the deck. Walking around the structure he moved to the bow area where four twenty-foot vans were secured to the deck. They were bolted to the deck with a four-inch spacer between the bottom of the van and the deck at each of twelve bolt locations. This allowed water to flow beneath them and protected the deck from rust because it could be washed down and coated regularly.

He looked over the forward railing to Level 1 bow section. On the starboard side a portable HIAB deck crane was secured in place. Traveling toward the stern again he took the steps down to Level 1. Eyes moving, he noted how clean the steps were and smiled.

Eight cabins were nestled in the bow of this portion. It was then divided by a walkway and the second part of the ship that contained the conference room and library, lounge, galley, and mess. Jim walked back through the galley to say hello to the crew working there. Whenever inspecting the ship, he made sure he made contact with his crew so he could encourage them.

Here Master Chief James Earl James ruled. Like Abe Lincoln he was an experienced chef and nutritionist. His nickname was JimJim. Unlike Abe, JimJim was not a body builder, but kept himself in good physical condition.

His right hand was Paul Jennings, or P.J. for short. Bob Hinkle and Frank Lafayette finished out the kitchen crew. All three of them were experienced and recently retired Navy personnel. Everyone called Hinkle "Winky" and Lafayette "Frenchie." They were hard at work and the smells from the kitchen made Jim's mouth water. He spoke to each man briefly and went on his way.

Sam Hammer was at one of the electrical relay stations near the stern working on a circuit. Tools were all kept in his tool belt because a toolbox tended to slide along the deck, which was dangerous. He nodded to Jim, since both his hands were busy. Jim nodded back.

"Problem?" Jim asked.

"Replacing the fuse, boss." Hammer said easily. "Just routine. Water and electricity don't always mix well." He added.

"Imagine!" Jim said sarcastically. "A new boat and already we're replacing simple parts!"

"Uh, boss? This is a ship. You bein' a Marine and all I thought I'd remind you." Hammer looked at the Captain as he spoke. "That little craft behind you is a boat. It's much smaller." He nodded his head toward the stern where one of the rigid inflatable workboats was mounted behind the crane foundation.

Jim chuckled. Hammer always joked around with a serious expression. He nodded. "I'll keep that in mind." He wandered off saying boat and ship over and over again. Hammer laughed as the captain disappeared into the DSOG electrical shop.

DSOG stands for deep submergence operations group. It was adjacent to the *Silver Bullet* upper hangar. As always, it was clean and ship shape. Nodding in satisfaction he walked down to the main deck and around to the stern where he checked the telescoping boom crane and the portable HIAB deck crane located on the starboard and port respectively. The A-frame for launching *Silver Bullet* was set to receive the craft after her present mission.

Moving forward he passed the flag sheave and entered the corridor between the DSOG machine shop, ROV bay on the portside, and the lower hanger for *Silver Bullet*. Passing through a hatch he walked between the hydro lab and wet lab, diver's locker, Shipboard Scientific Services Group (SSSG) electronics shop and turned left into the computer lab. The main lab was on the starboard side.

Most of the science crew was in the computer lab. They waved or nodded to Jim as he walked through, listening to the conversations, watching how the unit worked together. The lift door opened, and Dr. John Dinsmore stepped out with an armload of books. Everything going on in that lab indicated that his scientists were in their element, truly focused on what was happening. For a moment he simply watched the business unfold. He grinned.

Jim went back into the corridor and forward past the climate control chamber and freezer to his left, the biology clean lab, dark room and office, tech stores, and scientific storeroom. He found all as it should be and went back aft with some pride to finish is tour.

On the first platform deck there were thirteen cabins for crew, the exercise room, workshop, main control station, switchboard room, upper generator room, stores, winch room, and the Caley HPU. Jim was pleased to find everything in order, as he expected.

CHAPTER 9

"**H**ey7 Shep! Can you come to CIC?" Zeke's voice sounded in his earphones.

"*Pearl One* on the way." Jim answered, making his way quickly up the deck and climbing the stairs to the CIC. He entered and Zeke looked up.

"We're ready to find out who our secretive guest is." Zeke said. Jim wasted no time.

"*Steel Crab* and *Sea Bullet* execute test one." Jim commanded.

Both pilots were ready for the maneuver and the two submersibles moved into position. For the past few minutes they had been following a grid pattern that would take them close to the vessel, but not too close. Now they turned for their final section. *Steel Crab* was six fathoms shallower than *Sea Bullet* and slightly in the lead.

In the CIC and computer lab everyone who could was watching the monitors. Not only did the equipment work properly, it performed better than expected. The images that formed on the monitors were clear and concise. They were also disturbing. Jim, like everyone else, frowned in concentration and then in surprise as the images unfolded before them.

"It's a retired Juliett class submarine." Zeke's voice said matter-of-factly over the com-link. "Russia built 16 and retired them after the cold war ended. Displacement 3,174 long tons surfaced, 4,137 long tons submerged." The technical information rolled off his tongue from memory and Jim smiled. Zeke was one of the most intelligent officers he had ever had the privilege of working with.

"Uh, English please, Uncle Zeke, for us Marine types?" That was the voice of Chief Petty Officer Terrance Wade Red Claw, commonly called Chief.

"Long ton is the name for the unit called the "ton" in the avoirdupois or Imperial system of measurements. It's about 240 pounds heavier than our short ton, or 2,000-pound measurement." Zeke replied with a mock sigh. "For those of you who actually *finished* school of any kind it's 1,015 kg or 35 cubic feet of saltwater with a density of 64 lb/ft^3, which one will see designated as 0.9911 m^3." He concluded.

"I said English, not Geek!" Chief said cryptically.

"And proud of it!" Zeke replied instantly. "The sub we're looking at is 90 meters in length with a 10-meter beam and a 7-meter draft. She's propelled by two 4,000 shp (3.0 M) D-43 and one 1,750 shp (1.30 MW) 2D-42 diesel engines with two 3,000 shp (2.2 MW) PG-141 main and two 500 shp (0.37 MW) PG-140 creep electrical motors. You can see the dual screws that propel her."

"What does "shp" stand for?" That was Cup Cake from the Science Team.

"Sorry, Cup Cake. For you landlubbers "shp" stands for ship horsepower.

"Check! One more acronym to add to my growing list." Elizabeth Minor replied pertly. "Isn't there a limit to how many acronyms can be used?" She added petulantly, looking at her science team.

"Back to what I was reporting!" Zeke said, in a tone that brooked no more interruptions. "Her speed on the surface is 16.8 knots and she can do 18 under the water. She can stay submerged for up to 800 hours and has a test depth of 775 feet, designed to go 1200 feet. As you can see, she does not have a crew of 82, which she was designed to carry, but only six men.

"There are two divers in JIM suits in the water with a water sled towing something fairly heavy. It's registering a radio beacon at 356.44 megahertz which leads me to believe we are looking at a remotely detonated explosive device." Zeke paused for a moment, studying the device critically, his eyes taking in all the details, even as Jim did the same.

"There seem to be a dozen other such devices already planted on the ocean floor." He added.

"They're placed on a fault line." Cecilia and Smitty said in unison.

A long silence ensued as the teams on both ships absorbed this new information. This was a totally unexpected scenario and the implications were frightening. Jim broke the silence.

"Zeke, if I remember correctly, that boat has nuclear-capable cruise missile capacity of four. Is that correct?"

"Yeah, Shep. But the missile tubes are reconfigured to launch the sea sled and divers. She does have six bow torpedo tubes and four stern torpedo tubes. I've cleaned up the picture and you can see that there are 6 torpedoes forward and two aft. They're not standard. I think they're German make circa 1932." Zeke added after studying the pictures he was getting.

"I concur." Jim said.

"I concur." John added.

"I've locked on to their com-link frequency." Zeke said suddenly. In every earphone of the Omega team voices speaking Farsi could be heard.

"They're worried how close our research subs are getting." Jim said, listening closely to the interchange. "I think they're in communication with one of the surface vessels. Yes! The divers have been instructed to plant the explosives and return to the sub. *Steel Crab* and *Sea Bullet*, finish your final run and come on up." Jim added.

"You don't want us to check out the explosives?" FM's voice replied.

"We'll use the HROVs for that job. Once we know what we're working with we'll disarm them all. Zeke, please get me a secure line to Pearl Harbor. Science Team, please get the HROVs ready for a run." Jim requested.

Jim put his hand on Zeke's shoulder. He was thinking ahead, and he knew they needed to act quickly on this. "Also, please put all this together for a meeting thirty minutes after the subs are docked."

Zeke nodded, picked up a phone and handed it to Jim. He dialed the proper number as he handed the set to his Captain.

"Pearl Harbor, this is *Bring It Up One* speaking. I'd like to speak to someone in command, please, over." He said.

"This is Admiral Komentowski speaking. Go ahead Captain Shepherd, over." A gravely voice said over the phone line after a few minutes wait.

"Sir. We have a Juliett class submarine creeping around out here with a crew that speaks Farsi on board. There are eight men on the crew of the sub. Over a dozen explosive packages have been placed over a fault line on the ocean floor. The sub is using the electric creeper motor for propulsion and is taking some risks, considering her age, because she's in about eleven hundred feet of water. Over." Jim made his report.

"I know your reputation Captain, so I won't ask any stupid questions. Can your crew disarm the devices without detection? Over." Admiral Komentowski asked.

"We can. It might be a good idea to call us on the regular ship-to-shore radio and tell us you'll be running some hunting exercises with our subs as the targets. Ask permission politely and I'll have Dr. Alice Dinsmore respond. Once we get a good look at the devices on the ocean floor, we don't want them around to see that we're disarming their explosives. Over." Jim replied.

"Good plan, Jim. They'll hide that sub carefully and keep a low profile. What about the surface ships? Over." Admiral Komentowski asked.

"With your permission, we'll deal with them. I'll give you a full report. Over." Jim replied.

"Roger that. Duck asked me to give you whatever aid I could. He said you'd recognize that name and that you were good friends.

I guess that includes letting you deal with the terrorist element on those ships out there. If you need help, just give us a friendly call on this line. Over." Komentowski replied with a chuckle.

"Thank you, sir. If it's okay with you, let's keep a lid on this, and not pass on the usual reports for at least two weeks. There are those who can look at such reports who might report to our Farsi friends what's going on. Over." Jim waited for the reply.

"That's an unusual request, but I'll grant it. I will report to Duck. Is that satisfactory? Over."

"Thank you again, sir. Over." Jim replied and terminated the connection.

"We're going to get a ship-to-shore from Pearl Harbor Naval Base in a few minutes. Don't call Dr. Dinsmore until then, but have Alice respond to the call. I'll brief her. Thanks Zeke." Jim patted him on the shoulder, kissed Cecilia, and left the CIC.

"Dr. Dinsmore, Alice, as soon as possible would you please meet me in my office?" He said into his com-link. He took Cecilia's hand as he passed and gave it a friendly squeeze.

"Right away." Alice responded. She was getting used to Jim's manner of command on a ship. He asked, never ordered.

At his office door he paused to look into Tom's office and wave at his executive assistant. Tom was working at his computer station, looked up, and sketched a wave of his own.

Ives liked working for this Captain. Aware of the fact that Jim not only respected his abilities, but also trusted him to make decisions without his constant oversight was unusual in a Naval officer. Jim didn't pull rank and his men all respected him for that. He let Ives know early on that he was an equal among equals, and Tom had blossomed.

He watched Dr. Alice Dinsmore step into Jim's office. Jim never closed his door unless the person seeing him wanted privacy. That was another thing about this ship that Ives loved. There were no closely held secrets. Everyone on the crew knew about the entire mission.

Jim liked Alice Dinsmore. He liked her British accent, dry sense of humor, and her quick mind. She sat down demurely across from his desk, her high forehead framed by blonde hair with highlights, the latest fashion for women. Alice had deep lines at the corners of her eyes from laughter, and at the corner of her mouth. Dr. Dinsmore wasn't one for heavy makeup or hiding her natural features. Jim liked that about her as well. What you saw was what you got. Her brilliance was unquestionable, and he enjoyed talking with her whenever possible.

"They're going to trigger an earthquake on that fault, aren't they?" She asked as she crossed her legs.

"Not if we can help it." Jim replied without inflection. "And we will put a stop to that, I assure you." He added.

"What do you need from me?" She asked, coming straight to the point.

"We're going to get a ship-to-shore call in a few minutes. A Naval officer is politely going to ask if the U.S. Navy can take advantage of our presence to do some military exercises in targeting our subs. I want you to play dumb, as though you don't realize that their targeting exercises are just that, not actual shooting. Then I want you to tell them in no uncertain terms how delicate those subs are and how important your work is, etcetera." Jim replied. "The idea is for you to sound like you're in charge here."

"You want a submarine in the area to keep their sub out of sight and quiet while we defuse the devices." Alice said, nodding her head. "I'll give an Oscar performance, Jim." She replied with a slight smile. She thought about everything that had just been said and asked the obvious question. "Why me?"

"I want our enemies to think you're in command of this expedition. When the call comes, and you answer it, they'll realize my mission is to assist you in your work. In the Farsi mind that will make us even more vulnerable." Jim answered.

"Clever!" She said, rising. "I'll wander down to my lab so when the call comes it takes the usual amount of time for me to get to the CIC." She left with her usual stride and Jim smiled.

CHAPTER 10

"**D**r. Alice Dinsmore, please come to the Surface Control Station." Zeke's voice boomed over the loudspeakers. They were rarely used, and Jim smiled. Zeke had purposely used the SCS title instead of CIC, to confuse the enemy. Most ships did call that area the SCS. They would hear the announcement over the water.

In the CIC everyone listened to the radio conversation with smiles. It had taken Alice a few minutes to reach the CIC, much to the discomfort of the officer making the call.

"This is Dr. Alice Dinsmore. How may I assist you? Over." She said crisply into the microphone.

"This is Commander Reynolds, ma'am." The voice at the other end said. "We respectfully request that you allow us to take advantage of your activities around Pele Pit by practicing shooting solutions on our submarines involving your submersibles. Over."

"You what? You want to shoot at my research submersibles! Are you out of your mind, young man? Who is your immediate supervisor? Over!" Dr. Dinsmore snapped.

"No ma'am. We don't want to actually shoot anything at your submersibles. We have equipment on our subs that allows us to track and plot shooting solutions should we ever need to use the real thing.

This is just for practice. There is no danger to your equipment or personnel. Over." Commander Reynolds sounded flustered.

"Do you have any idea how delicate the equipment is on these submersibles, or what they cost to operate? I will not allow any exercise that will endanger any of that sensitive equipment. And do you have any idea how important this research is? It took us years to plan this! And now you want to jeopardize all that so you can practice something at which you should already be proficient? I fail to see any reason to allow this absurdity! Explain yourself! Over!" She waited to hear his explanation with a smile on her face, though her voice had been fierce.

"Ma'am, our exercise will not jeopardize any of your equipment. Basically, it entails using passive and active sonar to locate, plot, and anticipate the movements of enemy submarines. We have an untested crew on one of our subs and would like to train them. I personally guarantee that we will not cause any delays in your important research or endanger your research in any way. Please, ma'am. Over." Reynolds made the last request very polite. He had no idea that Alice made him wait thirty seconds on purpose before she responded.

"You're very polite Commander. I'm sorry I reacted so violently to your request. I am unused to military terminology and frankly bewildered by your idea for training. However, as long as I have your guarantee that no interference or harm will come from this exercise, you have my permission. Over." She replied.

"Thank you very much, doctor. Over." Reynolds replied sounding obviously relieved. "You will be informed when we begin and end our exercises, and we will keep in constant contact with your submarines, so they know what is happening down there. Over."

"Roger that. Over." Dr. Dinsmore put the microphone back. The CIC personnel stood and applauded her performance and she in turn stood and gave a bow. She was laughing with everyone as she did it.

On board the container ship Ya'qub al-Jameel raised his eyebrows. He looked across the consol at Tanfiq Abdulaziz. "A woman is in charge! The intelligence we received about this mission is verified now. *Bring It Up* is indeed doing oceanographic research. It is quite obvious that this Dr. Dinsmore is in charge. If not, it would have been her husband, would it not?"

"I have seen military men, and many of the men on board both vessels are military men. Or, at least, they were military men until very recently. Yet, as the intelligence suggested, they came straight here and began putting down those nodes for research. Najid is convinced he is still undetected. However, I am bringing him up until this exercise is over." Tanfiq replied after a moment of thought. "We need to remain undetected."

He did not like the sudden appearance of the *Coral* and *Pearl* where he and his men were setting up his most audacious attack on the Great Satan. Initial checks told him the two ships were doing research, and so far, everything they did pointed to that. Yet he had studied the crew carefully and determined that most of the men on board were military. Intelligence confirmed that they were once military, but now were retired and part of a search and rescue and salvage operation that was very successful.

Other facts concerned him. His plan was to drop charges along the fault line following the south rift of Loihi Volcano. The charges were designed to extend down into the earth and the result, according to his research, would be dramatic. A huge earthquake would spawn a giant Tsunami hurtling towards the west coast of the United States. Pearl Harbor would experience major damage and the Pacific fleet would, hopefully, be crippled.

This would rid the Persian Gulf and the Red Sea of the hated U.S. and Western European Naval vessels, for they would all be called into service to deal with the chaos of the Tsunami. Once they were gone Islam would have the window of opportunity to destroy Israel once and for all. He was only part of the plan, but he knew the importance of what it was he was about and was anxious to initiate the detonations. Few men knew the full plan, as he did. Only the limited number of people in that circle guaranteed success. That one thought had been drilled into him over and over. As missions go, this one was definitely one of the most difficult he had ever been entrusted. It would succeed. Of that he was confident. There were risks, but he did not take unnecessary risks.

Now there would be delays until these cursed scientists got out of his way. He spun on his heel and went to his office to think. Perhaps he could devise a way to deal with them. Ya'qub watched him go.

He had his own thoughts. Tonight, he would send Najid on board the research ship to disable their communications and perhaps poison their food and water supply. Tanfiq was too cautious. It was time to act, and to be sure that the timeline was not delayed for Jihad.

Najid brought the submarine up beneath the container ship and deployed the divers to attach it to the special airlock. Cables were attached bow and stern and winched up until the seal was in place and the airlock could be blown.

Once the water was cleared Najid opened the hatch of the conning tower and climbed the ladder into the ship. His men followed, the divers coming last. The last man closed the hatch properly before ascending the ladder into the bowels of the huge ship above him. Most of them were glad to be off the sub.

On board the research ship not far from them the sonar operator made his report. The Captain forwarded that report to Tanfiq. On board the two American ships the submersibles were returning after completing their assignment for the day. No one seemed to notice the submarine, and there had been no alarm on the base in Hawaii. Every frequency was being tested to make sure that fact remained. It would not do to be discovered now!

From the island Tanfiq's man reported that no submarines had left the base yet, but two were being prepared. So far there was nothing to alarm him, but he still had that nagging sense of impending disaster raising the hairs on the back of his neck. He ordered the watch for the night doubled. Sighing he realized it was all that he could do.

As usual, lights began to go out on the two American vessels shortly after nine that night. From the container ship Najid watched through his telescope as the night watchman came on deck to begin his patrol. The cagey Americans never patrolled the same way twice.

But one man could only see part of the ship at night, and he would not see into the shadows.

It was midnight before Najid made his way down to the cargo bay doors where he would leave the ship. Already in his wetsuit he padded through the dark hatchways without sound. In the waterproof container he carried in his right hand lay the two vials of poison he would use, his tools, and a schematic for disrupting communications.

Another waterproof case, carried over his shoulder, contained his Luger 7.65 commercial Parabellum carbine with an additional grip safety, rifle stock that could be quickly attached, and a silencer. He didn't think he'd need the gun, but he never went on a mission without it.

A team greeted him with his tanks, mask, and fins. Once he was properly fitted, he stepped onto a caged platform that would lower him into the water. It was the noise of the electric motors that alerted the divers in the water beneath the ship.

Unknown to those on the two ships from the middle east a group of divers was at work below, one person actually in the submarine, the others at work providing a way for Zeke to track both ships accurately wherever they might go from here.

One of them slipped away from the group and watched the surface, seeing the platform first, and then the diver. The diver, unaware that he was being watched, kicked off toward his destination. Mark Drumheiser returned to the group after making his report.

"We have an incoming diver from the container ship." Neil Meyers said when Jim picked up the phone next to his bed.

"On my way." Jim said, hanging up the receiver. Cecilia was awake but her eyes were filled with sleep. Leaning down he kissed her and told her to go back to sleep. Slipping out of the bed he quickly dressed and put on his communication gear. In silence he padded from the room, already thinking about the incoming diver and what he was going to do.

"Neil, have Team Sniper meet me in the weapons room." He communicated as soon as everything was in place.

"They're on their way down now, Shep." Neil said.

"Roger that. Keep us posted. Do you have a visual on the diver in the water?" Jim queried.

"Affirmative. One diver. He's using commercial tanks so his bubbles should be visible when he gets closer." Neil's voice was calm as he replied.

"Is the rest of Bulldog up on deck patrolling?" Jim asked quickly.

"Negative, Shep. Only Hayseed is topside. Chief and MP are at the weapons room." Neil replied.

"Thanks Neil. I'll see them there." Jim answered. "Do you think he saw our divers?" Jim asked.

"Mark says not. It was close though." Neil said.

"The grace of God." Jim said cryptically.

"Amen." Neil answered.

In the weapons room he found the four members of Team Sniper already suited up. Chief and MP of Team Bulldog were also getting into their suits. Jim joined them and in five minutes he too was suited and had his face grease painted for the night in shades of gray, black, and midnight blue.

"What's our story, Shep?" Chief asked as he checked the Captain's equipment.

"We're a SEAL team, sent on board covertly in a training exercise to protect the ship and science crew. Our orders were to stay well hidden and not make our presence known unless there was a threat. The Dinsmores will be summoned when we take this man down, further confirming their role as leaders on board our ship. Let's be real careful on this one." He looked around at the men.

Chief nodded and pressed his com-link. "Hayseed, you're nothing more than a crewmember who had guard duty. The SEAL team is a complete surprise to you. You don't know we're here. When we tell you, go get the Dinsmores and bring them to the deck to deal with the situation." He said.

"Roger that, Chief." Hayseed's voice came clearly over the channel.

It wasn't long before Najid's bubbles were visible off the stern diving platform. Jim and his men waited, watching. Najid was careful to keep any sound to a minimum but all the men heard the audible metal sounds of a clip of ammunition being checked and reinserted. Even the soft sound of the silencer screwed onto the barrel was audible to them. That made this enemy a very dangerous adversary.

Najid climbed the ladder slowly, peeked over the top, and waited until Hayseed's back was to him. He made his move, going after the guard, but was suddenly halted by the appearance of four red beams on his forehead and chest. He froze, raising his hands, pistol dangling from his trigger finger. He was hoping for a chance to shoot these enemies. Shadows seemed to take form and come to life as men stepped out to face him.

The cold barrel of a pistol settled on the back of his neck as a hand from someone behind he didn't even know was there reached over his shoulder to remove his pistol. It was at that point that Najid began to fear for his life.

"Uh oh! I'd say you're in a bit of a pickle, moron!" Chief's voice sounded next to his ear. He tapped the silencer of Najid's own pistol against his head. "This is a very nasty piece of equipment! Night guard!" Chief snapped.

On queue Hayseed turned and took a few tentative steps toward them.

"What the hay!" He exclaimed. He moved forward to where he could see them clearly. "You guys SEALS?" He asked, looking them over. "And you caught an intruder! What the hay!"

"Get whoever is in command of this operation up here, please." Jim asked Hayseed politely. Gene spun smartly and took off, grinning as he played his part. The look on the captive's face was one he'd remember for a long time. He knocked respectfully on the Dinsmore's door and quickly explained what was going on.

"What is this and what are you doing on our ship?" Alice snapped. She had thrown a robe over her nightgown and John had a robe on too, though loosely tied.

"We were assigned to keep an eye on you and your ship. My commander believes there's a Juliett class submarine hovering around your work area." Jim said. He felt Najid stiffen at that and smiled inwardly. "One of my team spotted bubbles and this diver boarded your ship. He was armed with this commercial Parabellum carbine, 7.65mm with additional grip safety. It's made by Luger. You will note the silencer on the end. I don't think this man was here for peaceful purposes, Doctor. He also has poison, if I'm not mistaken. It's in these two vials in his pack."

"You might have let us know you were going to be on board our vessel!" John said, playing his part perfectly.

"I'm sorry about that Dr. Dinsmore." Jim replied evenly. "Our orders were to come aboard covertly and remain hidden. We only patrol at night, and we've not interfered with your work. Again, I apologize for the inconvenience. You would never have known we were here if not for this perpetrator."

"Should I wake Captain Shepherd?" Alice asked.

"If you would. My men will escort this one to your supply ship. It has a brig, I understand. I'm sure Captain Shepherd will approve keeping him over night until the Navy can collect him in the morning." Jim kept his face schooled as he spoke.

Najid stood quietly, since Chief had his pistol pressed against the back of his head and an iron grip on his arm. Several of the crew were gathering around, many of them women. Inside Najid registered the fact that no one knew quite what to do. The leader of the SEAL team soon stepped in.

"Everyone, please stay back!" He ordered. "Go back to your cabins. We have everything in control." He added. "Please have Captain Shepherd meet us on your supply ship."

CHAPTER 11

Two of the SEAL team escorted Najid to the *Coral* where the giant Sturdy met them. He led them down through the galley to the brig where Najid was stripped, searched, and given a sweat suit to wear. Once the door was closed, he was left in darkness to await whatever fate would bring.

On board the container ship Dorf Bernard, Jack Boswell and Mark Drumheiser moved like ghosts among the huge metal trailers. Bill Kline was on board the submarine making sure it would not be in use for several days. It was near dawn when the four finally met up again, beneath the great ship, and engaged their sea sleds to bring them back to the *Coral*. Their job was complete, and they hoped the devices left behind would remain undetected. In this type of situation there were never any guarantees.

One of those devices was in the main communications fuse box, while another lay beneath the consol in the bridge. Two cameras had been mounted to help determine how many men were actually on the ship. They were both in the galley area where the men gathered to eat.

Both Ya'qub and Tanfiq would have been astonished to know that a team of four men not only boarded their ship, but also went undetected for the four hours they were there. They believed in the professionalism and thoroughness of their guards. The guards had indeed been vigilant, but they were neither trained by the American military, nor by Jim Shepherd. Seeing and hearing nothing they too believed that the ship was secure.

On the *Coral* Ned Vintner's fingers flew over the keyboards before him linking them with everything on the ship and submarine. By the end of breakfast, the crew of *Coral* and *Pearl* had an accurate count of the twenty-two-man crew.

On the bridge Tanfiq and Ya'qub pondered the fate of Najid. He had not returned and Ya'qub had been forced to reveal his plan. Tanfiq was still livid over the breech in security. Ya'qub dismissed his ravings as a sign of weakness, but he was wise enough to act contrite. He believed that Najid would return soon, victorious.

From the observation deck one watcher radioed the bridge that a small contingent from the *Pearl* was making its way to *Coral*. This was not unusual, so the two men in the bridge ignored the report. Both would remember it later.

Jim, in his full-dress uniform, walked beside John, also garbed in his dress uniform, to the brig. Najid studied them as they stood outside the glass door. They were cut from the same mold. John was slightly taller, had a slightly receding hairline, and an easy smile. Jim was more serious in nature, and somehow more dominant, though Najid could not put his finger on why.

Jim nodded to Dorf Bernard to open the cell door and it hissed softly as it raised out of sight. Najid had been waiting for this moment. His attack was lethal and instantaneous and failed almost before it began. John and Jim seemed to move together as one person, countering Najid's jabs and kicks easily, fixing submission holds so painful that Najid cried out.

"We may not be in the military anymore, but we have not forgotten how to fight. Cease struggling!" Jim snarled. Najid went limp, hoping they would release him, but they did not. Instead they waited until Dorf returned with a shotgun before releasing him.

Najid sat back down on the bed, rubbing his sore shoulders and wrists. Dorf remained impassively in the doorway with the shotgun menacing and still. He looked away, licking his lips. Thinking fast he spoke in Russian.

"I speak your language, coward!" Jim spat in Farsi, slapping Najid hard enough to knock him to his side on the mattress. Jim's words had been spoken in Najid's own dialect, as though Jim Shepherd had grown up in his own village. Startled he lay for a moment feeling the heat and power of that slap before slowly sitting up. He knew the time to think fast had come. Somehow the Captain knew where he was from!

"I am Najid Abu Kareem al-Jameel ibn Nidh'aai!" He said slowly. "I am a member of the crew of the *Sikandar*. Holding me against my will is very dangerous. There could be an international incident. I have committed no crime other than getting on your ship without permission. You have no right to hold me or treat me this way!" He said boldly.

"Save it for the Navy. They'll be by to pick you up in about two hours. Until then we will question you." Jim said without inflection.

"I will tell you nothing." Najid said.

"Give it to him." Jim said. John leaned forward, grasped his arm, and before he could resist slapped his other hand against Najid's arm. He felt the prick of a needle and a burning as whatever drug they had just given him entered his system.

Twenty minutes later Najid was telling them everything. Unaware that his tongue had been loosened he spoke at length of their plan and his part, told with true pride, in the grand scheme of things. Somewhere in the beginning of his second telling the Navy showed up to escort him from the ship. He was still talking animatedly when they put him in the boat to ferry him to shore, though he was unaware of his gregariousness.

From the pilothouse of the container ship Ya'qub watched through his binoculars as Najid was ferried to the base. He was ready to issue the order to weigh anchor when Tanfiq negated his idea.

"We do not know if he told anyone anything. Najid is strong. He will not be made to talk easily. The American Navy will not use a truth serum on him. The risk of reprisals is too great. Besides, the new President of this wicked country is one of us. He would never allow it. I will make a call and have Najid released."

Zeke listened to the conversation with interest, and immediately followed the call. It was to a leader in the Muslim Cordoba Initiative.

"Shep. The President is about to get a call from the Muslim Cordoba Initiative about Najid." Zeke said into his com-link.

"I discussed the possibility with Captain Cummings. They're going to give him the antidote for the drug we gave him, and act as if he said nothing. The story they'll feed him is that he was caught on board and they were called in to deal with piracy in American waters." Shep replied. "He'll be unaware that he talked because he just won't remember. That drug is a real boon to us!"

"If you're going to anticipate everything I learn, why do you have me around?" Zeke said with mock disgust.

"I don't know! Comedy relief?" Jim replied, getting a laugh from everyone on the ship listening in.

"Uncle Zeke is always watching you!" Zeke said in a serious tone.

"Copy that Seaman Kline." Jim shot back.

"Uh . . . Shep? I'm an Ensign!" Zeke corrected.

"Not if you rat me out!" Jim replied with a wide grin.

"Isn't that coercion of a junior officer?" FM drawled. "Dang! I feel like I'm back in the Navy!" He added.

"You Ducks should have stayed in the Marines!" Neil Myers quipped. "It's being wet all the time that makes you guys so weird."

"I represent that remark!" Hammer said, conversationally. The sound of wires sizzling came over the headsets followed by a loud "Ouch!" from Hammer.

Though Jim did not participate any longer, the banter went on as the men tried to outdo each other in outrageous remarks. Lynn Ross often broke in with a line of song from some play or movie. The banter was good for the crew and Jim welcomed it. The constant chatter was a sign that the crew was happy.

Later that afternoon *Steel Crab* and *Sea Bullet* were lowered into the water, along with the HROVs. The two submersibles were going to search a promising area for deposits of gold and cast iron. The

HROVs were disarming the cluster bombs along the ocean floor. Earlier the HROVs had been used to explore a lava cave. The footage of that was being offered on the Internet site, as if they were doing that study at the moment.

It was a ruse intended to keep the captains of the two spy ships from learning what was really happening. Jim had one man from the crew keeping a constant watch on both ships, and Zeke listening in to the chatter from the container vessel *Sikandar*. He reported that both Ya'qub and Tanfiq were riveted to the Internet site and watching the study unfold.

"No contact between the two vessels yet, Jim." Zeke said.

Thinking about that for a few seconds Jim turned over various scenarios in his mind. "How would you talk to the other ship if you didn't want anyone to realize the two of you were communicating regularly?" Jim asked suddenly.

"I'd go with coded messages through email." Zeke responded after a moment of thought. "I'm searching now." He added.

Jim walked down to the computer lab and found Alice and John hunched over a monitor. At the controls of an HROV Frank Miller was manipulating the claws from a thousand meters above. The delicate controls hooked to his thumb and forefinger on one hand, and thumb, forefinger, and middle finger of the left. Glancing at the monitor Jim saw what FM was doing.

Each package of explosives had a detonation device activated from the surface through a radio signal. FM was carefully removing the device with the two-pincher claw on one arm, and then depositing it in a net bag held by the three-prong claws of the left arm. He was pulling one out now very slowly. Concentrating so hard that sweat was forming on his forehead he finally pulled it free, and he heaved a sigh. Jim understood the intense concentration and sweat.

"Russian remote detonators." FM said by way of explanation. "Fulminate of Mercury with an electrical igniter. These things are really tricky and can blow up in your face. Plus, I'm not sure what the water pressure does." Carefully he rested the detonator in the bag as he talked.

"What happens if they go off in the bag, or while putting them in the bag?" Jim asked.

"The HROV looses an arm." FM said as he guided the vehicle to the last device.

"You blow one of those arms off and I'll rip one of yours off and beat you over the head with the bloody end!" Alice Dinsmore said, not looking up from the monitor. She didn't mean it, of course, and her face was fierce, but her eyes danced.

Jim grinned. Frank was one-inch shy of the six-foot mark and weighed one hundred and ninety-five pounds. His biceps filled his uniform sleeve without flexing. He waited to see how FM would respond. FM slowly and quietly disengaged his hands from the arm controls and then shouted.

"Hit the deck, this one's going to go off!" He yelled as he flung himself to the deck, tackling Jim in the process. It was a masterful performance with the desired effect.

John's reaction was to grab Alice and pull her to the deck, using his body as a shield against the metal floor. He grunted as they landed while FM and Jim stood up.

"Oops! I was wrong. It's not going to blow." FM said in his slow drawl. "But watching you pull her down like that was worth the effort." He reached down and helped John to his feet while Jim helped Alice to her feet. The look on Dr. Alice Dinsmore's face was ominous.

"Oops! Oops!" Alice snapped, the second one an octave higher. FM darted behind Jim as if for protection. "Bloody Yank and your bloody humor!" She snapped, and then grinned at Frank's antics as he peeked out from either side of Jim. Catching herself she turned the grin into a frown and put a ferocious look on her face.

"I don't get even! I get ahead!" She said, shaking a finger at FM. She straightened her hair and glasses and went back to the consol. "Now get back to work!" She said.

Without further comment FM went back to his station and reconnected the finger controls for the arm on the HROV. He guided the vehicle to the spot he wanted and adjusted the propellers until it would remain fixed there against the current. Not until he was positive it was as close to stationary as he could make it, did he attempt to remove the final detonator.

Jim watched him manipulate the arm and claws with respect. Some men had that connection with machines. FM was one of them and though his forehead immediately beaded in sweat he carefully removed the detonator and slid it just as carefully into the net bag. That done he guided the HROV east nearly a mile where the bag was carefully deposited on the bottom at a depth of 2,128 ft, nearly half a nautical mile from the last explosive.

"Why aren't we just bringing those bad boys up?" Jim asked as FM turned control of the HROV over to John Dinsmore.

"When they press the switch to detonate the first bomb, they'll hear a big bang. Hopefully they'll think their plan is working and continue. But I doubt it. Still, when they press the switch, we don't have to have those things in our bomb locker." FM replied laconically. "Then, there's always the chance that one or more will blow up with the change in water pressure. I was surprised they didn't blow when I took them so deep. These turkeys are idiots, Captain! They gotta know how dangerous those things are!" He added.

"I noticed you took your time getting them down there." Jim replied.

"You know how Dr. Wonderland gets when you blow an arm off one of her toys!" FM said, winking at Jim. "Since our company paid for the thing, and helped design it, you'd think she'd cut us a little slack."

"Cutting! I like cutting!" Alice said without turning her head from the monitor. "But I don't ever cut anyone slack, especially a muscle-bound slacker like you Mr. Miller!" She added.

"Hey Shep! Did I get a promotion I didn't know about? She called me, Mr.!" FM said with a serious face.

"She obviously doesn't know you well yet. Give her time and she'll drop that title." Jim replied with a straight face.

CHAPTER 12

"I'm the only titled person on this boat!" Lee Ainsworth said as he walked up to them. His nickname was Lord Lee. With his proper BBC English accent, he certainly sounded the part. Often, he acted the part well too, bringing real laughter.

"Spare me any titled British. They're all loony!" Alice said, with a theatrical toss of her head and a roll of her eyes.

"Off with her head!" Lord Lee retorted instantly. He made a passable red queen from *Alice in Wonderland*, mimicking her voice.

"Not in the computer lab!" John said with a smile. "It's almost impossible to get blood out of a keyboard." He added, and then danced nimbly out of the way as his wife swung her arm, intending to cuff him. "Not to mention the mess on the floor! Gruesome!" He slipped away again to the laughter of those watching.

Alice reached down and picked up the ship-to-ship phone, punched the announce button and spoke. "Mary Ann and Barbara, please report to the computer lab. I need your help disciplining some male crewmembers." She said.

"What's all this then?" Mary Ann said as she led her friend Barbara into the computer lab. "Which men need our discipline?"

"All of them, including my husband!" Alice said with a grin.

"Oh! A husband! What did he do?" Barbara asked, her brown eyes dancing.

"He suggested the keyboards of this room were more important than myself, and when I tried to chastise him, he fled in a most cowardly way." Alice said. Her own eyes were full of mirth.

"Ah! Then we know exactly what to do!" Barbara said. Her face was filled with mirth as she looked the men over.

"Oh yes!" Mary Ann replied. "Strap him in a highchair, and then force-feed him the most disgusting vegetables known to mankind!"

"And what would those be?" John asked, manfully keeping his face straight.

"Lima beans, boiled cabbage, and Brussels sprouts mixed with cod liver oil and pureed to a fine paste." Barbara replied without missing a beat.

The four men stared at Mary Ann and Barbara with their hands over their mouths.

"I'm gonna puke, boss!" FM said from behind his fingers.

"That usually happens." Mary Ann said sagely. Then she spoiled it by giggling. "We'll have to try that!"

"Uh Shep?" Lee said, letting his hand drop. "Zeke asked me to find you and send you up to the CIC."

"Roger that." Jim said, keeping his face schooled. "FM, Lee, John, follow me please." He added and led the way out of the room. He walked through the door furthest from Mary Ann and Barbara who were sharing a laugh with Alice.

"My hero!" FM said, slapping Jim hard on the back. "I think you actually saved our lives back there!"

"Wimps!" Jim retorted.

"Absolutely!" John retorted. "I'd sooner face a firing squad than eat that horrible concoction. How in the world do those women come up with that sort of thing?"

No one had an answer.

In the CIC Jim found Cecilia laughing hysterically and the rest of the crew in various stages of hilarity.

"Ha! Ha! Ha!" He said sarcastically. Then he burst out laughing as his wife broke out in a fresh burst, brushing her hand in front of her face for air, and wiping tears from her eyes with the other. Her laughter was delightful in his ears and he was more than willing to share in the laughter, even if directed at him.

Eventually the laughter died out. FM, Lee, and John left before it ended to return to their duties. Jim composed himself and looked at Zeke with a quizzical expression on his face.

"What's up?" He asked.

"The research ship is leaving." Zeke said.

"Do we know where they're heading?" Jim asked quickly.

"Off the Alaskan coast to the far north. They want to be in position to monitor the Tsunami." Zeke answered.

"That tells us they could not detect our disarming of their devices." Jim said thoughtfully. "Let's get the submersibles up, resupplied, and back in the water so the tests can begin. I don't want that sub disconnecting from the mother ship any time soon. Do we know the timeline?" He added after a moment of thought.

"That I don't know yet." Zeke stroked his chin, thinking carefully. His mind worked through all the probabilities. "My guess is it will be announced before it happens in a communication from *Sikandar* to whomever financed this little mission." Zeke replied.

"JR." Jim said into his com-link.

"Go ahead, Shep." John replied to his brother.

"Call *Steel Crab* up and resupply. Tell the crew to get some sleep. They'll go down again in eight, stay down for eight, and return. My crew will resupply during *Steel Crab's* eight, and so forth. Over."

"Roger that, Shep. Will-co. Out." JR replied.

"Zeke have Alice radio the Navy that we are ready. I'm going to send FM, Goody, and Dr. C down in the *Sea Bullet*. I'll brief them in my office. Make it so, please." He strode purposely out of the room intent on his work after kissing Cecilia.

Cecilia smiled as her husband left the CIC. He was always so polite with his crew. Her lips were still warm from the kiss he'd offered as he left. She turned back to her work, stacking the finished documents to one side before going on-line to complete the next.

In his office Jim met with Frank, Zeke Good, and Dr. Iris Copeland. He briefed them on the type of communications he wanted on the channel that *Sikandar* would be monitoring. They listened respectfully and when dismissed walked together to the locker rooms where they would change into their thermal wetsuits.

Ya'qub and Tanfiq watched the activity on the decks of *Pearl* and *Coral*. The fleet ocean tug was hoisting the submersible to its cradle while the research ship deployed *Sea Bullet* from the stern A-frame designed specifically for that purpose. From a radio scanner they listened to the crewmembers reading off the checklist.

They exchanged glances when the voice of a woman could be heard. The others referred to her as Dr. C. and they checked the list to identify her as Dr. Iris Copeland. She was a noted Marine Biologist with many awards for her work in her particular field. That she was on board meant that this was not a military operation. Both men relaxed a little.

Iris liked the accommodations of the submersible immediately. Instead of sitting, each occupant lay inclined on a comfortable pad. The table, as it was popularly known, was set at a comfortable angle with the head highest and feet lowest. There was a pad to rest her forehead as she watched the meters and screens on the consol below her face. Her arms were free on either side with an automatically adjusting elbow pad for support that followed the arm's movement perfectly.

Beside her, FM lay on his table, his strong hands on the control sticks. He was slightly in front of her. Goody, on his table, was directly in line with her on the port side. He had control of the manipulator arm on that side, and she had control of the Starboard manipulator arm. Both of them would control the video cameras, strobes, and digital cameras on their respective sides of the submersible. For her the thrill of her first dive far outweighed any fears she might have.

Beneath them was a retractable ski with sample basket attached that could be pulled out with the manipulator arms. To either side of that were two descent weights. Above them, on the conning tower, above the personnel hatch and towards the stern was the main ballast vent and communications transducer. Mounted on the front of the tower was the sonar unit.

Just behind them were two variable ballast spheres, one on either side. Behind those were the batteries, and above the batteries two more variable ballast spheres on each side. Just above them, in the center, were two high-pressure air spheres. Just behind the tower was the lifting "T" that connected with the A-frame to lift the sub out of the water.

Behind the spheres were six motor controller relay pressure vessels to operate the four thrusters in the rear and the two on either side in the front.

FM was an expert pilot and they settled into position without incident to begin a process they called mowing the yard. It was simply following a designed grid pattern to search for that large deposit of gold that would lead them to the sunken Spanish galleon. The instruments for detecting that deposit would register in the meters on Iris' side of the submersible.

She had a view port directly below her face, and another to the starboard side. Watching through the one below her she thrilled at the approaching darkness where light from sun or moon did not penetrate. Once they were below 650 feet, barely halfway to the bottom in this section of the ocean, darkness surrounded them, penetrated only by the strobes and searchlights.

Beautiful Moon Jellyfish (Aurelia aurita) pulsed past her side port in an elegant display of luminescent motion. She caught her breath when a Root mouthed jellyfish appeared, with colors of white, pink, and fuchsia cast against the black backdrop of water. The soulless face of a Blue Shark appeared, followed by its body with a scarred dorsal fin and tail. Looking closely, she saw that it had a tin can caught in the rear of its mouth.

"Somebody used this big guy as a can opener!" FM said with a throaty chuckle.

"Are we there yet?" Goody whined. "I never get to see anything! I have to go to the bathroom!"

"Spare me!" FM drawled. "Where do you suppose those jellyfish are headed?" He asked.

"It's getting late. They don't stay below 650 feet during the night. My guess is they're headed into shallower waters." Dr. Copeland replied.

"*Sea Bullet* this is *Hawaii* SSN-776, *Hawaii* One speaking. Be advised that we will begin our shooting solution practice at 16:00 hours." FM knew that the Captain of the attack submarine was Morgan Lewis, a 20-year Navy veteran. That information would not be given over the radio.

"*Hawaii* this is FM, pilot of the *Sea Bullet*. Let her rip!" Frank replied. "We're mowing the yard in a search grid registered with you folks. If y'all get lost and can't find us, refer to that to get back on track. We know how you Navy types get lost on this big ocean when y'all can't see land."

Ya'qub grumbled as the Navy attack sub approached his ship. They were deep enough that the sub hiding beneath would not be noticed but he worried about them coming to the surface. Tanfiq told him to quit worrying. Everything would be done far beneath the surface. Glaring at Tanfiq he continued to listen without making any response.

"So why are we looking around Loihi again?" FM asked.

"Because there were eight recorded eruptions in the nineteenth century, and the *El Dorado Espanola* sank in the nineteenth century." Iris replied, flashing her dimples at FM as he looked back at her.

"That's the historical evidence. But the records show he was much closer to shore." Goody said, looking up over FM.

"Hence the search grid that takes us in toward shore. I'm convinced there is a lava cave, or even dome down here with the *El Dorado Espanola* and two English vessels tucked neatly inside. The cast iron signature or gold signature should be heavy enough to read immediately." Iris replied. "And you need to be looking at your work, not at me!" She added impishly.

"You're much more fun to look at." Goody said with his handsome smile.

"Ooh! Butter! I love compliments." She turned her head back to her work.

FM and Goody exchanged a look and went back to watching what they were doing. Suddenly alarm horns sounded as the Navy sub locked on to their tiny submersible. Iris jerked her head too far and banged it on the instrument panel above her, reacting to the sudden sound in what had been a very quiet environment broken only by talk and the humming of the engines thus far.

"Ow!" She cried, grabbing the back of her head. FM reached up and switched the two toggles she'd depressed, shaking his head. "That hurt! You could have let me know what was going to happen!" She said, a hint of tension in her voice signifying that her head hurt.

"Sorry, Dr. C." FM said contritely. "We forgot you've never been in the Navy. Whenever instruments from another vessel lock on to our vessel the alarms sound so that we can radio who we are and hopefully not get blown to bits."

"In about two more minutes they'll have a shooting solution and radio us that we are dead." Goody added.

CHAPTER 13

"*Sea Bullet,* this is *Hawaii SSN-776, Hawaii* One speaking. We have a shooting solution. Bang! You're dead!" The voice of the Captain came through clearly.

"Copy that *Hawaii.*" FM said, bringing the sub to a stop. "Be advised that we had ample warning of two-minutes and forty-two seconds. Not that it would have done us much good." He added with a chuckle. "Dr. Copeland nearly jumped out of her thermal wetsuit when the alarms went off." He added with another chuckle. "Over."

"Dr. Iris Copeland?" The Captain of the *Hawaii* said. "Over."

"The one and only. Over." FM replied. "It appears that the warning buzzers startled her, and she hit her head on the instrument panel above. Histrionics here were worthy of your kill shot!" FM added.

"*Sea Bullet,* I don't suppose you'd be interested in a capture mission, would you? Over." The Captain said, the smile in his voice evident, even over the tinny sound of the radio.

"You leave my scientists alone!" Alice's voice came crisply over the radio. "She's not just a beautiful woman, she has brains! Over!"

"We're men, Dr. Dinsmore. We usually just notice the symmetrical alluring outside package. It can come with or without brains and we're just fine." The Captain said, laughing. "However, we will respect the parameters of this exercise. Get going *Sea Bullet*. Over."

"Roger that *Hawaii* One, we are on our way. Over." FM said, winking at Iris as he engaged the thrusters.

Once more they followed the grid pattern. It might have been boring had they not been exposed to such unusual beauty in the deep. A Jellyfish, genus *Atolla* appeared with its bottom facing the front portals. A perfectly round ring of orange, and eight polyps inside that ring, like bright orange lights in a display against the white background. Tentacles waved about, seeming to tangle with each other in the current, as they made contact with the portal and then slid up over the top.

An Anglerfish appeared beneath them, looking like a bulldog with fins instead of legs and tail. The tail and fins were lit up against the dark waters and it appeared to have tiny lights surrounding it. FM laughed as he studied the curious fish.

"Looks like he got his face and body studded with rhinestones!"

"Yes. All designed to draw curious fish to where it can strike and devour them." Dr. Copeland said, taking several pictures of the fish after turning off the searchlights. "This fellow was designed to live in these dark waters."

"What? You don't believe it just *evolved* into this?" Goody asked, emphasizing the word on purpose.

"That's preposterous!" Iris said, continuing to photograph the fish. "It would have ceased to exist long before it was able to develop this system for hunting in dark waters. What did it do? Decide one day it was going into the dark waters and wave a magic wand to make it so able a hunter. It would need experience and knowledge for that, and how could it experience that before it was designed that way? Besides, Hammer wasn't around to wire it up!" She added.

"Evolutionists would argue that over a period of perhaps millions of years it changed." FM drawled.

"Yeah. We have a name for scientists that still cling to that worn out historical science mojo over intelligent design. Instead of intelligence they exhibit thintelligence. They ignore what is right before their eyes and concoct some weird untestable historical idea about how the fish evolved. I tell you, it's impossible! Every one of those cells operating together to make that fish glow like that has to work in perfect harmony, and every part of that cell has to work perfectly, in order for that to happen, and that requires information, information that indicates intelligent design."

"I agree!" Goody said, watching the dials and LED readouts in front of his face. "I was just interested to hear how you would answer that."

"Yo!" FM suddenly exclaimed. "What in tarnation is that?"

"It's a Squidworm!" Iris exclaimed in excitement. She began to manipulate the camera.

"I'm gonna have nightmares for a week!" Goody said quietly. "That is one scary looking critter!"

The yellowish-gold body undulated past the portals with white whisker-like feelers protruding from its body and the squid tentacles up front now straight out, then coiled like a corkscrew as it maneuvered its body around the hull of the submersible. Iris took several pictures.

Half an hour later the alarms went off again and shortly thereafter they were informed that they were once more blown to bits and dead on the bottom of the ocean. Iris listened to the easy way FM communicated with the Captain of the attack sub. She shivered as she thought about being attacked this deep in the ocean. At this depth they would die quickly, crushed by the pressure, but still, it was a horrible thought. The men seemed calm.

"Doesn't it ever scare you?" She asked when FM was finished with the conversation.

"Yeah. It does." He'd understood the question immediately. Newbics always eventually asked because for the first time they realized just how deadly it was down here. He continued. "When you face death enough times you get to the point where you realize that when it comes there isn't much you can do about it. I stay focused on what I'm supposed to be doing and hope for the best." FM replied.

"What he said." Goody quipped.

"Whoa! Will you look at this fellow?" Goody said suddenly.

Swimming elegantly through the darkness came a Hawaiian bobtail squid. His luminous white body was covered in rust-colored spots, intermingled with dark blues and greens. Above its eyes a luminous greenish glow could be seen beneath the skin, like a pair of headlights. It had two ghostlike wings halfway back its bulbous body. It was quite a comical appearance.

"He looks like he's trying to be a clown!" Iris said, laughing.

"He's just beautiful, isn't he? Those colors can change, depending on the bottom he's hiding against. I've seen them in all blue spots. This one is of the genus Euprymna Scolopes."

"Show off! How the heck do you remember all those scientific names?" Goody asked.

"I don't know!" Iris laughed. "Sometimes I can't think of them, but if I'm just talking about them the name comes easily."

"I don't see a tail." FM commented.

"It's tucked under. If you saw it extended it would remind you of a bobtailed sled." Iris replied.

And so, the afternoon passed into evening as they continued searching the grid pattern established. About once every hour the *Hawaii* established a shooting solution and Dr. Copeland filled the time by teaching the men about Marine Biology. Both men wished they had faster hands to write notes. As it was, they filled twelve pages with notes about the creatures inhabiting these waters. Both men could understand why she was such a popular professor. Her comments were not just informational, they were interesting.

She noticed how intrigued and eager they were to learn, and the notes. It pleased her that men like these, one a mechanic, the other a professional soldier, had such brilliant minds. In the hours they spent together each had asked intelligent questions, made quick leaps to understand what some of her students in college took hours to comprehend, and discussed without fear contending theories.

"*Sea Bullet* this is *Pearl* One." FM raised his eyebrows. Shep was number One on the *Pearl* but Dr. Alice Dinsmore had just used that call sign. He decided it must be for the benefit of those monitoring on the *Sikandar.* That thought process was lightening fast and he answered immediately.

"Go ahead *Pearl* One. Over." FM replied. He wondered if Jim would mind, deciding immediately that he had probably suggested it.

"Mark your position and head to the surface. *Steel Crab* is ready to go and will pick up the search where you left off. Over." Dr. Dinsmore ordered.

"Roger that Doctor Dinsmore. We are marking in three, two, one, mark." FM said. "One our way up. Over."

Aboard *Sikandar* Tanfiq was questioning Najid, who had just been delivered from captivity. Najid thought he had been knocked unconscious when the SEAL team grabbed him on deck. When he woke up, he was in the brig of a Navy destroyer. He assured Tanfiq that he told them nothing, and he seemed quite confident that they had learned nothing. He wasn't even sure if anyone had questioned him other than to ascertain his name and nationality.

"Did they explain why they were on deck of the *Pearl*?" He asked Najid at the end of his questioning.

"I overheard them talking about it being fortuitous that they were practicing a covert boarding that night. Another said that they would have to keep guard over the scientists every night, whether they knew about it or not." Najid said. "If I understood the conversation correctly, they had been working their way back to the A-frame when they saw my bubbles and decided to stay hidden."

"And what did they say about the gun?" Tanfiq asked. It was his last question. Najid did not have the gun, and he never saw him without it.

"They took it. I was warned what would happen if I was caught with a weapon again, especially on a civilian craft in territorial waters. It was a very strict warning. I will heed it, for those devils were truly invisible, a shadow among shadows." Najid replied seriously.

Tanfiq turned to Ya'qub. "You see why I cautioned you not to send our Najid to that ship? I have felt dark forces gathered against us, and you're lack of discipline nearly cost the entire mission!" Ya'qub swallowed hard at the look in Tanfiq's eyes.

"It will not happen again, my friend. This I promise on my life!" He said, once moisture returned to his mouth.

"Your life will depend on it. Do you understand?" Tanfiq asked dangerously.

"I swore it. I understand." Ya'qub said, some color returning to his face.

"Then we will not speak of it again." Tanfiq said. He spun on his heel and left the bridge. Ya'qub drew a quieting breath and Najid remained seated, his head still groggy.

"The SEALS are fools." Najid said. "Had we caught one of them prowling about our vessel we would have tortured him for information, then cut him in pieces and thrown him out with the garbage for the fish to eat!" He spoke softly because of his headache, but he had been serious enough. True enough; that was exactly what they would have done. Ya'qub listened to the brave talk with no expression on his face.

"They caught you easily enough. Perhaps they are not the fools you think them." Ya'qub picked up his binoculars and studied the two research ships. Najid, after a moment, went to his quarters to get some much-needed rest. He was not overly upset over being captured now that he was free. The memory would serve him well.

In the *Steel Crab* Driver, Sparks, and Dr. Lowe descended to the mark where the *Sea Bullet* stopped the search and picked it up again. Despite her twenty-eight years she still looked like a stunningly beautiful young woman in her late teens or early twenties. Her wide-set blue eyes and soft brown hair, high cheekbones, and wide generous smile combined to make her pretty enough to grace the cover of a fashion magazine. Possessing a melodious voice with soft dulcet tones she was delightful in every way.

Driver thought about that as he kept the course. He'd seen many women scientists in his career. Some had been truly driven in their career, and some very happy, but he didn't remember the luminous beauty as one of the aspects of any of those faces from the past. Perhaps it was their faith that made a difference. The women on the ship were all followers of Christ, serious about their Christian walk, and careful to give the credit for everything good in their lives to their Lord. The Captain, John, Abe and Sturdy had been adamant that that be part of the hiring process.

Those scientists he met before were all self-assured, proud, arrogant, and condescending, as if they thought of themselves as the master race. Dr. Lowe was very different. For one thing, she seemed eager to share her world with anyone who was interested. Yet she did not look down on anyone who showed no interest in what she had to say, or anyone who did not understand. In fact, she was a patient teacher.

"Switch off the search lights please." She said suddenly. Sparks flipped the switch and darkness closed over them like a thick blanket. Suddenly something pinkish and amazing pulsed upward. It was a swimming sea cucumber. Through the translucent skin they could see a brownish colored intestine-like appendage.

"Nothing like showing everything, huh?" Sparks said in a quiet voice. The creature was beautiful. Dr. Lowe was busy photographing it. Driver thought about that amazing beauty so far below the surface. In shallower water, where there was ambient light, he had seen them crawling about on the ocean floor, almost fuchsia in color, all feet on the ground propelling it along. Here the two feet dangled from the bulbous body, three toed and used for swimming now. Amazed by its beauty and gracefulness he watched it swim along with appreciation and wonder.

Off to one side Sparks caught sight of a jellyfish in the medusa stage. "Hey! Catch that action!" He pointed, his voice filled with excitement and awe.

"Periphylla periphylla!" Dr. Lowe exclaimed. She smiled when she saw Driver quickly write down the genus. To help she spelled it. Sparks was too fascinated by the luminous colors of reds, blues, and whites, all cast against a backdrop of black water to notice. Its tentacles were all curled at the end, as though ready to lash out like a whip. When he did realize he'd missed something he sheepishly asked her to repeat the information. Smiling to herself she decided that these men, though military men, were eager to learn everything they could about the ocean.

"Amazing!" Sparks said, bringing another bright smile from Carol. She loved it when people appreciated the amazing beauty of creation.

"Goodness!" She said suddenly. The alarms went off signifying that the *Hawaii* was pinging them.

Since they were only a fathom from the bottom Driver dropped to the ocean floor, hoping to confuse the sonar signal. It wasn't enough. Two minutes later the voice of the Captain of the *Hawaii* announced a shooting solution.

"*Steel Crab*, this is *Hawaii SSN-776, Hawaii* One speaking. Nice try to become one with your environment. We gotcha though! Over."

Hawaii One, we bow to the amazing ability of your crew to target and kill us helpless little sea lambs. Ouch! Over." Driver answered, a big grin on his face.

"If this is the voice of Jack Boswell I'm hearing, I question the sea lamb comment. Over." Captain Lewis chuckled.

"Okay, okay!" Driver laughed. Two sea goats and a mermaid! We have Dr. Carol Lowe down here with us. Over."

"Roger that, *Steel Crab*. We would be more than willing to come to your rescue and take you all on board. Over." Lewis laughed.

"I told you before! Leave my scientists alone!" Dr. Dinsmore's voice was heated. "And you three get back to work!" She added.

"Slave driver!" Driver muttered.

"I wonder how a sea goat would taste broiled." Dr. Dinsmore's voice retorted.

"Uh! Back to work Captain Bligh!" Driver grinned, pulling the craft off the floor of the ocean and continuing on the grid.

CHAPTER 14

An hour later they approached a rise in the ocean floor with a cave entrance. Not until they were in the cave itself, did all of the equipment show them they had discovered what they sought. The cast iron deposits alone told them exactly what they had. There was more, much more showing up on the equipment! Driver pressed the communication.

"*Bring It Up Steel Crab* to *Bring It Up One!*" Driver said, his voice tight. "We have heavy deposits of cast iron, iron, gold, silver, copper, and a large deposit of gemstone on our scopes. We are in the cave. Repeat, we are in the cave. Signatures indicate three separate ships! Over."

Driver smiled as he heard the whoops of excitement from the crew on the surface. Zeke's voice came over the com-link.

"Roger that, *Steel Crab*. Well done. Dr. Dinsmore was right. Not that I doubted her for a moment!" Zeke added. "Photograph the entire cave system that you can reach and return to surface. Over." He commanded.

Driver complied as his crew took photographs that allowed the entire cave system to be mapped. When they had completed that part of their mission, they exited the cave and a moment later the voice of the Navy Captain in the submarine shadowing them spoke. Driver winced. He'd momentarily forgotten his shadow.

"*Steel Crab*, this is *Hawaii SSN-776, Hawaii* One speaking. Over."

"Go ahead *Hawaii One*." Driver said quickly.

"You were invisible to us in that cave. Nice move in figuring out how to hide from us. Over." The sub Captain said. Just then the alarms sounded, signifying that their sub had been "lit up" by the Navy sub. "We kept our equipment on the spot where you disappeared, figuring you had to come out sooner or later. So, bang! You're all dead. Again. Over."

"I'll have to remember to wait until you leave next time, *Hawaii One*." Driver said laconically. "That cave is large enough to hide an enemy sub, so keep that in mind for the future!" He added. "Thanks, Captain for the exercise, but we've been ordered to the surface, over." He ended.

"Roger that. We are heading back to base. Thank you Dr. Dinsmore for allowing us to use your sub for practice. Perhaps when you come to shore, we can meet, and you can show us some of your discoveries. Over." The Captain spoke.

"Since none of my vessels were damaged and all my equipment seems to be working, you're off the hook, Captain. We are always ready to help our Navy. Yes, I'll be glad to share our discoveries. Over and out." Dr. Dinsmore replied.

Aboard the *Sikandar* Ya'qub cursed. "They know about the cave now!" He said tersely. "I curse those researchers and their interfering ways!" He spat, leaving the bridge in a fury. Tanfiq wisely remained silent. There were ways, he knew of dealing with interfering elements, but that was perhaps for later.

The explosives were all planted, and the detonators were still sending out their signal. If everything worked according to plan the cursed researches and their ships would be crushed by the initial explosions and upheaval.

CHAPTER 15

"**W**e should move our schedule up." Tanfiq said later that evening.

"No. Everything must be in place before we detonate. We keep the schedule." Ya'qub said after a moment. "Part of the plan is to cement Bahdijn's place in the Cabinet and Admiral Jacks as men who could both anticipate and respond to an emergency. They will not be ready for six days. We will wait. The submarine will not go out to check the explosives again."

In the CIC of *Coral* and *Pearl* eyebrows were raised. Zeke was first on the com-link. Knowing that someone with itchy ears could be trying to penetrate the secure com-link he pushed the talk button and in a very calm voice spoke. Everyone on the ship was being very careful of what they said on every frequency but those absolutely protected.

"Bright Eyes, would you please round up your miscreant husband and bring him to my station at your earliest convenience." He winked at Cecilia.

"Roger that." She said in a flat voice, got up and headed out to find Jim.

"Hey John!" News said immediately afterward. "I've got the

sports statistics up here. Can you come up and take a look? I think you owe me some money!" He added.

"No way they lost!" John's voice came on. "I'm on my way and you better have proof!" He sounded flustered and irritated.

Twenty minutes later Jim contacted his brother by radio, not their com-links. Several times they had used the radio frequency to talk so that those listening on the other ship would not know they had the com-link system to communicate.

"Hey JR, this is Shep, over. Do you copy?"

"Go ahead Shep, I copy, over." John replied after a pause.

"Why don't we have dinner on the observation deck of *Coral* to celebrate our find. Over." Jim said evenly.

"I was thinking along the same lines. Over." John replied blandly.

"After dinner we can meet in the conference room and discuss the find and how to bring it up. Over." Jim said.

"I'll alert the crew. Dinner will be served at 18:00. Over." John said.

"Roger. Over and out." Jim replied.

Ya'qub had indeed listened as best he could to the radio transmission. The boom microphones they had pointed at the ship provided a little conversation, but not much. Nothing had happened since he and Tanfiq had their conversation in the bridge but he still worried. What was going on between the two ships seemed not only likely, but also reasonable, so he dismissed it as normal. That did not decrease his concern.

As evening settled, he watched through his binoculars as the two crews met on the observation deck and ate what looked like prime rib and crab. No one was left on board the research vessel, but the temptation to board it died as soon as it rose. There was the possibly of Navy SEALs on board. *Besides, no one with something to hide leaves a ship without a guard.*

Dinner, he noted, included some dancing before the entire crew moved below decks to discuss their salvage operation. Now both decks were deserted, with the exception of the kitchen crew clearing away the tables, chairs, and dinner remains from the observation deck. With eight crewmembers the cleaning did not take much time.

Below decks Zeke closed and sealed the door to the conference room and squeezed into his seat.

"We are secure." He announced.

"A six-day window does not give us much time. I want a plan by the end of this meeting, and I want us to be ready to move by 03:00 in the morning." Jim said tersely. "What can you tell us about Merlin Bahdijn, top advisor to our new president?"

"Off hand I'd say he's a sleeper agent who has been in the U.S. since before 9/11/2001. Everything I've been able to gather on him describes him as the voice of reason from the Muslim point of view, a man of vision, and a first-generation American citizen." Zeke replied, manipulating his keyboard to give pictures and news cuts on the man in question. He nodded at Pen. "Pen, go ahead."

"MI6 has a bit more on this character." Pen replied. At age 22 he graduated from the American University in Cairo, Egypt. Smart, well educated, and highly motivated he created a circle of influential friends from America. However, his tuition was paid by Kareem al-Jameel ibn Nidh'aai. Kareem's sphere of influence included the very worst of our terrorist leaders and financers. Merlin, it seems, was groomed for this moment in time." She looked around the table as she spoke.

"We are of the opinion that Kareem al-Jameel ibn Nidh'aai is the famous Ghost. Ira of Mossad agrees. Stephens, your new president, is from Illinois, and his campaign funding raised many questions with your FBI. No proof of wrongdoing was ever produced. Ira is of the opinion that much of it came from Kareem, but none of us have taken the time to trace the actual money source. I think now that was an oversight on our part.

"That, at least, is in keeping with the Ghost. If this plan of theirs worked, Bahdijn and Jacks would be sitting pretty, and our new president would have the adulation of the multitudes, at the cost of thousands of innocent lives. Has anyone else noticed how this president and his wife act more like a king and queen than an elected civil servant? They act poorly, but the words and actions are there for any who dare to look close enough. Whoever is behind your president may have promised to make him a king, or emperor, and he's naïve enough to believe it."

"Ya'qub has been on our radar several times. It seems he is al-Jameel's most trusted and successful agent. Up until now he has been mostly involved in assassinations. Kareem plans and Ya'qub carries out his plans." Pen sat back.

"Has Duck sent us anything since you alerted him?" Jim asked Zeke.

"The news isn't good. Bahdijn is working on beefing up FEMA and Jacks has put the ships in the Med, and Red Sea on notice fearing an attack on American soil. Jacks claims that he has a hunch forces are at work against America to weaken her and plans to be ready, whatever may come. Hogg backed him up.

"Naval Intelligence is wondering where he's getting his information, because so far Homeland Security, NSA, CIA, FBI, NATO, and other intelligence agencies have no inkling of a pending attack." Zeke shrugged his shoulders. "Stephens is listening to Hogg."

"Of interest to me is the fact that Jacks background gives us a few hints to his hatred of Israel. Back in 1980 his sister was killed in Israel. She was an exchange student and got caught up with Hamas. Her parents are extremely anti-Semitic and Jacks senior was high up in the KKK. Israeli forces attacked a known Hamas leader in his home and Jacks' sister happened to be there. Through an admiral we all know was a traitor to his country Jacks managed to keep her name and part in the organization secret." Zeke sighed and looked up.

"Options?" Jim asked the crew after they pondered this last bit of news.

"Take out Ya'qub, Tanfiq, and Najid first. Sweep the crew from their ship. At the same time two teams take out the research ship that is heading for Alaska. We teach this Ghost character what real ghosts look like!" John said quietly.

"Expose the plot afterwards and name Bahdijn and Jacks as co-

conspirators. We'll need rock solid proof for that." Jim added after a moment of thought.

"How do we get that?" FM asked no one in particular.

"Ya'qub knows the whole plan. We get it from him, along with whatever written records are available, while Ira works on the other end with Kareem." Pen said quietly into the silence that followed the question. "Even if the Ghost escapes, this particular plan must have taken years to set in motion. He may have a back-up plan if this fails, and we need to consider that. If not, we've hampered his operation enough to slow him down considerably."

"He'll have a back-up plan. Ira will need to get the details on that if he can, but I think Ya'qub will be our information source on that particular plot." Jim said; his brow knitted in concentration. "Israel is involved somehow. We need to discover what Kareem's plans are for Israel while he has all eyes turned to America! His hatred of Israel is something we all know very well. Let's make sure that Israel is protected, despite our new president's views on that particular subject."

"Bahdijn must know both plans, boss. Pull him out in the open, grab him, and make him talk." Chief said suddenly. "You know he's going to pull strings to have us searched and followed and everything else once the crew on both ships disappears. Pushed men often make stupid mistakes."

"We will have to continue our research to maintain our cover, and to frustrate him enough to make a move on us. He has to come to us in that case, because we're here legitimately, working with several universities, and we don't have to move." Jim nodded. "Pushed men do make stupid mistakes, so let's push him at every opportunity."

"Uh, how are we going to get the research ship in Alaska if we don't move?" Numbers asked.

"Let's call in a favor. We'll put two teams in the water and have them picked up by a submarine, and we'll borrow a C-130 to transport the team to Alaska." John said quickly.

"A C-130! Can't we take the CH53D?" Fagan whined.

"What? Don't they have comfortable seats on a C-130 and a beverage cart?" Driver asked facetiously.

"Gawd! Wouldn't that be awesome!" Fagan grinned.

"How exactly will we get Ya'qub to talk?" Wade asked after the laughter died down. "If he's as fanatical as he sounds, he won't tell us anything, even if we torture him."

"We use the right mixture of drugs, and a look-a-like for Kareem and Bahdijn." Jim replied immediately. "I've been thinking about that. He would certainly tell them anything if he was confused enough to believe they were actually talking to him, and perhaps a little upset with him."

"When I grow up, I want to be able to think just like you, boss." Viper said, bringing another outburst of laughter. Jim grinned with the laughter and didn't mind the interruption.

"Well, they do say that wisdom comes with age, and I haven't seen any sign of the former yet, so it may take a while for that growing up." Sid Barrett commented; his head tilted to one side and his face serious as he looked at his team leader. "I hear with some it takes a whole lifetime!"

"We'll go on the C-130 boss." Dodge said quickly. "Sid loves flying in the belly of one of those birds." Sid usually threw up on flights on transport planes.

"Thanks, boss!" Sid said with a grimace.

R.C. slapped Sid on the back of the head and everyone laughed. Jim cracked a smile at the interchange and cleared his throat. When things settled down, he continued.

"This will take precise timing. 12 Team 1 will take the research ship. Night insertion, silent and deadly! No evidence we were ever there. We clean up every single piece of brass and wipe every surface we touch!

"12 Team 3 will take the container ship. When you're finished sink the sub. We'll let the Navy recover it later. Night insertion, silent and deadly! No evidence we were ever there.

"12 Team 2 will have security on the two boats, and we'll be running a recon of the cave to determine how to get at the treasures in there. Dr. Dinsmore believes they are in the cave at the highest elevation, which is shallow enough for divers in the Newt Suits, once we determine how to get in there. With one sub down and activity on both vessels no one will know we're gone." Jim sat back.

"And how will we catch Bahdijn?" Norm Geissler asked quietly.

"He'll try to grab someone from the crew. My guess would be a woman or two. That way he'll think he has more leverage against us." Smitty said after a few moments of silence. "Isn't it odd how God seems to put us in the right time and place?" He added. "No one would have known about this! And whomever he kidnaps will put him in our hands!"

"I volunteer." Pen said with a grim smile.

"Me too." Cecilia said quickly. Pen nodded at her.

"They would be the best two to grab, boss." FM said. "We could put them on the island, shopping or something, give him the opportunity. We're all chipped so we'll be able to see where he takes them. He'll want to be there when they try to get the information, so we should be able to nab him then. Kidnapping will put the final touch on his demise. Life in prison is a suitable punishment for this scum, and I'd like to see that happen!"

"Since the two of you volunteered, I'll go along with the idea." Jim said. He'd taken a long time to consider all the possibilities, and he knew this one was the safest. Pen and Cecilia were years ahead of the other women on the crew when it came to self-defense and poise in tight situations. Inside his gut was twisting hard, as he knew John was experiencing the same sensations. They looked at each other and nodded at the same time. Their eyes were grim, but the decision had been taken out of their hands.

"Okay!" Jim said. "Let's get the details of this plan down on paper and get to work!"

Two hours went by as they hammered out the details of their plan. Those new to Jim's crew were amazed at how carefully their own ideas were considered when offered. Some of them went into the master plan. Those that didn't were recorded for possible use in another mission.

An expert at letting people know their input was valuable to him, both Captains encouraged the best from every member of his crew. By the end of the meeting every person on the team was more than ready to go. They knew the plan was well thought out, the contingencies considered carefully, and subsequent actions planned to meet each one. At the end of the session Jim led them in prayer. It was perhaps that final action that gave them the most courage.

12 Team 1 went into the water almost immediately after the meeting, welcomed aboard the submarine waiting beneath the surface for a temporary ride to the island. Once on base they were transferred to a C-130 transport and were in the air only seconds after everyone had taken a seat.

Ya'qub watched as the submersible was launched from the research ship. Frank was operating the controls, while the Dinsmores lay on either side of him. Raider team was on the *Coral*, shadows among the shadows for security. Knife was providing security on the *Pearl*. He could not see either team in place but suspected someone was there, watching over the crafts.

Finally, after watching them for an hour, he put down the binoculars and turned to Tanfiq. "We don't need to watch them work on the treasure. I'm going to bed." He said simply. In an hour all of them were quietly asleep, never suspecting what was about to take place. Even had they known they could not have prevented it. Their best guards in place were no protection.

At the prescribed time the two 12 teams hit the ships of the terrorists. In his berth Ya'qub awakened to the touch of cold steel against his neck. He stared up into the cold eyes of C.G. Franklin, whose face had been painted for a night insertion, blacks and grays, a wicked mask behind a black balaclava. In Farsi Franklin told him to lie still.

Other hands frisked him, found the gun beneath his pillow and the one just under the mattress. Roughly they rolled him over, used special restraint plastic ties to bind him, putting his hands back to back and even binding his fingers and thumbs so that he was completely helpless. Sitting in his underwear on his berth he listened as the men spoke together over their headsets. He didn't have to wonder about Tanfiq or Najid for long. They were tossed into his cabin, bloodied and bruised.

Najid got to his knees and spit at Wade. Wade avoided the spittle, took one step back, and then lashed out with a kick that put Najid out for the count. The kick had been fast, accurate, and powerful. It wasn't the type of kick he would have expected from a Marine or a SEAL. He had seen kicks like that in full-contact martial arts contests. Usually military men lacked the speed and finesse of such moves. Every man spoke English when speaking to each other, but there were odd accents among them making him wonder if they might be a NATO force.

Shots rang out, the sound of AK-47 fire loud in the night, and the spitting of silenced weapons. Shouts of "clear!" in English followed each volley. Eventually two men arrived at the doorway. One was a giant, the other rather short for a man, but athletically built. The smaller one spoke.

"All crew accounted for, Captain. Driver has detached the sub and it is sinking as we speak. The current will carry it a fair distance before it grounds on the bottom. It won't be hard for the Navy to pick it up and salvage it." Mark said, snapping off a quick salute.

"Good work. Dorf, please supervise the policing of the decks and make sure nothing is left behind. We'll transport these three to the *Coral*." The Captain said. It was he who lifted Ya'qub bodily from his berth, slung him over his shoulder in a fireman's carry, and without another word ducked through the doorway. Everything he'd just seen confirmed his suspicions. The very tall man and the shorter man were the final pieces. Ya'qub remained silent. It was the crew from the *Coral*! *How did they know? What do they know?*

They were, at the moment, anchored over one of the explosives set to go off in six days. The blast would cripple their ship, and even possibly sink it. He hoped he would not be on board when that happened! Self-sacrifice had not been in the plans. Still, he would be a hero if he remained silent, and he was not about to betray Kareem.

CHAPTER 16

Jim's plan was carefully thought out. As the rigid raider moved silently toward the *Coral* Dr. Dinsmore gave orders that the CH53D was to go up and monitor the sensors that had been placed on the ocean floor to be sure all were in working order. It was a ruse, of course, because the equipment to monitor those nodes was on the research ship and in universities on the island and mainland. However, it was also possible for that to be done, if some of the equipment went with the helicopter. None was transferred to the bird.

Dorf and Mark quickly made the chopper ready to fly, and before dawn painted its light lines on the horizon the helicopter lifted off and flew to an atoll exactly forty miles from the ship. This tiny island was home mostly to birds, had no beach and few trees or brush of any kind. What it did have was a cave that during high tide wasn't accessible, which was most hours of the day and night. With the tide at its lowest the cave was not only accessible, but there was enough space in front of it to land on the rough volcanic rock that formed the atoll.

Forty-five minutes later the three prisoners were on a ledge inside the cave, shackled together by their ankles, with heavy steel balls to weight them down. Each man was given a canteen of water and two MRE packages and told to hold tight, someone would be back.

Mark chuckled as he watched the three fend off crabs that seemed to inhabit the cave in multitudes. They wouldn't get much sleep.

As the helicopter lifted from the rocks the first waves washed over them. Soon the cave would be full of water, and the ledge, though above the surface of the highest watermark, would get wet repeatedly as the water moved back and forth with the surf of the sea. It would also be pitch black inside that cave. Mark had been inside during high tide earlier when they passed the atoll and explored the cave on their way to Hawaii. He remembered the darkness and the feel of the water moving across his legs.

With the weighted shackles around their legs they wouldn't risk swimming. A man didn't swim well with a hundred and fifty pounds of steel holding him down! No, he guessed they would sit tight and wait it out, fear mushrooming inside until the tide went out and there was at least some light from the mouth of the cave. Purposely lights had been withheld from the prisoners. The psychological affects would include disorientation, sleep depravation, and above all, fear.

That too was fitting. Somewhere deep inside their soul was a deadly darkness. People who took thousands of innocent lives without remorse possessed that darkness in their souls, that deadly darkness that allowed them to step across the boundaries of decency and righteousness into horror and death. Mark also knew that every man was but a thought away from that line, that every human being possessed that deadly darkness in his soul that only Sovereign God could fill with light.

Knowing that if he allowed himself to dwell on the evil that these men were perpetrating in his world against innocent people, he could become just like them in dealing with the prisoners he lifted a prayer to his Lord. "Keep my heart from vengeance, Lord. Don't let me *want* to kill these men." He immediately felt better and pushed those dark thoughts from his mind.

Later that day, after 12 Team 3 returned from taking the research ship, Jim received a call from Admiral Komentowski.

"*Bring It Up One,* this is Admiral Komentowski. One of our subs discovered a diesel sub, Russian in origin, sitting on the bottom of the ocean near your location. It appears to be intact but is currently full of water. Do you know anything about that? Over."

"Good morning Admiral. Is that what has been showing up on our sonar. Every time we pinged the reading though it disappeared. I'm assuming the crew was aboard. Did they radio for help at any time that you know? Also, can we assist you in raising the sub? Over." Jim replied.

"We've got a barge coming out to raise the sub now, Captain. I'll let you know if any crew were aboard. No one picked up a distress call of any kind. Do you have any idea what they were doing down there? Over." Admiral Komentowski's voice sounded tinny over the radiophone.

"No sir. However, I would check the container ship anchored out here. That sub had to come from somewhere, and it is possible to attach a submarine to the hull of a ship. It's possible it became detached and sank somehow. It would be interesting to know what they were doing down there. Let us know if there is any way we can help. Over." Jim waited patiently for a few moments.

"I will send the Coast Guard out to inspect that ship, Captain. I'll have to send them to inspect your ship as well. Over." Admiral Komentowski was covering all the bases and Jim could appreciate his position.

"Roger that, Admiral. We will give them a friendly reception and permission to board our vessels and do a thorough search. Over." Jim replied. He smiled at the transmission and knew his cover was secure. Because they were on two ships, it was very possible the Coast Guard would do random drug testing on both vessels, but Jim never worried about that.

"Thank you, Captain. Your cooperation is much appreciated. Over and out." Admiral Komentowski put the radio down and looked at the men gathered in the ready room.

"Have a Navy destroyer stand by the Coast Guard when they approach the *Sikandar*. Let's keep them safe." He ordered.

"I'd like that assignment, sir." Commander Cummings said.

"Thank you, commander. You have your orders." Commander Cummings saluted and left the room.

Jim kept everyone above the surface while the Navy raised the submarine and sent the Coast Guard cutter to the *Sikandar*. With Zeke in the CIC he listened to the reports of the Coast Guard as they swept through the ship. They found the hatch where a submarine could be fastened to the hull of the ship and sent divers down to see what had gone wrong. Only the crew of *Bring It Up*, Komentowski, and Duck Ashley knew what had taken place. This charade needed to play out exactly as planned for it to work.

An NCIS crew arrived to work the crime scene. Jim already knew what they would find. Each AK-47 would have more bullets in the magazine than shells on the floor. His men had taken extra ammo for that purpose, to make it look like the firefight was between people carrying the same weapons. His men had carried the silenced H&K MSG90 that fired the same caliber round. Any autopsies would show the men were shot by that caliber of ammunition, suggesting a falling out amongst comrades, rather than an attack by American or international forces. Knowing he'd covered the bases he waited patiently.

It was what they would find in Ya'qub's cabin that would shock the world. Detailed plans to create a tsunami that would hit the western shores of the United States were all there. Among those plans Zeke had planted a digital memory card with the conversation between Ya'qub and Tanfiq about moving the deadline up, mentioning Bahdijn and Jacks by name. A digital recorder, small enough to be hidden, was among Ya'qub's things bearing his fingerprints. Jim hoped they would be on file somewhere.

Later, toward evening, the Coast Guard cutter came alongside the *Pearl*. Commander Packer was a trim man of medium height with gray hair and hard eyes from years of service. Captain Shepherd was polite and welcomed his men aboard the vessel. Jim personally conducted a tour of the vessel for the Commander while his men searched the ship from top to bottom.

Packer hated wasting his time, knowing that searching these two vessels would produce nothing. Yet he had his orders and he wasn't about to disobey an order. He found Jim's crew professional, careful, and able seamen. The ship was spotless and cared for better than any he had ever searched. His estimation of Captain Shepherd went up a notch as he looked around and met various crewmembers at work.

After the search he stood at the railing looking down at his own cutter and sighed. "I'm sorry I had to waste your time and mine in this search. It's pretty obvious that a firefight went down on that ship sometime last night. Your crew was working last night. Did you hear any shots? Is it possible any of your crew noticed a boat approaching the ship over there?"

"With the deck crane running and all the activity on board we did not hear any shots." Jim replied. "Our equipment did pick up the sound of two outboard motors around 03:00 but we paid little attention to it, since it wasn't close. I'm sorry." Jim said politely.

"At least we have a starting point." Packer replied. He shook hands and went down the gangplank to his own boat and moved over to the *Coral*. There he met John Shepherd, wearing the rank of Captain, who gave him a tour of his tug. John was much more talkative than Jim and took Parker on an extended and animated tour of his ship. Like the research ship this was kept up and spotless. He found himself envious of such a pristine ship.

Everywhere he went he met professionals he would have gladly had as members of his own crew. Most of them were ex-military, which was obvious. Packer decided he never wanted to come up against this crew. Yet they were quite friendly, open, and showed no nervousness with the search or presence of the Coast Guard. What he also saw was the cohesiveness of the men, and he felt rather than saw their resolve and ability. It was truly inspiring.

At the brig, in the kitchen of all places, he saw that it was spotless and obviously unused. Meeting Sturdy and Abe was an experience and the food he tasted was marvelous. Accepting an invitation to eat while his crew searched, he joined the men in the dining room for supper. By the time he was finished he was wishing he could be part of this crew.

Commander Packer reported to the Admiral that evening. His crew had inspected both ships owned by *Bring It Up*, identified and checked all crewmember's identification and seaman card status, and even drug tested a few of them. In order to serve on a ship, one had to possess a seaman's card, and undergo random drug testing to maintain that card.

"Both Captain Shepherds run a tight operation, sir." Packer said with appreciation. "Those two ships are kept in pristine condition and crews are professionals. Medical staff does random drug tests regularly and keeps good records of the results. It might be interesting to go looking for lost ships at sea and find treasures from the past. I don't know what his pay rates are, but the food on the ships is first rate. A transfer to another duty at sea sounds pretty good right now." He ended.

"NCIS thinks the three missing crewmembers may have killed their own crew and fled so that no one would talk." Admiral Komentowski said slowly. "That may have been the outboard motor Shepherd was talking about. We're searching for them by air, but nothing has been spotted. What doesn't make sense is the research ship that was here with them was found this morning adrift, all members dead, the same signature. Only this time no crewmembers were missing. That doesn't make any sense, since the purpose of the research ship was to register the effect of their plot."

"What about the explosives on the ocean floor?" Packer asked, registering that thought and deciding he needed to think about it.

"We've asked *Bring It Up* to suspend operations beneath the surface and move away while we gather them all up. Can't have civilians and researchers blown up if somebody makes a mistake down there, can we? Anyway, we'll have those by the end of tomorrow. They may tell us a great deal. NCIS is working on getting proof that Bahdijn and Jacks were indeed involved in this nefarious plot. Expect blowback, especially from the president's pet man." Admiral Komentowski sighed.

"I don't think I ever would have pegged him as a terrorist, sir." Packer said quietly. "If it is true, it goes to show that we can't let our guard down for even a moment anymore. I remember a time when all we did was rescue idiots on the ocean. Now we're police!"

"Do you think *Bring It Up* had anything to do with this?" The Admiral asked quietly.

"I searched their ships, sir. There were no assault weapons to be found anywhere, and my people know how to search a ship thoroughly. We even searched the keel and hull of each ship. I had my people search the helicopter, submersibles, and even the ROVs and HROVs. Sir, we opened crates in the hold and even had a few containers moved to be sure nothing was hidden beneath. I can guarantee that." Packer said earnestly. "Most of those men are highly decorated soldiers we should never have let go, sir."

"I concur." Admiral Komentowski sighed. "We have some criminals to catch Commander. Let's get to it. Ya'qub, Tanfiq, and Najid must be found. Dismissed, and thank you for your cooperation." Packer saluted and left. His work was just beginning, and he was anxious to get started.

In the evening the CH53D helicopter left *Coral* once more, bound for the atoll. Again, the excuse was in calibrating the equipment beneath the ocean. No one questioned the filing of the flight plan. In the cave Mark found three demoralized men, starved for sleep, bitten and bleeding at various extremities. Ox stepped up and treated the bites and cuts, giving each man a shot.

This time they swept the ledge clear of crabs and other creatures, providing a cage to keep the men safe from them. Made of a simple frame with screen wire stretched over it and weighted at the bottom it provided ample protection. An air mattress was inflated for the bottom to make them more comfortable, and battery-operated lights were provided, with extra batteries. Psychologically this change would confuse all three men.

Again, Mark left them with a canteen of water and two MRE packs each. Water and food had been treated with the proper drugs, and the shot the three men had just received was the beginning of their treatment. By the following evening they would be ready for the appearance of Bahdijn and Abu Kareem al-Jameel ibn Nidh'aai.

Meanwhile the crew was making progress toward the next step in their plan for the prisoners. Working off recent pictures and videos of the men Bill Kline and David Carr had been transformed through the use of latex masks and modern make-up techniques into perfect mirror images of the two men. It was uncanny to see just how much the two men resembled the terrorists.

In the morning Commander Cummings pulled alongside the *Coral* and asked permission to come aboard. John greeted him and welcomed him formally. Cummings didn't wait.

"I have orders to search both these vessels. I'm sorry. I know it's a waste of time, but orders are orders. You should know these came from Washington, and not from Hawaii." He added. He waited, curious how John Shepherd would react.

"By all means. Search to your hearts content." John said with a grin. "I'll get my men on finding out where that order originated, and we'll have information about officers that can't be trusted. Thanks for being so polite about the search, sir." Cummings smiled and nodded in agreement and motioned his men to come aboard.

Four hours later he left the two ships to report to Washington that there were no assault weapons on board the two ships, and no prisoners being held against their will. Bahdijn received the report and spat. Jacks cursed. They were in a safe house in West Virginia, an hour's drive from civilization. Zeke had recorded the phone call between a Captain Derringer and Bahdijn. He also had the address of the safe house for future use.

"Uncle Zeke sees all." He said softly as he put the report in a folder and sent it down to Jim.

Evening fell and the CH53D took off again, this time for a different spot. Inside the Rigid Raider was ready for unloading three miles from the atoll. Kline and Carr were dressed as Bahdijn and Abu Kareem al-Jameel ibn Nidh'aai respectively. Carr looked nearly sixty and waited until they arrived at the cave to insert the contact lenses in his eyes.

The first Ya'qub knew they were there was a powerful flashlight shining in his eyes as the screen cover was ripped away and tossed into the cavern. He swallowed hard when he saw the face leaning over him. Sweat formed on his forehead and he hunched into himself. This, he knew, would all be bad!

"Fool! Carr spat in Afrikaans, the language Kareem spoke most often. "Your incompetence has ruined everything! Bahdijn is exposed and our influence with the president is gone! I should kill you right here!" Kareem's favorite pistol, a Luger .22 with silencer appeared and filled Ya'qub's vision.

"Wait, Master!" Bahdijn's voice sounded raspy as he put a browned hand on Kareem's shoulder. "He is instrumental in our back-up plan." To Ya'qub's relief the pistol, which had not wavered, slowly lowered.

"These two know nothing of that plan." Kareem said. Dispassionately he shot them both. It had been agreed unanimously that both men should die. Carr fought to keep his face still and not show the repugnance he had for such an act. Yet it had to be done, and he was not one to shirk his duty. After all the evidence was weighed and the kills sanctioned, he had volunteered. "What have you told the Americans?" He spat, bringing the pistol back to bear on Ya'qub. Quailing before that threat Ya'qub hunched into himself again.

"Nothing, Excellency! They have not questioned us yet!" Ya'qub sputtered, watching the smoke curl up from the silencer.

"Who has not questioned you?" Kareem asked dangerously.

"Those men on the *Coral*. They were the ones who captured us. I do not know what they intend."

"They questioned Tanfiq! Did you know that? He told them everything. The drugs they gave him made him talk. That is how the American's knew so much! Before he woke up other drugs made him forget! How do I know that you have not been questioned in the same way?" He asked dangerously.

"Such drugs, I am told, create other memory problems. Let us ask him to divulge the entire back-up operation. If he can do this, he was not drugged as Tanfiq was." Bahdijn coaxed.

"If you miss one of the pieces of information, I shall kill you." Kareem said in a dangerously soft voice.

"Excellency! I do not know the whole plan! Only my part!" Ya'qub wailed, terrified at this unexpected turn of events.

"I know that fool!" Kareem slapped him hard. "Why would I trust you with that kind of information? Just tell me your part. All of it!" The slap nearly convinced Ya'qub he was really talking to Kareem. Nearly.

"If the tsunami did not follow our plans what were you to do immediately after that information was provided?" Bill asked softly.

"I was to remain with the container ship until the container from El Diazair arrived in Hawaii, pick it up, and go to Puerto Vallarta in Mexico. There I was to load it on a truck driven by Aziz, and accompany him to Washington, D.C. In Washington it would be stored in a facility for two weeks, and then we were to park it in close to Franklin Square on the eve of the United Kingdom Prime Minister's speech. I am to call 911 and inform them that a dirty bomb has been parked in the vicinity of Franklin Square.

"During the evacuation of the buildings I am to assist Aziz in his work. He is a skilled sniper and will kill Lord White and Ira Lehman, who will be dining not far from the square. I am his spotter. This I have done before, Excellency. I swear I will not fail." Ya'qub watched as the gun came up to point between his eyes and he swallowed and held up a hand.

"I have not forgotten, Master. I but needed to know you were indeed who I believed you to be!" He begged. The gun did not move so he swallowed and continued, now sure he was talking to Kareem. "When the two are dead I am to call Mr. Bahdijn, posing as a diplomat from Iran, and protest the imprisonment of two freedom fighters. He will know by that call that Ira Lehman and the Prime Minister are dead. I have memorized Mr. Bahdijn's private cell phone number!" He gave it haltingly. For a long moment he waited, feeling his heart beating too quickly in fear. His eyes wandered to the two dead men and he shivered.

"He has obviously not been drugged." Sparks said. "We must get him away from here."

"He cannot know how we do this, or if he is captured again, he will tell all!" Carr said, still pointing that deadly gun at Ya'qub's head. "Spray him. He will awaken in his birth back on the container ship. I will send you a new crew and you will carry out your assignment! Do not fail me again!"

"I swear that I will not, Master. We were captured because of those two. They were careless!" Ya'qub said, kicking the dead body of Tanfiq. "They would not listen to me."

"The men I send will listen to you. Tell them nothing." Carr replied.

Sparks leaned down and sprayed something in Ya'qub's face and everything faded.

CHAPTER 17

"How are we going to play this one?" John asked his brother as the two sat at the conference table on the *Coral*. Wade, Dorf, Mark, Viper, Zeke, Sparks, Smitty, Hobbs, and Ox sat around the table with them. Cecilia and Pen had not yet arrived.

"A good sniper always goes for center chest. Heads tend to move too much so I don't think this sniper will go for a headshot. We'll make sure our doubles for Lord White and Ira know what's coming, and that they wear our special body armor. A bullet with that velocity will knock them both down and hurt them. We'll have to make sure there are two burly fellows right behind them, so they don't get thrown down too hard." Jim said after a moment of thought. It was an interesting problem and his expertise helped him think it through.

Wade grimaced, rubbing his chest as if remembering the pain. "Our body armor did stop the sniper bullet, but it sure did bruise some ribs and hurt some!"

"I seem to remember a Lieutenant Commander that insisted since he designed the body armor, he should be the one to test it. In fact, I distinctly remember being threatened with a true Marine beat down if that particular officer was not permitted to test his own invention!" Jim grinned at Wade. "It wasn't easy to let my best friend take that bullet!" Jim grinned and punched Wade on the shoulder.

"We did test it on a dummy first, so I knew it would work." Wade said, grinning back. "Sharky wasn't on the boat at the time, if I remember correctly." He added. "Can you imagine what a fuss he would have put up? Little Mr. Prim and Proper would have pitched a fit!"

"What do we know about the shooter?" Jim asked quickly, steering the conversation away from Finn, whom many of the men detested despite his efficiency.

"He uses the Steyr Tactical Elite .308. For his best shot he will want to be within twelve hundred yards. We've identified several locations he can get to for his shot. Our best guess is this parking structure, third or fourth level. He can work from inside a van or car, but most likely a van. Range is preferable, less than a thousand yards, which makes it a sure shot. That's what I would do." John answered, showing the locations on the computer screen.

Jim studied the locations and decided his brother was correct. The parking garage was the best location that provided the simplest means of setting up, taking the shots, and provided three escape routes. This particular parking structure would be constantly busy with vehicles entering and leaving at all hours. The only real difficulty he could see was procuring a parking place, and that could be done only by arriving very early in the morning, or perhaps the day before, and simply leaving the van. One could not drive around hoping that the right spot would open. Shooting from inside a van made it difficult to determine where the shot originated. After a few moments of consideration, he nodded his head.

"We have to let them believe they have succeeded, and we have to be able to trace that call to Bahdijn, record it, and identify the voices." Zeke continued. "I can do that." He added unnecessarily. "Even from here I can do that!" He grinned and nodded. The man could do things with cell phones, landlines, and computers that defied belief. Some of it was even legal.

"Ya'qub has several options for making that call. He can use a prepaid phone that he will toss immediately after use. He can use a payphone, probably on location or near the location to make the call while the shooter makes his escape. My guess is he will have a rental somewhere near for his own exit. Another option is a phone provided by Kareem's group for the purpose, which will also be untraceable and easily discarded." John said quietly.

"I will have control of the cell towers nearest the location, and a tap on every payphone within a mile radius." Zeke said as if this was an everyday request. "Uncle Zeke sees and hears all! Just don't tell Finn!" He added.

"Have we considered how Kareem and Bahdijn will respond to what happened on the ship?" Wade inquired.

"One or both of them will try to snatch somebody from the crew to question." Jim replied. "My guess would be one or two of the female crew. I recommend giving them Pen and Cecilia. They are both trained and strong enough to hold out until we go in for the rescue. We've all been chipped, and I've seen Zeke target one individual to within a fraction of an inch of where he was. Perhaps the worst part will be waiting until we know we have them cold."

It was a fairly new technology. The chip itself was inserted with a hypodermic needle beneath the skin on the top of the left foot. Tests had determined that the foot was the least likely to cause any reaction to the chip. Every team member and crewmember voluntarily accepted the chip because it meant that in the event of an accident at sea he or she could be found quickly.

Zeke had fine-tuned the system so that he could track members of the crew up to a hundred and eighty-two miles. Once beyond that point he had to tap into the satellite system and accuracy was lost. From a satellite the chip could be pinpointed to within a mile radius.

Hand-held units had been created to locate the wearer of the chip. One advantage the chip gave them was that the vital signs of the body could be accurately recorded in real time. Each unit could also detect every human heart within a thousand yards, telling them accurately if a team member was surrounded by enemies, how many they were, and exactly where they were in a given location.

"We need to warn the female crew not to go ashore without a team of four men. And I think we should ask Pen and Cecilia if they are still willing to be bait." John added with a grin for his brother. Jim knew why John made that suggestion as the two women entered.

"Ah!" Jim said, putting on his poker face. "In my family the man is the head of the house, and the women do what he says." He knew that Cecilia was coming into the room behind him as he spoke. She smacked the back of his head hard. Hard on her heals Pen arrived and she walked over to John and grabbed his ear.

"Don't listen to your brother and get any ideas bub!" She said through her laughter.

"Submit woman!" Jim said in a rare display of playfulness, dodging as Cecilia tried to hit him again. All of them laughed at each other as the two couples hugged each other.

"What exactly was I going to willingly submit to?" Cecilia asked Jim.

"We were thinking of letting Bahdijn and possibly Kareem or men who work directly for them kidnap the two of you. Both of you have come a long way in your training and we think you could handle the situation better than any of the other female crewmembers." Jim said, reluctantly letting Cecilia go. "Kidnappers usually strip their victims for the psychological effect. Can you handle that?"

"Neither of them would resort to torture or drugs. We're too high profile. My guess is they would try to terrify us with threats and possibly rough us up a little, but no more than we get during martial arts training. A team would come in and rescue us before things got out of hand." Pen said after a moment of thought. "And, if we play this right, we can plant some false information in the heads of these terrorists." She added.

"She still thinks like a spy." Zeke said.

"Spy?" She asked, raising her eyebrows.

"What is it you did for MI6?" Zeke asked innocently.

"Well, mostly I was a spy." Pen replied. "But that's no reason to suggest that I think like a spy! That word has such negative connotations. I'd rather one said I thought like a counter-terrorist operative, or a counter-intelligence operative. Those sound so much more sophisticated and up to date than the word *spy*. I think of myself as an operative.”

“Yep. She still thinks like a spy.” John said, nimbly stepping away as she swept her arm around to backhand him.

“I have a constant tap on Bahdijn’s phones, including the secure phone he uses to contact Kareem. Figuring such a thing existed I asked a friend to put a few things in place to catch encrypted communications. With News working with me, it only took a few hours to crack the encryption. Any time he uses that phone we will have a recording. We also have the ability to decipher the encrypted email messages. SOS actually helped us put that whole program together. She’s good!”

“I thought those phones were supposed to be secure.” Pen said, raising an eyebrow.

“Uncle Zeke sees all!” Zeke replied automatically. “Normally they are. However, the Russian model they are using was designed to use specific encryption that we can easily hack once we know the proper parameters. But, you spies already know that.” He grinned at Pen.

Pen took her Sig Sauer P-226 Para from her holster and checked the clip. With the clip out she examined the shaft of the pistol with a critical eye. “I don’t like the word spy anymore.” She said with a straight face. Zeke swallowed dramatically. A year ago Pen would never have engaged in such frivolity, but now she was part of the unit, friends with all of them, and she joined in the fun these days without hesitation.

After the laughter died down the two girls decided to plan a shopping trip to Honolulu on O‘ahu. Jim watched them as they walked off, heads bent toward each other, talking quietly. His eyes looked over at John and the two shared a moment of pride in their wives. Only the danger of the mission dampened their spirits.

“How do you think the President will react to his Cabinet member’s duplicity?” Jim asked the men in the room.

“He will try to save face.” Mark said. “Bahdijn and Jacks were both his personal appointments.”

“Let’s look at his options.” Dorf said, ticking them off on his fingers as he spoke. "First, he can claim he knew nothing of their duplicity and that he was duped. I don't think he'll do that because it makes him look either stupid or easily manipulated. Second, he can attempt to discredit the information, and in consequence he will have to discredit us. I don't think he'll go that route, because it will involve too many people. Third, he can put a lid on this in the interest of national security. That's his best option. He'll have to trade some favors and owe some people, but I think he can accomplish his goals."

"That means he'll shut down our operation, at least temporarily." Hobbs said calmly.

"We've registered the find and rights to the salvage through proper channels. Of course, we'll complain about the loss of time and money, as well as the loss of time on the important research we're doing here. It will give some of us a chance to fly to Washington to make our point, and we'll be on hand for the assassination attempt. That, of course, will put a stop to the President's ability to do much of anything and we'll be free to come back and salvage the ship." Jim said after a moment of thought.

"We should write a thank you letter afterwards, you know, to thank him for giving us the excuse to fly back to Washington and help out." John laughed.

"Let's not give away trade secrets!" Wade grinned.

"How did you yanks ever get to this place?" Ox asked. "What country elects a bloody traitor to the office of President?"

"One easily duped by the media." John said sarcastically. "We've been doing it for years. The all too handsome and clever draft dodger and friend of communism, and then the president from Illinois who would be king, obviously the result of too much inbreeding within the royal family, etc.! At least we had eight years with Jack Royce after that stupidity!"

"And now you have another economy killer congress and a traitor president!" Hobbs said. "Will you blokes ever grow up?"

"Shall we talk about Great Britain's government? Or Australia's?" John asked pointedly.

"Most embarrassing, what?" Hobbs said in his best Eaton accent.

"Okay! We're all in barney!" Ox grinned. "Our respective governments, pelicans all, are lucky to have us to keep things together while they play the patsy." His grin was infectious, and the men laughed together at his quip. "The reality is, statesmen are a very rare breed these days." He continued when the laughter died down. "Men who really care about doing what's best for the nation usually don't get elected!"

"Hear! Hear!" Hobbs said, raising his glass of orange juice.

"Either way, we need to prepare for the worst-case scenario." Smitty said quietly. "We're up against a powerful enemy!"

Sobered by his comment the men got back to the discussion at hand, making plans carefully. Pen and Cecilia returned to share their plans for their pseudo-shopping trip as bait. Sparks, after a nod from Zeke, left the room and returned a few minutes later. Once Pen and Cecilia shared their ideas Zeke, who had been watching his computer spoke up.

"The crew we put together has arrived on the *Sikandar*. Delta Force found nineteen men who could speak fluent Afrikaans and Farsi. Ya'qub put a call in to Bahdijn. I routed it to Sparks who confirmed the team was his. Ya'qub is briefing the crew now on their duties, and the ship is set to move into international waters and await the arrival of the container." He grinned at his brother.

"What if Bahdijn calls?" John asked.

"I warned him not to talk about the new crew. Bahdijn actually requested a crew from Kareem. Ira was able to intercept them secretly and they are being held until the assassination goes down." Sparks said.

"So, neither knows that the crew on board is American?" Jim asked.

"Correct, boss." Zeke said with a happy smile. "Only Duck and Romantowski know."

"Okay. Let's allow our bait to wander through the shops of Honolulu and see what happens." Jim said, taking Cecilia's hand gently. She smiled encouragingly.

CHAPTER 18

Kareem did not disappoint the crew of *Bring It Up*. His team of four men arrived in Honolulu the day after the disaster on the *Sikandar*. Their orders were to kidnap a woman from the ship and question her. Kareem had been very careful in choosing his men and giving them their orders. The women were not to be tortured for information, only frightened. His ideas on frightening them were quite extensive. Confident his men would succeed in getting the information he sought he waited patiently for their play.

What he did not know was that Pen Shepherd was one of the finest operatives in MI6, or that Cecilia was at least physically, mentally, and in martial arts ability nearly a match for her friend. Both women were quite attractive, and that only increased their fame when it came to press releases and news stories. Pen had soft blonde hair she kept tied back behind her head, blue eyes, a very pretty face, and a strong chin. The only indication of her physical prowess was a slightly thicker neck and shoulders that were broad enough to make her choose a size above her own to fit properly. Purposely she wore black to hide those features.

Cecilia had more of a long-distance runner's physique, though she had been blessed with a full figure. If she wore the right outfit that accentuated her figure, she liked how her husband looked at her. In public, she did not, choosing rather to wear professional attire that did not draw attention to her more salient features. Her hair was reddish blonde, hung to the middle of her back, and her hazel eyes were a devastatingly blue today because of her outfit.

Both women sat in the back of the boat as Driver taxied them to the port. He would be returning to the ship immediately and the four men watching the two women step up to the dock and wave goodbye nodded to each other. These were the first two to arrive alone. Others had come, but always with four to six men accompanying them. The thought that these two women might be bait never entered the minds of the would-be kidnappers.

No sooner had the women entered the city proper than they were suddenly confronted by four men; all discretely showing them wicked knives and insisting they come quietly.

"Don't be ridiculous!" Pen said haughtily.

"Don't be stupid!" The leader said, showing her the gun under the coat draped over his arm. It had a silencer screwed to the end. He watched her eyes and was confused for a moment when instead of fear he saw anger. Sometimes he surprised this look on one of his victims, but it was rare enough to give him a moment of doubt. But he soldiered on.

With a look at each other they nodded, and the men formed up around them, led them to a rented Suburban with tinted glass, and drove them to a rented beach house just off of Waikiki Beach. Silently both women watched the scenery as they headed south on H1, exiting on Kalakaua Avenue. To the right they passed Embassy Suites Hotel on Beachwalk, the Yard Hotel, the Sheraton Waikiki Hotel, Duke's Restaurant and Barefoot Bar, and finally they turned left on Kaiulani Avenue. The house was one of the newer ones. One of the rooms, hastily altered in an attempt to soundproof it, proved to be their prison.

In that room, the girls were secured by hand and leg cuffs to two wooden ladder-back chairs. Once they were secure one of the men took out his knife and began to cut away their clothing until both were naked. Although both women had been prepared for this, a standard procedure in kidnappings, they were still deeply embarrassed. Yet they maintained their courage, sharing a glance at each other. For both of them the friendship they had developed over the past year, and their faith in God and in their husbands, was more than enough to help them keep it all together. Cecilia, who had been the most concerned, breathed deeply and thanked God for her courage.

She truly hadn't known if her courage would be enough in this type of situation, but her training and faith proved to be exactly what she needed. Fighting down the panic and fear inside she sought to comfort Pen, and saw that Pen was doing much the same for her. Cecilia almost giggled at that point, and suddenly, instead of fear and embarrassment, she felt only anger towards any man who behaved this way toward any woman. Fighting that feeling down she tried to look meek.

The man who had cut away their clothing made a great show of dumping it in a trash can and telling them that later the clothing would be burned in the barbecue outside. A slow smile spread over his face as he decided the women were putting up a good front of bravery. It was time to frighten them.

In Afrikaans he called out an order. Another of the kidnappers arrived, pushing a serving cart covered by a towel. When the towel was removed various tools of torture were revealed. Ben Aziz was the leader and he lifted a pair of locking pliers, testing them, snapping them open, and closing them several times. He moved over to Cecilia and slapped her breast hard, putting the pliers up to suggest he was going to fasten them.

"What do you want to know?" Pen said tersely. Cecilia spit at her captor, showing no fear at all. Ben was taken aback. Pen's question however was what he wanted, so he turned to her, keeping the pliers poised to clamp. In his mind, American women were puffed up with their own importance not knowing their value was less than that of farm animal. He wished he'd not been cautioned not to actually harm them.

"What do you know of the *Sikandar* and her crew?" He asked.

"The container-ship?" Cecilia asked, as though confused. "We're not part of that crew!"

"It weighed anchor a few hours ago and left the area where we are doing research." Pen added.

"Just tell me everything you know about the ship." Ben's voice was resigned.

"Get that thing away from me, you creep!" Cecilia responded, spitting at him again. He slapped her hard on the face, rocking her chair with the force of his blow. For a moment her head spun, but it cleared quickly, and she looked up at Aziz with real loathing.

"My husband will probably kill you for that." She said, spitting blood from a split lip and feeling the blood flowing out of her nose. When she looked at Aziz, he saw that there was no sign of fear in her eyes, only anger, loathing, and resolve.

"And who is your husband?" Abdul asked sarcastically.

"Jim Shepherd, Captain of the *Pearl* and commanding officer of *Bring It Up*." Cecilia said, unashamed of the tears flowing down her face. That slap had hurt! "When he sees what you've done, he will tear you apart, you bloody wanker!"

That shook Ben. He looked at Pen. "Is this true? Are you also married?" He asked.

"My husband is John Shepherd, Jim's brother. We're sisters-in-law. Yes, it is true." She said.

"Identification!" Ben shouted in Afrikaans. Both women had brought only money and their American identification. A third man arrived, and he showed the identification to Aziz. He cursed fluently. He had not intended to personally tangle with Jim Shepherd, or his brother. Their reputation was such that he was now deeply concerned. Almost he regretted slapping Cecilia.

"Good!" He said.

Liar! Cecilia and Pen thought at the same moment. They shared another glance, almost triumphant.

"You will know much. Tell me what you know of the ship I mentioned."

"They were boarded by the Coast Guard a few days ago, and the

Coast Guard had a Navy Destroyer as escort, so I'm guessing there's something funny about the ship or its crew. Judging from the name I'd say it's probably from one of the Middle Eastern countries. The Coast Guard didn't take anything off the ship, and they didn't arrest any crewmembers that we noticed. Of course, we were busy with our own research, so we didn't pay much attention." Pen said.

"We were more interested in the research ship." Cecilia said when Pen stopped. "There was some talk that they might be trying to butt in on our research project. Our grant coordinator checked and found out that no grants had been offered the ship toward studying volcanic activity on the ocean floor, so we stopped worrying about them. They left soon after we arrived anyway." Cecilia was running her tongue over her lip, tasting the blood. Jim would be furious when he saw her. Good!

"What of Ya'qub, Tanfiq, and Najid?" Ben pounced with the question.

Both women just stared at him as if confused. Pen was the first to speak.

"Who?"

"No one by that name is on our crew." Cecilia added.

Aziz grabbed Pen's hair and jerked her head back hard, smacking it against the back of the chair, and with his left hand slapped her breast and then stepped back. His face was livid.

"Do not lie to me woman! You know who these men are!" He snapped.

"You know, when John sees the bruise on her breast, he's going to want to help my Jim kill you." Cecilia said, smiling crookedly through swollen lips. "You're a stupid man."

"We don't know who those men are you bloody bastard!" Pen snapped, shaking her head and glaring at Ben. It was at that point Ben began to worry. The women were too cocky, not afraid at all. There was a loud knock at the door, and he jumped at the sound.

"See who that is and get rid of them!" Ben snapped in Afrikaans to the third man who had come into the room. The fourth man was supposed to be on guard outside to make sure no one came close enough to the house to hear any screams. That someone had come to the door did not bode well, unless the outside guard was walking around the back when it happened. Even then he would know someone was at the door and run to the front. He should have seen him pass the window in the next room. Certain he had not seen him pass he thought about the situation. Now he was beginning to really worry, and he bit his lip, hesitant to do anything at the moment.

The sound of a scuffle was heard, and then silence. Ben quickly pulled his pistol and moved around behind Cecilia, putting it against the back of her neck. The other man did the same to Pen and they waited. But no one came. Silence reigned.

After a few minutes Ben Aziz ordered the other man to take off the restraints. He intended to have both women standing when whoever was out there came in for more protection. Pen looked at Cecilia and nodded fractionally. As soon as Cecilia was free, she stood up and rammed the back of her head hard into Ben's chin, knocking the man backwards, while at the same time turning quickly and kicking him solidly between the legs. It was a calculated blow, delivered with all the power she could muster.

Pen had been more creative, using her chair to push her assailant backwards, flowing around it to get behind him. Her chop sent the gun to the floor and her kick dropped him to the floor, holding himself and groaning. Both kicks had been delivered with amazing force and the two men were lucky they were not killed outright.

Jim and John entered the room, each handing their wives clothing, each being careful to keep their eyes on the two men. Cecilia took her clothes and began to dress right there in the room, with Pen beside her. When they were dressed again Jim called out and Ox appeared with the first aid kit. Jim waited until the two men were patted down and all weapons removed before stepping back.

"Which one hit you?" He asked Cecilia. His eyes were filled with the need for violence. Mutely she pointed to Ben Aziz while Ox pressed an ice pack over her battered face. In her eyes Jim saw only pride in her accomplishment, no fear, and his heart skipped a beat. For a moment he merely stood, taking in her beauty, and she saw the appreciation in his eyes and understood it, feeling her own spirits swell up inside her.

"Get up!" Jim ordered. Ben slowly stood. "So, you like to hit women? Would you like to hit me?" He asked, handing his gun to Terrance Red Claw. "Spit at me and you eat with a straw for the next six weeks!" He said, watching Aziz carefully. He tried to spit at the Captain, but Jim's hand shot out, blocking it. Slowly he rubbed the spittle from his hand onto Ben's face. It was at that point that the kidnapper knew he'd made a terrible mistake.

Jim's fist lashed out with the force of a pile driver, shattering Ben's jaw and sending the man reeling across the room to slide down the wall unconscious. Pain does not allow one to stay unconscious long, however, and Ben's eyes fluttered, and he groaned, and then screamed as the pain hit. Screaming only made the pain more intense but he could not stop.

John walked over and smashed the heel of his boot down on Ben's left hand, shattering bones, crushing the hand, grinding it hard into the floor. "That's for hitting my wife you coward!" He said tersely.

Chief's knife slammed into Ben's right hand, pinning it to the floor. Aziz tried to open his mouth to scream, only making the pain worse, and he howled in agony through clenched teeth. Chief walked over, pulled his knife free while holding the hand down with his foot, and then showed the bloody blade to Aziz. For a long moment he made sure Ben was watching his eyes. They were dark eyes, filled with resolve and they frightened the poor man.

"Next time you touch one of the women from our crew, or our country, I will tie you to a tree, dig a pit between your legs, and fill it with hot coals. I'll make sure your arms are free, so that you'll put your hands down to protect yourself. Usually men are burned all the way up to the elbows when they do that by the time they die. Your gonads still get cooked. It's a slow and painful way to die, fitting for cowards. Do you understand me?" Chief had spoken in Afrikaans to be sure Aziz got every word. He saw the knowledge fill Ben's eyes. Red Claw's eyes were empty pools of death.

Jim nodded to the other man. He was still doubled up, holding himself. Hayseed and Neil lifted him to a standing position, pinning his arms painfully behind him. He looked at Aziz, and then at Jim. Trying to keep the fear from his eyes he drew upon his courage, but it was no good.

Jim slipped a bullet into the man's pocket. He patted it once and then looked the man in the eyes. "I have a message for Abu Kareem al-Jameel ibn Nidh'aai." He spoke in Afrikaans. "Give him this bullet, and then tell him to look in his safe behind his desk." Ira had placed one there personally. "He will find another that has the same markings. The next time he interferes with me, or anyone from my crew, I will visit him once more. I have one more of these bullets, here in my gun. Tell him I will shoot him in the eye, so he can see that the bullet was kept for him alone and know that justice has been done. I have written this message, so you forget none of it." Jim tucked the index card into the man's pocket with the bullet. "You may go."

"What of Aziz, Quasim, and Tha'Labah, my brothers?" The man asked. Panic was in his voice and his eyes were stretched wide. *How did these men know about Abu Kareem? My life is forfeit!*

"They will be arrested for kidnapping. The punishment for kidnapping in the United States is life in prison. You will not see them again. Consider yourself lucky, Ameer." Jim replied.

"You know my name?" Ameer asked, startled. *How did they learn my name so quickly? Who are these people?*

"You may go now." Jim said once more. Ameer did not wait. He ran from the house, jumping into the Suburban and sped away.

"I'm sorry, my love, but if you wouldn't mind?" Jim said, indicating the chairs.

"We'll have to get naked again. Go ahead. We'll leave our clothes on the bed, so we have something to change into when the police free us." Pen said. "Take the clothes they cut off from the trash and don't worry, we'll tell a very good story!"

"I'm proud of you." Cecilia said, touching his lips tenderly. "You didn't kill him."

"Not yet." Jim said, his eyes still stormy.

"Best get going then." She pushed him out the door as the men left. Ten minutes later the police arrived. By then the bruises were fully formed, and Cecilia was hurting. They looked at each other as the police came in, hearing the confusion in their voices.

"What the hell?" One voice said. "There's another one unconscious by the front door Captain!"

"Whoever tipped us said that the kidnappers were no threat. Clear the rooms carefully!" An authoritative voice spoke. Shouts of "Clear!" echoed through the house until their door was opened.

"Shit!" The leading police officer said, raising his weapon, looking at the two women and Aziz, moaning against the wall. None of what he'd seen so far made any sense at all, and he didn't like it.

"Aptly said. Do you think you could release us?" Pen said quietly.

"What the hell happened here?" That was the authoritative voice, and a medium sized man stepped into the room wearing shorts, sandals, and a Hawaiian shirt.

"I don't really know." Pen said, her eyes beginning to show the pain she felt. "Four men accosted us and brought us here. They were questioning us about some foreign ship named *Sikandar*. We're from *Bring It Up*. I rather think they grabbed us thinking we were part of the crew of that other ship."

"Four! We only found three! Get a BOLO out for that Suburban that neighbor said was parked here." The Captain snapped. He turned back to the room and studied it carefully, noting everything in the minute he took before speaking again.

"How did these three get in this condition?" He asked.

"Would you mind if we put on our clothes before we answered any other questions?" Cecilia asked through swollen lips.

"I am sorry!" The Captain said. "There's a bathroom across the hall."

Gathering their clothes, once they were freed, the two women dressed in the bathroom. Although they were both in some pain neither felt any fear or frustration. Humiliation could be dealt with, as could the fear both had felt. Pen kept the atmosphere light as they whispered to each other.

"I swear! You're no better looking than I, but because you have those huge *bosooms* every guy in that room was practically drooling. Nature is so unfair! I was fully expecting to hear one of them ask, 'Got milk!'"

Cecilia giggled at that one, her motions stopped for a moment, her eyes dancing with mirth. "I felt like every one of them was thinking about that bed against the wall! How do strippers do it?"

"Probably the same way we do!" Pen said with a straight face, getting another laugh out of Cecilia. "Oh! You didn't mean that!" She added. Cecilia burst out laughing at that until tears poured out of her eyes.

"What's so damned funny?" The Captain asked suspiciously as they entered the room.

"We were discussing whether or not your men were all bottle fed." Pen said flippantly. She had the pleasure of seeing the Captain flush.

"Yeah. Well!" The Captain said, glaring at his men who looked sheepish. "How did these guys get trashed?"

"Our husbands stopped by to rescue us with four men from our crew. When Jim saw what this one had done to his wife, that's Cecilia, he hit him once. After he fell, my husband stomped on his left hand. One of the other men, Terrance Red Claw threw his knife through the other hand, and then proceeded to tell Ben Aziz what he would do if he ever touched another female member of our crew. I think Aziz believed him." Pen watched the Captain digest it.

"Your husbands left you here?" He asked in amazement.

"They didn't really want to go to prison for killing those men. I'm sure you can understand that, Captain. Talking them out of taking us away with them was not easy, but we managed. We usually do. We decided they needed to be arrested for kidnapping, tried, and punished accordingly. Cecilia and I will be more than happy to testify." Pen replied.

"I was truly afraid Jim would actually kill this slime. When he left, I told him I was proud of him for not killing Aziz." Cecilia said.

"What did he say to that?" The Captain asked.

"Yet." Cecilia said matter-of-factly. "I'm Cecilia Shepherd, an

Ensign on board the *Pearl*, our research ship. This is Pen Shepherd. She's a Lieutenant on board the *Coral*, our deep ocean tug." Cecilia offered her hand and the Captain shook it.

"I'm Captain Danno, and please!" He looked pained. "No comments like 'Book 'em Danno'."

"Captain Danno, I believe this man needs medical treatment. My husband may have shattered his jaw. He did warn Aziz that if he spit, he would be drinking his meals out of a straw." Cecilia said. "I too would like to get some medical treatment on board our own vessel for this." She pointed at her lip. "Perhaps you would be willing to have dinner with us aboard the *Pearl* tonight."

"You can take our statements then." Pen said, nodding.

For a few moments Captain Danno looked at Aziz, and at the ladies, and then he lifted his hands as if in supplication. He sighed. "Fine! I'll bring one of my men with me and we'll get your statements tonight. What time?"

"Dinner is at 18:00 hours Zulu. That's 6:00 P.M. in landspeak." Cecilia said with a crooked smile that obviously hurt.

"I know what Zulu time is. We use it." Captain Danno said.

"Thank you, Captain. I believe our husbands are probably waiting outside for us." Pen said.

He followed them outside and watched as two men got out of a Taxi, opened the back doors for the ladies, and one sat in front while the other joined his wife in the back. Shaking his head, he went back to his investigation. This was a first.

CHAPTER 19

When Jim and Cecilia returned to the ship Cecilia was met with an ovation by the men and women, all who looked at her swollen face and split lip with various reactions. She was surprised by the comments and gentle touches and gratified. She hoped Pen was experiencing the same. In her cabin, after being treated by Dr. Penny, Cecilia held tightly to Jim and wept, finally letting go. He held her tightly, gently stroking her hair, kissing the top of her head as she sobbed. Eventually the tears stopped, and she smiled up at him, grateful for his caring touch.

"When they took my clothes off all I could think about was that animal who killed my parents." She said shakily. "For a few moments I wasn't sure I could hold up. But then I realized that I was not afraid, but truly angry, angrier than I've ever been before!"

"You're amazing!" Jim said softly, kissing her salty lips gently, and very gently wiping the tears away.

"And only a year ago my crying would have made you very uncomfortable!" She smiled up at him. "And don't you dare say it's because you're getting used to it, James Shepherd!" She retorted correctly reading his thoughts.

"I guess before, when you cried, I had no right to hold you like I wanted to, and comfort you." He said after smiling at her quip. "I was afraid of deep emotion." He added quietly.

"Yes, you were." She said, snuggling into him. "It's a good thing I wasn't wearing make up. My face would look like a pair of dirty railroad tracks!" Cecilia laughed. "My grandmother used to say that."

"You look ravishing even with puffy swollen red eyes." Jim smiled at her and kissed her gently again. Over the next hour she told him everything that had happened, what she thought, and how it made her feel. His unwavering attention and quiet helped to draw it out of her, and when she was done, she felt whole again. That was especially true after they spent time praying together with thankful hearts.

"You know, we're very fortunate we have this amazing relationship with the Lord!" She said when they finished the prayer. "All the time I was in the hands of those men I knew that He was watching over me with all the love and attention I'd enjoyed before. His presence was a tangible thing in that room, Jim!"

"Yes! I felt it while I thought of you in enemy hands. No one can protect you better than God, so I guess I need to start thinking about that. He certainly proved He is watching after his people Israel by sending us here at this point in time. I'm just so very glad you weren't injured any worse." Jim hugged her fiercely. "Thank You, Lord!" He breathed.

Jim welcomed Captain Danno aboard personally just before dinner, watching the man look around with keen interest. Danno's eyes were quick to take in every possible detail and Jim suspected that this officer missed little. The two men stood looking at one another, measuring each other as such men do. Their smiles went from polite to friendly in a very short period of time. Both had measured the other and discovered that here was a kindred spirit.

"This is Sergeant Paul Gaston." Captain Danno introduced his second. "I'm Jeff Danno."

"Let me show you the ship." Jim said. He took the two men on a tour of the ship and by the time they were finished with the tour Captain Danno knew two things. Jim Shepherd was a true leader of men and he had the best-kept ship Danno had ever seen. Second, the men who worked on this ship were in top physical condition and deadly combatants.

He'd been dazzled by the beauty of many of the women on the science team as they talked about their research. Not only were many of them extremely lovely, they were intelligent on a level he not only recognized but also appreciated. There was something about the entire crew that he couldn't quite grasp. It wasn't until he was seated in the dining room that it came to him.

A silence fell as Jim led them all in standing. The chef, JimJim, stepped forward and led them all in a prayer of thanksgiving. It was short, but real, not memorized or quoted, but straight from the heart. It was then he realized that he was seeing an entire crew that not only believed in God, they followed the Lord Jesus. These were people of high moral standards, with good hearts, whom he knew instinctively he could trust.

Pen and John were guests at Jim's table, and it was a happy hour of delicious food and conversation that followed. Tonight's dinner was prime rib, red potatoes, mixed vegetables with watercress in honor of Pen who loved them, mushrooms, onions, and an amazing tossed salad. The men who served were also in top physical condition and had names like Winky, P.J., and Frenchie. With the chef, they managed to serve dinner to eighteen science, and thirty crewmembers in a reasonable amount of time, and then sit at various tables with their own meals.

Once dinner was over the Captain took them up to the observation deck where the interviews took place. Danno appreciated the candor of the two couples. He now understood how they had located the two women held captive thanks to the chips. Terrance Red Claw came up to give his statement. Danno was really surprised by the honesty he read in the statement. Chief even offered the Ontario Navy Knife he'd used to pin Aziz's hand to the floor.

"Why did you do that?" Paul Gaston asked, more curious than anything else.

"He used that hand to hurt two of ours." Chief replied quietly.

For a moment Gaston's hand paused in writing the reply and

he looked up into Red Claw's eyes. After a moment he nodded. He understood completely. So did the Captain. When Chief offered the knife to the two officers he was waved off.

"No need for that. If necessary, and I'm sure it won't be, we'll ask for it." Jeff Danno said with a smile. "I don't often get people who are absolutely straightforward with me." He added, nodding his approval.

"Honesty is always the best policy." Richard Kagan said, arriving on the observation deck. He was bringing a message to Jim. Captain Danno looked at him and chuckled.

"You I would arrest on sight!" He said.

"We call him Fagan." John replied, laughing.

"Very fitting!" Gaston laughed with them.

"It's the haircut, right?" Fagan asked no one in particular. "Too extreme?" He wore the usual "jarhead" cut, short on the sides, about a quarter of an inch on the top. His he had combed straight up in front and around the edges, using gel. As he said it, he put on his most evil look and everybody burst out laughing. Fagan was a great joker and a first-rate soldier.

"Captain Danno, when you get back to shore, you're going to be met by a delegation from Algiers demanding the release of your prisoners. I thought you should be forewarned." Jim said when Fagan retired, laughing. "Official delegations are usually quite full of themselves, but they can be frustrating." Jim added.

"Those men committed a federal offense. Even non-citizens have to stand trial for such offenses. I'll send them packing." The Captain said with feeling.

"Will your superiors back that play?" Jim asked candidly.

"Yes, they will. I've already had the three of them before a federal judge. He was adamant that they must be tried here and punished here. Not many of our judges are men like this one. He won't back down for anyone. I anticipated such a move when I saw their passports." Jeff smiled. "None of my superiors would dare to go against this particular judge. And, if you're wondering, I will indeed enjoy sending those interfering politicians packing!"

"Good!" Jim said with feeling. They all stood and escorted the two police officers back to the police cutter that was waiting for them. After they left John and Pen stayed for several hours visiting with Alistair and Gwyneth. Finally, they said goodnight and returned to the *Coral.* Jim and Cecilia watched them until they were safely aboard the vessel and then with a wave left the observation deck and headed for bed.

In the morning two pieces of news reached them. The first was from Washington demanding that they stand down from both research and the salvaging of the ship. Second, and more disturbing, Ameer did not get off the island. His body was found floating in the ocean near Honolulu International Airport. He had been shot in the back of the head execution style.

"So, Kareem is in Honolulu, or was." Jim mused quietly.

"I don't think so." Zeke said. "Ira has him under surveillance. I did pick up a name on a flight manifest that we've seen before!" He added. "Abu Muhammad al-Filsieeni left for Japan this morning."

"He's the third." Jim breathed. "Bahdijn, Kareem, Muhammad! Two of the richest troublemakers in the world behind Bahdijn."

"The FBI thought there was something hinky about the campaign funding behind our new president. They came up empty. I think we can do better." Zeke said. "With Ira, Sir Edward, and our team working on it I imagine we can find the missing pieces. You are also a marked man if Muhammad has your bullet and message. I hope you realize that."

"Good. They'll come to us." Jim replied bluntly.

"Just a heads up, boss." Zeke said with a smile. Jim nodded.

"May I request that you make plans for Cecilia and me to go to Washington to protest this official cease and desist order?" Jim's voice was very polite. "Twelve-Team-Three will go with us. "Please ask Sniper, Bulldog, and Nightfall meet me in the conference room."

"Right away Captain." Zeke said with a grin. "You get to have all the fun!"

"Keep the home fires burning. Move both ships out of the area. Why don't you let the crews enjoy the pleasures of Hawaii until I get back? No work. Lock down the computers and equipment and leave the ships unguarded in the harbor. No female crewmembers go anywhere alone, and I want groups of no less than four for any trips." Jim grinned at Zeke. "Maybe you can get in some surfing!"

"Hawaii will never be the same." Zeke said with an answering grin.

Jim walked down and picked up Cecilia in the computer lab of the science section. They walked together to the conference room where the twelve-team joined them quickly. Sitting down at the table they looked at Jim expectantly.

"We're going to Washington to protest the cease and desist orders. According to Zeke, I am now a target for Kareem and friends. Abu Muhammad al-Filsieeni is one of those friends. Zeke thinks he killed Ameer and has my bullet." Jim paused.

"Bahdijn, Kareem, and Muhammad! Who would have thought?" Lee Ainsworth said quietly.

"I suppose they learned the committee of three idea from the communists who were training them years ago." Mel Pierson said.

"Weird!" Donut said, shaking his head.

"We're going to take down the assassin Aziz and Ya'qub when they go after Ira and Lord White. Counselor, you're going to be Ira. Santa, you're going to be Lord White." Jim said. "Practice looking, talking, walking, gesturing, and especially laughing like those men until you have them absolutely perfect."

"Once you get shot you fall back and stay down. No movement! Breathe very shallowly and keep your eyes open, stare at a fixed point. Pull the blood capsule chord when you go down so there's blood they can see. We've rigged those vests so that there's a good stain forming when you fall." Jim looked down at his notes. "The call has to go through before we can move on those two. Also, we have to be ready for the President and his friends to try to keep track of all of us. You boys are going to fly on Alias 2, and you're going to come into D.C. by air, train, and car. I want you on twelve different flights."

Each member of the *Omega Force* had six passports from six different countries with six different names, all registered and legal with complete background histories. Each identity came with three credit cards, also legitimate, with the usual ten to fifteen thousand dollar limit. Jim continued addressing his men in a quiet voice.

"Ira and Lord White are expecting you two." He pointed at Norm Geissler and Steve Coleman. Ira knows your alias, so you'll get in fine. You'll have a few days to practice. How do you feel about playing your parts?"

"I'll film Santa as Lord White. We'll play them side by side until you can't tell the difference." Kagan said.

"We'll do the same with Counselor. He'll have Ira down pat." Rock responded.

"Good. The switch will take place after the bomb alarm. I want confirmation that it is indeed a dirty bomb and set to go off. Bulldog, that's your department. Be careful. Defuse it as soon as it's placed and make sure no one checks it. Get some cops to patrol the park 24/7 until the alarm. It will be interesting to see who checks to discover what went wrong. I would like a name on that person, and perhaps a little background. All of you are professionals when it comes to this sort of operation, so I'll let you handle the details. This is one time when what we do saves not just our country, but Israel as well.

"Once we take down Abdul and Aziz we get out of Dodge. Switch to Alias 3 and leave by a different route than you came in. Stay in character and everything should be fine." Jim finished.

"Uh, boss? What about the threat against you?" Hayseed asked.

"Ira is having a couple of his boys keep watch over me." Jim grinned. "So is Sir Edward."

"Teacher's pet!" Tom Izbicki said with a wide smile.

"See you all on the other side. Stay alive!" Jim said, nodding to the men.

When that meeting was finished, he had Frank Miller take him over to the *Coral* to confer with John. John listened to Jim's plan without comment until he was finished speaking. They were in the bridge at the moment with Driver at the wheel.

"What am I supposed to do with Sharky?" John asked, shaking

his head. It had been his idea to keep Sharky on *Coral.* "You know he won't want to take a vacation and have any fun!"

"Order him to do it." Jim replied with a grin. "Tell Spanky and Babs to make sure he enjoys himself." This final addition had John laughing.

"I'll do that. Watch your topnotch!" John replied. "Meanwhile, we'll keep Hawaii safe."

They hugged briefly and Jim left to motor back to the *Pearl.* Two hours later they were paying for slips in the harbor while the crew lined the railings in bathing suits, T-shirts, sandals and tennis shoes, shorts and Hawaiian shirts, and other warm-weather outfits. It was obvious that shore leave had been granted.

A woman sitting on a bench feeding ducks watched and counted as people came off the ships. Thirty-three walked off *Coral* and forty-eight exited *Pearl.* That was everyone! Waiting until they all left the harbor she finally moved, walking slowly to a payphone, and making the call. Ten minutes later a man on a bicycle stopped to ask directions and offered her a newspaper. Tucked inside was the two hundred dollars she'd been promised. Neither noticed the teams watching them from various locations around the wharf. Those teams weren't interested in the woman; she was merely a pawn.

The man on the bicycle did not waste any time. Boldly he walked up the gangplank to the deck of the *Coral* and spent a few hours searching the vessel. Frustrated he moved to the *Pearl* with the same results. The ships were clean and there were no assault weapons to be found. No paperwork suggesting what was going on other than research could be found either, with the exception of the cease and desist order, and Jim's plan to fly to Washington to protest. He was going with his wife.

He made a call from the deck and then left the ship. As he neared his bicycle three men stepped out onto the pier. All three flashed badges identifying themselves as NCIS. His cell phone was confiscated, and he was arrested for criminal trespass. Since he'd stolen nothing and taken no pictures, he was confident he would be released fairly quickly, so he cooperated without making a scene or demanding his rights or putting any kind of struggle. In the interrogation room he began to have his doubts.

"You made a call as you were leaving." The lead agent said in the interrogation room.

"I was paid to look at those two ships." Ivan Kristoff lied easily. "A rival agency hired me to do some industrial espionage. I found nothing, so I made the call and reported that." That was a half-truth.

"What company?" The agent asked quickly.

"You have the number! Check it yourself." Kristoff replied after a moment of searching his mind for an answer. He had none. Just the way the officer looked at him made him wonder what was going on.

"Yes. We have the number. You're lying. Abu Muhammad al-Filsieeni is a person of interest in the death of an American soldier. You are now considered a person of interest in the same death. Aiding and abetting in a murder is a serious business Mr. Kristoff. We are waiting for further information regarding your fingerprints from Interpol." The leader of the NCIS team replied.

"Then I think it's time for me to say I want an attorney." Kristoff said, his face frozen. *How did they know that phone belonged to Abu Muhammad al-Filsieeni? Somehow, I must get a message to him!*

"Unfortunately, this was an act of terrorism on American soil. We can hold you without charges indefinitely. Until we actually charge you, no attorney will be provided, and you will not be allowed to contact one." The team leader gathered his paperwork, stood up and left. Kristoff cursed. Two Navy personnel appeared to escort him to his maximum-security solitary confinement cell.

That evening Jim and Cecilia boarded the first-class section of their jet. Only three others shared the compartment to Los Angeles. At LAX six more stepped on board. The flight to D.C. was uneventful. Jim slept, and Cecilia read and slept.

Much met them at baggage claim and loaded them into the limo to drive them to Live Oak Retreat.

CHAPTER 20

Ken Worthington arrived the following day with a legal team from Bethesda that was considered the best when it came to maritime law. He introduced Jonathan Luther Samuelson, lead attorney for the company. Jonathan was in his early forties and towered over everyone at six feet eight inches. Jim correctly read his physique and even remembered his name from the not to distant past.

"Princeton football." He said, shaking hands with the giant. "J. Luther Samuelson, middle linebacker, all-American!"

Jonathan chuckled. "Years ago." He said with a laugh. "Most fun I ever had until I started coaching inner city kids last year." He added. Jim and Cecilia both had positive reads on the giant.

"That's a worthy endeavor." Cecilia said, shaking hands with Samuelson.

Jonathan introduced his team. His assistant was an attorney named Jeffrey Nolan. With him he also had a lead researcher, an elderly gentleman named Benjamin Rawlings, also an attorney. Two legal aids named Iris and David, a married couple, took notes. They met in the library on the second floor around one of the mahogany tables.

By noon the case was drawn up and a deposition prepared to go before a federal judge. Samuelson was confident that a threatened lawsuit would end the cease and desist order immediately, since the law was clearly stated. He would personally present the letters to the appropriate parties.

Samuelson also wanted to go ahead with the suit, to teach the powers that issued the cease and desist order a lesson. An hour of discussion followed. Jim finally agreed to the suit with the stipulation that any money gained from the suit go to the three most prominent oceanographic institutes in the United States.

No sooner had the legal team disappeared than the unit from Ira and the men from Sir Edward appeared at the door. They had been invited for lunch, and Jim was pleased to see looks of anticipation on their faces as they came to the door of his imposing home. It wasn't often that operatives were given the kind of treatment this assignment offered. They would be guests in the house and travel with the couple wherever they went.

A sweep of the area was carried out after lunch while a few of the team studied vantage points around the property for possible sniper sites. Several were identified but no snipers were uncovered. It was early in the game so the team was pleased to have the possible sites identified so they could be watched. Jim wanted to capture the sniper team alive. So did Ira's team, because those men or women would give them needed intelligence.

Ken Worthington joined them for lunch to go over some of the investments. Jim was not surprised to discover that Worthington had almost doubled their investment funds once again. *Bring It Up* Corporation now owned several goldmines, and invested heavily in gold and gold shares. Prime property had been bought and sold or leased at huge profits. There were also investments in natural gas and oil wells in Alaska and off the Florida coast, though most of the oil and natural gas investments were in energy provider companies and the small businesses that supplied them.

What Jim appreciated most about his business partner and investment banker was the absolute joy he took in his work. Ken was enthusiastic about investing, even when the economy threatened to tank at any moment in countries in which investments were made. He took risks with a small percentage of the investment funds that often gave returns of 300% or more! Winning those challenges seemed to excite him the most.

Discovering that the cost of purchasing a second ship and equipping that ship had already been recovered gave Jim a sense of intense satisfaction. It had been a gamble to put out the funds, and everyone in the company had willingly submitted a yes vote on the expenditure. A period of six years had been determined for recovering the funds, and Ken had done it in less than a year! Also, two patents awarded to the company promised steady income for several years.

If any one at the table found it uncomfortable or odd that Jim asked them all to bow their heads so he could give thanks for God's blessing on his company, no one looked sideways or appeared not to join in the prayer. Jim had a tendency to talk to God as if he was speaking to his very best friend, and his prayers were not full of flowery speech. Instead his words were simple and real. Several of the men at the table were moved by his simple faith, and one or two voiced their own faith in Jesus Christ.

Ira's men, all devout Jews, did not participate in the conversation, but they understood that many Christians believed that God's chosen race was to be honored, and in a world where most religions, including some Christians, preached hatred of the Jewish people they were grateful for the ones that did not. America and England had been strong supporters of Israel, and though some of that support waned from time to time, it was still strong.

During the afternoon, calls came in on a regular basis on the progress of Aziz and Ya'qub in the truck crossing the U.S. Well versed in picking out surveillance both of those men watched everything around them with suspicion. So far, according to the reports phoned in each day on different disposable phones they had spotted none. Jim would have been surprised if they had.

In California, a family in a motor home had noted their route out of that state and reported it. In Utah where the 15 and Highway 70 intersected a Utah Highway Patrol had noted the vehicle taking Highway 70. It appeared they were making their way to D.C. on

Highway 70. In Denver, an FBI agent followed them for a short time, making them nervous, but exited shortly afterwards.

In Oakley, Kansas a Christian Biker club picked them up and followed them all the way to Kansas City, passing them several times. A custom car club in St. Louis noted their passage and followed them as far as Dayton. Two agents hauling used currency to be destroyed kept them in sight all the way to D.C. Their forty-foot trailer had no markings to identify it.

It was in D.C. that a team of twelve NCIS agents picked up the surveillance. Each was in a separate vehicle, some utility vehicles, most nondescript autos rented for the occasion and paid for by *Bring It Up*. Switching off often, and then switching vehicles at Enterprise rental agencies in the city, they kept the pair under close watch.

Aziz paid to store the truck in a storage facility near the Dupont Circle, not far from where they were going to park it. Individuals paid to park vehicles or rent one of the storage units by the month, and Aziz wisely paid for three months in advance, stating that he was looking for an office in D.C. and in a few weeks would need all his office furniture and equipment which, he claimed, was stored in the truck.

He and Ya'qub split up at that point. Ya'qub took a room at a nearby motel where he could check on the truck daily to be sure no one tampered with it. Aziz began visiting used car lots until he found the van he wanted, bought it with cash, and with a false identification registered and insured it. Neither man detected any surveillance during their activities.

Jim made sure none were spotted, by insisting that tails and watchers be switched out hourly and never used twice. Duck followed his advice, keeping the pair under tight surveillance. Those used in the surveillance were experts drawn from various NCIS stations around the U.S., all supposedly vacationing in D.C. Each pair of agents actually received expense money for the trip, courtesy of *Bring It Up* so that no trace of their assignment would appear in military financial records. The families were more than happy to cooperate for a few hours of work.

Jim insisted they bring their families, enjoy the city for a full two weeks; all expenses paid, for one eight-hour tour of duty. Duck chose his agents well, and when they discovered the vacation package offered, they were more than willing to comply.

Each family had a rental car, traveled first class, and stayed in the finest of hotels. It was, Jim knew, a dream vacation, and he was more than willing to go the expense. NCIS agents, he knew, were not paid large salaries. To make sure the whole set-up looked legitimate all of the vacation packages were handled through AAA travel and within the means of each family. Families kept receipts of all expenses and they were reimbursed through *Bring It Up* before they returned home.

Six days after returning to Washington the assassination team was deployed to kill Jim Shepherd. He and Cecilia had not left the house in those six days, forcing the attempt to be made as they walked about the grounds. The team was spotted immediately as they took a position already scouted by the security detail. It was the British team that took them, and it was done quickly and quietly.

Both men were surprised to be taken to the house, rather than to a police station or military base. In the massive basement beneath the house a very large room lay empty. Worse, at least for the captives, the two men were shackled to heavy steel chairs, quickly assembled in the center of the room, in a small pool of light, leaving the remainder of the room in darkness.

Ira's team had the somewhat disturbing task of extracting information from the pair. Experts at this line of work they completed the chairs and equipment in a short period of time in absolute silence. Both men were then locked into the chairs, wrists, ankles, and chest strapped down tightly. Once the men were secured Ira's team introduced themselves, showing their Mossad identification and explaining their purpose very clearly.

No one heard the screams from that basement room, for the walls and ceiling were designed to eliminate sound. Three days later Ira's men had the information. In secret, the assassins were taken out of the country for trial in Israel, all three requiring medical transport and care. Jim knew that the sentence for their crimes would be death. Only in Western European "civilized" countries were psychotic killers allowed to live. It made no sense to Jim that his country almost categorically refused to adopt a death penalty for such men. Even in prison they killed. Such people knew nothing else.

The day arrived, at last, when Aziz moved the truck at four in the morning, to park it by some buildings under construction just across the street from Franklin Square. No one questioned the container truck showing up and being parked there, for there were a half dozen construction firms working on the buildings. Aziz spent about twenty minutes inside the container and then closed the doors and locked them.

Bulldog moved in thirty seconds after Ya'qub picked Aziz up in the van and drove away. Mel Pierson was an explosive's expert, but the best the team had was Sparks. As soon as the doors were checked to be sure they weren't booby trapped Mel made his entry and began to take pictures, sending them to Sparks in Hawaii. Sparks sat over his computer in a hotel room and whistled.

Literally hundreds of leads were connected to the device in a series he had seen only once before. Bombers tended to have a favorite system, and this one was tied to a known al' Qaeda operative for which, until now, no one had an identity. Sparks fingers flew over the keyboard as he typed instructions on how to defuse this particular system. It was extremely complicated, and it would show an exponential run of time as one went through the steps.

Pierson, who had been through the most rigorous training read the directions and made sure he had them memorized. Then, with sweat beginning to run down his forehead and face he began to cut the proper wires. Steeling against the feeling of running out of time because of the accelerated time flashing in the corner of his vision he worked steadily and cut the last wire with a sigh to see everything go dark.

"Good job MP!" Hayseed said, slapping him on the back as Pierson dried his face outside the container. "How bad would it have been?"

Peering out from beneath the towel, Mel looked at his tall friend. "It would have contaminated about twenty city blocks and killed a lot of innocent people. Certainly, anyone on the street or near windows within a block would die." He said, his eyes bleak as he looked at his team. "Aziz, it would seem, has piled up one too many attempts at bombing innocent victims, and before very long he will certainly pay." He went back to wiping the sticky sweat from his face and hair. "That was scary, watching the seconds tic away faster and faster!" He grimaced as he wiped away the sweat.

"Cowards! Always ready to bomb innocent people! I want to see just how brave this Aziz is when he faces us!" Chief said, shaking his head.

"Brave and honorable people don't kill unarmed non-combatants on purpose." Neil said quietly. For a moment the men looked at one another bleakly, knowing Neil was correct. "We don't do that because we know the value of human life. Far too many have forgotten that in this day and age." He sighed.

Shortly after the team left the bombsite District police vehicles passed by the truck every few minutes. Volunteers were put into marked vehicles to do nothing but circle the blocks around the truck. Ya'qub cursed when he saw another police cruiser coming. He had meant to check the bomb once more but there would be no opportunity. The neighborhood was obviously under heavy watch because of the dignitaries coming to hear Lord White and Ira Lehman.

He made the call from a public phone at the appointed time and hurried up into the parking garage. Using his door key, he unlocked the van and stepped in. Aziz was already prone with his rifle at the ready, the barrel a good six inches back from the open rear window. Ya'qub nodded, made his way to his perch, picked up his binoculars and waited with them focused on the doorway the two intended victims would use for evacuation.

Alarms sounded, sirens went off, and in the pandemonium, Aziz smiled as his two targets were ushered out of the door. He shot Lord White first, since he was on the left, and moved his rifle a fraction to shoot Ira Lehman next. Both men fell back and lay still. Better still, Ya'qub could see the blood staining the shirts and jackets of the two men. Their eyes stared at a fixed point, as dead eyes do, but he could not see the glazed stare of death from this distance. After a few moments he was quite sure both men were dead.

It took Aziz less than two minutes to break down his rifle and stow it away. They had already wiped the van clean and left it where it was parked. Each took a separate vehicle and left the parking garage. Half an hour later Ya'qub made the call to Bahdijn. As he put the phone back on the receiver, he noticed four men converging on the phone booth. Even when he recognized them as men from *Bring It Up* his mind could not quite fathom how they were here.

Bahdijn and Jacks looked up as a window crashed and a gas canister filled the room with tear gas. A heartbeat later a Secret Service Team entered, taking the two dazed and angry men into custody. Confused, because Bahdijn was sure the house was completely safe, he felt the cuffs tighten about his wrists and realized that his failure was complete. *How had the infidels known? This is not supposed to happen to me! I am unknown to the Great Satan!*

Aziz pulled into the parking lot of the rental car agency and went to the trunk to remove his rifle case and suitcase. Four men suddenly surrounded him. He recognized them as Israeli soldiers and was soon subdued. Ira Lehman and Jim Shepherd appeared, and Aziz cursed. Ira looked at Jim.

"You will take care of the details?" He asked quietly.

"Exactly as you ordered." Jim replied. Aziz didn't like the sound of that, but he had only two days to consider what it might mean.

Two days later Aziz hung from the ceiling of the container in which he'd built his bomb. It was armed again, and the time was ticking away furiously. Unable to move he could only stare as the seconds ticked by. Far out in the Atlantic the old barge that had been towed to a spot chosen by the Navy, began to sink. It was nearly sixty feet below the surface when the bomb went off.

Reconfigured by Sparks the bomb did not send radioactive materials out into the water. Instead, helped by the copper now lining the container, the heat sealed the container solid. Aziz died quickly his body consumed by the heat. Duck Ashley watched the upheaval from the explosion and smiled grimly. *One less killer of innocent people to worry about!*

CHAPTER 21

Admiral Hogg, Secretary of the Navy, read the reports in the Oval Office, surrounded by the President, and the usual men and women that directed the various departments involved with national security. It was the first time in many years he felt the beginnings of doubt tugging at his inner core. Most difficult of all was keeping his face schooled so that he showed no emotion.

Sitting alone Donald Ashley, Director of NCIS, watched Hogg intently. Minute signs were there to read. Body language always revealed so much. Good gamblers learned to hide those "tells" and Hogg was a good gambler. Yet even the best gamblers learned to read each other, as much as the odds on a wager. Duck saw the signs, reading them correctly, knowing his own derisive glare every time Hogg looked his way made the man even more nervous. He waited patiently for the perfect moment, and when it came, he cleared his throat and looked at the President.

"Permission to speak frankly, Sir!" He said, just as Hogg was about to speak.

It took the president a full minute to decide. He knew he was in trouble and his mind raced for a way out. At last he cleared his throat and nodded his head reluctantly. He hated feeling trapped like this.

"I am not a regular member of this group, and this is probably the first and last time I will be invited." Duck said in an even voice. He knew he was on very shaky ground here and he needed to step carefully. "England's top government officials and the Prime Minister of Israel have both expressed their deep gratitude for saving the lives of Lord White and Ira Lehman.

"They expressed deep regret that the office of President of the United States was compromised by unscrupulous individuals bent on the destruction of the United States and the discredit of our President. Both men personally cautioned me to let you know they will do everything necessary to uncover the details of this attempt and urge you to do the same, sir."

Having set the groundwork for his next statements Donald looked around the room, assessing the mood. Only the President, his Chief of Staff, and Hogg showed any signs of resistance. *Good!* He went on.

"Although I do not think the original intent of this operation was to discredit you, Sir, or the office of our Commander and Chief, it has surely become exactly that! I urge you, sir, to root out every person even remotely involved with either Bahdijn or Admiral Jacks, and to make a public example of them for the world to see. Unless you take a strong stand here, sir, this event will undermine everything else you attempt, whether here in the United States, or abroad."

Heads were nodding. The director of the FBI and CIA, along with everyone except Hogg and the Chief of Staff were agreeing with Admiral Ashley. Watching the President become aware of the nods of agreement Duck nodded once.

"I really don't belong here, sir. But it was my duty to speak for the good of the office of our Commander and Chief." His admission that he did not belong among the top leaders of the country would be received as proper submission to authority and rank. Speaking of his duty to protect the Office of the President would be interpreted correctly, he was sure, but not commented upon negatively.

"Do you know how deep this goes?" That was the Director of the FBI. Duck liked the man and respected him.

"Yes, sir. I do." Donald replied evenly. "I have a list of the people directly connected to both men."

Without asking for permission he handed it around. Notably absent from the list were the names of the President and the Chief of Staff. Both men relaxed slightly when they saw this fact as they read down the list. Some eyebrows were raised, and Hogg grimaced when he read his own name on the list. He had known it would be there.

"I also think it would be best for you, sir, if these men willingly stepped down from office, resigning their posts. Most of them are of retirement age. Resignations would not be too closely questioned or commented upon, sir." This last was to give them an honorable way out. Duck knew few would accept this proposal willingly. Hogg proved that by speaking.

"As SecNav I should have been informed of this information before it was ever brought to this meeting!" He grunted, glaring at Duck. "I could have cleared up some misunderstandings and misinformation in this list." He stated baldly.

"Admiral Ashley brought this information to me because you were implicated." The Director of the FBI said quietly, his eyes boring into Hogg. "He didn't want it going further if the information did not prove to be true. My own department did a full investigation to determine the veracity of these accounts."

"Director Bradley brought this information to me as well." CIA Director Runner said quietly. George Runner did not have an extensive background in intelligence, but Jack Royce had appointed him when then Director Van Horn had been implicated in trading secrets with China. Runner had been helpful to Jack and sat on his Cabinet. From California, the man had a sterling reputation and maintained that in D.C., an accomplishment in itself.

George Runner wasn't an imposing man, but when he spoke people listened carefully, because he talked sense. Never perturbed or angry he usually spoke with a slight hint of humor in his voice. Today there was no humor.

"Unless you want charges brought against you, and to serve time in a Federal prison, I suggest you say nothing further, Mr. Hogg. We did indeed strike two names from the list because we felt that in the interest of protecting what little dignity their offices still possessed and that both parties could easily have been duped because of their lust for power was in the best interest of our country." Runner looked at both the President and the Chief of Staff as he spoke, letting them know he was in possession of all the facts and nodded when both looked down and, if possible, a little ashamed. Duck thought it was probably shame at being found out more than any moral guilt.

"We know exactly how much money was paid, what off-shore and foreign bank accounts the money was deposited in, and who provided that money." George Runner said quietly into a suddenly very silent room. "Because of some recent intelligence provided to us, we also know where large sums of money for a national election campaign came from."

The President looked up at George Runner with two white spots in his cheeks signifying intense anger. George Runner returned the gaze steadily and it was the President who looked away, and then back as if in disgust with himself for looking away. George Runner tapped his forefinger on the report in his lap as if to let the Commander and Chief know that he was holding all the cards. The President's shoulders sagged, and the Chief of Staff suddenly could not look at anyone.

"What is said in this room today will be held in confidence by all present." Director Runner said softly. He looked at everyone in turn, receiving a nod of assent.

"Good!" Director Bradley said, taking the reigns once more. "Abu Kareem al-Jameel ibn Nidh'aai is now a person of interest to the United States. So also is Abu Muhammad al-Filsieeni ibn Abdul Aziz. Because they plotted to kill millions of Americans, they go to the top of the most wanted lists of all of our agencies. Justice will be served, as it has been on other terrorists, whether by our country, or by Israel.

"Mr. President, may I suggest that you have a private talk with each of the members on this list and insist on letters of resignation. Refusal will result in criminal charges being brought, which could create no little difficulty for you, sir." Bradley said blandly. He could see that the President was in a rage, trapped and unable to find a way out he could only agree. Schooling his face to keep his repugnance for this man who held the highest office in his country from showing the Director nodded. It galled him that he was willing to trade with the enemy and allow this man to remain in office, but it was prudent.

At a signal from Director Bradley the directors of the various agencies gathered in the middle of the room, excluding the President and his Chief of Staff and Hogg they shook hands. The message was clear. Duck felt honored to be included in that group and took full advantage of the situation to shake each hand, saying nothing as instructed. It was a blatant message to the President that he was now excluded from this group.

Finally, the President stood, and as he did so everyone turned to face him. He waited to see what might happen, but he met only baleful stares in poker faces. Clearing his throat, he spoke.

"This meeting is adjourned. Let's put this all behind us, gentlemen." He said authoritatively. Only Hogg and the Chief of Staff nodded. The rest merely gathered their things and left.

He was furious when the door closed and his Chief of Staff and Hogg both remained silent. President Stephens knew now that all his plans, all the promises made to him by so many others, were not to be. His rage burned and finally he clenched his fists and lashed out at the two men still in his office. The tirade lasted for twenty minutes before he wound down and ordered them out. White faced and shaken the two men who also had lost all left defeated.

CHAPTER 22

In his private office some distance from the White House the President of the United States swore and threw a full mug of coffee smashing against the credenza bookshelves across the room. His hands shook as he read the message once more. Without a word he thrust it out toward one of the Secret Service operatives occupying the room. Agent Channing took the message carefully.

A very public assassination is fitting for your failure. Channing's eyes bulged as he read the missive. In his own hand it had been written and signed by Kareem! That it had made its way to the inner office could only mean one thing!

"I want this assignment to go to Naval Intelligence, under the direction of Admiral Donald Ashley!" The President snapped.

"With all due respect, sir, we usually handle these matters." Channing said.

"Not this time." The President ground out between clenched teeth.

Channing nodded. He left the office, went down to his SUV and in the privacy of the vehicle made a call to his director. To his surprise Director Wisemueller chuckled.

"Admiral Ashley will work with us, allowing us the lead on this, even if that lead is covert in nature. Go ahead and give him the note.

Let his forensics team work on it first and then pass it and everything they have to us. Also, ask him if he thinks a mutual friend might eliminate this threat."

As soon as Channing was off the phone Dean Wisemueller called Admiral Ashley.

"Hey Duck! This is Dean over at the not so Secret Service!" He said with a chuckle. "You won't believe what I'm sending your way. Kareem has threatened the President's life in writing. My man Channing is on his way with the note. Let's work together on this one, and do you suppose our mutual friend might help us out on this one? I'd like to keep the tightest lid possible on this." He said.

"At least you remembered to use a secure phone!" Duck laughed. In his first assignment Dean had forgotten that rule and those who knew the story never let him forget it. Every agent makes mistakes, and Dean knew it was a way to remind each other to be careful.

"Since you brought that up, stay away from any pretty redheads!" Dean said with real laughter in his voice. Duck had been seduced by one, and nearly lost his life because he believed her story. He would never forget that lesson, Dean knew. Both men laughed. The reminders were good for them. "I'm certain that some people, who shouldn't, already know about the threat." He added soberly. That had prompted his "not so Secret Service" remark.

"Too true." Duck said. "I'll put my best people on it, and even bring a few out of retirement. Stay clear of politics." The phone went dead.

Dean grinned. They used to tell each other to stay alert and stay alive. Now the warning was always to stay clear of politics. Sighing Dean hung up the phone and began to make plans to protect his current President.

Kareem's note had been included in a diplomatic parcel delivered to the President. The parcel had come from Saudi Arabia. Slipped into the pages of a proposal the letter had not been detected. Chief of Staff Krantz saw the note and passed it immediately to the President. It was his final error. The letter should immediately have been brought to the attention of the Secret Service before anyone even touched it.

Dismissed from service and publicly humiliated he took a vacation to Belize where he had his money secreted away. Kareem, aware of the danger of leaving such a loose end took swift action and the body of the former Chief of Staff was found floating in the surf some weeks later. Identification was difficult because fish and crabs had been at the body for some time.

Aware that financial transfers left a footprint that could be followed Kareem moved the money swiftly from bank to bank, eventually covering the trail from watching eyes. What he did not know was that Zeke Kline not only followed the trail effectively, but with the information he now had he was able to access Kareem's personal computer. Kareem had firewalls designed to protect him, but to a genius like Zeke they were no more than a speed bump in his entry. Lock, stock, and barrel, he had the terrorist cold.

Bring It Up was back on location at 18° 55' N by 155° 15' W, just over the lava caves in which their treasure ship had perished. Activity on the decks of both ships was evidence of the ongoing mission of bringing up whatever treasurers were buried in the lava below.

The HUGO site was three kilometers southwest of their position. All the nodes they had planted were working perfectly and new information was flowing in daily on the seismic activity of the ocean floor. This information would insure the upkeep and safety of the 40-kilometer long permanent cable powering HUGO from the Big Island, among other applications.

At present the most complicated part of their plan had to be executed. Finding a way to uncover the treasures trapped in the lava beneath the surface was no easy task. The challenge was multifaceted, and Jim watched his crew with pride as they tackled the many difficulties. Every crewmember believed that the impossible was possible, thinking accordingly. It was amazing!

First, only those in atmospheric diving suits (ADS) would be able to work at those depths. Of course, the submersibles could go down there with them, and *Steel Crab* was designed for this kind of work. With the purchase of the ship the company had also purchased four new exosuits, the newest generation of the Newtsuit. Designed by

Phil Nuytten the suit has fully articulated, rotary joints in the limbs providing great mobility virtually unaffected by high pressures.

The suits operate untethered, a plus for working in a lava cave where hoses and communication cables could easily be cut by the sharp rock. Fitted with thruster packs the suit was very mobile in mid-water, navigating with foot controls. The left foot operates vertical control, and the right foot lateral control. Each suit was fitted with twin video cameras, color imaging sonar, and an AMS (Advanced Monitoring System) that transmits information to the surface including CO_2, HPO, and percentages of O_2, depth, temperature, and cabin pressure.

Communication with the surface is achieved through digital voice/data transmission via water and umbilical cord. Certified at 300 meters the suits had been tested as deep as 900 meters. The cave where they would be working was at 596 meters. Testing the suits at that depth was a risk, but a calculated risk, and most of the divers cleared for this equipment were confident there would be no problems, considering the tests at 900 meters had been so successful.

Pinpointing the wreckage was accomplished by using the technology on the HROV so that the science team could probe the lava bed for minerals. The two British ships were pinpointed by the heavy deposits of cast iron and lead from the cannon and cannon balls. The *El Dorado Espanola* showed a mixture of stone, gold, silver, and copper jumbled together. Theories about that abounded, but it was Dr. Gregg who provided the most viable.

"The ship was obviously burned very quickly in the hot lava allowing the various materials in the holds and storerooms to come together before being captured in the cooling lava beneath the surface." He said. "If they stored some of it in barrels and crates, I would imagine those burned as well. Of course, the heavier metals would melt and run together, so we may find that we have to separate the elements. However, practice those days was to put the precious metals in chests and separate them, so we may find huge lumps of melted gold, silver, and copper already separated if they were stored far enough apart. The signature on our probes seems to indicate the latter."

"I concur." John Dinsmore said as he studied the data on the computer screen.

"If that's true, we'll have to purify the minerals from trace elements in the lava. I know the proper temperatures for each mineral to separate and purify it." Neff said quietly.

"Isn't that just a little dangerous?" Hammer asked, raising an eyebrow.

"Not if one is careful." Neff replied with a grin.

"I knew we'd find something for him to do eventually!" Lord Lee said with a wide smile. "A weatherman who can purify gold!"

"I'm a meteorologist." Neff corrected, striking a pose.

"You study meteors too?" FM drawled, keeping a straight face.

"I think the chances of us pulling off this mission might be above some of our crew and soldiers!" Alice said dryly, shaking her head at FM's quip.

"It's easy, Dr. Wonderland!" FM replied with a deadpan expression. "You put a couple of guys in these zoot suits, drop 'em down the rabbit hole, and Hey Presto! You find the treasure!"

"They're Newtsuits." Tiffany said into his ear.

"You gonna fill 'em with newts?" FM asked, his eyebrows climbing his forehead as he looked at her comically.

"Would someone get that lump of muscle out of my laboratory!" Alice laughed.

"Abe's in here! I ain't gonna try to move him!" FM quipped.

"I said lump, not mountain." Dr. Dinsmore replied dryly.

That brought a burst of laughter from everyone, but after a moment the team returned to the task at hand. Jim stepped beside FM and patted his shoulder to let him know he appreciated the humor. There were men on his crew that always seemed to know just the right time to bring down the house, lighten the atmosphere, and encourage everyone.

"Getting back to business!" Alice said with a light laugh. "From the information we have all three ships were taken down quickly and seem to be very close to each other. We don't need to concentrate on the two British ships. Our Galleon is here." She used a laser pointer to indicate the spot on the big screen showing all the views from the various computers in the lab. Everyone looked at the pictures and at the location with critical eyes.

"Depending on what type of stone those tablets were written on the material might be fairly brittle because of the intense heat of the lava." Neff said quietly. "It's been my experience when working with lava rock that it comes away from whatever it is covering but can also mar the surface because of the high acidity of the water."

"Let's hope we can read the stone tablets!" Dr. Gregg breathed.

"I believe we ran into some good fortune on that." Dr. Dinsmore continued. "From the readings I believe that we will find the ship hull almost intact, though burned beyond recognition. The waters seem to have cooled it before all of it burned away, and our treasures should be inside it, preserved, if you will, in a coffin of seawater. Whether the acidity was high enough to burn away symbols on the stones is another matter entirely. I've never had experience with this type of situation before. What say you, Dr. Gregg?"

"In excavations beneath the ocean where volcanic activity has been prevalent carved stone is still readable in most cases." He said after a moment of thought. "I did see some stone tablets recovered from Kilimanjaro. They were pieced together like a puzzle, but also readable. I think we have a good chance." He added.

"Izzy, Lord Lee, Rock, and Dr. Dundee will be in the dive suits. Driver, Sparks and Inchworm will pilot the *Steel Crab*. FM, Goody, and Sparkles will pilot *Sea Bullet*." Jim said, stepping to the front of the group beside Dr. Gregg and his mother. Support staff is now on call 24/7 so everyone grab some shuteye. Divers and submersibles will be down 24 hours, up 48, and down 24. No arguments, no discussion!" He added when he saw a few heads come up.

"Safety first. Divers will work until they need rest, no more than eight hours. If you work eight you rest twelve. If you work four you rest four. No arguments. You get cold you come up. You feel sick you come up. Slow and steady wins the race.

"Submersibles can stay down 24 with the same work schedules. Working together will probably produce better results. Constantly monitor each other and be sure to watch each other's backs! I want all of you to be as safe as possible. Be careful down there!" He finished.

"Uh, boss?" FM raised his hand.

"Yes, Frank?" Jim asked with misgivings.

"I've never slept with a woman before. Since Sparkles is going to be down there with us, can you give me some pointers?" Frank's face was comical, and giggles filled the room. To Jim's surprise it was Dr. Dinsmore who stepped forward.

"You have nothing to fear, Mr. Miller. We women know how to deal with children. You'll be quite safe. Just don't wave your blankets and share your farts with everyone in the submersible." She added, bringing a roar of laughter from everyone. Her husband blushed scarlet as she fixed him with a baleful glare, her hands on her hips.

Everyone in the subs would be wearing thermal wetsuits for warmth, not sleeping in blankets, but Dr. Dinsmore knew this. Her quip had come at a proper moment as everyone was thinking about the danger of going to those depths and working. Any accidents down there were deadly, and everyone knew it. FM knew it too, and he was grinning at the doctor and nodding his head. Once again Jim marveled at the creativity of his people.

Slowly, still sharing quips and jokes, the crew filtered out of the laboratory and went to their quarters to rest. Bulldog had the watch for the first four hours. Jim and Zeke, with Santa and Fagan took the second watch.

CHAPTER 23

Wade Adams, Loony, TRT, Papa Orvieto, Goody, Hammer, and Wrench designed the structure that now held the two ships side-by-side. Made of a lightweight aluminum alloy the structure was strong, flexible, and tested in a force-three tropical storm with fourteen-foot waves. Its purpose was to join the two ships into one working platform. Crew could even pass between ships on the structure if the waves were gentle enough.

Using the bow thrusters in tandem the two ships could remain stationary over a site, the pilots keeping the boats pointed at the same heading even in heavy weather.

All four men in the Newt Suits were finally comfortable. Since they were going to be down for 24-hours they had self catheterized for urine elimination and made sure the bags were secure. In preparation for the dive they had done a cleansing under the direction of Dr. Penny and his wife. Physically, mentally, and emotionally they were ready for the dive and pronounced good to go. Carefully the suits were assembled over the men until they were completely encased in the exoskeletons.

In the wetlab all that remained was to lift them with the winch and drop them into the water. Once in the water they would be able to use the controls of the suit to move. All four of them would be lowered until they reached the cave entrance, where they would disengage from the crane cable until they were ready to be lifted back to the ship.

At one hundred feet they came to a stop, checking all the systems to be sure they were operating correctly. This took nearly half an hour, but no one minded the delay. Every safety system, life support system, and navigation system was checked and rechecked before the cables began to unwind once more. Four men were able to relax even more as they ascertained the suits were working as designed.

Driver and FM followed the suits down, ready to help if it was needed, their powerful lights turned off at the moment until they neared four hundred feet. In the wetlab the thermal wetsuit had made things uncomfortably warm. At four hundred feet the divers began to feel the cooling effect of deep-water operations. Finally, the divers touched the sandy bottom of the ocean.

Minutes passed as the systems were once more checked. Izzy was first to speak as he finished his systems check. His voice was strong though tinny through the speakers.

"Suit One, good to go." He said.

"Suit Two, good to go." Mike Putnam followed.

"Suit Four, good to go." Rock reported.

"Suit Three, ruling the ocean depths!" Lee Ainsworth said.

"56.5541 atm, including 1 atm ambient air pressure at sea level. 831.116 psi. Articulation nominal." Dr. Dundee reported in his Australian accent. "That's 56 and a half atmospheres or approximately 831 pounds per square inch of pressure for you non-science types." He added.

"Gee! Thanks Dr. Dundee!" Izzy said.

"*Coral*, this is *Steel Crab*, over." FM spoke into his headset.

"Go ahead *Steel Crab*." John replied from the bridge.

"The four Michelin men are on the bottom." FM said dryly.

"Roger that." John grinned. The men had taken to calling those in the Newt Suits Michelin men, because of the similarity to that mythical cartoon Avatar for the tire company. All four suits were painted a bright yellow, easily seen when it reflected light at the depths in darkness.

"I am the real Michelin man. These others are mere stand-ins!" Lord Lee said.

He pressed the control with his left foot that lifted him from the bottom, seeing that the others were doing the same. For a moment they faced one another and looked into each other's faces through the helmet bubble glass faceplate. After only a few minutes of practice they turned to the cave entrance and glided through about a fathom from the bottom, with the submersibles following.

"This is cool!" Lord Lee said as they moved.

FM guided the *Steel Crab* to three points where powerful battery-operated lights were set on the cave floor illuminating the entire wall that would require the attention of the demolition team. While this was accomplished Dr. Van Haaten studied the wall with the practiced eye of an archaeologist. Using a laser pointer, she indicated where the charges should be set to clear the first twelve inches of rock.

Using the traditional trunkline designed for mining and quarrying PRIMACORD® 4R was quickly attached to the wall at the points she indicated. Soon the red lines of explosive were in place. Sparks watched the application with a critical eye, made a few adjustments, and then ordered everyone out of the cave.

This was necessary because water, unlike air, is incompressible. Technically, it can compress, but it takes a massive amount of pressure to apply a small amount of compression. Therefore, in an underwater explosion, the surrounding water doesn't absorb the pressure like air does, but it moves with it. Underwater explosions transmit pressure with greater intensity over a longer distance. No personnel or equipment could be in the path of that pressure wave! It would crush them instantly.

All six units moved out of the cave, up to three hundred feet, and behind the direction the blast would spread. When Sparks was satisfied the divers and submersibles were safe, he detonated the explosive. Above, on the *Pearl*, the scientists watched the blast move through the water, gathering strength seemingly as it went. From behind the blast inside the Newt Suits the four men manning them had a moment of discomfort as their instrument panels flashed on and off, flickered, and then settled back to normal.

Two hours of work, and two hours of getting to the cave had passed and it was time to rest. To keep the current from moving them apart the men in the Newt Suits hooked on to the two submersibles and then relaxed. Izzy, Lord Lee, and Rock were soldiers, and they knew the benefits of sleep. Within minutes, despite the cramped quarters and odd environment, they were asleep.

Mike Putnam had grown accustomed to the ways of soldiers as he'd trained with these men but getting to sleep took him longer. He dozed, rather than slept, but at the end of four hours felt refreshed and ready to go. The men talked together about sleeping in the suits as they detached from the submersibles and followed them back to the cave. Despite the discomfort, sleep had been possible.

"Did all of you consume your requisite liquids?" The voice belonged to Donna Penny.

"Roger that," came from ten voices. Some called her D.J. for Donna Jane, while others called her Nurse Penny, and still others just called her Donna.

"Any problems eliminating?" She asked quickly.

"Nurse! I'm blushing!" FM quipped.

"That will be the day." Donna replied quickly, smiling despite her serious question. "Just answer the question."

"We've all been to the head on this crew." FM replied.

"Same here." Sparks replied.

"It's a little weird with the catheter. 800 milliliters in the bag at the moment!" Izzy said.

The others in the Newt Suits read off their amounts to indicate they had indeed been able to eliminate. She wrote down the numbers and nodded, checking her chart. They were on schedule.

"You are cleared to go back to work." Donna said. "Over."

Inside the cave the lights were hooked to the batteries once more and Dr. Van Haaten smiled. One portion beneath that first level of rock showed the burnt wood of a hull. Dr. Dundee and Rock arrived at the wood first, tested it, and were able to pull large pieces away, revealing an open space and horizontal ribbing of the inside of a ship, and a second wall of wood.

"Time for the diamond wire saw." Mike Putnam said.

He and Rock moved back to allow the *Steel Crab* to inch forward. Using a diamond wire saw attached to the left manipulator arm Sparks carefully cut a hole tall enough for the Newt Suits to enter without difficulty and wide enough for three of them to go in abreast. An hour passed as the hole was cut and finally the submersible backed away to allow the divers to look inside.

Hot lava had poured through various spots, but it was not deep inside this hold. Crates, made of wood, now rotting away, were burned about three quarters of the way up, but still visible. Izzy and Lord Lee moved to one crate and easily lifted the wood top away. Whatever had been inside floated away in the lazy current as burnt ash, filling the water with black flakes.

Dr. Dundee and Rock used their manipulator arms and tools to open a hole into the next hold. As they worked the two talked together over their COM links.

"Light hasn't penetrated this hold in over three hundred years." Rock said, his voice calm. Working the arms didn't require much physical effort. His hands and arms worked the controls of the machines attached to his exoskeleton. "We'll be the first humans to look in here."

"Too true, mate." Dr. Dundee replied. "The anticipation of discovery is one of the reasons I became a scientist."

"What were the other reasons?" Rock asked. He liked Dr. Putnam because the man didn't put on airs like so many scientists he'd known in the past. None of their science crew did that. Because Mike Putnam was analytical in social style, and a beaver in his personality type, he didn't talk much unless asked direct questions. Rock knew this so he asked.

"When I was a kid, I learned that God created this world we live in. I wanted to know Him, but I also wanted to know about Him. So, I began to study what He'd made. The more I studied the more I realized that human intelligence is far too limited to fully understand the nature and vastness of the intelligence of God. It was fascinating and a bit of a challenge. God was challenging me to use the mind He'd created in me to dig deeper than the usual bloke." Mike replied. "Now pull this piece out of the way and I think we'll get a lash at what's behind door number two!"

Working perfectly together they pulled the wood away, revealing an opening into the next hold. Once they'd carefully deposited the piece they cut away where it wouldn't fall on one of them or impede progress in any way Rock waved his right arm.

"After you, Doc." He grinned at his friend.

Marveling at the almost human motion of the waved arm Putnam moved in and to his left and Rock followed. Mike loved the way his whole unit glided through the water, like flying, making him feel almost weightless. Strangely graceful in this deep water the suits glided through the water like ethereal spirits in air. His lights picked up five skeletons jumbled together near the forward bulkhead. Only the upper parts of their bodies were evident, suggesting that lava had literally burned away the lower halves of their bodies.

"They must have suffered horribly when they died." Rock breathed.

"Only for a second or two." Mike said, his voice strangely quiet. "Makes one think. In the time it takes to blink an eye we can die. What do you suppose they were doing down here?"

"My guess is guarding the gold and other treasures in case the ship was boarded." Rock replied.

"Yes. You are in the area where the heavy deposits of gold, silver, and copper are coming from." Dr. Dinsmore's voice sounded in their ears.

"We have what looks like a cornerstone, or something similar!" Izzy suddenly said.

"Cool! Let's have a lash!" Dr. Dundee said to Rock.

Rock grinned at the Australian slang and followed Mike out into the other hold. Moving carefully to the lights of their fellow divers they looked at a large square stone. Dr. Gregg's voice came over the radio.

"Each of you take a side and photograph it, please. Over." He said. They could all hear the excitement in his voice.

They did so and Dr. Gregg looked at the photos as they came up on the screen before him. Zeke, working in the computer center, enhanced the photos as they came up. Within ten minutes there was a very clear set of photographs of the four sides and top of the stone. Gwyneth watched her husband's face light up as he poured over the ancient text.

"It's from Sacsayhuamán, the Inca stronghold of Cusco!" Dr. Gregg announced.

"Sacks of humans?" Lisle Mirelle quipped, grinning.

Dr. Gregg smiled at her and pronounced it slowly. "It was quite a city in its time!" He added happily.

"Hey Beer Bottle!" FM spoke into his headset. "Got any ideas on how we're going to get that monstrosity out of this cave?"

"Monstrosity?" Dr. Gregg said in disbelief.

"Marines always know how to do difficult things." Wade Adams shot back.

"Yeah!" FM drawled. "If you mean blowing stuff up!"

"Don't you dare suggest blowing up my stone!" Dr. Gregg sputtered.

"Don't worry Dr. Museum. We'll get it out of there and up on deck in one piece." Sparks said into his headset.

"They were joking with each other, dear." Gwyneth said, giving her husband a gentle shake of his shoulders. He winked at her, to show he knew that. It had taken some adjustments to his more austere nature to finally accept the joking for what it was. That the men did it almost without thought impressed him somewhat.

"Okay divers!" Jim commanded. "Take what you can carry out to the sand box over the next hour. After that you head to the surface. Slow and steady, caution first!" He ended. "Over."

"Roger that, Shep." Four voices replied in unison.

From above scientists watched the live feed from *Sea Bullet's* cameras as the men moved slowly out of the hull of the ship with items they could carry. Mike Putnam came out carrying what looked like an old-fashioned pirate's chest. It was half his size. When he lowered it to the sea floor in the sand box a huge puff of silt rose up, signifying it weighted an enormous amount. That he'd been able to lift it with his suit's strong mechanical arms had impressed him.

The men were only able to make three trips in the hour, and to conserve their power they stepped into the sandbox, each grasping one of the corner cables running to the hook at the end of the hoisting block. Slowly the platform began to rise toward the surface. Facing each other the divers grinned at one another as they made the quick trip to the surface. They had the privilege of being the first to see these things in hundreds of years, and it was an honor. As the sandbox rose their suits adjusted to the outer pressure automatically. Still, they watched the gauges carefully.

CHAPTER 24

Three hours later the men in the suits were finally able to climb out. Tired and satisfied with the knowledge that their first test had been nothing but positive they sat comfortably at the conference table and answered questions about how the suits operated, any difficulties they experienced, and what it was like to sleep inside the suit. When the debriefing ended, the four were allowed to go to their cabins for much deserved rest in a real bed.

"I think I can fix that problem with the forward counter-clockwise motion of the left arm." Wrench said. His freshly shaved head broad shoulders and muscular hands were accented by the cleft in his chin and his ruggedly handsome features. He was first and foremost a mechanical engineer and he had proved his skills already on this maiden voyage. Mike was not boasting when he spoke.

"How would you fix it?" Jim asked, interested.

"I noticed it when I was studying the suits earlier. Two brackets holding one of the pulley arms interfere with that motion. I think I can twist the brackets to clear the interference. If I can then hinge the pulley arms to swivel about 22.5 degrees in either direction the problem should be solved." Romentowski replied. He drew a diagram to show everyone what he was talking about. Although complex, it was also amazingly simple, once drawn.

Goody nodded his head in agreement. Zeke Good was the other mechanic on the boat. It had been at his request that Jim sought out Mike Romentowski to serve under the Master Chief. In his opinion, Romentowski was the best he'd ever worked with. Jim trusted the men he hired to know who was best for the job and he was able to entice Mike away from his Navy career.

"Build a prototype and we'll test it." Jim replied. "If it works, we'll build four, and then a fifth to send to the company that built the suit. We'll offer them a joint patent. Thanks, Wrench." Jim held out his hand and they shook hands.

After the Captain walked away Mike looked at Zeke, a strange expression on his face. Zeke, thinking he knew the reason smiled.

"What?" He asked.

"He didn't even bat an eye when I told him I could fix that problem. Shep didn't suggest that the engineers that built the suit probably designed it that way to avoid other problems. The Captain just listened to me, looked at my drawing, and told me to build it! I don't think I've ever been treated with that kind of respect for my expertise before by a Captain!" Mike said.

"He's always that way," Zeke Kline said, coming up to the two. "He expects us to know what to do, and to do it. That's why he hired you. It took some getting used to." Zeke admitted, clapping them both on the shoulder and moving on.

"We better get to work on that prototype." Goody said, leading the way out of the conference room.

"Roger that!" Mike said with a wide smile.

"Our Captain has a way of bringing the best out of his crew." Angela Rysdale said as she and Dr. Carol Lowe followed the two men.

"He does seem to trust us all to do our jobs, and not to hesitate to make suggestions." Carol replied.

They hurried up on deck to look at the artifacts that had come up. Dr. Alastair Gregg was in charge of that project and he was leaning over a saltwater tank as they approached. Both looked down into the liquid at what appeared to be an ornament made of gold encased in lava. Words had been carved into the gold.

"What's this one?" Dr. Rysdale asked, waving her hand in front of her nose as she got close enough to really smell the water.

"The writing is Quechua, which was the official language of the Incas, and I can see some indications that it belonged to the Kingdom of Cusco. *Qusqu'Qosqo* is Quechua for Cusco.

"See this word?" He pointed a finger at the word. "That's *Tawantinsuyu*! *Inca* really refers to the ruling class or the ruling family in the empire. There were many people in the regions that did not belong to that class. They spoke Aymara, Puquina, Jaqi, Muchik, and scores of lesser-known languages. It was the Spanish who called them all Inca. *Tawa* is four with the suffix *–ntin* which means a group. *Suyu* means "region" or "province." It is believed that the empire was divided into four *suyus*, whose corners met at the capital, Cusco!" His voice was filled with excitement as he deciphered the writing he could see through the water.

"See here!" He suddenly said as they all bent lower to look closely. "That's *Sacsayhuamán!* It was the Inca stronghold of Cusco! I saw that word in the photo under the water. This is quite a find!"

"Are you two ladies distracting my husband?" Gwyneth asked, stepping over to the tank. Dr. Lowe and Rysdale looked up with smiles while Dr. Gregg remained fixed on the object in the tank.

"Is that even possible?" Carol asked, giving Gwyneth a hug. Angela held her hand and then hugged her in turn. The three women moved off while Dr. Gregg continued his study of the artifact, totally focused on his scrutiny.

Jim watched his science team working at the tanks for a moment and then moved off toward his office. He'd been aft to check on the *Sea Bullet* after the dive. Life support systems and batteries were being recharged, all the filters were changed, and the Envirovac flushing system was being serviced. According to his crew the vessel had worked properly and was in good condition. He thanked them personally for their work before leaving.

Sea Bullet did not have the fishbowl glass bubble that the *Steel Crab* was equipped with. Yet the pilots agreed that with the video cameras in operation they had a good line of sight on everything around the sub. All it took to pilot the craft was a mental adjustment to viewing things from a computer screen rather than actual line of sight. Jim knew the men who piloted the craft were adept and he marveled at their skill.

What always concerned him, as Captain, was safety. Having a crew down that deep where any problems could become a major disaster in seconds was a high-risk proposal. This time he'd sent a woman down, and that had been hard. Cecilia had helped him see the importance of the decision, but it still was a concern. None of the Science Team had been trained in high-risk assignments, life and death situations, like his own team and crew.

Dr. Van Haaten was calm the entire trip, professional, showing no signs of stress and no fear of being in cramped quarters for a full twenty-four hours. Jim was impressed, but not surprised. Dr. Dinsmore trained them. Feeling much better about the situation he made his way to his office.

Tom Ives was at his desk, pouring over the reports from the dive. Ives was Jim's height, but weighed only 175 pounds. An avid long-distance runner and basketball player Ives added a new dimension to the crew as Jim's administrative assistant. Like Finn, Ives was a detail person, missing nothing when it came to minutiae. He had an amiable side to him, making him easier to work with. Knowing that the Captain didn't need the details he provided them only when asked. And he had a happy nature. His rank meant little to him, only his job was important, and he knew his responsibilities. Because of that the entire crew had taken to him almost immediately.

"Hi Shep!" He said with an easy smile as Jim came through the door. "There are some forms to sign on your desk, and Admiral Ashley asked that you call at your earliest convenience." Sitting back and stretching his back he grinned at the Captain. Jim Shepherd might be Captain of this vessel, but he always treated his men as equals, and Ives had come to deeply appreciate that.

"Thanks, Ives." Jim said with a nod. "Would you please get the Admiral on the horn for me?" Tom nodded as Jim walked past, reaching for the phone to make the request to Uncle Zeke.

At his desk Jim signed the forms after quickly scanning them and stacked them in his out box. His secure phone rang, and he picked it up.

"Captain Shepherd." He said easily.

"Good afternoon Shep." Admiral Ashley said.

"And good day to you, sir." Jim replied. "The weather is a balmy eighty degrees here in paradise. We have calm seas and the wind is at my back. It rained earlier this afternoon, a very pleasant occurrence each day."

"Go ahead! Rub it in!" Duck laughed.

"To what do I owe the honor?" Jim asked after sharing the laugh.

"Kareem." Duck said without preamble. "And his compatriot." He added. "Sanctioned. May I ask this favor of your team?"

"They will be coming after us soon enough." Jim said quietly. "I take it your meeting with the President went well." He added.

"*He* didn't resign." Duck said with derision in his voice.

"Are you safe, sir?" Jim asked.

"Sir Edward is minding my back. I'm as safe as I can be for the moment. Ira suggests using his assets if you need them." Don replied. For some reason his own safety had not been a consideration and he silently berated himself.

"Get Captain Gridley on your six, sir. You won't find better." Jim said after a pause.

"You think it will get that bad?" Admiral Ashley asked, his voice suddenly sharp.

"Worse. I'll be in touch. Remember, money is key. Follow the money. Good luck." Jim replied.

"Same to you, you pirate." Donald laughed and hung up the phone.

Almost immediately Duck picked up his phone and asked his administrative assistant to get Captain Gridley on the line. He smiled as he gave his orders and felt immediately that a heavy load had been lifted from his shoulders.

"Ives, will you come in here a moment." Jim said from his office. Tom was there almost immediately. "I need a meeting with the

Team. Ask Zeke to set it up for 16:00 this afternoon. We'll meet in the conference room on the Coral. I'll let John know."

Ives nodded, took the forms from the out box and left the office to make the call up to Zeke in the CIC. Jim smiled and picked up the phone, dialing his brother's number. Sharky picked up the phone on the first ring.

"Good afternoon, Finn. I'd like a word with my brother, please." Jim said when Finn answered.

"Immediately, sir!" Finn replied.

"Thank you, Lieutenant." Jim replied. He could almost see Finn's smug smile as his rank was mentioned. While he waited for John to come on the line, he looked at his schedule, automatically memorizing what he needed to do that afternoon. With a pen he made a few changes to make room for the meeting.

"Yo Shep! What's up?" John's voice came over the line.

"Hi John. How did *Steel Crab* do, being down that long?" Jim asked.

"He was in excellent operating condition when he came up. How about the *Sea Bullet* and *Newt Suits*? John asked.

"Same." Jim replied.

"You were really sweating sending Sparkles down there, weren't you?" John asked.

"Definitely." Jim replied emphatically. "She did great though. I called to let you know Duck is asking a favor. I'm calling a Team meeting at 16:00 on the Coral."

"Roger that. Team meeting at 16:00 hours! I'll get News on it right away. How do you feel about the rigging that's keeping our two ships together?" John had been inspecting the rigging earlier and was impressed.

"Helm says it works a treat. Goody says it lessens the stress on the bow thrusters." Jim replied.

"Master Chief Warner says the same thing, but he cautions that in heavy weather, if a bow thruster should fail, the whole thing will get crushed or worse." John said.

"My Master Chief warned me of the same danger." Jim chuckled. "We got a pair of winners with those two, didn't we?" He commented.

"Roger that. I'll see you at 16:00 hours." John disconnected and Jim put the phone down with a real smile of pleasure. He and his brother were kindred spirits, best friends, and it made him feel a strong sense of belonging to something very special. Fondly he considered the years the two had served together, thinking that it was great to love your work and the people you worked with. Just then Cecilia walked through his door and his smile got broader.

Deciding to surprise her he leaped from his chair; picked her up in an embrace and spun her around. She laughed after the spin and a passionate kiss, her cheeks coloring in a fetching way.

"My!" She said almost breathlessly.

"To what do I owe the pleasure?" He asked, putting her down and sitting with her on the bench instead of behind his desk.

"Kareem and Muhammad are going underground for a while. They both have safe houses, fortresses actually, where they can stay for months, even years if necessary. Kareem also ordered an attack on our ships. Zeke will have all the details for the meeting this afternoon."

"Does Zeke have a twenty on their safe houses?" Jim asked quickly. Cecilia smiled. How easy it became to pick up on the lingo of the soldier!

"Both men have a GPS locator on their computer, and both are convinced that no one can penetrate their firewalls of security. That's a mistake none of us would make." She replied, snuggling into her husband as he held her gently with his arm around her shoulders. His display of affection was something very special and she meant to enjoy it.

"Actually, I believe there are only a few people in the world who can actually defeat multiple firewalls of the kind those two use. We're fortunate to have one of those on our crew." Jim said. "We can't expect them to keep believing they are secure. If they do go underground, we need to know where."

"We do." She said with a complacent smile. "The same courier who gave up bin Laden has visited both safe houses when Kareem and Muhammad were there. Real estate records show ownership to both men as well, though we had to wade through several dummy companies to finally get to the real owners!"

"I have a great intelligence team up there. That deserves a kiss to the one I'm holding in my arms." Jim said, kissing his wife once more and standing up.

"Yes, you do." Cecilia said, leaving the office in a much better frame of mind than she had entered it. Her husband had surprised her with an exuberant greeting, something he rarely did. She was still flushed when she reached the CIC, her mind going over the emotions she'd just experienced, and the smile on her face mute testimony of her present attitude.

"I see the meeting with the Captain went well!" Zeke said as she took her seat at her computer station. She flushed even deeper and he laughed. "It must be nice to be the Captain's pet Ensign!"

"I think being his wife gives me some advantages over everyone else." Cecilia said haughtily, and then giggled.

"Leave my wife alone, Mr. Kline, or we will be calling you seaman Kline around here!" Jim's voice came over Zeke's headset. "Uncle Jim sees all!"

There was a roar of laughter over the headset as Jim's comment had been heard by all on the boat. Jim had guessed correctly that Zeke would be teasing Cecilia.

"I retire bested." Zeke laughed over the radio with the rest. "Jeeze, Shep, you're gonna ruin my reputation!"

"What reputation?" Wrench drawled.

"I might reply by asking why you have your head practically in that toilet bowl!" Zeke shot back.

"I'm thirsty." Wrench replied evenly without hesitation.

"Gross!" Echoed over the headsets, mostly in female voices.

"How'd you know?" Wrench asked.

"Because Uncle Zeke really does see all, the Captain only guesses correctly from time to time." Zeke replied urbanely.

"There's no camera in the head, you dufus!" Wrench replied.

"Obviously not. However, there is a work order, properly noted, that says the bottom bracket on a certain toilet tank is loose, and that you are currently fixing it, which I know requires you to lean over the toilet bowl in a precarious position. Simplicity!" Zeke replied.

"Somebody put a bun on that hot dog!" Wrench grunted.

More laughter followed and Cecilia decided she was very happy to be a part of this crew. They had rescued her once, in the near past, and God in His mercy had put her among them so that they were responsible for most of her healing. Satisfied that she was right where she needed to be, she went to work, ignoring the bantering between the crewmembers that continued for a few minutes. Zeke, she noticed, had not stopped working his computer consoles the entire exchange.

The man could certainly multi-task in amazing ways. She turned her eyes to her own screen and began to study the information popping up. At the moment she was linked to the New Scotland Yard system looking for a name she was sure had come under the scrutiny of her aunt's organization. In a few moments she had the information on the screen. Someone else was also looking in on that server!

A warning flashed on the screen that someone was trying to trace this connection. She saw, out of the corner of her eye, that Zeke was aware of the attempt and was not only blocking it but tracing it!

"How can you do that?" She asked.

"Uncle Zeke sees all!" He said under his breath as his fingers flew over the keyboards of two computers. "Got you! You thought you were one bad hombre but you're mine now!"

A picture of a man desperately working a computer keyboard suddenly appeared in a pop-up screen. He looked for a moment at his computer camera in surprise, his face and eyes registering shock, and then with a foul oath he asked the question that came immediately to his mind.

"Who are you?" He waited, working his keyboard, his face sweating heavily. "Show yourself!" He snarled. And then his computer showed a single picture, a human skull with the jawbone askew and the top of its head exploding outward, and the man swore as his computer slowly became useless, no more than a paperweight on his desk. Cursing at the top of his lungs he tore it free of wires and hurled it.

CHAPTER 25

Alexander Soracco sat at his desk staring at the pieces that were, only moments before, his laptop. He cursed New Scotland Yard vehemently, shoved his chair back, and stood up to pace his office. Someone at New Scotland Yard had traced his connection all the way back to his computer, something that wasn't supposed to be done in mere seconds, and that same someone had downloaded all his information and then destroyed his hard drive.

Only minutes passed but Soracco was a man of action, a former GIGN agent turned rogue who had been on the run and staying under the radar of various law enforcement agencies for six years. Cleaning up the parts of his computer he quickly tidied his office, dusted all the surfaces carefully, and then vacuumed the floor as he slowly withdrew. Everything else was already pristine, wiped clean daily against the need for a quick retreat. Soracco knew the drill well, and he practiced it religiously. In thirty minutes, he was gone, leaving no trace of his presence.

Zeke and Cecilia analyzed the data from his computer, calling Stephanie Morris to join them. Using key word searches they soon found the information they needed, and Zeke sat back with a low whistle. Stephanie Morris gave Cecilia a hug and patted Zeke on the shoulder as she left the CIC and headed back down to the laboratory.

Zeke watched her slender body, swaying easily with the motion of the ship, as she left the center.

"She's much too young and pretty to be so smart!" He said at last, turning back to his computers.

Cecilia smiled. Zeke was infatuated with SOS, as everyone affectionately called Stephanie Morris, as he was with several of the women on the science team. Morris had been too close to Morse, and the code originally developed by Alfred Vail in the early 1840s for Samuel F. B. Morse's electric telegraph was familiar to all the military men on the crew. Hence her nickname SOS, the international call for help. Cecilia wasn't sure just how the call for help fit in, but she thought it might just be the men subconsciously admitting that such beauty left them helpless. It wouldn't do to say it out loud, but she smiled again as she thought it.

"What do you think Soracco will do?" Cecilia asked, having formulated her own theory in the second it took to think all that. She knew now that anticipating the actions of criminals wasn't always easy but working with these men had honed her skills and she was getting much better at putting it all together. Even her aunt had noted her newfound ability and commented upon it. For Cecilia, that was high praise, for she held her aunt very high in her estimation of law enforcement agents from Scotland Yard.

"He's a dangerous man with dangerous military training. I don't know what he'll do, but I do know he'll find a way to attack us. We have to expect the unexpected, and hopefully we'll see the attack before he has a chance to do any real harm." Zeke replied as his fingers flew over his keyboards. He looked at her, his boyish smile suddenly lighting up his face, which was often locked in a look of utmost concentration.

"I'm making sure that if he leases any aircraft, or purchases any serious weapons, the information will come to us first, and then to all the law enforcement agencies in place. Red tape will keep them from doing anything useful until after the crime, so I want to be ready to avert disaster!" He went back to his computer layout, the smile gone as he worked. Once more those agile fingers flew over the keyboards, sometimes typing on two at a time. She didn't know how he did it.

"As young as I am, I can still remember a time when a policeman could act on an accusation. Now it is so sad that policemen are hampered by the legal system and jaded so that they will not respond unless an actual crime is committed. Often it is too late, then. I hate that." Cecilia said softly. Zeke turned to her.

"It has to do with values. When we took the ten commandments and prayer out of schools, and so many people worked so hard to infiltrate and destroy churches throughout our country, we lost our innocence, our value of right and wrong, and our appreciation for law and order." For Zeke that was a fairly long and fairly deep speech, and Cecilia thought about it, nodding in agreement.

"Here we are most vulnerable from the air." Cecilia nodded, voicing her own opinion as she agreed with Zeke's analysis of Western European Society.

"I believe that our AH-1W Super Cobra will balance the scales." Zeke said as he worked. He was referring to the newest purchase the company made. It was a modified AH-1W Super Cobra, and though it could still be armed when necessary, the armaments had been replaced with very sophisticated and delicate research equipment. At the moment, the craft minus any equipment was stored in one of the containers on deck, out of sight and protected from the elements. It could be assembled and ready to fly in twenty-minutes, fully armed and ready for battle.

Radar on the *Pearl* and *Coral* would detect any craft coming in under normal radar thirty-five minutes out. That was sufficient time to get *White Knight* in the air for defensive purposes. The craft was not painted white, as it had originally been when purchased, but now matched *Bring It Up* colors of burgundy, pearl white, and aqua blue. *Bring It Up*'s logo Eagle on either side was a fitting symbol for that particular gunship.

Powered by two 1212-kW General Electric T700-GE-401 turboshafts (1,625hp each) the 58-foot craft was capable of flying at 352 kmh or 218 mph. With her 10 ft. 7 in. wingspan and 14 ft. 2 in.

of height she fit into a container designed especially as an on-ship hangar.

This AH-1W's chin houses the Night Targeting System, Laser Designator and the Forward Looking InfraRed (FLIR) sensor. The gunner, who sits forward and lower than the pilot, uses this sensor suite to aim and fire the host of anti-tank missiles, rockets, and 20mm cannon in a typical AH-1W loadout. When armed the helicopter boasted an M197 three-barrel 20mm cannon (750 rounds) @ 650 rounds per minute. TOW wire guided missiles, Hellfire laser-guided anti-tank missiles, FFAR rockets, and Sidewinder air-to-air missiles completed her armaments. Formidable weapons all!

Her avionics included the Night Targeting System (NTS) (FLIR, laser-designator) AN/APR-39(V)2 Radar Warning Receiver and AN/ALE-39 chaff and flare dispenser. She was called *White Knight*, because when it came to being rescued by an aggressor, she fit the bill. It was an aircraft built for one thing, battle in the air and especially air to ground fighting. There was none better.

Especially critical the craft's unique design also allowed for serious research advantages, especially after dark. Highly sensitive cutting-edge design equipment was developed to allow *White Knight* to measure wind currents, air temperature, and collect information from the research nodes on the ocean floor, while tracking various forms of marine life beneath the surface. She was also capable of measuring the variations in water temperature up to a hundred and twenty fathoms and plot currents to that depth. One of the rocket launchers could also be used to tag larger denizens of the deep with uncanny accuracy.

Inside the hangar the helicopter was always fitted with the research equipment. Armaments were kept in the hanger in secret compartments, much like the compartment in the hold of the ship, virtually hidden in plain sight. That way, whenever an inspection was made, no evidence of military capability could be detected. Zeke knew that even then, if *White Knight* was needed, it would lead to suspicion, but without proof, that was all anyone ever had. By the time there was an inspection, the armaments would be hidden again.

In the cockpit Jim Shepherd as pilot and Terrance Wade Red Claw as gunner proved to be the best pair of the *Pearl* crew, while Chance Edwards and Phil Eustus were the best pair of the *Coral* crew. At the present moment Shep and Chief had the edge in points scored. If the Cobra needed to be used for defense, they would be the first up. That thought chilled and thrilled Cecilia at the same time. She was immensely proud of her husband, he worked hard to be the very best, but also knew one mistake in the air could lead to his death.

Yet she would not change him, even if she could. Jim was a man of courage, honor, and deep patriotism. He believed in what he did for his country. Now, even more, he did things for the good of the world. She too risked her life willingly for God and country and did not consider the risk too great. With those thoughts wandering through her mind she went back to work on the more immediate problems they faced.

CHAPTER 26

Izzy, Lee, Lloyd, and Mike met in the wet lab once again and hoisted themselves into the bottom of the Newt Suits. Once they were situated comfortably the middle section was lowered and sealed, and after a full systems check, the helmets were lowered and sealed in place. One by one they were lifted from the deck and lowered through the opening into the ocean.

Hooking onto the *Steel Crab* they sank slowly back to the wreckage of the galleon. Today they would be working in teams of two to uncover and load more of the contents of that fated ship's various holds. Driver, Sparks, and Inchworm kept up a steady conversation with the ships on the surface and the divers as they sank to the bottom, as well as communicating with FM, Goody, and Sparkles in the *Sea Bullet*.

Once on the bottom a full systems check was done once more of the Newt Suits and the submersibles. Nothing was left to chance. Only when all systems were determined to be nominal did the strange looking group move into the cave once more. Once the lights were in place and powered up work got underway. Manipulator arms on the *Steel Crab* and Newt Suits moved rock and heavy loads with comparative ease. *Sea Bullet* took things set aside out to the sandbox.

Four hours later the men in the Newt Suits settled in to rest for four hours. *Steel Crab's* crew set down inside the cave for their four-hour rest, while *Sea Bullet* settled beside the sandbox. Dr. Van Haaten watched FM and Goody flip a coin to determine who would take the first two-hour watch while the others slept.

"If all three of us kept watch each of us would get an extra forty minutes of sleep." She said easily.

"Done!" FM said, grinning at her. "I get first watch, Goody, second, and you third."

"Just like that?" She asked, hardly believing what she was hearing.

"Just like that kiddo. You proved you can handle it." FM said. "Now close those pretty eyes and get to sleep!"

Goody did waken her at the allotted time, and she sat quietly, watching the instruments, while the two men breathed the quiet rhythm of sleep. They were soldiers, so they slept lightly, and she'd learned both would wake if she moved much. On her way to the head both men had opened their eyes and looked at her, then gone back to sleep. The same occurred on her return trip and she decided that next time she'd use the head before the watches began or after it was over.

When she apologized for waking them both men just smiled and nodded. She'd figured it out by herself. Work began again in the cave and went on for two hours, followed by a six-hour rest. It was during the latter two hours of this period of time that the plane appeared on radar.

"I have a contact out of the usual air-traffic lanes, thirty-six minutes out. Course is set to fly over our position!" Bob Neff spoke into his microphone. Everyone who heard his voice began to move. Immediately he picked up the phone and dialed Jim's stateroom. The Captain picked up on the second ring.

"Sir, sorry to wake you, but I have a contact out of the usual air-traffic lanes, thirty-five minutes out. Course is set to fly over our position." He said.

"Roger that. Sound the alarm and alert the diving teams. Get Chief to the hanger, please. Thanks Bob." Jim replied, hanging up the phone. In one minute and thirty seconds he was fully dressed and running out to the hanger.

Team Sniper was already changing the fittings on the Cobra. Jim climbed into the pilot's seat and began to go through the preflight check, while Chief, only seconds behind him, appeared and climbed into the gunner's seat. Practice makes perfect and in this case their rehearsal of this exercise proved useful. Nineteen minutes later the rotors began to turn as the chopper was pulled from the hanger. Once clear the crew moved back into the hanger and pulled the doors closed so Jim could power up and get into the air. This he did quickly and turned to intercept the incoming plane. He wished fervently they had a better detection method that gave them more time. The enemy was almost upon them.

It was, he saw, an old cargo plane, and worse, it bore no markings. The pilot, whoever he was, was also flying without lights. Jim knew immediately that this was the threat to his crew. He hit the microphone switch on his helmet.

"Unidentified aircraft on heading 201.7° south by southwest, you are flying outside of the designated flight lanes, without identifying markings and lights. Identify yourself immediately and turn 15 degrees north. I am reporting you to FAA authorities. You will be instructed to land on the main island for immediate inspection. Do you copy? Over." He said.

In answer the plane dove to within one hundred feet of the ocean. It did not alter course. Chief lit up the front of the plane with the spotlight and an angry face looked out at them and then back to the instruments. It was Soracco in the pilot's seat.

"Fire across the front of the plane." Jim ordered.

Chief aimed the guns to fire across the nose of the aircraft, the tracer rounds alerting the pilot. The rear of the plane opened, and two barrels went into the water.

"Depth charges! Take him down now!" Jim ordered.

Below him he saw the cockpit of the plane disintegrate as Chief emptied the cannon, not needing Jim's warning. He'd seen the barrels roll out. The explosion shook the air and it took the plane only seconds to hit the surface, burning wreckage littering the surface for a moment before sinking out of sight. Jim heard Bob Neff telling the divers and submersibles to prepare for impact and get somewhere safe. But where was safe?

Inside the cave the *Steel Crab* rose toward the ceiling of the cave, pulling two divers with it. Dr. Dundee and Izzy moved inside the inner hull of the Galleon. Out by the sandbox FM pointed the *Sea Bullet* toward the glow on the surface, just as the shock waves hit them. He had just touched down on the bottom and the submersible slid backwards, the front end coming up.

Adjusting instantly FM hit full power and the blast rolled them backwards. Fortunately, he was far enough from the bottom to escape having the submersible smashed against the rocks of the bottom. Lights flickered, went out, came back on, and went out again. Sparks flew in one corner were the batteries were located. They were all holding on for dear life until slowly the submersible began to sink, and hit, on its side, bouncing once and coming to rest silently at the bottom. Even then Frank remained fully in charge of his facilities.

"Damage report." FM said in the darkness.

"Checking the batteries now." Goody said from the back corner. A flashlight shone in the darkness and Goody carefully checked the batteries. One connection had come loose, and he fixed it, tightening it down properly. Sparkles was at the life support unit, checking it with another flashlight. FM noted that her hands shook slightly as she worked over the unit inch by inch, checking gauges and connections in the proper sequence. All three of them had trained for this. Making his way to the reset switch FM waited for Goody to signal he was ready.

"Hit reset." Goody said calmly.

FM pressed the engage switch and the lights flickered, and then came on. The steady pump of the oxygen unit could be heard, and Sparkles looked back at them both and gave a thumbs up. She'd taken a blow to her forehead, just above her right eye, and blood was pouring down her face. Goody had blood coming from above his right ear, staining his ear and hair. FM had some bumps and bruises, but he felt okay otherwise. It was a miracle they had not been broken and battered, dying at the bottom of the ocean. He breathed a prayer of thanksgiving.

Sparkles pulled out the first aide kit and using a small mirror began to dab at her cut. It wasn't bad. FM moved over, took the cotton swab from her, and gently washed the blood away from the cut. He dried the area around it and applied two butterfly bandages to close it, and then put a piece of gauze over it with medical tape. Goody sat quietly while Sparkles shaved the hair around the cut and FM attached the butterfly bandages to keep the edges together. It had stopped bleeding, so he left it at that.

"Look at my finger. Follow it with just your eyes." Sparkles said, holding one finger up in front of Goody. His eyes moved together, following the finger naturally. "How do you feel?" She asked. Goody knew she was afraid of concussion.

"If I told you it hurt, would you kiss it and make it all better?" Goody asked with a boyish grin. He was a handsome man with a nice smile, dark stubble forming on his chin and above his lips, with deep dimples in his weathered cheeks. Heidi smiled at him, leaned in and kissed him lightly on the lips.

"It ain't his lips are bleeding!" FM said, mimicking a pirate. "I hopes ye brought enough for everyone!" FM added, puckering his lips and closing his eyes. Heidi rolled her eyes, gave him a light kiss, and pushed him away.

"Let's take stock of how the submersible took that battering!" She said, and tears formed in her eyes. FM knew she was finally allowing her emotions to come back on-line after the emergency. Knowing the drill, he continued his antics to keep the atmosphere light.

"I be cap'n of this here vessel, and I gives the orders, lass!" FM said, sliding back into his pilot's position. "Git to yer stations or I'll have yer guts for garters!" He commanded imperiously. "Aargh! The floggings will continue until morale improves, don't 'e know?" He added comically. Goody and Sparkles smiled at his antics and quickly moved into position.

"Com-link is down." Goody said, checking the wires. "Antennae lead is not connected." He proceeded to reach awkwardly around the radio set to reconnect the lead. A moment later the radio sounded.

"*Sea Bullet*, do you copy. This is *Pearl Two*, over." Andrea Orvieto's voice sounded calm over the radio.

This is *Sea Bullet*. We are back on-line and assessing damage. Over. At present all systems seem nominal." FM replied.

"I'm going to use the manipulator arm to push us upright." Goody said, settling in place and putting his hands on the controls. Slowly the ship came upright and settled on her skids.

"*Steel Crab*, this is *Sea Bullet* One speaking. Do you copy, over?" FM tried to reach the other submersible.

"*Sea Bullet*, this is *Steel Crab* One. A few segments of the ceiling came down in here and we got battered by a rock or two, but other than those dents we seem to be operational. What is your situation, over?" Driver replied evenly.

"Checking now, Driver." FM replied, sighing. "How about the divers? Over."

"Divers are on-line and all systems are nominal. It seems that Dr. Dundee got buried by some debris and we're clearing that away so he can join us for the ride to the surface. Over." Anyone who didn't know this crew would assume that they were all calm and that everything was okay. FM could hear the tightness in Driver's voice, as he was sure Driver could hear the tightness in his own voice. They knew each other well enough to recognize the danger.

"Once we nail everything down in this tub, we'll join the efforts. Over." FM signed off.

He turned to the others and watched as both of them went over the craft carefully. Turning back to his own work he checked all the systems, adjusting the carbon dioxide levels automatically, noting that everything seemed to be working. He noticed a flashing light on one of the panels and moved a camera to look at the thruster indicated by the flashing light. Sliding along the ocean floor had jammed some rocks in the propeller.

"Hey Goody, can you use the manipulator arm to clear the right rear thruster?" FM asked.

Goody slid back in his place, and a few minutes later the last of the debris was removed. Both men checked the propeller with the camera until Goody gave the order to try the thruster. They could hear the whine as the prop turned and eyes were fastened to the panel.

"It's running a little hot." Goody said. "It must have some sand in the bearings. Did anybody get the name of that 18-wheeler that ran over us? I want his insurance to pay for that bearing! Best not use it unless we absolutely have to, FM." Goody ended. FM quickly shut it down.

"*Sea Bullet,* this is Dr. Dinsmore. Status report. Over." FM could hear the near panic in her voice. She, like all the crew, understood the dangers that lurked beneath the surface of the ocean, and that the ocean took what she wanted. But she had friends down there and FM understood that as well. He took a deep breath and concentrated in keeping his own voice level.

"Hey Dr. Wonderland. *Sea Bullet* One speaking. This is one amazing piece of equipment. She got run over by something nasty, rolled a few times and slid along the ocean bottom, but she's back on her feet, shaking off the dizzies, and ready for round two. Over." FM grinned at Goody as he said this.

"How is Dr. Van Haaten? Over." Alice spoke, her mouth close to the microphone, her knuckles white as she held the shaft with a grip tight from fear. Everyone around her was waiting quietly, equally worried.

"Oh sure! What am I? Chopped liver? Jeeze, doc! Sparkles is just fine. I even got a kiss! She's coming on to talk to you now. Over." FM joked, feeling the release of tension in his shaking hands and tendency to want to laugh.

"Hi, Dr. Dinsmore. This is Heidi. I'm just fine. You wouldn't believe what babies these guys are! A few bumps and bruises and they need somebody to kiss it and make it better! The ship is in great condition considering. We're about to move back into the cave to help extract Dr. Putnam. Over." Heidi took her finger off the speak button and FM saw that it was shaking slightly. She laughed then.

"Roger that. Just be sure everything is operational and come back to us in one piece. Over." Dr. Dinsmore sighed and let go of the shaft of the microphone and sat back. Tears ran down her cheeks and she sobbed, and her husband put his arms around her shoulders.

"Doesn't that fool realize he could have killed all of us?" She sobbed.

"He didn't get much of a chance to realize much of anything. Captain Shepherd and Chief demolished the cockpit with that cannon on the front of that Cobra and the plane blew up and splashed into the ocean." John said quietly. "I think killing all of us was his plan." He'd seen the destruction, felt the heat and strength of that blast in the air, and remembered the violence of the moments before that blast. Captain Shepherd had been desperate to protect his divers. The man could fly, that was something to see. Watching that chopper maneuver and attack had been an eye-opening experience.

Jim landed the chopper in front of the hanger and watched his crew roll the craft into the protected space and close the doors. They would work fast now, taking the armaments off the craft and replacing them with the research equipment. For a moment he simply stood watching, his feelings a tumult in his stomach, turning it sour. He turned to Chief.

"Thanks, Terrance. That was some fine shooting up there." He said, holding out his hand.

"Thanks, Shep. That baby makes it easy to hit what you're aiming at." Chief said, shaking hands. "You fly well for a white man." Chief added with a grin. Jim's eyes lit up with a smile that didn't touch his lips or face. *This guy is scary when he's this focused.* "Let's go see about getting our people off the ocean floor. Chief added, shaking his head."

Jim nodded and the two ran down to the ready room, took off their flight gear and weapons, and dressed quickly in their work uniforms. Once the bulkhead was closed and Jim was satisfied his weapons room was hidden, they headed topside once more. Stopping by the hanger Jim saw that the weapons were already stored away and most of the equipment was back in place. He was glad he hadn't balked at buying the chopper now. Very glad! Vulnerability from the air had been a real concern but he realized they now had at least a fighting chance. Sighing at the memory of those moments in the air he watched his men work.

Earl Duncan was carefully cleaning the barrels of the 20mm M197 cannon. By the time any inspection of the craft was done the gun would show no signs of having been fired. The other men were working quickly and silently, knowing they had to get the job done in a brief period of time. Nodding at the men he walked through and out the back door and into the laboratories. He found Dr. Dinsmore and her crew gathered around the radio.

"May I have a report?" He asked politely, coming to a stop in front of John Dinsmore.

"Dr. Putnam is stuck in some debris, but all the divers and the two submersibles are okay." John said. Jim could hear the tension in his voice.

"How much time do we have?" He asked quickly, checking his watch as he did so.

"A little over two hours." John said, turning back to look at the computer screens showing the activity in the cave.

"141 minutes, to be exact." Lisle Mirelle said, checking.

"Time to call in the Navy if we need help." Jim said quietly.

"I don't think we will, Shep." Bernie Finlay said, coming into the lab. "They will have Dr. Putnam free of debris in about five minutes."

"I'd best get up to the CIC then." Jim said. "Thanks for the good work folks." He said as he sketched a wave and left.

Up in the Command Intelligence Center he found Zeke and Cecilia. As soon as he entered Cecilia leaped from her chair and threw herself into his strong arms. His green eyes softened as he looked into hers, and he kissed her gently, holding her tightly. Knowing why she had been so demonstrative gave him a warm feeling of deep contentment. After a moment he put her down.

"Dr. Putnam is free." Zeke said, his eyes glued to the pictures coming up from the cave.

In the CIC they listened to the chatter between the divers and the submersibles.

"You okay, Dr. Dundee?" Izzy asked. Jim could see that he was facing the scientist. From where he was Jim cold actually see the faces inside the helmets. He studied Putnam's face and it was calm, even smiling. The arm of the Newt Suit came up and the claw appeared to be trying to do a thumbs up maneuver. After a few moments Putnam spoke again.

"Sorry, Izzy, that's the best I can do!" Putnam laughed.

It took a few minutes, but soon the submersibles and divers were on their way to the surface. Jim joined most of the crew at the rear of the ship and saw that the crew of the *Coral* was doing the same thing. Cheers and tears greeted the arrival of everyone to the surface.

CHAPTER 27

Jim saw a destroyer moving toward them, with several patrol boats moving around it. From the opposite direction a Cobra appeared in the sky, heading for the destroyer. Watching it set down on the deck Jim smiled. Commander Cummings was protecting him. Everyone in the patrol boats would assume the assault helicopter belonged to the navy.

From the mainland a pair of hands lowered the powerful binoculars. Someone had tipped off the military and the American researchers had been protected. He ground his teeth. There would be no cry of "foul!" The plane had been American. With a deep growl he turned to move to his car. Kareem would not be pleased.

Captain Shepherd kept the patrol boat personnel from boarding until the submersibles and divers were up and safe. Nearly an hour had passed since the chopper had been in the air. By now the hanger would be pristine, the chopper fully fueled, ready for research. Still, he was in no hurry to comply with the request to board his ship. He had divers to see to, to determine their mental and physical wellbeing. Not until he was satisfied his divers were good to go would he deviate from his intent.

"Hawaii patrol, as soon as I've seen my divers in sickbay, I'll escort you on board. Thank you for your patience." Jim said into the radio from the bridge. He left immediately and headed down to sickbay, with Cecilia in tow.

Dr. Putnam stood with Izzy, Lord Lee, and Rock, as though they were a team. None of them had any bruising or cuts and they were talking lightly amongst themselves. As soon as Jim appeared, they straightened and saluted. Smiling a little he returned the salute.

"Good work under pressure, men." Jim said easily, shaking each man by the hand. "I'm glad things weren't worse."

FM was sitting on the examining table as Dr. Penny treated a bruise above his eyebrow. He grinned at Jim. Goody was sitting next to him, and Dr. Van Haaten was having her own forehead stapled by Nurse Penny.

"I think there's something wrong with my lips, doc." FM said lightly. "They're kinda tingling! Of course, it might be because Dr. Van Haaten kissed me." He added, laughing.

"Whuss!" Heidi said. "You get a little bump and you need somebody to kiss it and make it better! Both of you!"

"I don't see any cuts on their lips." D.J. said with a smile as she put in the final staple.

"It was the only way I could get them to stop whining!" Heidi said with a laugh.

"Hey! I wasn't whining! I just said you needed to bring enough for everyone when you kissed Goody. He was whining." FM quipped.

Heidi hit FM on the arm, which was like hitting a piece of oak. She shook out her hand and made a face.

"Shall I kiss it and make it better?" FM asked, puckering up his lips and leaning toward her.

D.J. elbowed him aside easily and everyone laughed. "See what you started?" She asked Heidi, her face suddenly stern. Heidi couldn't help it and she giggled.

Jim cleared his throat. "How is everyone, Doctor?" He asked, keeping his face schooled and not smiling. Cecilia, next to him, was hiding her mouth but her eyes were sparkling with laughter.

"Ornery, moving when they should be sitting still while I'm stitching them up, and quite annoyingly healthy." He replied, putting in the last stitch and tying it off. He winked at Jim as he put away his equipment before speaking. "No kisses on that, Mr. Good!" Doctor Penny said sternly. "Too many germs, too much chance of infection."

"Put a Band-Aid on it! Girls can kiss the Band-Aid, can't they?" Goody asked plaintively.

"It will heal better without a covering." Dr. Penny said, making a motion that he needed to get off the examining table.

"See what I mean about the whining?" Heidi asked with a giggle. Zeke glared at her, raised his hand with one finger up as if to make a point, then shrugged his shoulders and left the infirmary. The Captain saw the open grin on his face as he left.

Jim and Cecilia left shortly after that and returned to the deck where Jim gave permission for the crew from the patrol boat to board his vessel. Everyone wanted to know what happened, everything about the plane and the crash, and it took hours to get the statements. For a while it seemed futile. Knowing that by the time the order was given whoever had been involved in this crime would be long gone, with the exception of the dead pilot and crew. Jim bore it with mounting frustration.

CHAPTER 28

Kareem was not a man given to emotional outbursts. He received the news of Alexander Soracco's failure with silence, his mind racing. *Soracco had not even been able to get close enough to the ships to do any real damage! Who were these men and women that thwarted him at every turn? How did they manage to know his plans? What will it take to destroy them?* Several thoughts passed through his mind in the passage of but a few seconds when he finally spoke.

"Very well. Get out of Hawaii. Someone may connect you with the plane. I will contact you in two weeks." He said to his agent in Hawaii. Both men would have been shocked to know the call was monitored and the crew of *Bring It Up* was on top of the situation.

"Shep, I have a contact to Kareem from Hawaii International Airport." Zeke said. "I'm pulling up the security cameras now to see who our caller is." He added as his fingers flew over two keyboards.

"I'll be there in two." Jim replied. He had just ushered the Coast Guard team off his ship once more. As they pulled away, he turned and walked normally to the steps that would take him to the bridge.

People were busy on the deck, washing down the submersible, and cleaning and checking the Newt Suits. For once he was not thinking of his crew or watching them work. Instead his mind wrestled with the problem of how to deal with Abu Kareem al-Jameel ibn Nidh'aai and the third member Abu Muhammad al-Filsieeni ibn Abdulaziz. Duck Ashley asked him to deal with them and he needed to move as quickly as possible.

Worse, Kareem must know that he and his crew were responsible for unmasking him and effectively blocking his play at Israel, and then Lord White and Ira Lehman. MI6, he knew, was scrambling to pull together all the information they could on both terrorists. Ira already had a head start. Mossad was never idle when it came to investigating terrorism. Still, it would fall to *Omega Force* to remove the threat.

Kareem considered himself the Ghost. What did Muhammad call himself? Jim didn't know. Both men had billions of dollars to use in terrorist activities. *What would I do if the plane attack failed? How would I attack Bring It UP?* Everyone was in harms way until he could figure that last question and plan appropriately. Walking in a normal manner his face did not reveal the thoughts raging through his mind.

Stepping from the humid hot tropical air of Hawaii into the CIC Jim breathed in the cold air with pleasure and walked over to stand behind Zeke. Cecilia was still down at sickbay or in the computer lab. He missed her presence, looking once at the empty seat. Zeke nodded.

"That's our guy." He said, pointing at a man with middle eastern characteristics hanging up the phone and looking around quickly. Maybe he felt that someone was watching him. "He bought a ticket under the name Alex Mahir. He's flying to San Francisco." Zeke filled in.

"Any hits on that name?" Jim asked, studying the face intently.

"None under Mahir. However, Ira has his face on record under Benjamin Aziz. It's interesting how that last name crops up constantly in this investigation. We might want to look into that. Two years ago, he was busy in Yemen. Ira thinks he killed two top NATO advisors involved in the peace talks and is responsible for supplying arms and explosives to PLA activists.

"I ran the name through the usual channels and came up with

a house in Georgetown. He leased it a few months ago and paid the first year in cash. The real estate agent reported the transaction to the FBI, but they haven't done anything with it yet." Zeke sat looking at his computers as Mahir moved toward the departure gate.

"No luggage. Simple carry-on bag." Jim noted. "He'll go to Georgetown. He thinks he's safe there."

"I concur." Zeke nodded.

"Pass the information to Ira. Tell him of the connection to Kareem. What is Muhammad doing?" Jim said after a pause.

"Muhammad moved ten million dollars in American currency this morning to a bank in the Cayman Islands. The numbered account belongs to a mercenary group operating out of Nicaragua. They have two Aérospatiale Super Frelon 321G choppers. One carries the Sylphe panoramic radar and dunking sonar while the other is armed with four homing torpedoes. Both are available to whoever wants to pay the fee, and it's a hefty one.

"A purchase of four homing torpedoes was completed an hour after the transfer along with two crates of FAMAS assault rifles and several boxes of ammunition for that gun. Another purchase of 40 Glock 17's was recorded at the same time, along with boxes of ammunition. I'd say someone is putting together a force to attack something in the water." Zeke looked up at Jim.

"Do they have a boat?" Jim asked.

"Two Archer Class patrol boats." Zeke replied. He brought up pictures of the boats, docked at the present moment, though men were very busy around them. Jim winced at the amount of rust on the boats, the broken rails along the sides, and the general mess on the front deck. A sudden blast of black smoke belched out of the back of the boat signifying that the diesel engine had been started.

"Sloppy." Jim said. "How do you estimate they plan to get the choppers close enough to attack?"

"See that barge over there?" Zeke pointed at one of the screens. If possible, the barge was in even worse condition than the patrol boats. It would hold two choppers. Both choppers were already chained down on the deck. A small seagoing tug was tied next to the barge. Like the rest of the boats it was in deplorable condition.

"Do we know the speed of that tug?" Jim asked.

"Eleven knots in prime condition. In that condition they'll be lucky to get eight out of it." Zeke replied. "Also, it's a long trip for a boat like that." He added, studying the picture. "And on a long trip, things can happen." Zeke looked up at Jim.

"Yes. To stop them from attacking our ships we should plan a little surprise while they're still on their way. If we disable their boats and choppers, they can't do much." Jim said levelly.

"We should do the world a favor and disable the men too." Zeke said without looking up.

"We'll bring that up at the planning meeting. You should probably cut back on the caffeine." Jim added without inflection.

"Too much red meat." Cecilia said, coming in on his final comment.

Zeke grinned at the two of them as he continued working. Jim hugged Cecilia before leaving, his mind now focused on what needed to be done with two threats.

Kareem and Mohammad were more than accessible. Both had their safe houses in the United States. Kareem was in New York, and under another name was the CEO of a very successful security services provider company making and selling the latest technology in electronic locks, surveillance, and infrared detecting devices. In America he hid behind the name Jameel Aladdin and used his company for industrial espionage against major American companies that operated in his part of the world.

Muhammad lived in Southern California, moving between two houses, one in San Francisco and the other in Pismo Beach. There he posed and made a very good living as head of an investment firm that specialized in overseas oil investments. Klepenheim, Goldstein, and Kemper Associates were fictitious names and no one by those names worked at the offices. Muhammad used the name Abraham Goldstein in America. That, Jim knew, was a mockery and showed the nature of his mind. He was very careful to keep attention away from that business and his activities on the coast.

Ira was using assets in place to keep tabs on both men and Zeke already had blueprints for all three houses and daily schedules. When it was time both of those men would be terminated. Former President Royce, Admiral's Runion and Duck, Sir Edward Marsh, Ira, Petros, General Marsh, and Ken Worthington had all cast a yes vote for a sanctioned kill. So had the entire team and crew.

A thought struck Jim as he walked to his office and he immediately pressed his talk button.

"Zeke, do we know if Kareem is involved in this transfer of funds, or did it come specifically from Muhammad?" He asked.

"It all came from an account controlled by Muhammad. Kareem is trying to get some Russian assets together to take us out." Zeke said immediately. "I'm watching both of them carefully. "Muhammad has also been in contact with some pirates from Somalia. They want one hundred million dollars up front to do the job. I doubt if they'll be hired, it would take them too long to get to us."

"Keep on it, Zeke. I'm sure Muhammad will find another group or arrive at a price soon." Jim said. "Thanks for being so thorough." He added.

"Uncle Zeke sees all." Zeke repeated his mantra once again. Jim grinned.

In his office Jim dealt with the paperwork Ives had for him, made the appropriate decisions for resupplying the ships, and read through the repair reports for the day. Satisfied that things were well in hand he appeared in Ives office two hours later with a stack of papers.

"Thanks for the hard work, Ives. File these please, and if anyone needs me after lunch, I'll be in the labs or on deck." Jim put the papers in the appropriate slot on Ives desk and walked out.

Ives smiled. If anyone wanted the Captain, they had but to press the talk button on their communication gear for instant access. However, the Captain always let Ives know where he'd be in case an outside call came in. It was merely another link in communication, and the Captain believed in good communication. Filing the paperwork Ives remembered his Captain's words "good paper makes for good friends" and smiled again.

Jim arrived at the CIC just as the lunch bell sounded and willingly escorted his lovely wife Cecilia to the dining room. Outside it was beginning to rain, as it often did in the tropics, and the cool dry air-conditioned comfort of the dining room was much appreciated by the crew.

Excitement ran high as the finds from the bowels of the ship were discussed around the tables. Alistair and Gwyneth often ate at Jim's table and he was glad to welcome them today, along with John and Alice. From Alistair Jim learned the details of the finds, listening as he ate a Salmon Caesar salad that was a delicious surprise.

He drank half a glass of White Riesling wine with the lunch, enjoying the way it perked up his taste buds to enjoy the fish and subtle seasonings. As usual, he was finished long before anyone else at the table, but he continued to listen carefully, sipping from his glass of iced tea. That too was a pleasant treat.

JimJim made his own version of the famous Arnold Palmer tea, half tea, half lemonade. Instead of lemonade he used limeade, giving the tea a very tart taste that stimulated the taste buds on Jim's tongue satisfactorily. Twice, Winky stopped by to top off the Captain's glass.

Seaman Hinkle liked Captain Shepherd. In all his years in the Navy he'd never served under an officer like Jim Shepherd. An avid martial artist in his own right Bob was encouraged by the Captain to participate in the daily training of the team, and he sparred often with Jim. In top physical condition Winky could easily have been one of Jim's soldiers, and Jim treated him as if he was one!

In his daily service in the kitchen, which he loved to distraction, Jim was constantly stopping by to compliment the men on their work, the neatness of the kitchen, and the way they treated the crew. On this ship seaman Hinkle was treated as an equal to the highest-ranking officer, never as an underling, and he knew he was respected by one and all. It had taken some getting used to, but he now did his best, as he always did, with a much lighter heart.

On his regular day off he worked in the science labs with Cup

Cake, Little Miss Sunshine, SOS, Hot Lips, Tiffer and Miss Chief, helping where he could and learning everything he could. This also Jim encouraged. If one of the crew wanted a certain book it was usually in the library within a week, ordered by Zeke and approved by the Captain. Marine biology and chemistry were passions of Hinkle's, and he constantly soaked up everything he could. He was determined to be of the utmost usefulness to this crew. Loving the learning and study was just icing on the cake.

Winky grew up with five older brothers and one younger sister, and it had fallen to him to care for his younger sibling often. She was ten years younger and the duty was not unwelcome. He looked at the lab technicians as sisters, and he treated them as such. They were at ease with most of the men on the crew for that very reason.

Jim nodded and thanked Winky each time he filled his glass. He liked the young seaman. Handsome and young, like the lab technicians, Jim had worried he might become attached to one in a shipboard romance. However, Winky had surprised and pleased him by treating them all like younger sisters, teasing and roughhousing as adult siblings often do, all in fun and innocence.

Hinkle had a strong faith in the Lord and devoured his Bible daily with the rest of the men, attending chapels and Bible studies with an eagerness that enticed others. Watching the easy grace of the man Jim quietly thanked the Lord for men like this to lead. Strongly he felt that his crew was more of a family than anything else, despite its size.

With lunch behind them the crew returned to work, as artifacts were uncovered, and new discoveries made. Dr. Wonderland had been correct in the sudden heating and cooling of the ship, and the gold, silver, and copper were in lumps of melted material, easily transported to the surface.

Jim stopped in the machine shop and found Bob Neff purifying the gold and pouring it into bricks. The ingots were marked with the *Bring It Up* logo and neatly stacked on a skid, ready to be hauled to the ship's safe where it would be properly stored to keep its value at top dollar. He noted the fire equipment easily at hand for the dangerous task of doing this on board a ship that constantly moved.

Team Sniper was helping Neff with the job. Relaxed and confident the men worked at a steady careful pace under Bob's careful tutelage. All of them wore heavy fireproof aprons and gloves, and their boots were fire resistant as well. Jim nodded with satisfaction.

Every gold bar was highly polished, and it looked impressive, stacked five feet high on the heavy-duty skid. A second skid was nearly full. Jim looked at it with a sense of pride. It wasn't about the huge amount of gold or the payoff, it was about the skill of his men and crew.

A reporter from the island wandered in, gasped, and began taking pictures. First, he talked to the men about the process of purifying the gold, and how they did everything so that the gold would have top value. He had the usual questions about what the Captain planned to do with the treasure. Jim was happy to answer.

"Half of the money we make on this venture will be invested. Twenty percent of it will be given to charity. Ten percent of that will go to oceanographic study charities, and ten percent will support missionaries in various parts of the world." He said easily. "The other thirty percent will go toward operating costs and our next treasure hunt. Most likely that will take place on land because some of the artifacts we found suggest there are Inca cities we have not yet uncovered." Jim finished.

"Missionaries?" The reporter's eyes narrowed. "From what religion?"

"We support Evangelical Christian missionaries that are providing education, medical services, building schools and hospitals, and reaching disaster victims all across the globe." Jim said without hesitation. "Most of those are providing these services to people that have never experienced them before. But the most important work they do is introducing people to Jesus, the Savior of the world."

"I would think you could find a better use for that money." The reporter said testily. "Why not give it to organizations that don't include proselytizing and leading people to believe in some non-existent exacting and judging God! We've put that myth to rest in the civilized world!" Jim sighed. Understanding very well the underlying hatred of Christianity, he replied.

"What could be better than providing an orphanage for children living in the streets, or a hospital in an area devastated by natural disasters? I can't think of anything better than providing an education to kids somewhere who would not have one if there weren't missionaries willing to go there. Doctors that could make millions here would rather use their gifts to serve. That's worth supporting. Nurses that could make a good living and be comfortable in America would rather go to some dank, disease infested jungle, to care for people and help the doctors there. That's worth supporting." Jim replied.

"Sure, if they can proselytize poor ignorant people into believing in a myth!" The man said derisively.

"We don't believe it's a myth. You may, but we don't. Obviously, you've never met Jesus face to face, as I have. My relationship to the Lord Jesus is the most important thing in my life. Next to my love for Him my love for everything else should look like hatred in comparison! Every person on this crew believes in the Lord Jesus! You should too, because He died for you." Jim said softly.

"Oh, come on!" The news reporter said. "You have Dr. John and Alice Dinsmore, Dr. Iris Copeland, Dr. Carol Lowe, Dr. Lisle Mirelle, Dr. Michael Putnam, Dr. Angela Rysdale, and Dr. Heidi Van Haaten on your crew. Surely they do not believe in that piffle!"

"Why don't you ask them?" Jim invited.

Quickly leaving the machine shop the reporter went in search of Dr. Alice Dinsmore first. He was at a disadvantage, never having read any of her papers or books, but he knew her reputation. Jim followed with a smile on his face. Dr. Wonderland would frustrate this young reporter and he wanted to watch.

"Dr. Dinsmore, I'm Allan Callahan, reporter for *Omni*. What are your feelings about the Captain's decision to give ten percent of the money made from this venture to Evangelical Missionaries?" He said, without preamble.

"Oh! That wasn't the Captain's decision. The entire crew voted on how to use the money. We always do, because we're all partners. I'm certainly in favor of efforts to bring the Gospel to the neediest people in the world. It's a message of hope and love, Mr. Callahan." She replied, hardly looking up from her study of a section of volcanic rock. Although she looked intent on her work Jim knew she was thinking furiously.

"Surely you don't believe in that nonsense?" Callahan asked.

This time she did look up, her eyes sharp. "Nonsense? I'd hardly call faith in the Lord Jesus Christ nonsense. Would you tell a Muslim that his religion was nonsense?"

"Of course not! But Christianity?" His voice rose in disbelief. "Surely we've put that myth to rest! I mean, nobody of any real intelligence believes in God and Jesus and the Bible anymore!" Callahan said. Alice raised an eyebrow and Jim almost laughed out loud.

"Would you consider me intelligent, young man?" She asked dangerously. Callahan nodded.

"Of course. Your credentials are well documented. You are one of the leading minds in Marine Biology today." He answered.

"And would you consider my husband intelligent?" She asked.

"Yes, of course. All of the scientists on this crew are quite well known." Callahan replied.

"Yet we all believe in Jesus. We all profess to a personal relationship with Him, worship Him, follow His words in the Bible with all the religious fervor that a Muslim might follow Allah. Have you forgotten that this great nation, founded by the greatest minds of their time, was founded on the very principles I espouse?

"I believe in creation, intelligent design, not just because the Bible teaches it, but because nature itself shows it! Some of the creatures that live in our oceans are so amazing and so perfectly fitted to their environment that only intelligent design can explain their existence!"

"You're putting me on, right?" Callahan asked, laughing nervously.

"Are you really that obtuse?" Alice asked sarcastically.

"I was under the impression that serious scientists embraced the theory of evolution." Callahan responded, stung.

"You are that obtuse! Evolution is not a theory. A theory can be tested. Evolution comes from historical scientific study, not practical science. It is merely an interpretation of how life came about, and it cannot be tested or proved. Life does not consist of matter (chemicals) alone, but of matter and information. Information is not reducible to matter, but it is a different kind of thing altogether! An interpretation of life thus has to explain not just the origin of the matter but also the independent origin of the information involved in each complex cell. Also, complex, specified information of the kind found in a book or a biological cell cannot be produced either by chance or at the direction of physical and chemical laws. That was Berra's blunder!

Michael Behe, if you're familiar with him, wrote *Darwin's Black Box*. Did you ever read it? No? I thought not! He points out clearly that molecular mechanisms are *irreducibly complex*. They are made up of many parts that interact in complex ways, and all the parts need to work together. Any single part has no useful function unless all the other parts are also present. There is therefore no pathway of functional intermediate stages by which a Darwinian process could build such a system step by tiny step.

"Molecular mechanisms, according to Behe, are as obviously designed as a spaceship or a computer. You can't explain the origin of any biological capability (like vision) unless you can explain the origin of the molecular mechanisms that make it work. Behe claims that evolutionary biologists have been able to pretend to know how complex biological systems originated only because they treated them as black boxes. That's a term that grew out of the efforts of scientists to expose medical hoaxes. But now that biochemists have opened the black boxes and seen what is inside, they know the Darwinian theory is just a story, not a scientific explanation or a theory.

"Do you accept what people tell you without checking out if it is true or not before printing it?" She looked at him as he struggled for words. Finally, he nodded in the negative, though he realized that she could take that confession and use it against him. He often did print things that weren't true, simply because he couldn't bother to check the veracity of every statement!

"But you accept what pseudo scientists tell you, what thintelligence teaches in our colleges and universities today? Really?" She snorted.

"But the evidence!" Callahan blurted.

"What evidence! Richard Dawkins published *Climbing Mount Improbable* around the same time Behe published his book. It was sometime in the late nineteen nineties. That blithering idiot made the claim that the genetic database of a human could not be created all at once. To do that would require a prodigious mind and hence would amount to supernatural creation, but of course he ignores that. He claimed that just as a mountain climber has to go up a mountain step by step, biological evolution has to go through a series of intermediate, functional steps in order to create each biological system. According to him each step represents a random mutation, usually defined as a copying error in the reproduction of DNA. However, unlike Behe, Dawkins fails to create any serious effort to lay out plausible, testable scenarios for the step-by-step evolution of molecular mechanisms.

"Oh, I know some of these thintelligent pseudo scientists claim that we may not see the intermediate steps today, but they must be there! So, they engage in useless shams like 'hand-waving.' New molecular steps mysteriously 'stand forth,' or 'emerge,' or just 'appear'– without any realistic mechanism. They don't even *try* to fill in the Darwinian theory with specific examples because they don't know how to do it! And you just accept what they say?

"Yet what do they do when the *facts* cast doubt on the philosophy of evolutionary science? Instead of bravely facing the *facts* as a true scientist would, they suppress the facts and protect the philosophy! Fools! Science is about discovery, not suppression! It should be about facts, not philosophy! What evolution has become is a religion, not science, and therefore useless.

"You disappoint me, young man. Instead of allowing that fine mind you've been gifted with to search for the truth you have allowed yourself to be blinded by popular tripe! If you were a thinking man, Mt. St. Helens would have opened your eyes. Things that were said to take millions of years to form, formed in less than forty-eight hours!

"I know that the Darwinian mechanism doesn't work and

that complex biological systems never were put together by the accumulation of random mutations through natural selection. It's virtually impossible! This is not a mere gap in a theory that is sound in other respects, either, young man! It isn't just that the Darwinists have failed to provide a complete explanation; they've failed even to *understand* what needs to be explained. Their so-called *theory assumes* that *variation* is all they need to explain and that the accumulation of small variations over immense amounts of time can produce complex organisms from simple beginnings.

"No, young man, once the problems of informational content and irreducible complexity are out on the table in plain view, well-informed people are going to be amazed that these 'thintelligent pseudo scientists' took so long to see that random mutation is not an information creator and that the Darwinian mechanism is therefore irrelevant to the real problem of biological creation!" She folded her arms and watched him. He was obviously trying to keep up, and Jim guessed he would reject it out of hand.

"Come on, Doc!" Callahan said. "You can't ignore textbooks and museums that exhibit fossils that are transitional forms between major groups! I've seen them myself."

"Are you aware, young man, of the vast absence of ancestors for the major animal groups that appear in the 'Cambrian' explosion? Yet the museum exhibit in San Francisco goes so far as to supply *imaginary* common ancestors for the animal groups! I'm not impressed by claims that specific fossils prove the theory of evolution. Instead, unlike you, I ask the right question: Does the fossil evidence, considered as a whole and without bias, tend to confirm the predictions of Darwinian theory? Fossils were formed in hours after the eruption of Mt. St. Helens!" She looked at him again, her eyes piercing.

"No, I wasn't aware of that." He said.

"This rock I'm studying would probably be dated in the hundred's of millions of years. I know it was formed less than 400-years ago! Therefore, as I study it, I don't let appearances interfere with my hypothesis. Here's my mantra when it comes to sharing what I believe to be true. I try to give all the information to help others to judge the value of my contribution to science, not just the information that leads to judgment in one particular direction or another. Darwinists cannot make that claim. Now let me get back to work!" She turned back to her study of the volcanic rock.

CHAPTER 29

Jim watched Callahan go from scientist to scientist, growing more and more frustrated by the hour. It made him sad that instead of thinking about the evidence he rejected it out of hand. The article, he knew, would be derogatory. His scientists were used to that. In a world where truth was suppressed, and students were indoctrinated rather than educated it was a fact of life.

He wondered how the nation had come so far from its roots. The very men that wrote the First Amendment to the Constitution of the United States also wrote books, none of which would be permitted in a classroom today because they "violated" the separation of church and state clause of the First Amendment, which, of course, didn't exist. What fools! People accepted the rulings and lived their lives without demure as the results of those decisions destroyed society in America and provided government the opportunity to become more and more socialistic.

Grants might dry up for his research team, but the money from the *El Dorado Espanola* would ensure that they could continue in their efforts to bring light, the true light of scientific discovery, to the world. God had a way of providing what was necessary to continue His purpose in a world broken and darkened by sin. Smiling at that thought he continued to watch the reporter.

Callahan came last to Dr. Copeland. Openly he challenged her belief in intelligent design. When he was finished, she smiled at him, her dimples forming in her most winsome smile.

"Prove it." She said.

"What?" Callahan sputtered.

"I said to prove it." She replied. "Science demands proof. So, prove it."

"You wouldn't believe me if I did!" Callahan stated baldly.

"Really? You know me that well?" She replied calmly.

"This whole crew is whacko!" He snapped, closing his notebook and putting down his camera.

"Is that a scientific observation?" She asked, her smile still in place, her eyes sparkling with pleasure. He spun and headed for his boat.

"I see you chased the odious little man away." René Millstein said, coming to stand beside her. Tiffany sauntered up and they watched Callahan flounce into his boat and stare balefully at them. All three waved cheerily at him which only seemed to increase his ire. They laughed.

"*Coral One*, this is *Pearl One*, over." Jim spoke into his headset.

"Go, Shep!" John responded immediately.

"Let's get the team together at 21:00 in the conference room on the Pearl, over." Jim said evenly.

"Roger that. See you at 21:00, over." J.R. replied.

"Omega 1, Sniper, Bulldog, and Nightfall, did you all copy that, over?" Jim said as John finished speaking.

A chorus of "Roger that, Shep," or "yeah, boss," sounded in his ears as each man indicated the message had been heard and understood. Jim pressed his speaker once more, looking out over the water to see what boats might be hovering around. There were none close enough to monitor his equipment.

"Science team and crew. Please, could all of you meet in our conference room to be part of the meeting at 21:00 hours, over?" Jim asked politely.

"We'll need some time to get our make-up on correctly, since we'll be on camera, Captain, but we'll be there." Barbara said into her communicator. Jim smiled. Barbara and Mary Anne rarely wore make-up.

"I need my men to be able to concentrate on business, ladies, over!" Jim replied.

"Yeah, boss, like you concentrate on Bright Eyes during all the meetings, over." FM piped up.

"It's the drool that gives him away, over!" Hayseed quipped.

"I'll keep a towel handy, over!" Jim responded quickly.

"So! You admit it?" FM said laconically.

"She is the most beautiful woman on either ship, at least in my eyes. Over." Jim answered easily.

Lynn Ross danced across the lab singing the popular Carpenter's song, "Close to You." As her beautiful voice went over the radio Jim could hear laughter all over the ship.

"Hey boss! I think there's something wrong with our radios. I'm picking up the golden oldies station!" Fagan said.

"Maybe Sparks can fix the problem." Zeke said.

"Duct tape usually works." Hammer said. A sizzling sound and a loud "Ow!" came over the radio. For a moment the lights on the ship went dark. "I got it!" Hammer added amidst the laughter. The lights came back on immediately.

"Serves you right!" Lynn Ross said.

"Did somebody rain on Little Miss Sunshine?" MP asked.

Jim smiled and continued his journey through the ship. The banter continued for some time and he often burst out laughing at a particularly funny remark. He also understood the need for the comedy relief. They were meeting tonight to discuss dealing with the threat against them, and a mission that was fraught with danger. Enjoying his crew's sense of humor and camaraderie he finished his inspection in a much better frame of mind.

That night at the meeting everyone was in attendance, and for that Jim was grateful. He had some serious questions to bring to his crew and he wanted an answer from everyone. It was he who led them in opening prayer before the session began.

"Okay, Zeke, please give us the INTEL we have on this one." Jim said, sitting down with the rest of his team and the crew in the conference room on *Coral*. Out of the corner of his eye he saw that everyone on the *Pearl* had been standing for the prayer too. Somehow that made him feel better.

"This is a small army of Mercs, all from Nicaragua, most of them former guerilla fighters. When they're not doing a job, they spend most of their time carousing in local bars, being arrested, getting into brawls, and other nefarious activities. I found one correlation that raised some red flags. Twenty-seven prostitutes have disappeared from the town these Mercs usually visit in the past six months. Police down there think it is the work of not one, but three separate serial killers. Their three suspects, all members of this unit of mercenaries, always have an airtight alibi.

"In the town and surrounding area there are a slew of unsolved murders, all very violent, most of them pointing to the mercs, but the police don't have enough evidence to convict them. At least that's their story. Since the mercs outnumber the police department in that area I think they might just be taking the path of least resistance. These men are protected by powerful people as well.

"In the past three years this group has planned and carried out six abductions of American and European company representatives, receiving a ransom amounting to sixteen million dollars when you add them all together. Company reps are returned roughed up, but alive. Debriefs of the reps indicates that the group is ruthless and kills easily.

"Three European reps disappeared with no trace when the ransom demands were not met on time. That has spurred other companies to pay up the ransom when the demands are made.

"Several police officers have been assassinated over the past three years, probably contract killings ordered by drug cartels. The mercs are suspected in six of them because of the brutal nature of the deaths. An army, even a small one, with air support is a very serious matter. That alone is worthy of consideration.

"Those two Aérospatiale Super Frelon 321G choppers are a serious threat to anyone on land or in the water. One carries the Sylphe panoramic radar and dunking sonar while the other is armed with four homing torpedoes, along with the usual armaments. The men are armed to the teeth as well and will be highly motivated by the payoff to succeed. Anything they plan will be violent and deadly." Zeke sat back with a sigh. On the computer screens pictures of the mercenary organization flashed by in a slide presentation that took a few seconds.

"The Coast Guard is always boarding and searching us for weapons. Can't we let them handle this?" Dr. Rysdale asked, her pretty young face appearing in the small screen in the upper righthand corner of the laptops.

"If the crew of those boats see a Coast Guard cutter won't they launch the choppers and take it out?" Dr. Mirelle asked quickly.

"They could lose several people in a pitched battle at sea." Dr. Putnam said. "This is going to take a specially trained military group to handle, isn't it?" He added.

"If conventional enforcement agencies are used these men will be out of prison in a short period of time and just come after us again, won't they?" Dr. Flush added, wondering why none of the military unit had spoken yet. He wondered if they were still processing the information.

"They don't like the decision they have to make. That's why they're waiting." Alice said, putting a hand on her husband's arm. "They know the only effective response in this instance is a lethal one." Her calm voice had an effect.

"These are very bad men. They like the killing, and they will continue to kill as long as there are people willing to pay them to do it. The Lord reminds us that those who live by the sword will die by the sword, Jim. I don't think we have any other choice in this one." Abe said.

Jim looked at Abe as the muscle-bound cook spoke quietly. Abe rarely spoke at these meetings, but he'd gone to the heart of the issue, as the scientists had, and he was right. There was always that moment of hesitation when it came to deciding that certain people had to die. Everything he believed and knew to be true warned him of the danger to him if he made such decisions alone. Glad that he didn't have to make them alone he looked at his team.

"All right." He said with a sad sigh. "Let's put this before the jury. All in favor of a death sentence for these men respond by saying aye." He listened to the chorus of voices, male and female. In his own men he heard the reluctance in their voices, and it made him proud again to lead them.

"Those against respond by same." He said after a moment.

Silence was his answer. One by one the support team in their various countries nodded and signed off. The vote was unanimous. Sighing again Jim squared his shoulders. A decision by jury had been reached and it was now time to decide how to carry out the death sentence. His mind raced as he thought for a moment before speaking again.

"We're going to have to do a night insertion with the Rigid Raiders and take all four boats at the same time. I recommend we render the sleeping men unconscious and deal with any guards, and then send the boats to the bottom." He said.

"The choppers too?" Viper asked, one eyebrow raised.

"No evidence. No mayday calls, nothing to mark where they went down, and we need to sink them somewhere deep!" John Shepherd said emphatically. "The deeper the better. If anyone looks for them, which I doubt, I want them hard to find."

"What about the Middle America Trench? They'll be over that for part of their journey." Bob Neff offered. "Everybody dumps garbage there." He added.

"Smitty, can we get an accurate read on when they'll be over the Middle America Trench at night?" Jim asked.

"Give or take an hour from one hundred hours I can do that." Smitty replied.

"Ideas on sinking the boats?" Jim asked, looking around.

"Fill them with water." Andrea said quietly. "We can pump them full of water and let them sink to the bottom of the trench. Even if they are discovered there will be no evidence."

"We can bury the bodies at sea as well." Richard Nelson added after a moment of silence.

"No bodies on the boats, boats and choppers at the bottom of the trench, no evidence of damage to the hulls or attack! Diabolical!" Chief said. "Kareem will think they took the money and ran."

Over the next hour the men discussed how to divide the labor and take the boats with the minimum of risk. As the plan drew together Dr. Lowe shivered. *Those men will never know what hit them! They think they are the killers, but they are just thugs with guns. Our men will bring them to justice!*

It surprised her that she was thinking of the men as "ours." Truly, they were a team. Now that she knew all the men, and knew that they were good men, and that she was in a safe relationship with every single one, it was like being part of a large family. She smiled at that thought. Even on research ships she'd never felt this safe.

"They're talking about this mission like it's just another day on the job!" Lisle Mirelle whispered to Carol.

"It is." Heidi whispered from the other side. "They know this job better than any other job they do. Almost I pity the men who are coming to attack our vessels. Almost." She ended with an emphatic nod.

CHAPTER 30

Taking moving ships in the dark was a risky proposal at best. Rigid Raiders were faster than the boats, and quiet enough to creep up unnoticed. One advantage was that the boats were designed for stealth and to confuse maritime radar. Only if someone posted as a lookout saw them would they be in danger of discovery.

Jim sat in the bow of the Rigid Raider with 6-Team-1. Driver, Uncle Zeke, Sparks, FM, and Smitty were with him, shadows on the dark waters moving toward the lead patrol boat. From his vantage point he could see one pilot and gauged the speed to be close to eight knots, maybe a little more.

The Guatemalan's fast training boat was made by Watercraft Marine and powered by two Rolls Royce M800T diesels. Her hull speed was normally 14 knots but considering the condition of the boats, Jim guessed correctly that top speed at the moment was only eleven knots. Interestingly, the hull was designed for up to 45 knots but limited due to the type of engine fitted. The engines in the boat he was shadowing were belching black smoke indicating they had not been properly maintained and were struggling to keep the speed.

Soldiers that didn't maintain their equipment were often lazy and careless. He hoped this would be the case, making his task of taking down the crew of the lead *Archer* easier. So far, the pilot had not touched his radio to contact any of the other boats, which indicated that contact was made only if one boat fell behind. Again, it was an indication of carelessness.

"We'd be checking in every fifteen minutes, boss." FM whispered close to Jim's ear.

"Roger that. Rather nice of them to be careless. It makes our job easier. But don't underestimate them!" Jim added.

"Go mission!" Smitty said, looking at the position of their boats.

With night vision the men stepped from the Raider to the diving platform on the rear of the boat, which bowed under their weight, indicating that the boards had been allowed to rot. Jim tested the ladder carefully and crept over the stern, a shadow among the shadows. Even the pilot in the boat behind did not notice what was happening on the boat in front of him. Jim was proud of that fact as he and his men crept on board. No alarm was raised. He hoped and prayed his other teams would fare the same.

To his surprise the doors to the bridge were chained open and banging against the reinforced plastic outer shell of the boat. Using the constant noise and timing his steps he crept up behind the pilot, rose behind him, and quickly snapped his neck. The automatic pilot was on, so Jim left things as they were and joined his men in dispatching the rest of the crew. Once all the men were down the boats could be stopped and sunk in the proper place. He grimaced as he moved through the boat.

This particular boat was designed for a crew of 5, but six slept in the open on the bow, and four were stuffed into storage, and six more in the regular crew quarters. Once it was ascertained that the men inside were all asleep, FM slipped a canister of gas through the hatch and closed it fast. In seconds the men inside would be dead.

Up on the bow Jim, Jack, and Sparks moved silently, shooting each man in the heart with a silenced weapon. Death was instantaneous. When they finished their grizzly task, Jim waved to the men to follow him and they moved carefully back to the bridge.

"Report." Jim said into his communicator.

"6-Team-1 clear!" Zeke reported. "No injuries or wounds to the team. All packages canceled and ready for transport."

"6-Team-2 clear!" J.R. reported. "No injuries or wounds to the team."

"6-Team-3 clear!" Viper said. "We're fine."

"6-Team-4 clear!" Sean reported. "No injuries or wounds to the team."

"6-Team-5 clear!" Chief responded. "We own the shadows!"

"6-Team-6 clear!" Izzy said easily. "Good to go, Captain."

"Well done. Stop all boats and rig pumps." Jim replied with a sense of accomplishment. "Let's transfer the bodies to the *Stallion* and prepare them for burial at sea."

Over the next hour the men worked at a fast pace, transferring the bodies to the *Stallion* where they were wrapped and weighted for burial at sea. Pumps normally used to empty hulls now filled the hulls of the enemy boats, tug, and barge. One by one the boats slipped beneath the surface just as the last pump was transferred to a Rigid Raider. Last to go was the barge and it settled upright until the last possible moment before it rolled over and slipped beneath the surface with a surprising amount of noise.

Moments later the CH-53D settled on the water and the raiders were winched on board. Jim checked each man as he came up to take his seat, counting in his head until he'd reached the number thirty-five. That was John, making sure all his men were on board and safe. They bumped shoulders and grinned at each other. Knowing the dangers they had just faced, both felt an overwhelming sense of gratitude to see each other.

Ponderously the CH-53D lifted from the waters, shedding a shower of white in the darkness below as it gained altitude. When Pipi was sure they had enough altitude, she tipped the nose forward and increased speed until they were skimming a hundred feet above the water at a speed of 136 mph. Mark Drumheiser slipped into the co-pilot's seat and put on his headset.

"How did it go?" She asked immediately.

"Like clockwork." He replied. "Start ejecting the bodies." He said.

One by one the bodies of the enemy soldiers were rolled from the rear platform of the chopper until all forty were gone. Each body had been weighted to sink immediately and disappear beneath the surface. Two hours later, just before dawn, the CH-53D settled on the pad on the *Coral* as Finn and Loony rolled under to chain down the skids. Seconds later the engines were turned off while the teams trudged down the ramp and down to the weapons room.

Before breakfast they met in the conference room to debrief. Jim listened to the comments about the condition of the boats and the condition of many of the soldiers that were so drunk they had soiled their clothing. The boat he'd taken had been the same. Filth and garbage were everywhere under foot and the smell of alcohol almost overpowering to the senses.

"Yeah, boss! When I opened the hatch to the lead boat it smelled like a distillery in an outhouse in there. It was pretty rank." FM said.

"I think we may have added to the pollution of the ocean dumping those bodies." Bond quipped. "Q would have found a way to neutralize the pollutants." He added with a smug smile.

"You mean Q-tip, don't you?" D.C. laughed.

Bond shook his head sadly. "This from a man who thinks he's a car, and he can't even spell it correctly. Car has one 'r'."

"My mother was Italian. She rolled her 'r's'." D.C. responded quickly. He pronounced his last name with a rolled 'r' sound. "See?" He asked, looking around.

"If I may bring us back to the discussion at hand?" J.R. asked with a laugh.

"Our teams performed perfectly, and the carelessness of the soldiers only made our job easier. We won't always get easy ones like that but they're nice when they come along. Even then no one got careless or allowed his concentration to wander. Are we keeping an ear open for any communications from Kareem?" Jim asked.

"They were communicating by email." Zeke said. "Rojas, the commander of the mercs, emailed regular updates every morning. Kareem will know approximately where they were when they disappeared. Our advantage is that I was able to make sure there were no satellite images available for that part of the world. I'm going to be monitoring how Kareem responds to the silence this morning."

"Keep us posted on that and on Muhammad's plans." Jim nodded. "Thanks."

"Our satellite feeds were right on for the positioning of the raid." Smitty said with a pleased smile.

"How deep was the water where the boats sank?" J.R. asked.

"18,660 feet where they went down, boss." Zeke replied. "Were you planning on salvaging them? We could put them on film as a 'How not to' instructional video."

"No. I think we'll just let them sit down there and rust. No one will notice the difference." Jim replied sarcastically.

By the time breakfast was open on both ships the crews were back in place and enjoying a festive meal. Jim watched the science team move through the room hugging and patting shoulders, glad to have the men back safely. Cecilia smiled at him and he hugged her close, knowing she'd been watching him observe the interaction.

"We have a great family." He said simply, kissing her passionately on the lips.

"Indeed we do!" She said somewhat breathlessly.

Later that morning Zeke called Jim to the CIC. He left the engine room where he'd been talking to Goody and Loony about the power plant and walked quickly up the steps of the various decks to the CIC, sketching waves as various crewmembers said hello.

"It seems that our friend Kareem has access to some satellite technology he shouldn't have." Zeke said as Jim came in, bent and kissed Cecilia, and stood to look at the computer screens.

"He's looking for Rojas." Jim said, looking at the photos that Zeke was putting up on the screens.

"Here are the last four emails he sent. It seems that Kareem bought the idea that Rojas took the money and ran." Jim read through the emails, promising horrible death to Rojas if he did not fulfill the contract. What worried him most was the satellite photos Kareem was able to access. Normally access to such satellites was restricted to military and law-enforcement agencies.

"Zeke, please make sure Duck gets this information. How in the world did this guy ever get access to our military satellites? And who was stupid or careless enough to allow that access. Somebody made money on this and can't be trusted! We don't want the wrong people to have access to our satellites." Jim said emphatically. "What do you recommend?"

"I'll let Duck know I can set up an algorithm, firewall, and access code that can be used on all the satellites in question, locking Kareem out, and tracing any users instantly." Zeke said, his fingers flying over the keyboard.

"Then we'll be exposed." Cecilia said.

"Bright eyes! Please! If I write the programs, we will have unfettered and unmonitored access to the system! Plus, I can set it up so that system can access any other satellites in the sky, again keeping everyone in the dark. I've been waiting for the chance to do this for four years!" Zeke grinned at her.

"Are you really that good?" She asked seriously.

"I'm really that good." Zeke said softly.

"That's a go mission, Zeke." Jim said softly.

"Roger that, Shep." Zeke replied. "I'm going to need News and SOS on this one. Cecilia, you too." Zeke added. "Four keyboards and four Crays will do the job."

"You're going to have me hack the Scotland Yard Cray, aren't you?" Cecilia asked with a sigh.

"Absolutely. I'll take one of the Pentagon Crays, News will go for the FBI, and SOS will use the Cray at USC. I'll orchestrate and we'll enter the data at the same time using enough power to overwhelm the entire system and give us our secret entrance. The only Cray anyone will be aware of is at the Pentagon. They'll miss our backdoor installation and think they've got a system that is currently impenetrable." Zeke kept his eyes busy.

"Kareem got a shot of the boats leaving and at the half-way point. There are no pictures during the hours we took them down. He's searching every grid looking for them, trying to figure out where they went." Zeke said, following Kareem's progress. "Won't he be disappointed?" He grinned wickedly at them.

"We have to lock him out of the system before we go in to take him down." Jim said, his mind moving forward. "I wonder if he saw our CH-53D leave the ship. We'll need a cover story for that."

Without looking away from his screens Zeke handed a sheet of paper to Jim. It was a flight plan to an Atoll to collect a core sample for analysis of volcanic activity related to the Loihi site.

"I called in a favor and a sample is already on board. Commander Cummings arranged the delivery by submarine under the cover of darkness. It's in the lab." Zeke added.

Jim chuckled. "Tell me, why am I here again?" He asked, throwing up his hands.

"You look really handsome in your uniform, honey." Cecilia said with a mischievous twinkle in her eyes.

"Gee, thanks!" He said sarcastically, and then he kissed her.

"Good work, you two." He said as he left the CIC.

Kareem, not willing to leave any stone unturned, did indeed arrange to have that verified. Callahan, the reporter from *Omni* returned to do a story on how the new nodes were helping with information on the volcanic activity around the islands. He brought with him Dr. Fred Dunnebier, the director of the HUGO project. Nothing would get past Dr. Dunnebier, and Callahan knew that.

Jim thought it was a good thing that Dr. Dunnebier didn't know the sample in *Pearl's* lab was from his own lab back on campus. Dunnebier was very excited to meet Dr. Dinsmore and he was more than willing to accept that this sample was recent. He was even able to identify the Atoll from which it came.

Callahan, who didn't know he was being used, tried to restart his conversation with Dr. Dinsmore about intelligent design, but he was unable to steer the talk away from the volcanic studies and the information that the new nodes were providing the university. Discussions on the Murray Fracture Zone and plans to put nodes down along the ridge followed. Following the talk Callahan wrote notes furiously.

Later the editor who suggested the story called to see what Callahan discovered. After talking to the young reporter, he called the number he'd been given and reported that the CH-53D Sea Stallion that left the *Coral* did indeed take a sample from the Atoll in question and that it had been confirmed and verified.

Kareem hung up the phone and cursed in impotent fury. His plans of vengeance were not to be. Rojas and his men had simply disappeared. In a few hours when the satellites were not positioned correctly, they had faded away. Now he knew that it had not been the CH-53D that attacked his forces. He hadn't thought they'd know his plans, but he was cautious. There would be another way to deal with them.

CHAPTER 31

By morning Zeke had permission from the Pentagon to protect the Satellites that had been compromised. Late that afternoon he sat with Cecilia, Ned, and Stephanie explaining what they had to do.

"Cecilia and Stephanie, you're going to be operating the Cray XE6 model with scalable interconnect capabilities. I've printed out the exact data entry you need to make on my mark. We will have to go as quickly as possible, and we all type at about the same speed. Just make sure you don't make any errors!" He grinned at them.

Ned and I will be operating an XE6m supercomputer. Mine at the Pentagon is the only one that will appear in use. The other three will be setting up that amazing firewall and back door I talked about. Since we will be doing this simultaneously with Crays no one will be able trace what we are doing. This, my friends, is streaming information on steroids! On my mark! Mark!"

Four pairs of hands began to enter the data simultaneously. At the Pentagon intelligence computer gurus watched Zeke's work, following only what he did with that Cray, nodding as they followed although they did not understand the complex algorithm but did understand commands for the firewall and security code. They were waiting for Zeke to turn control over to them to enter the codes, so that only level 6 security clearance individuals could access the satellites from this point on. They believed that once control was theirs, no unauthorized persons could access the system without detection.

Once they understood the concept of the security programs now being entered, they saw both the simplicity and the complexity of the programs Zeke wrote. More and more, computer security was an art as well as a science. Most of the security personnel understood they were entering a new era in security. Zeke knew that some of them would question this act, wonder if he could enter through a "back door", but he also knew that in their arrogance they would believe they could catch him at it. So, he made his plans accordingly.

As planned the military experts soon were given control and entered the codes, at the same time that Zeke entered a set of codes of his own, giving him unfettered and untraceable access to the system. He designed the program so that the computer system did not register his keystrokes or usage and effectively hid any activity with the satellites from the systems of the military.

Kareem's security company director Manju Agnimukha called him later that evening to inform him that access to the satellites was no longer available. Attempts to hack the system had triggered an alarm and federal forces had descended upon the building. The director confessed to setting up one of the newer hackers with promises of protection and a huge payoff for going along with the plot.

Kareem listened to the report with mounting frustration. Everything he had worked to build over the past fifty years was crumbling around him. His most daring coup had been infiltrating the satellite system. Years of work were suddenly useless after only a few days of access. He hadn't even had a chance to offer this new access to his friends in the Muslim world.

"There is no way we can get back in?" Kareem asked quietly.

"My experts claim that something new is being used, a program even more advanced and dangerous than the last upgrade to security. The government can now follow any attempted access almost instantly! It took them only four minutes to get to our office! We can't even study the new program without being detected." The director of the technology department of Kareem's network paused.

"Can we discover who wrote this new program?" Kareem asked.

"Our source at the Pentagon says that everything was done from the Cray supercomputer on location, and that the access codes were written by the technicians working in that section. Access to all of the U.S. military satellites is now limited to level 6 security clearance." Manju responded evenly.

"We still have access to the Russian and Chinese satellite systems, as well as the academic systems around the world. Response time is slower, and only a few areas are not available. It limits us somewhat, but we can make do with that." Manju hoped that they could.

"Very well." Kareem said after a pause. "Keep looking for those boats! I want Rojas and his men punished publicly!" He cut the connection, unaware that Zeke had recorded every word.

On his desk Kareem looked at the two bullets, one sent from Jim Shepherd, the other he found in his safe, as Jim had said. That was just not possible! Cursing again he stood up and paced his office. At least here he was safe. No one could reach him here.

From the air vent above him the dart flew through the air, piercing his neck. Almost as soon as he registered the prick of the dart the poison coursed through his brain. Later that day his secretary would find him, his face a rictus of pain and agony, blood having poured from his eyes, ears, nose and mouth. No evidence of the dart would be found, and no one would suspect the use of the air duct for some time.

Xun Hao slithered out of the air duct and looked at the coveralls she was wearing. They'd been black when she entered the ductwork, now they were sticky and gray. Carefully she removed the clothing, her tiny frame wearing dark pants and shirt, dark shoes, her hair covered in a sort of black Fez hat. She removed the hat, let her long luxurious hair hang down, and put on her sunglasses. The coveralls went into a shopping bag. Careful to avoid the camera points she made her way from the maintenance catwalks to the stairwell. There she waited until a group of women exited the door and headed down the steps two floors to the restaurant. Dropping behind them she joined them, just one of the crowd. Xun was always careful to avoid detection because she was literally a ghost, an unknown assassin.

With her brother Yao Xiake Hao, both had been assigned the task of assassinating Kareem and Muhammad. Yet the minds behind these assassins were unaware that their efforts to keep themselves hidden failed. Not only did the assassinations tip off the men of *Bring It Up* and other intelligence agencies, but the assets seized by various government agencies inevitably led to them.

It was Zeke who first saw the connection. With Cecilia, MI6, and Scotland Yard hard at work it didn't take long to link the money to the Zhanzhu triad. Although they had covered their tracks well, sifting through the companies finally revealed them.

"Three brothers, boss." Zeke said, sitting down at the conference table and looking around at the men gathered for the meeting. Cheng De, Hu Meng, and Wu Yi Zhanzhu. Cheng is ninety-two. Hu is ninety, and Wu Yi is eighty-seven. They've been plotting this for sixty years!" He sat back, letting the computer show the pictures and the history of the three Chinese men.

"We are sure it was their money behind Kareem, Muhammad, and Bahdijn?" Wade asked.

"Most of it. Kareem and company had a lot of money to begin with, but they were definitely funded by the Zhanzhu Triad." Zeke replied.

"Why?" Jim asked in the quiet that followed.

"Yeah, mate. Good question." Leroy Brown said emphatically.

"World domination." Pen said quietly when no one ventured an answer. "If they could get the Jihadists to create enough chaos in the world they could step in and bring peace." Pen had been reading Zeke's in-depth report on the Zhanzhu brothers. "They might very well have pulled that off, and China would become the world power. It appears that they pull most of the strings in Chinese government!"

"Why now?" Jim asked, reading the report himself, his eyes busy with the words on the page and his thoughts centered on understanding what he had in his hands.

"Jihad was convenient." Mary Ann said. "They finally had a

group crazy enough to kill millions, a group without a conscience, a religion of death, and they took advantage of that and used them."

"And they had the means to pull off a master plan, and it was a master plan!" Chief said, looking around the table. "Even the backup plan was a master stroke."

"Do we have any assets in place to find out if we're even close?" John asked, looking at Jim and Cecilia.

"Duck has a few assets in place. He'll let us know what he finds out." Jim said. "But I think Chief and Mary Ann are correct. They had a group crazy enough to kill millions, and the means to pull off a master plan of world chaos. That they were willing to use such a group says a great deal about them, and bears scrutiny. How amoral does one have to be to sanction the killing of millions of innocent people?"

For several minutes no one spoke. That was a question that was hard to answer, and Jim admitted that he didn't have a clue how someone could become so depraved.

"At least they saved us the trouble of taking out Kareem and Muhammad." Viper finally spoke. "Whoever did that job was good." He added.

"What gets me is that this triad has never come under the radar before, never done anything dodgy." Phil Eustus spoke up.

"It's called a triad because there are three of them, not because they're like other triads that are criminal organizations." Bill Kline said. "Up until now they've been involved in quasi legitimate business."

"Why quasi legitimate?" Jim asked, looking at Bill, who rarely spoke during the meetings.

"Nobody gets that rich and knows people like Muhammad and Kareem without bending a rule or two." Sparks replied after a moment of thought. Jim thought about that, and he noticed many of his men nodding in agreement. John spoke and he gave him his full attention.

"Good point. As we dig further, we may find some skeletons along the way they don't want found." John replied. "We want to be very careful! Those two assassins left no clues! That means we don't know who we're dealing with."

"They left two." Ox said quickly. "Those men died a horrible and painful death through the administration of a rare poison mix. Each had a pinprick on his neck, suggesting a dart of some kind."

"How did they get the dart back, leave no evidence of entry into the room from any point of egress, or evidence of leaving the room from any point of exit?" Pen asked, curious.

"My guess is a blow gun, with a very small dart attached to the end of the gun with a bit of fish line. Once the poison has done its work, they can pull the dart out and slip away. I've read about an assassin that did that twice, using the air ducts." Mark Drumheiser said.

"Xun Hao?" Jim asked, raising an eyebrow.

"Or her brother Yao Xiake." Mark nodded. "Word is they're both very small, but masters of some scary martial arts."

"No one checked the air vents. The vents were in place and the screws had not been removed." Zeke said, looking at the report quickly on his computer. "Someone should have checked that, Shep." He looked at Jim for a moment. "We would have."

"Call Duck. See if NCIS can get in to look at the air vents." Jim said. Zeke picked up his phone and made the call.

"This triad is going to be somewhat upset with us, if they discover it was our work that uncovered their nefarious plot!" Lord Lee said with a grin. "We should watch our backs."

"Perhaps we should rattle their cage a little, see if they get careless." Banks suggested lightly.

"Fair dinkum, mate!" Chance said, making a fist in the air.

"Just realizing that people know them now will be enough, I think." Jim said with a smile. "So far we've been able to keep our company out of the mix. People investigate us, find we're bona fide, and pass over us because we are legitimate. We're still ghosts. You are correct, however! We need to watch our backs. These three men and those who work for them do not value human life, and do not believe in the concept of 'innocent' people. Remember that the author of every false religion in this world is Satan, and his agenda is to destroy all that God has created!"

"We are always very careful not to leave evidence and to stay under the radar." Cecilia said quietly after a pause. "I think we're safe from the triad."

"So that leaves us free to go after Z!" Dr. Gregg said with a huge smile.

"Here we go again!" Mary Ann quipped.

"Yeah! Right to the back of Bourke!" Phil Eustus muttered. "I hate the jungle!"

Jim grinned at PU, nodding. Evidence of the City of Z had been discovered in the treasures taken from the depths, and Dr. Gregg was ecstatic about that particular find. To those who studied ancient cities, and especially those that were lost to us, evidence like this was a major breakthrough. The city existed and had communicated often with Cusco. His musings were interrupted as Pen spoke.

"Okay, Dr. Museum! Let's talk about the lost city of Z!" Pen said with a huge smile. Jim and J.R. both smiled at her taking command, noting that she had become quite confident in her place now on the team. They both appreciated her expertise and Jim grinned and winked at J.R. who knew he was thinking about the other things J.R. enjoyed about his wife. He almost laughed.

"I think that Colonel Fawcett and Richard Burton were both quite convinced that the lost cities did indeed exist, and they both had clues to help them find them. Yet they both overlooked something. First, let's ask the question, how does a city become lost?" Dr. Gregg began.

"It's abandoned because of pestilence, war, or other catastrophic event to the people living there." Hobbs said, his pen tapping his chin as he spoke.

"That's one way." Dr. Gregg nodded. "Cities like that are overtaken by the jungle and consequently are very difficult to find if one doesn't know what to look for. Roads, like the one mentioned in Manuscript 512 would lead to such cities. But there's another way a city is lost!"

"Natural disaster." Loony said immediately.

"Quite correct, lad!" Dr. Gregg said. "What did they say about the city in Manuscript 512? They talked about an upheaval as if an earthquake struck the city. Yet there is one more way to make a city disappear! Remember the buried city we uncovered? It was built in a cave system!

"Many of the Inca's were miners of great skill. If they pressed westward from Peru into the Mato Grosso region, they would have encountered the fierce tribes. I believe, because of the evidence we've found from *El Dorado Española*, that there is indeed a city in the Mato Grosso, but that it is buried beneath the earth, and may not be accessible because of earthquakes! It may literally be buried beneath the surface of the earth, waiting for someone to discover it and uncover its mysteries!"

"Do you have an idea of where the city might be?" Jim asked his stepfather, with a smile.

"Actually, yes!" Alistair said, his eyes bright with anticipation. "I've been studying satellite photos of the River Araguaia, from its source. There are certainly a series of waterfalls that may indicate what the explorers who wrote Manuscript 512 saw. I also believe that the city they discovered had been abandoned as the Inca people moved beneath the ground! It may be that simple!"

"If we had a location, we could airlift everyone in, set up camp, and explore in a grid pattern search for heavy deposits of gold and silver, or perhaps even diamonds." John said with excitement in his voice. "Remember how we traced the caves in Italy? We could do something similar here, perhaps even uncovering a cave system that would lead to the city!"

"Has that region been explored and mapped?" Wade asked.

"Actually, it has, though most of it is inaccessible and none of the settlers that poured in during the last forty years have claimed any of that territory." Cecilia said, studying her satellite images of the area. "Here's an interesting fact!" She looked around before sharing it. "Most of them live along the River of Death."

"Rio das Mortes!" CG said with a startled voice! "Why is it called that?"

"My guess is that when the water rises any attempts to try to navigate that river end up in death!" Bob Neff said.

"So, we're not talking about Piranha or Anacondas, then?" CG said.

"Actually, there are probably some of both in those rivers." Dr. Gregg said, his eyes crinkling with a smile.

"Oh good!" Neff said, nodding sagely. "We'll take Abe and Sturdy along to frighten them!" Abe grinned and flexed his huge torso, making a scary face.

"Doctor!" Rachael Hague said, putting a hand over her mouth. "This man seems to be swelling!"

"Don't worry about that, miss!" PU said with a wicked grin. "They've got mosquitoes down there that can suck a man dry, leaving just an empty skin and some bones! Of course, it will take three or four of them for this big guy. One will do for you!"

Rachael stuck her tongue out at PU.

"Let's get back to planning how we're going to find this lost city." Jim said with a chuckle. His own thoughts were filled with excitement at another such coup for the company. The historical benefit of such a find alone would add to their reputation.

CHAPTER 32

"**V**ents!" Sparkles said suddenly. Everyone jumped but Alistair looked up with excitement.

"Yes! If they built a city beneath the ground, they would need vents. There are no mines in that area, so any vents we located would be vents to their mines, or the city itself! Well done, Miss Van Haaten!" Dr. Gregg almost never used the nicknames of his staff.

"Finding those vents would be a snap. We have access to the satellites that can measure the difference in air temperature on the ground. A plume of colder air coming up out of the vent would show us an exact location!" Zeke said, his own eyes aglow with excitement.

"Alright." Jim said when the conversation died down again. "Zeke and Cecilia will extrapolate the location of any vents and we'll decide where to put our base camp. We now have two important projects going. We need to know everything we can find on our Chinese triad and their pet assassins, and we need to find those vents.

"I want Delta to work on the camp site and materials we'll need for any conceivable situation in locating our lost city." Dorf nodded and almost immediately his three companions put their heads together and began tapping the computer keys. Jim was certain that when they were finished all the bases would be covered.

"Zulu, you have weapons and defense." John nodded at Jim

and Wade, C.G. and Vince put their heads close to his. John began scrolling down through the catalogue of weapons and equipment for battle they had available on both ships.

"Firefox, you have energy. Find out what we'll need, and what we might need in the way of lights, flashlights, lanterns, etc. Get us a diesel generator for base camp and some small generators for inside the caves." Bill Dodge waved his acquiescence and his team began to mumble among themselves.

"Omega 1 has explosives. Knife has biological hazards and defense against insects, snakes, frogs, poisonous plants, etc." Sean nodded and his men put their heads together. "I want everyone prepared for any biological danger!"

"Raider, your team has SAT NAV and maps. Get us the best and most recent photos and maps, rainy season, dry season, and everything in between. Study the rivers movement for the past ten years and how that effects the local ecology and fauna." Hobbs saluted and his men gathered closer.

"Sniper, you have possible enemies and organizations that may try to stop, hinder, or get in ahead of us. You also have the local government and the contracts issues we'll face. "Let's be sure we cover all our bases before we go feet dry, men. We don't want any legal surprises!" Norm Geissler waved a hand, propped his feet up on the table, and looked at his team.

"You guys get all that?" He asked laconically. "Get on it then."

"I'm doin' my nails PO1!" Lee Ainsworth said plaintively.

"I got a sore toe, boss." Lloyd Brookstone offered.

"How do you spell organizations?" Duncan asked, looking up as if trying to spell out the word.

"You're a sorry lot!" Norm said, putting his feet down as everyone laughed. Jim appreciated the humor. When the laughter died down, he went back to assigning details.

"Bulldog, you have local tribes and military. Give us a full report of how they are armed and how they do battle. Any military in that part of the world cannot be trusted." Jim said.

"Is this because of my Native American heritage?" Chief asked.

"Cause them Injuns in that part of the world ain't like us American Indians." His face was set in a serious mask as he asked the question and Jim grinned at him.

"I don't think it's politically correct to call them Injuns, Chief." Gene Hardesty spoke up.

"Is it politically correct to call him Chief?" Mel Pierson asked with a grin.

"You had to stick me with a bunch of paleface wannabes!" Chief said, throwing his hands up. "Paleface, heap big chief speak now. We have wampum in the wigwam!"

"Wampum sounds like delicious fun!" Mary Ann quipped. That brought the house down but Chief just shook his head.

"Wampum means I wampum on these idiot's heads until they get the job done!" He said.

"We could watch, and then comfort them when he's done wampum 'em!" Barbara said to Mary Ann.

Once again Jim waited for the laughter to die down. When it finally did, and all the bantering came to a stop he cleared his throat.

"Nightfall, you have transportation." He said.

Fagan began to rub his hands and put on his most sinister expression. "Let's see! We'll need to lift a few six-wheel trucks from the local military, steal enough diesel fuel for the generator and trucks, and I'll take charge of any gems or jewels we may find." He sang a verse of the tune *You can go, but be back soon,* from the movie. Jim decided that Fagan was actually quite good at playing the part and joined in the fun in an unusual display of humor.

"I'm reviewing the situation!" Jim sang off key, but a recognizable likeness of the movie character from Oliver.

Cecilia laughed at her husband as the whole room erupted in laughter. Fagan was continuing his sinister routine. It was upon that lighthearted mood that the teams went to work. For Cecilia, it was a scene she loved about this crew, and her husband's role in it was a surprise. He rarely joined in the actual acting. She wiped tears of mirth from her eyes and settled in to listen to the talk about explosives. Until Jim was finished with Zeke, she wouldn't be able to work on the satellite photos anyway.

Six days passed at anchor and the final work for the grant at Hawaii was completed, while other teams brought up all of the relics from the ships in the cave. When the men weren't on actual work duty, they were doing research for their assignments. Only in the evening did all work stop and the crews gather for some rest and relaxation. On both ships the R&R routine was something every member of the crew enjoyed.

Abe, Sturdy, and TRT taught the Bible study from the *Coral* and the crew on the *Pearl* watched it on the big screen in the observation room. Jim noticed that everyone had a Bible, a notebook, pen or pencil, and was busy jotting down notes. His own pen slid over his paper as he carefully printed the words he wanted to remember from the study. He noticed that his Bible, a Thompson Chain Reference in the New American Standard translation was beginning to show signs of wear and tear. That made him feel good.

After the study they went down to eat, and after dinner every crewmember joined in the evening games that were scheduled. Some crossed between the ships, some stayed where they were, and everyone had a lighthearted time of social interaction and fun.

The tournaments were drawing to a close in Texas Hold 'em and Monopoly. Jim's Rook tournament was also drawing to a close, but the rest of the games were going full steam. Cecilia was a great partner for Rook and he and his lovely wife took the tournament, winning the last game by shooting the moon. Hobbs and Banks sat there looking at the two, Hobbs blinking like an owl, and Banks stroking his chin. Banks smiled at the two.

"We let you win." Banks said. "Bond only loses on purpose, you know!" He added.

"He let you win!" Hobbs corrected. "He was the one who dealt the hand!"

"Quite right." Banks said sagely.

"Well thanks." Jim said, sliding his arm around his wife. "Thanks for taking it easy on us! I'm going to take this gorgeous creature up to the observation deck to watch the submarine races."

"You're gonna get lipstick all over your collar, boss! Dames do it every time!" Hobbs said knowingly.

"Lip wrestling often leads to that." Jim said easily, standing up and lifting Cecilia with him.

"Who wins?" Banks asked with a too innocent look on his face.

"It's usually a draw." Cecilia answered with a light laugh.

They went up on the deck and stood in a corner against the railing. Jim did indeed spend some time kissing her passionately, but soon they simply turned and looked out over the ocean.

"It's all very beautiful in this part of the world, isn't it?" Cecilia asked.

"At least until one of those babies erupts." Jim said, nodding his chin at one of the active volcanoes from which a red glow could be seen. A few nights past lava ran down the sides and into the ocean, orange, red, yellow colors blending, glowing in the darkness like fireworks in slow motion. It had been an amazing sight to watch.

"Another tropical island being born." Cecilia said softly. "I think it's amazing that such beauty comes out of such ugliness."

"Where we're going is a beautiful place too, but it is filled with ugliness as well." Jim said pensively. "I worry about taking everybody."

"I know, dear. But they are up to it, you'll see. I think every one of them will contribute something important to our trip." She added.

"Yes. Yet I remember the last city we explored hidden beneath the earth. Talk about deadly darkness!" Jim said. Cecilia could hear the tenseness in his voice as he thought of the dangers. She put a hand on his arm and felt him relax under her touch. That always amazed her.

"Those injured did not heed your warnings or follow directions." She said. I think there will be enough stories about that to keep everyone in line." She said softly. "We are in God's hands, my dear. You are not responsible for anyone's life. Please remember that. He decides matters of life and death."

"That sense of responsibility comes with the command." He said, looking down at her. Leaning in he kissed her. "I'll do my best to put it all in His capable hands."

Later that night, in their berth, they knelt together by their bed and prayed about the upcoming adventure. Jim had to admit that praying about things like that always made them seem easier to bear. He thanked God for being his very best friend, and asked God to remind him often that nothing ever catches Him by surprise. Cecilia smiled as he prayed; so simple, yet so profound a faith!

Cheng De Zhanzhu, half a world away, listened to the report of his two best agents. Though small in stature, like himself, they stood tall in a different world, the world of martial arts. Xun Hao was finishing her report on *Bring It Up.*

"As far as we can tell it is a bona fide deep-sea search and rescue, and now ocean research team. The scientists on board that research vessel are the top in their fields. A grant awarded the company was legitimate and they accomplished the work. At the same time, they discovered three lost ships. It is believed that they will go after the Lost City of Z." She bowed and handed the scroll to her employer.

"Do you believe they will find the city?" He asked as he took the scroll. His voice was as dry as his personality, but his eyes still shown with amazing vitality.

"I do not believe the city exists. My brother does not agree. If, however, it does exist, there are few companies more capable than *Bring It Up.* If it exists, they will probably find it." She replied.

"Very well. Monitor their progress, and if it appears they have found the city see if we can steal the treasures without an international incident, and without loss of life." Cheng said. "If it happens that we make an attempt, my protégé Nie Ke Jing will assist you. From this point on you will copy him on everything you do for me. I thank you both for your excellent service." As he turned to walk away Nie Ke Jing silently handed them a leather pouch filled with gold. Both assassins bowed to him, which was proper, and he dismissed them.

Inwardly he was thrilled to meet the famous assassins. Outwardly he schooled his features and kept his thoughts hidden. It was his ability to hide his thoughts that brought him to the attention of the infamous Cheng De Zhanzhu. Now he was second in command to the great master. Thinking of his responsibilities he moved away to get to work. Cheng insisted on discipline at all times.

Zeke got a memo on that meeting less than half an hour after it happened. The Haos took their gold and left the building. No one took note of the window washer that photographed the entire meeting. MI6 now had a new name to add to the list. Cecilia emailed the information to her aunt at Scotland Yard and Zeke sent it all to Admiral Ashley at NCIS.

"We'll need to know if the Haos fly to South America and if they are in country." Jim said when he read the report. "I don't want to lose anyone to either of those two, so let's keep our eyes sharp. Since we have the facial recognition programs at most of the airports, that should be possible."

"At present they're on assignment in Beijing cleaning up something for the Zhanzhu family." Cecilia said, putting her hand over his. He'd rested his hand on her shoulder when he came to hear the report. "I think they're going to let local assets handle everything. Zeke is watching for transfers of large amounts of cash."

What assets might they have in that region of the world?" Jim asked. Zeke looked up from his smart board.

"DeGaul has a troop of mercenaries he uses to help the government of Bolivia. My guess would be him. He's closest and considered the best."

"What's your assessment of DeGaul and his troop?" Jim asked quickly, knowing that Zeke would already have information.

"They're actually a step above the troops that Marta Hess used." Zeke said, punching keys and then using a pen laser pointer to draw Jim's attention to the video playing. "This was taken by a policeman doing some under cover work. It shows them at training."

Jim watched the thirty-minute video with interest, taking pains to note how the men moved, how well they shot, what weapons they used, and what style they were being taught in combat. When the video ended, he nodded at Zeke, his eyes still on the photograph of DeGaul.

"Some of them are masters of Brazilian Jujitsu." He said, looking down at Zeke for a moment. Zeke watched Jim's stormy green eyes as he pondered what he'd seen. "The rest are adequate. DeGaul is obviously proud of his men. How old is he?"

"Forty-seven." Zeke said, looking at a screen even as he spoke. "His men are afraid of him."

Jim nodded. "I caught that." He said softly. "The way they watched him, and their body language said volumes about that fear. We didn't see any reasons for it in the video, but it's there. Keep a sharp eye." With a sigh he turned back to Cecilia, leaned down and kissed her rather passionately. She blushed prettily as he walked away.

"That was nice!" She sighed, laughing at Zeke.

"A certain Captain distracted my assistant in CIC, and I regret to inform everyone that Ensign Shepherd will be useless for the remainder of the day." Zeke said into his headset. Cecilia laughed.

"Seaman Kline! Leave my wife alone!" Jim replied sternly.

"Uh, skipper, I'm an Ensign too." Zeke corrected him.

"Not if you pick on my wife!" Jim shot back. "Babs! Go kiss Uncle Zeke so he stops brooding and gets back to work!"

"Yes sir!" Barbara said into her headset with real laughter in her voice.

Cecilia laughed as Zeke sprang up from his chair and began to comb his hair, his boyish face alight with devilish plans. As soon as Barbara and her cohorts came into the CIC, he grabbed her and bent her backwards, imitating the cartoon character Pepé la Pew.

"Oh, my darling! How long I have waited to hold you in my arms, to press my lips to yours!" Using a phony French accent, he sounded quite funny, and Cecilia knew that cameras were showing this entire scene on both ships. Zeke reached into his pocket and pulled out a breath freshener and purposely aimed it so that it missed his mouth completely. In the process he dropped Barbara on the deck amidst the laughter. Indeed, it was a comical moment filled with mirth and riotous laughter.

Barbara did not miss her chance. She scissored his legs, bringing him to the floor and was on him before he could fully recover, also imitating the cartoon skunk. She kissed his forehead, cheeks, neck and eyes over and over, covering his face with lipstick marks while telling him what a beautiful little pussycat he was. Zeke pretended to be helpless, screaming and waiving his arms from the floor.

When Barbara moved to get up, he pulled her down and kissed her passionately on the lips.

"You missed my lips!" He said. "I think you should see the doc about glasses!"

They sat on the floor laughing with everyone else. Jim smiled as he made his way to his office. When Zeke decided to ham it up it was always a showstopper! No one was disappointed.

"Captain James Shepherd, this is J.R." John's voice came over the COM link. "Your crew lacks discipline! Shameful!" He said in a haughty British accent. "Most insidiously heinous!" He added.

"Honey, could you hand me my bra!" Pippi's voice came over the COM link.

"Discipline!" John said haughtily again, not missing a beat. "Here darling." He added.

Laughter followed.

CHAPTER 33

Both ships dropped anchor just off the coast from Lima, Peru. They were far enough offshore that no one could see the ships without a powerful telescope. As arranged, Calvin Beardsley arrived with twelve of his crew to do some work on the two ships while they remained at anchor. He climbed aboard the *Coral* and saluted John.

"Beardsley and his forty thieves, reporting for duty, sir!" He said.

"Uh, Calvin, you only have twelve men." Wade pointed out.

"Thirteen thieves is bad luck! Besides, forty thieves are better than thirteen!" Beardsley said in his gravely voice. "Now get your crew off this tub so I can fix it!"

"Aren't pirates supposed to steal the ship?" Penelope asked facetiously.

"Not until ye bring back the treasure from the lost city!" Beardsley answered grinning at her. "Do we look daft to ye? Don't answer that!" He added.

"Good enough. We'll be gone for at least a month." John said with a chuckle. "See you then."

John was last to hop on board the CH53 and as he closed the hatch Dorf pulled back on the cyclic, lifting the machine into the air. He watched the pilot maneuver the controls with easy movements and took his seat glad that Dorf was his pilot.

The helicopter is maneuvered by the cyclic in pitch and roll, by the rudders in yaw and by the collective vertically. The cyclic and collective are connected to the main rotor primary tandem servos by mechanical linkage. To smooth out pilot's roll it inputs a viscous damper that is incorporated in the roll linkage. The damper permits limited continued flight with reduced damping if the damper fails. The FAS actuator also acts as a damper. The rudders are connected to the tail rotor tandem servo also by a mechanical linkage. To prevent overstressing of the helicopter from too rapid movement of the rudder pedals a damper is incorporated in the AFCS yaw servo that functions with AFCS systems on or off. It really was an amazing craft.

John's group was the last to leave the ships and join the base camp near the head of the Araguaia River. Because of the nature of the exploration thousands of dollars had been handed out to local dignitaries to purchase permission to search. With the contract signed by the governor of Mato Grosso and President of Brazil *Bring It Up* now had exclusive rights to the area of exploration for a period of twelve months. A contingency plan was in place in case more time was needed, but they were confident a year would cover their needs.

National Geographic was offered the rights to the films of the adventure, provided they did not edit any of the commentary by Dr. Gregg or Dr. Putnam. Although they did not like that requisite, and put their legal team to fight against it, Ken Worthington refused to budge on that issue and in the end, they grudgingly signed the contract. It didn't hurt that the film crew, professionals from Austin, Texas led by a former SEAL team member refused to film if the contract wasn't approved. Don Patterson made a name for himself filming the most dangerous explorations of the past decade and his crew was known throughout the world as the best of the best. National Geographic bowed to necessity, aware that they indeed would have a first-class production to air when the time was right.

Don's team was streamlined. He did the filming. His boyhood friend and fellow SEAL team member Tom was his "mule", the person who carried all the heavy equipment. A full-blooded Seminole Tom stood six-foot four-inches tall in his bare feet and weighed an impressive two hundred and forty-five pounds. Don and Tom were perhaps twelve years older than Jim and John, and both showed a little gray around the temple, and Tom had a gray spot in the middle of the top of his head.

Both were powerful men and neither carried any extra weight physically. None could question that this was the best pair of photographers in the business. When Jim simply signed the check to pay their expenses both men had blinked once and smiled. Jim guessed that one blink was about all the surprise either would ever show.

For Dr. Gregg, choosing the location of base camp had been an easy decision. There was only a small portion of Mato Grosso that had, as yet, been unexplored and untouched. Two small tributaries of the River Mortes began just twenty-five miles west of a section of the Araguaia River just a hundred miles from where it began. It was rugged high country that would be difficult to traverse. Satellite images revealed five vents in the mountain, all spaced in a twenty-mile stretch of the river. Intuitively he knew they connected the cave system.

Base camp was a little over two hundred miles south of where Colonel Percy Harrison Fawcett disappeared in 1925. Fawcett missed a major change during a particularly deadly flood season along the Araguaia and Dr. Gregg was convinced he was looking for the wrong waterfall. The one mentioned in Manuscript 512 had most likely dried up after the flood, although he thought there might be another reason altogether. That, he kept to himself, until a later time. Careful study of topographical maps and satellite images helped him locate a likely spot for that waterfall.

Jim's team erected base camp about ten miles from the waterfall location in the only spot available. Small huts, each capable of sleeping four individuals had been built using aluminum studs, marine plywood, and tin roofing. Each hut was twelve feet square. Along three of the walls, windows had been cut, three-foot high by six-foot long, and the wall facing the inside of the square had a door and two windows. Covered by a very strong aluminum alloy grid placed over a screen every window was doubly protected. Grid and screen were held in place between two sheets of marine plywood on the outside wall. The inside wall was also marine plywood.

Instead of insulation in the walls, a grid of brass tubing that carried water ran through the joists and between them, allowing the walls to be cooled by pumping water through them. Even the floors had pipes beneath for the water. Every crack and opening was carefully sealed against insects, and a week before anyone took residence in the huts they were sprayed for insects.

It was a neat and tidy camp with twenty-two huts surrounding a flagpole, neatly landscaped quad, and a medical hut. Opposite the medical hut was the main conference tent, a huge structure complete with air conditioning and a working kitchen. As evening closed around them the entire group met for dinner and the final briefing before starting the adventure.

Abe and JimJim, working together, provided a dinner of delicious fruit and green salads, cheeses, and freshly squeezed juices. After a sumptuous dinner Jim sat back and watched his crew as they carried on various conversations. Don, sitting two seats away, leaned forward and touched his hand.

"This is a tight crew." He said, nodding his head once.

"We've been through a lot together." Jim said with a smile. "Thanks." He added. At last he rang the bell by his plate, a small brass bell, and instant silence settled around the table.

"Thank you, Abe and JimJim, and both kitchen crews for an awesome dinner!" Jim said. There was a moment while everyone applauded. Things got quiet again and every eye turned to Jim. He appreciated the attention of his crew. For a moment he sat, looking around the room at everyone, marveling again at the number of people he and John now commanded.

"Tomorrow, at 04:30 hours we meet here for breakfast. Before we go to our rest, I want to remind all of you to review the dangers we're facing from animals, insects, snakes, and arachnids in this area. Our gear is designed to minimize the dangers, so regardless of how hot you get, don't take off any of your gear. How is everybody doing getting used to your new boots?"

He looked around as everyone nodded approval of the new footwear. The boots were waterproof, snake proof, and extremely comfortable. A company in Australia made the boots and Jim had ordered three pair for every member of the crew, and the two cameramen. He noticed that Tom was lifting his shoe to study it, appearing quite satisfied. It was the first time he'd ever worn such a boot and decided that from that time forward, he would not go out in the jungle without them.

"How did you get shoes big enough to fit Sturdy?" That was News, who at only five feet five inches in height always felt dwarfed by the giant Sturdy.

"That was easy, mate." Sean piped up. "They sowed two canoes to a tent and hey presto! Boots!"

Sturdy got up and walked over to News, lifted him out of his chair with one hand, and set him down so they could compare shoe sizes. Pointing down Sturdy spoke.

"I have a better understanding than you!" He said, nodding his head sagely.

"O pun the door!" News said. "Shut up or I'll punch your kneecap!"

After the laughter died down the two touched fists and took their seats again.

"There are two biologicals that I want to remind everyone again are the most-deadly to us. The Wandering Spider is one we need to constantly look for. But even more dangerous is that Lonoma obliqua. These are hard to see and any contact with their venom can send you back here to the medical hut. So be careful. Be vigilant. Don't put your hands on anything unless you're sure it's safe!

"We won't be wading through much water unless absolutely necessary. Remember the dangers there as well. Now we need to talk about noise." He looked around and noticed that every eye was on him.

"In the bush we need to move with caution, be as quiet as possible, talking only when necessary. Talk in a quiet voice if you have to say something. The people flanking you need to be able to hear what might be coming. Some of you were with us in the Amazonas region, so you know how to walk. Those of you who weren't have done well in training and are getting good and keeping the sound down. Slow and steady wins the race here. I'm going to ask Sturdy to lead us all in prayer before we go to our huts. Sturdy!"

The soft-spoken giant led them in a very passionate prayer for protection and keeping eyes focused on the Lord, no matter what might happen along the way. Grand success or utter failure was in His capable hands, and Sturdy wanted everyone to think about accepting whatever God brought into the lives of the adventurers. When he was finished Jim felt confident that God had listened carefully to every word, and that Sturdy had asked nothing that was not in keeping with the will of God. Sturdy's faith amazed and inspired Jim and he made sure to compliment the giant on his prayer before leaving with Cecilia.

To leave the tent, one stepped into an airlock, was doused with insect repellant, and put on a pith helmet with a very fine net that had elastic around the neck for a tight fit. Jim and Cecilia put on their helmets and walked out into the evening air. No bugs landed on them, but they buzzed around them in a frenzy. Jim wondered aloud what they lived on when they couldn't eat a human getting a giggle from his wife.

A fan over the inside mantle of the door kept the bugs from their hut. Jim entered quickly and zipped up the screen protector inside the door that sealed it from insects. The huts were about fifteen degrees cooler than the outside temperature, but the humidity made it feel hot in spite of that. Once the lights came on the constant sizzling of bugs hitting the screens in the windows was evidence of the danger.

Each screen was electrified and killed insects that touched them. Every morning they had to be cleaned or the dead bugs would literally shut off the ventilation those screens permitted. Jim turned on the overhead fan and sighed. That seemed to cool things down a little.

It also produced a breeze, something that was sadly lacking in the jungle, even at this altitude.

He allowed himself four hours of sleep, having rested the last two days, and eaten foods that would stock up his energy and stamina levels. Rising in the dark he shook Cecilia awake, kissed her, and stepped into the tiny shower in one corner of the hut. The water was tepid, not hot, not cool, but it was clean and after sixty seconds he stepped out, clean and ready to dry off. Cecilia made her way into the shower and took quite a bit longer.

Jim didn't mind. He sat on their bed, which he'd made, and watched her dry off, do her makeup, brush her hair, tie it back, and get dressed. She smiled often at him as he watched her, knowing that he enjoyed simply looking at her, taking in what he called her beauty. When she was fully dressed, she faced him.

"We're both going to stink to high heavens by the end of the day!" She said, adjusting her clothing. Their snake boots came to the top of their calves, and each person had a pair of Kevlar leggings to go over them to further protect them from biting fish, electric eels and stinging rays. Jim was sure they would have to traverse through water often and wanted his people protected. Clothing was a bit heavier than usual to protect against biting insects. The union suit they wore beneath it all was designed to soak up sweat, dry quickly, and cool the body. She was right. They would both stink of sweat and grime by the end of the day. But that was the nature of such ventures and both were used to the hazards and difficulties.

Without comment he stood up and they went to the door. Before he unzipped the screen, Jim put on his pith helmet and netting, and made sure that Cecilia had hers on before he switched on the fan. Switching on the fan automatically opened the door. Unzipping the screen, he stepped out, and after Cecilia came out closed the door. Air hissed into the rubber seals around the door, sealing it from insects.

They made their way to the tent for breakfast and Jim noted with pride that most of the crew was doing the same. Dr. and Mrs. Penny and Dr. and Mrs. Wozniac were last to arrive, on the heels of the Millstein twins. Breakfast waited them in a buffet that included scrambled eggs, bacon, sausage, grilled onions, various vegetables to add to the eggs, and fruit.

Jim ate his usual large breakfast, as did most of the team, getting ready for a day of exploration. He sighed when he finished, knowing that for the next few days they would be eating MREs and meals from tubes. The food was nourishing, but hardly what he had just enjoyed. At least the fruit would be fresh.

After a time of prayer Jim helped clean up the breakfast area, as did everyone else, and within half an hour they were finished. He looked around at the expectant faces and smiled. Excitement was high, and he felt the same way.

"Bulldog, you have point." He said. Chief, Hayseed, Neil and M.P. turned and headed for the air lock. "Firefox, you have the rear guard." Jim added. Viper saluted and moved his men to the side to wait. Scope, R.C., and 45 were relaxed, but they checked their weapons a final time while waiting to leave. Jim took note and smiled again, proud that his men were as thorough and careful as the best of soldiers. Bumping fists or shoulders with each man as he passed, he nodded to each, a silent approval.

In small groups they moved through the air lock into the predawn darkness. Everyone knew where he or she belonged, and Jim took note that his science crew was right where they were supposed to be before he joined Omega 1 team and followed Bulldog. Cecilia took her place with the Greggs.

Moving through this part of the country was done slowly and cautiously. Still, they made good time, and by noon had covered nearly four miles. No one sat on the ground to eat lunch. Each person carried his or her own folding camp chair, very light weight but very strong, upon which to sit.

Men like Sturdy, Abe, and Dorf had chairs designed for their height and weight. Sean, the Wozniacs, D.J. and Cowboy walked around checking everyone's canteen to be sure they were drinking the proper amount of water. It was the first time and Jim noted that not one person had failed to take in the appropriate amount. Proud of his crew, he made sure they all knew his thoughts, keeping morale high.

No one, thus far, had complained about the humidity, the intense heat, or the exertion necessary to make one's way through the jungle. Jim watched the men trade parts of their MREs with others. It was a common sight amongst soldiers. There was usually something in the pack that a person didn't care for, while someone else did. So, the men, knowing each other's tastes, knew with whom to trade and did so.

"You did a lot of work with that machete!" Cowboy said, stopping in front of Jim. "How much fruit are you eating at lunch?"

Jim smiled at him and showed him the two oranges, two bananas, and a bag of blackberries. Cowboy smiled, nodded his head, checked Jim's canteen, and finding it empty nodded again. "Don't forget your water purification tablets and don't forget to strain the water! You certainly don't want to swallow a Candiru by accident. He was speaking of a species of fish, and babies were very small, small enough to crawl up a urethra. Jim had heard him say the same thing to every member of the *Pearl* crew and was sure Doc was saying the same to the *Coral* crew. Satisfied that he had the best medical crew anyone could find he followed the good doctor's recommendations to the letter without really thinking about it. That was the real power of routine. One didn't have to think about it if the routine was often practiced.

CHAPTER 34

Two latrines had been set up at the edge of camp and the ground around the holes raked clear of any debris. Each latrine had a lightweight cloth tube that hung from a tree to provide privacy, and a three footed toilet seat upon which to sit for the ladies. Both doctors and Sean noted with pleasure that everyone had to use the latrine to urinate. Jim was rather pleased that the science team women did not complain about the smell, which one could not avoid, though they did tease some of the men about the sounds emitting from their side. It was the kind of banter one might expect from a sister.

"When should we expect the disaster?" Cecilia whispered in his ear.

"I'm sorry. I don't understand." He whispered back, nibbling her ear lobe through the netting and kissing her. He didn't like the netting between them.

"Ew! Get a room!" Cup Cake said, interrupting Cecilia's response, so when she gave it, she was giggling a little.

"Everyone is doing what they're supposed to do, morale is high, and we're making good time. That's usually when disaster strikes." She whispered.

At that moment Jim leaped from his chair, his Ruger .44 Magnum seeming to leap into his hand, and the shot that roared from the huge barrel stunned everyone to instant silence. Hayseed's face paled as he looked at the Viper that had been hanging from the branch above him. The bullet had neatly severed the diamond shaped head.

"You had to say it!" Jim said, grinning at Cecilia as he ejected the spent shell and inserted a fresh round. After making sure his safety was on, he holstered the pistol again. It went into a holster on his vest, low and to the left, within easy reach.

"Thanks, Shep!" Hayseed finally said. Jim noted that Chief was sliding his huge hunting knife back in its sheath.

"You shoot straight for a white man!" Chief said. He was serious.

"That was a Pit Viper!" Hayseed said, looking at the severed head, the jaws still working the biting motion, venom dripping from the fangs.

"Out here they call it the three-step snake." Chief said, pulling out his knife, sticking the head, and flinging it into the river. "It bites you, and you take three steps before you die." His voice was light, but his eyes were serious. "It's a good thing Shep saw it, because I wasn't sure I could reach it in time."

None of the science crew missed the tension that had come into the soldiers, leaving just as noticeably when the gunshot was explained. Tiffany looked at her twin sister, trying to smile. "This is a very dangerous group of men!" She whispered. "I'm glad they're watching over us!"

"How long did you know that snake was there?" Cecilia asked, her hand still up to her mouth.

"I caught the movement as it dropped from the branch and extended its body toward Hayseed." Jim said. He sat down again after righting his chair and making sure no insects were present.

"I'm glad your good with that cannon!" She said, putting a shaking hand on his.

"He's the best there is, Bright Eyes!" Zeke said with pride. "No SEAL has ever beaten his score with the pistol. Mrs. Museum, when he was born you didn't happen to feed him gun oil, gun powder, and put a pistol in his hand, did you?" Zeke asked, turning to her.

"He was born after only twelve minutes of labor!" She said with a smile. "The doctor who delivered him commented that the kid was fast. His father was a Marine through and through, so he might have received gun oil and gun powder while I wasn't looking." She smiled at Jim as she said it. "If so, he found his mother's milk more palatable. I could never produce enough to satisfy him!"

Jim blushed as everyone laughed and Cecilia looked at her ample figure and smiled.

"I always wondered why his eyes wander to these so often!" She said, lifting them lightly. Her laughter was light as her husband turned crimson.

"You have to be firm!" Pippi said, looking at John. She pointed her two fingers at her eyes. "My eyes are up here!" She said sternly. John simply reached out and fondled her breast, staring at her as he did so.

"These are equally tantalizing, darling." He said dramatically. Then he licked his lips.

"John Russell Shepherd!" Mrs. Gregg snapped. Everyone laughed as John snatched his hand away and looked sheepishly at his mother. Pippi was laughing so hard she had tears in her eyes. "The middle name always does the trick." Gwyneth said with a prim smile. "Alistair Winston Gregg!" She said suddenly as her husband whispered something in her ear. Now she was blushing.

Once everyone had finished using the latrine, it was cleaned and packed away while others found a spring and filled canteens through the filter. Jim noted that the science team had volunteered for the job. One would drop in a purification tablet and the other would hold the funnel with the screen, while the third dipped and poured water into the canteen, filling it. Once the canteen was filled another dropped in another pellet that added electrolytes and tasted a little like Gatorade.

Jim took his canteen, thanking the girls, and waved for Delta to take point. Sniper had the rear guard. He grunted a little, noting that his pack didn't seem much lighter minus only the fruit and MRE he'd eaten. Pulling his machete, he went to work clearing brush away from where people would follow, ignoring the weight as only a soldier can.

They camped that night on a flat slab of rock overlooking the jungle about two thousand feet below. Routine called for dinner, devotions, use of the latrines, and then inflating the tents. While the tents were inflating people sprayed each other with bug repellant. It was odorless and so far, no one had shown any signs of being allergic. Two-by-two people crawled into their tents. Knife had the first watch.

Morning began predawn, as before, and after a breakfast of fruit and bread, camp was packed, cleaned, policed, and the latrines sterilized and put away. Just as the sun touched the horizon they stood in a circle for prayer. By mid-morning they would reach the first of the vents they were going to explore. Everyone was excited, but also wary of the danger. Prayers that morning were honest, and Jim noted that many did not ask for protection, but for trust that God would care for them.

Three hours later they stopped over the first vent. Reaching it would require some climbing skills, but nothing too difficult. The terrain was rugged, overgrown with plant life offering many purchases, and the slope, though steep, was not a cliff face. Sniper drew the first task of getting a man down to the vent and then sending Dr. Gregg down to join him. Norm Geissler checked Lloyd Brookstone's gear as the man prepared to make the descent. Of the four of them, Brookstone was the best climber. He was also a world-class free ascent climber. Nodding to Norm he looked behind him, and then slowly and carefully began to back down the slope.

This process was slow because Lloyd needed to check every step to be sure there were no poisonous insects, arachnids, or snakes to alarm. Since the vent was on the north side of the mountain it was cooler here, and he hoped the insects and snakes would bed down where it would get warm quickest. Though that was probably the case, his vigilance did not waver.

His sharp eyes picked out a group of Lonomia Oblique caterpillars on a fallen log. They looked very much like moss and lichen growing on the shady side of the log. It never ceased to amaze him how deadly creatures in this part of the world seemed to be.

"Avoid this fallen log, Dr. Museum!" Lloyd called up in his cultured British accent. "Lonomia Obliqua Caterpillars!" He added.

Moving around and avoiding the danger he continued down, making sure his rope was nowhere near the caterpillars. If some of their venom got on the rope and someone touched it with bare hands it would mean big trouble. At last he reached the vent, feeling the cooler air rushing up at him. The odor on the air was something he knew well. There were dead bodies below, probably human, judging from the smell.

"Somebody went down before us, Shep!" He called up. "I can smell dead bodies! Dropping lights now." He cracked the lights and dropped them as he spoke.

They fell a long way, perhaps seventy or eighty feet before landing on hard rock. No one looked up the chimney or approached the light. That was a bad sign. Whoever was down there had not fallen down the vent, which meant they might have been exploring and discovered a trap.

"Toss down the hundred-and-fifty-foot line!" He yelled up at his team.

Norm looped the coils over his powerful shoulders and hooking onto the rope made his way down to Lloyd. Taking one whiff from the vent he turned to Lloyd. "Bloody dead bodies, Rock!" He nodded in the affirmative. "Been there a bit, eh what?" He added.

"Ripe for sure." Lloyd replied.

Dr. Gregg was not afraid of climbing, had been doing it his entire life, and with great anticipation hooked onto the rope and began his journey down. He arrived without mishap and smiled at the two soldiers waiting for him. Looking into the vent he saw the lights far below.

"Look how uniform this vent is!" He exclaimed, examining the lip carefully. Using a tape measure, he measured each side. "A perfect square. And see how it widens as it goes down? That provides the perfect draw for a chimney! The air gains pressure as it compresses and pulls other air up behind it."

"New or old work, Dr. Museum?" Norm asked, raising one

eyebrow in a comical way. The doctor's answer would be critical to their exploration, for if it was new, they were in the wrong place.

"Quite old. These marks were made by hand tools made of stone!" He showed them some marks but to Norm they looked just like weather marks. However, he knew that Dr. Gregg was an expert and accepted his assessment without question.

"Rock goes down first, then you and I go down together." Norm said, looking down the vent.

"You're the expert." Dr. Gregg said with a grin.

By then Lee had joined them, and he and Norm lowered Rock down the chimney. When he put his feet on the floor it was with great care. Finding the landing solid he unclipped his rope, drove a spike into the rock floor, and attached the rope, keeping it taught.

Norm and Doctor Gregg came next, tethered together, making a steady descent without incident. Lee came last, repelling down the chimney in easy stages while others gathered at the top. Dr. Gregg turned on his light and carefully looked around the entire area. Rock was testing the floor carefully, step by step in an ever-widening circle.

One by one the rest of the crew came down the rope, until C.G. repelled to the bottom, the last to arrive. His boots touched down with a barely audible thump as he turned his head, taking in all he could see. In the cool of the cave they sat down or stood in the area that had been deemed safe, waiting for Dr. Gregg to arrange the exploration to his satisfaction. Here he was in charge and everyone deferred to him, including Jim. His expertise was inspiring, and the men all trusted him.

Alistair liked his stepsons very much and respected them more than they knew. Their deference to him filled him with a sense of belonging to something he'd missed for a long time. He was part of a loving family, and he had men he could count on in any situation.

"Mark and I will take point." Dr. Gregg said, smiling at Jim as he used the military term. "Dorf can handle the weight of the two of us if something goes amiss. We're going to try to find those dead bodies."

Slowly the two men set off, stepping carefully, looking not only at the floor, but walls and ceiling. At one point, Dr. Gregg paused, looking ahead, noting that there was a pit in front of them. With a hand-held whiskbroom he swept away dirt from the floor, uncovering the rock. Finally, he brushed away the dirt around a diamond shaped stone set in the floor, perhaps an inch below the regular surface.

First, he pushed on it, but the stone didn't move. Finally, with Mark's help, he pulled the stone up to the level of the floor. There was an audible click as something beneath the stone snapped into place. When he was sure they hadn't activated another trap he swept the floor, finding seven more of those diamond shaped stones.

Going back to the first stone he pushed it down, and it slid down that inch and stopped again. Curious he studied the next stone, and finally put all his weight on it and stepped away. For several seconds nothing happened, and then quite suddenly the stone dropped an inch!

"Clever!" He said shaking his head. "There's some type of time delay being used here. Let's get that first stone out and see what's below it!"

He and Mark pried the stone out of the floor and for nearly half an hour Dr. Gregg studied the device. Finally, he called for Wade.

"Mr. Adams, please come here and tell me how this thing works!" He said with exasperation in his voice.

Wade squatted down and studied the mechanism uncovered when the stone was removed. Finally, he touched a small leather pouch. Lifting his finger to his nose he sniffed and nodded his head.

"Stepping on the stone depressed this pouch, causing this substance, which I believe is sodium bisulfate to be released, eating through those thick cords. Once those cords snapped the trap was activated. The snap you heard when you pulled the stone up was this piece of bamboo moving back in place."

"Clever buggers!" Dr. Gregg said, and then winced at his language. "Sorry dear." He said to his wife. "Clever Blokes." He dusted off his hands.

Slowly he and Mark approached the open pit in front of them, avoiding the diamond shaped stones. Some sixteen feet below them five men were impaled on sharpened bamboo stakes set in the floor. Some of the stakes were long, some were short, and every single body had been pierced at least half a dozen times. It was obvious that the men had died in considerable pain, bleeding out or dying of dehydration.

"See that hand?" Dr. Gregg pointed at a hand with his flashlight. "That poor lad was alive after he fell, long enough to get his hand off that short stake there. The floor seethed with scorpions that had gathered for the feast. Turning to face the other crewmembers he spoke quietly, his voice carrying easily in the stone corridor. Knowing the dangers they faced here, he wanted everyone to take the utmost care.

"There are five dead men below us. Judging from their clothing and hair I'd say they were Oriental, possibly Chinese. The smell is bad here, but once we're past this trap the vent will carry it away from us. Try not to look into the pit when you are crossing it." He said softly.

Sturdy and Abe made their way forward with some special folding ladders. It was all they carried, because the ladders were heavy, and each one had two. Judging the distance, they set up the ladders as scaffolds with legs eighteen inches high. Then, their huge muscles bulging with the effort, they extended them over the pit and set the far leg in place on the other side of the pit. The pit was sixteen feet wide. Now, with two scaffold platforms, everyone could cross safely.

Mark grinned at the giant Sturdy and stepped onto the scaffold, walked easily to the other side and studied the floor carefully. Dr. Gregg, slower in crossing joined him, and after stretching out on the scaffold and brushing away all the dirt so they could see the floor of the corridor Dr. Gregg allowed Mark to step down.

"Why are these darts here?" Mark asked, helping Dr. Gregg to his feet and down onto the rock.

"The trap probably released them in case anyone escaped the pit." Dr. Gregg said, lifting one gingerly. "See this sticky substance that's dried on the head?" He showed it to Mark who nodded. "It's probably poisoned. Whether or not the poison is still viable is something I'm not willing to test. We need to be very careful!"

"The fact that these traps are here tells us that there is either a mine here, or that lost city we're looking for!" Mark said with an excited grin.

"Indeed." Dr. Gregg replied. "My guess is both." He said after a moment. "The Tawantinsuyu the Spanish incorrectly dubbed the Inca Empire was really a conglomeration of hundreds of cultures under the ruling class, which was the Inca. Tawantinsuyu literally means The Four United Provinces.

"The most populous suyu, Chinchaysuyu encompassed the former lands of the Chimu empire and much of the northern Andes. At one time it was believed the suyu extended through much of modern Ecuador and just into modern Columbia. Collasuyu or Qollasuyu was named after the Aymara-speaking Qolla. They encompassed the Bolivian Altiplano and much of the southern Andes, running down into Argentina and as far south as the Maule River near modern Santiago, Chile. You can see that they covered the most territory.

"The second smallest of the suyu, Antisuyu, seems to have been located northwest of Cusco in the high Andes. It is actually the root of the word "Andes. Smallest was the Cuntisuyu or Kuntisuyu, located along the southern coast of modern Peru, extending into the highlands towards Cusco, which was the central city.

"By the time the Tawantinsuyu reached its greatest influence it included civilizations such as the Caral, Chavín, Valdivia, Nasca, Moche, Tiwanaku, Chachapoyas, Wari, and Muisca. Those would have been the Andean civilizations.

"What I think is amazing is that the capital area, Cusco, was probably akin to a modern federal district, like Washington, D.C. Cusco sat at the center of the four suyu and probably served as the preeminent center of politics and religion. By the time the Spanish had begun to conquer them they were desperately trying to hold on to the republic they created.

"Smallpox wiped out at least sixty percent of the population before Francisco Pizarro's campaign. Some say the deaths went as high as ninety-four percent. I don't know, but it was devastating. Other diseases and internal struggles really led to the downfall of the republic." Dr. Gregg paused for a moment and noticed that everyone had been listening closely, many taking notes. He smiled.

"How in the heck do you remember all those names, Doc?" FM asked, scratching his head. "And how do you spell Tawantinsuyu?"

"Well done, FM!" He chuckled. "You actually pronounced it correctly!"

"I did! Heck, Doc, I can't even spell it!" FM put on a confused look.

"You might try reading my notes." Dr. Gregg suggested.

"Have they come out in comic book form yet?" FM quipped.

"You said we had to bring him along!" Dr. Gregg said, pointing to Jim. Jim chuckled.

CHAPTER 35

What FM had done was take everyone's mind off the horrors of the pit, and the dangers that were yet to come, lightening the moment, allowing everyone to breathe normally again. Jim clapped him on the shoulder.

"College notes don't come in comic book form." He said, causing everyone to laugh again.

Mark and Dr. Gregg set off again, and when there was room, Abe and Sturdy pulled the ladders and folded them, helping each other pack them to carry on their broad backs. Almost silently now the group moved on, sometimes taking five minutes to cover ten feet.

Half an hour later Mark and Dr. Gregg paused where a series of irregular holes in the walls on both sides puzzled them. Mark stretched out his bamboo walking stick in front of one of the holes. Nothing happened. Then he waved the pole and a wooden dart hit it with enough power to stun his hand. He looked with awe at the dart sticking through the end of his pole.

"Is it just me, or do these holes line up with each other?" He asked Alistair as he cut off the end of the dart and pulled it out of his bamboo pole.

"They line up." Alistair said, looking carefully.

"Shields!" Mark called quietly.

C.G. and Vince came forward carrying riot shields commonly used around the world. They each moved close to a wall and in perfect step with Mark began to walk along the corridor, while Dr. Gregg kept checking the floor and Mark kept his eyes on the ceiling. Heavy thumps marked the flight of darts that bounced harmlessly off the shields.

"Stop!" Alistair's voice was shrill. Mark saw the danger, but it was too late. Even as he pulled his foot back a rack of sharpened spikes slammed up from the floor, while another swung down from the ceiling. Even as it happened Mark could see the trajectory of both sets of spikes. His own voice was shrill.

"Down!" He screamed, hitting the floor as he yelled the warning.

All four men dropped to the floor and the spikes came together with a crash. Then, just as they thought they might be safe, another loud thunk sounded and a dozen darts arched up from the floor heading to where they might have been impaled. The darts passed over their heads and skittered along the floor while those behind dodged them, not willing to even stop them with their snake proof boots. Those points were as sharp as a snake's fang, and would not have penetrated the boot, but the poison made them ultra cautious.

"Anyone caught in those spikes would now be stuck with poisonous darts!" Alistair said, propping himself up on his elbow to look back and make sure everyone was okay. He was glad now that Jim had insisted on a thirty-foot gap between he and Mark and the rest of the group.

"Anyone injured!" Sean called out in the silence that followed those words.

"We're good to go up here!" C.G. called out with a feral grin.

"Are we there yet?" Loony quipped.

"That's enough children! We'll get there when we get there!" Barbara said with a nervous giggle.

A few voices said almost in unison, "I have to go to the bathroom," while a few more said "I'm hungry." Laughter followed and everyone sighed.

"That was close!" Mark said to his three friends as they slowly got to their feet. It had been the quick reflexes of the men that saved them from death and he was thankful no one was injured.

"And nasty!" Vince said, looking at the bars and spikes. "These were meant to freeze the prey and the darts would finish them off!"

"Look what was hiding behind the bars!" Mark grinned, pointing with his light to several large hairy tarantulas. "Those guys are pretty harmless, but I think some of our ladies might not like that many in one place." He added softly.

"Whatever is beyond these traps is indeed valuable. Let us proceed with caution!" Alistair said, dusting himself off.

Once more C.G. and Vince moved to the sides, ducking under the spikes, and together they moved to the end of the section with holes in the wall. They went back and escorted four at a time up the corridor, in case any more darts were released. After the third trip they held the shields high, releasing the highest darts. There were but four, but Sturdy or Dorf might easily have been hit by one of them.

"I don't like this." Alistair said, looking at the walls now. "Doesn't that look like it might be a runway for a large object?"

The walls indeed were cut so that a ledge seemed to curve from higher up to the floor, and in the deeper shadows ahead they could see the ceiling rose. A few feet beyond the end of the run a simple door could be seen in the wall to their right. On the ground, just outside the door, a few pieces of gold glittered in their light, beckoning the unwary to immediately open the door to find more treasure. No one was surprised when several of the men figured out that this was another clever trap.

"So, we open the door, a big rock rolls down, and traps us inside an empty room!" Vince said. "Anyone seeing that gold would rush to the door, open it, and rush in." He added.

"There's probably enough gold inside the room to keep everyone interested long enough for the plan to work." Mark said.

"Look at the floor!" Alistair said. "I think the plan is that anyone making it this far is crushed by the stone!" He pointed to the octagon shaped tiles on the floor, each with a different symbol.

"See how the wall is rounded out here?" Alistair asked, pointing to the side. "That's to stop the rock, or ball, or whatever is waiting up there."

"So, what do we do?" Mark asked.

"Look at the pictures on the tiles!" Dr. Gregg said, his voice suddenly excited. "The Tawantinsuyu had many local forms of worship, most of them concerning local sacred Huacas. See that symbol?" He pointed his light. "That's Viracocha, also called Pachacamac, who created all living things. He's the main or head honcho, or whatever you call them these days when it comes to their gods."

"Is that made of gold? It looks like gold that has not been properly protected." C.G. said.

"Yes. Well done!" Alistair said.

"He's a stubby weird looking dude, isn't he?" C.G. commented.

"Over there is Apu Illapu, the Rain God. And that's Ayar Cachi, the Hot-tempered God that causes earthquakes. Next to Apu Illapu is Illapa, the Goddess of lightening and thunder. Some called her Yakumama the Water Goddess.

"That's Kuychi, the Rainbow God, connected with fertility. That one is Pachamama, the Goddess of earth and wife of Viracocha. People gave her offerings of coca leafs and beer and prayed to her for major agricultural occasions."

"Oh! A lush who likes chocolate!" Vince quipped.

"Grow up, Marine!" Mark said, slapping Vince on the back of the head.

"Do shut up, both of you!" Alistair said with a grin. He continued to shine his light.

"That's Qochamama, goddess of the sea, and Sachamama the Mother Tree, the snake with two heads. And that is Inti, the sun god and patron deity of the holy city of Cusco, which in Quechua means home of the sun."

"You missed one." Mark said, pointing his light.

"Ah yes. That's Mama Kilya, wife of Inti, called Moon Mother." Alistair said.

"Sad that nature was their true god. They worshiped that which was created, rather than the Creator." Mark said, shaking his head.

"Notice that a small man like me could step from Inti stone to Inti stone? That's the way through this maze. I'm sure of it." He added when Mark looked at him.

"Don't step on Inti himself. Step rather on the dais upon which he stands! Note the holes in the figures!" Dr. Gregg said.

"All the figures have those holes!" C.G. said.

"Correct. Don't wave your arms about while you're moving from stone to stone!"

"We normally do that for balance, Doc!" Vince said, looking at the stones.

"I know. This is a test. Let's take a leisurely stroll with our hands behind our backs, shall we?" He asked. Without waiting he stepped forward, and carefully planting his feet on the dais moved from stone to stone in a strange meandering path. Mark followed quickly. C.G. and Vince stayed behind to tell everyone what to do.

"Hey Dr. Museum! What about guys like Abe and Sturdy and Dorf, with those huge broad shoulders?" C.G. called.

"Wait there! We should be able to figure out how to shut the thing down!" Dr. Gregg called back, keeping his concentration on the stones. "Send Wade up." He added.

Wade made his way carefully along the winding steps to the other side and joined Dr. Gregg and Mark looking for a way to turn off the mechanism. After nearly an hour passed Dr. Gregg paused before a stone in the floor. He smacked his forehead and groaned, and Mark and Wade came over quickly.

"What's wrong?" Wade asked.

"We've been walking past the controls for the last hour. It's under that stone!" Dr. Gregg said with a wry grin.

"How do you know? It's got two holes in it!" Wade said guardedly.

Dr. Gregg pointed to a rusted iron handle hanging on the wall over the stone. It was hinged in the center, allowing the ends to fit in the holes of the stone, and then locked in place to lift it away. Wade carefully inserted the ends of the handle, pushed it down until it clicked into the locked position and squatted, studying it for a few minutes.

"Those ancient people were pretty smart!" He said. "That's a clever design!"

"Well, professor, when you're done studying the design, maybe you could employ those Marine muscles and lift the cover clear!" Mark said.

Grinning at Mark he shook his head. "It won't come up yet." He said. "Push the rod this handle was hanging on into the wall please." Mark raised an eyebrow and did as he was bid, finding that the rod did indeed slide into the wall. An audible click sounded beneath the rock and Wade grunted, his shoulders swelling, the cords on his neck standing out as he pulled on the stone. Slowly it slid from its resting place.

Something else caused Mark and Dr. Gregg to step back quickly. A dozen of the huge scorpions poured out of the hole beneath the rock. The movement of the two men probably saved Wade a nasty sting, because the scorpions skittered away. Mark, ready for that eventuality, used his walking stick to kill them quickly. One, however, leaped upon Wade's boot and tried to plunge its stinger into his foot.

"Where's the other one?" Mark asked, breathing quickly.

"I introduced him to the bottom of my other boot. It made quite an impression!" Wade said facetiously. He made a face as he wiped the mess from his boots.

"Scary, aren't they?" Dr. Gregg asked. "Scary, but usually harmless."

All three looked into the hole now uncovered. With bleak expressions they looked at each other. There were three levers, made of stone, in the hole. Two faced one way and the third faced the opposite direction. It was up to them to figure out which stone controlled which trap and decipher the riddle the ancients set before them.

"My guess is that one of these operates the big stone set to roll down and seal us in here forever. One controls the darts, and the other controls false steps." Dr. Gregg said, squatting down and studying them. He looked across at the group crowded on the other side of the tiled walkway.

"Jim!" He called out in a voice that could be heard but wasn't too loud. "Can you move that door about half an inch, no more?" He asked.

As Jim moved to the door, he put his hands lightly on two of the levers and motioned for Wade to put a hand on the third.

"If yours moves even a fraction, grab it and stop it!" He said. Wade nodded. It was one of the two that Dr. Gregg was touching that began to move. "Stop!" He commanded, and Jim let the door return. He sighed and looked at Wade, and then at Mark.

"Okay! That's the big stone. Let's keep it there, shall we?" He asked, not expecting an answer. If no one opened the door, they would remain safe. Now he nodded at Wade and they each took one of the levers.

"Okay, Jim. Now use a walking stick and push on one of the false stones, lightly, just enough to make it move." He called out. This time Wade's lever moved, and Wade grabbed it, calling out for Jim to stop. Dr. Gregg looked at his two companions.

"Everybody over there move back a safe distance." He called out, waving them back. Jim moved everyone back. Finally, when he was satisfied, he moved the lever they hadn't tested slowly. Nothing happened until it reached the end of its arc and there was a very loud sound of something metal moving over something else metal. At the end of the screeching there was a solid sounding thunk.

"Okay! Wave a walking stick over the holes in the stones." Dr. Gregg yelled.

Jim returned to the tiles, waved his stick, and nothing happened. Dr. Gregg smiled and nodded. "Bring everyone over following the safe path already established. Make sure no one steps wrong!" He said. Jim nodded and started people moving into the next section.

Linking hand in hand and stepping carefully everyone made a human chain to help each other across the tiles. Great care was taken with each step and Jim came last. Once everyone was in the new section Dr. Gregg pulled the lever back and motioned for Wade to return the cover.

"Let's not make it too easy for anyone following." Dr. Gregg said softly. Wade nodded.

After the cover was in place, he pulled the handle out, pulled out the rod in the wall, locking the cover down, and hung the handle on the rod as before. Once more Dr. Gregg and Mark took the lead, their ropes hooked to Dorf who followed at a safe distance. Finally, they came to the place where they could see the huge round stone set to roll down on anyone who opened that fateful door.

"Somebody is following us, Shep." A soft voice said from behind. Jim turned and saw Fagan had moved up to a few feet behind him. Jim held up his closed fist and everyone became silent. He pointed back and people saw the two lights coming along the corridor far behind.

Using hand signals Jim gave commands. There were raised eyebrows at his commands. Don Patterson moved up beside the Captain and showed him his infrared camera with a telephoto lens. Smiling at the former SEAL he nodded. Don set his camera on a tripod and looked through the lens. Jim faced the crew after taking a look as well.

"Hold hands if you want to, sit down, and turn off your lights." Setting up their folding chairs the crew sat down in four rows spread across the room. Jim saw that the science team girls were holding hands as their lights extinguished. He didn't blame them. Sitting down behind Don Patterson Jim turned off his own light.

In the blackness of that underground corridor the darkness seemed sudden and heavy, settling around them like an ominous mantle. Jim felt Don's hand on his shoulder, and he allowed the man to guide him to where he could look into the camera again. It was a good lens and Jim immediately saw a group of five, four men and a woman. He was certain the man and woman in the lead were the Hao assassins.

Eventually they came to the door. Jim remembered his footprints on the doorstep and held his breath. One of the men pushed the door and it opened. Above them that horrible stone crashed to the runway and slowly and ponderously rolled over their heads and gathering speed rushed toward the hapless explorers.

Three of the team broke away and ran toward the tiles, while the Hao brother and sister team ran the opposite direction. When the stone smashed against the wall at the end of the runway the Haos were on the other side, sealed off. Their men, however, ran onto the tiles in their terror, too spooked to watch where they were stepping.

Tiles dropped beneath their feet and they were hurled into a deep pit. Their screams echoed in the corridor and the length of those screams told the explorers watching how deep the abyss beneath them was. All three screams ceased suddenly as the poison on the darts paralyzed them. Then, a few seconds later, the sound of their bodies smashing on the rocks some hundred and twenty feet below them echoed hollowly in the cavern. The drop had been long and deep.

Jim switched on his light. He pointed to Dr. Gregg and Mark and headed back toward the tiles. The two men followed. Every tile had dropped with the men, leaving a gaping chasm. Mark shone his light down on the broken and twisted bodies.

"I guess we won't be going out that way." Mark said quietly. He pointed his light to the huge rock now blocking the corridor.

"Those poor men!" Dr. Gregg said, turning away, feeling sick.

"I think the Haos will return, probably ahead of us." Jim said to the two men softly. "If not, they will probably post men about the chimneys and wait for us to surface."

"What do you think they will do?" Alistair asked.

"I think they will try to steal our treasures." Jim said sadly, and then continued. "They will also probably try to kill as many of us as possible. That seems to be their usual tactics. They are assassins and thus without conscience."

"With this many they could easily hide and try to pick us off one at a time." Mark said, nodding his head.

"No. They'll go for Dad first." Jim said. Alistair looked up at Jim with a smile of pleasure on his face. Being called "Dad" was something he treasured.

"I have an idea!" Alistair said, putting his finger to the side of his nose and grinning at the two men.

CHAPTER 36

Moving his head and neck experimentally Dr. Gregg nodded. Everyone smiled. Using material they brought to cast impressions Fagan, who was an expert at make up, fashioned a second layer of skin for Dr. Gregg's neck. It was carefully made up and fashioned so that it blended perfectly with his skin.

"It's a little warm under there, but nothing I can't handle." Alistair said, touching the fake skin. "It feels like kelp!"

"If they shoot a dart at you, it will be to the side of your neck, aiming for the carotid artery. Remember to drop immediately if you feel it hit, raising your hand as if to touch it, but never reaching it. The poison they use acts fast and paralyzes the victim, killing he or she slowly and with great agony. None of the bodies have been pretty.

"As soon as Alistair goes down Bulldog and Zulu pin them down. They will have an escape route, so be sure that Knife and Raider cuts that avenue off. Once they're pinned in a crossfire they'll surrender. We'll deal with them then." Jim nodded at the men as they listened, giving a thumbs up that they understood.

Once again, they moved through the corridor. The next trap was discovered before it was activated. In the center of the corridor a single large stone had been cut out. If one put weight on it a counterweight would be activated, and once that person was several feet out on the slab it would simply tip vertically, dumping the hapless victim into a pit full of sharpened stakes.

Alistair motioned Mark away from the slab and they moved along the wall, carefully checking every step, each side and the ceiling. Mark shot a spike into a crack in the ceiling, and using that rope, he tried the mechanism. When the slab tipped it tipped quickly, so quickly that the other side of it hit Mark hard enough to bounce him several feet away.

"Ow!" He said, hanging from the safety rope and looking down into the pit as he came back in contact with the slab. Just that quickly it tipped back up, but not all the way. Wade, who had been studying some iron rings set in the wall pulled one and the slab snapped back into place and everyone heard the audible click of something sliding into place.

Dorf pulled Mark's safety rope sideways so the gymnast could shimmy down the rope to safety. Using their ladders Sturdy and Abe erected an A-frame that Mark could climb to retrieve his spike and rope from the crack in the ceiling. Once everything was back in place they moved on, marveling at the engineering skills of an ancient race. Wade, locking down the slab, allowed everyone to cross safely, but they still used the edges for safety.

They made camp that night in a cavern dug out by nature and filled with rose quartz. Geodes dotted the floor of the cavern and after being cut open showed various crystal habits such as acicular, bladed, dendritic, equant, prismatic, striated, and tabular. Some of the crystals were twined in contact, penetration, and repeated forms, which are the most popular. Neff explained all the various forms and explained that geode was an aggregate form common in crystals.

"How does a Navy guy get rocks on the head?" D.C. asked, scratching his head as Neff spelled some of the habits they were seeing inside the geodes. Grinning Neff looked up.

"I wasn't born in the Navy." He replied, going back to his teaching.

From inside his tent, later that night, Jim stretched out with Cecilia snuggled against him, her regular breathing telling him she was asleep. The dim lights used to mark the trail to the latrines made the tents translucent, and Jim watched a particularly large wandering spider walk across the top of the tent. Two scorpions were on one side, and a beetle of some sort wandered into their territory and paid the price.

Slowly he relaxed and allowed himself to sleep for six hours, waking seconds before his alarm went off. He and Cecilia were not damp with sweat as they had been above the cave. Moving away from her carefully he managed not to wake her, and after making sure no spiders were near the opening of his tent he stepped out.

After a quick visit to the latrine he moved off to take his turn at guard duty near the entrance of the cavern. Bear was peering out of the cavern when Jim reached him and reached out to touch his shoulder. The man jumped and spun around and then sighed heavily. His face was chagrined.

"Dang, Shep! Don't do that! You nearly gave me a heart attack!" He said.

"Sorry. What had your attention out there?" Jim asked.

"I can feel cooler air coming from somewhere up the corridor, and a few minutes ago I cold swear I heard something plastic hit the rocks. I'm not sure, but it almost seems like a greenish glow down there, like someone dropped some light sticks down a chimney!" He replied.

Jim took out his infrared binoculars and trained them down the corridor. Soon he had a flare of light. He grunted. Bear's instincts had been quite correct, and the enemy was out there. Someone was coming down the chimney vent, and he thought quickly, his brain turning over scenarios until he settled on one he liked.

"Let's take them now!" He said. "Six Team 1 and Six Team 3 to the cave entrance now!" Jim commanded in his COM-link.

Seconds later all twelve men were present, and they made their way cautiously down to where the light sticks cast off their sickly glow. Whoever was in the chimney was coming down slowly. Jim motioned with his hands and his team spread out, finding good hiding places. Finally, two sets of legs appeared. It was the Haos.

When they landed, they unclipped from the rope and looked

around. The sound of a dozen safeties switching from on to off position froze them in place. Red laser sights dancing on their black uniforms were enough to let them know they were in deep trouble.

"Xun Hao, Yao Xiake Hao, this is a sanctioned archeological exploration, and we have the rights to this maze of caverns for the next eighty-eight days. You are in violation of the government of Brazil." Jim said in Mandarin. "Keep your hands where we can see them and don't make any sudden moves. We have no desire to kill either of you."

"You speak that dialect like a native." Yao replied quietly. "Is it not Captain James Shepherd to whom I speak?" He added.

Jim stepped out from behind the rock formation he had chosen, as did Mark. The two men walked toward the two Chinese nationals. Neither carried a weapon of any kind. Xun and Yao looked at each other and moved in tandem, as if speaking in each other's minds. Xun went for Mark and Yao went for Jim.

Both men met the attack calmly, and within seconds the Haos were rolling on the cavern floor. That was a fatal mistake for Yao, for he rolled into the presence of a Wandering Spider, and the spider, alarmed by the sudden movement, pounced, sinking its fangs into Yao's neck, hitting the carotid artery on its first bite. Xun leaped to her feet and ran to her brother, who had killed the spider. Jim squatted down.

"We have medical supplies. There's no antivenin for this poison, but we can treat him and perhaps save him. He is strong." Jim said in their home Yue or Pinghua dialect. Xun looked at him quizzically and then nodded.

"You are kind to offer aid, even after we attacked you." She said.

"We are honorable men." Jim said simply. Bear lifted Yao carefully and carried him back to the cavern, where Millie and Doc, Will and Donna and Sean were already setting up. As soon as they heard what had happened Doc set up an IV and Will began a series of shots.

"That spider got him in the carotid artery, Jim. I don't know if we can save him." Doc said. He was working quickly around the now suffering patient. "We may have to intubate if he stops breathing, and we may have to breathe for him for a while. Even then there's no guarantee he'll survive. Bites like this close to his brain are very bad. How big was the spider?"

"Big enough." Jim said softly.

Dr. Gregg emerged from his tent, and Jim watched Xun reach for her dart gun. Mark, who was guarding her, pressed his own pistol against her neck and drew back the hammer.

"That wouldn't be very nice, considering we are trying to save your brother." Mark said quietly. "Zip tie her hands. "Pen, why don't you and Cecilia search her and take away all of her weapons? We'll zip tie her feet until you're done." He added.

The two women searched Xun carefully and thoroughly. When all her weapons had been removed, including the container of darts, both women stepped back. Mark cut the ties on her feet and her hands. Xun looked at him with a raised eyebrow.

"If you want another crack at me, lady, go for it." Mark said, handing his weapon to Dorf.

Xun went for it, learning a very hard lesson. Mark held nothing back and the third time Xun hit the floor she stayed there, holding her side and moaning.

"I think I might have broken a rib or two." Mark said as Millie bent over the woman.

Gently Millie tried to determine what damage might have been done but was rebuffed.

Xun fought her off, drew up her knees, and grunted when a breath caused pain. Her eyes found Mark and she simply stared at him. After a few minutes she spoke in clear pedantic English.

"Your style is all defense." She said through clenched teeth. "Who taught you?"

"I've had many instructors over the years. What I used against you was a combination of styles. You are well versed in the Bajiquan or eight extremes fist style, Hei hu quan, the black tiger fist, and Hung Fut, Hung Kung Fu. Worthy styles, but no match! My styles are all practical, easily defending against yours. If you attack me again, I will kill you." Mark said evenly. One look in his eyes and Xun knew he spoke the truth.

"Does that one fight with the same style?" She asked, pointing her chin at Jim.

"He is much more skilled than I." Mark said. "That's one thing we all learn in martial arts. There's always someone who is better, faster, or more skilled."

"How badly are you injured?" Jim asked, coming to stand beside Mark. He looked down at the tiny figure on the ground and his eyes were fierce, stormy, and commanding. Xun found she could not long look into those eyes.

"My ribs are bruised, but I do not think they are broken." She said.

"You fought off my nurse. Why?" Jim was all aggression and Xun almost flinched. She was angry with herself for showing such weakness in the presence of a hated enemy she'd sworn to kill.

"I did not want to be helped." She said through clenched teeth, trying to find the courage to stare back at Jim.

"Go easy, Jim." A giant stepped up behind the Captain, a man so tall he dwarfed everyone, and so wide and muscular Xun marveled at his physique. "Her kind may never understand goodness." The giant's voice was filled with sadness as he spoke.

Jim drew in a deep breath, let it out, and sighed. He looked up at the giant. "Thanks Sturdy. I'll calm down." Moving away the two men talked quietly but Xun watched them. The giant was all muscle and power, but the man who stalked beside him was like a tiger, and though it defied belief, the mightier of the two.

Yao Xiake Hao died, despite every effort to keep him alive. The spider had injected enough poison to kill an elephant in that attack, and it had gone into the carotid artery, carried instantly throughout the body. After three hours of suffering his heart simply stopped. Will and Charles covered him with a sheet sadly.

"We came to kill you! Why do you look sad?" Xun asked, coming to stand beside the body of her brother.

"We believe in the sanctity of life, young lady. This young man was in the prime of his life, and he is dead. That is sad. His tattoos tell me he did not worship the One True God. That too is sad." Doc Wozniac said.

"There are those in my land who worship this God of yours. They call themselves Christians, and they are willing to die for their faith. Some have spoken to me of sacrificial love. They are weak, easily taken in battle, and easy to kill. There is no power in their religion, other than their unyielding faith." Xun said slowly.

"And this tells you nothing. Are you truly so obtuse?" Will asked.

"Does faith make one strong?" She asked, looking Will in the eye.

"It makes us strong enough to embrace the principles of our God, and to die without wavering in our belief. We do not worship physical strength, for no matter how strong one is, there is always someone stronger! And God is strongest of all. None can resist His power." Mark said softly.

"Then why does He not make me a Christian?" Xun said derisively.

"Because He wants you to choose to love Him, He does not wish to make you love Him." Mark replied evenly.

"I do not wish to hear any more of this God!" Xun said stubbornly.

"Then we will not speak of Him directly to you." Will Penny said respectfully. "I am very sorry for the loss of your brother."

"I watched. You tried to save him, despite the fact that he came to kill you. Thank you." Xun said, and her eyes began to tear. Then she broke down and wept for her brother.

After a time, she set up a makeshift alter and burned incense and lit a candle. She put her brother's picture beneath the candle. For a long time, she sat quietly as if in prayer and then she stood easily. Turning about she looked for Jim. When she found him she walked to face him.

"My brother is dead, killed by a poisonous bite. But you are responsible for striking him and putting him in the way of that insect. For that I have sworn to kill you."

She struck then, a blow that would have crushed Jim's chest had it landed. Her eyes opened in disbelief as Jim went from standing still to high speed motion, blocking her thrust and countering with one that sent her sliding across the stone floor stunned. No one had ever moved with that speed in all her training! Mark had not lied!

"Do not try to strike me again." Jim said quietly. Xun climbed to her feet and took a wide stance with her feet, her arms waving in the air. Jim recognized a mixture of the black tiger fist and hung fat. He took his own stance and waited. In his head his focus became total.

Xun realized that she was free to continue her attack as people gathered in a circle. Her blows flickered almost faster than the human eye could follow, and Jim backed up, step by step, blocking every attempt to reach him. The mistake seemed small as Xun over-extended on a thrust. Jim's hand clamped on her wrist as he fell backwards and his feet caught her middle, sent her flying, and as she sailed over him, he rolled violently to his right, tearing her arm out of the socket.

As she slammed to the rock floor with stunning force, he was already making his move, and she found herself in a choke hold, her left arm useless, her right now in Jim's mighty grasp, her air cut off. Xun's right arm snapped and she would have screamed, but slowly she was losing consciousness. To her surprise Jim released her and leaped away. He landed like a huge tiger, his balance perfect, and Xun cried out in agony.

"Doc, will you see to her needs?" Jim asked, his eyes never leaving her tortured face.

"You must kill me!" She rasped.

"I will not." He said sternly. Doc plunged a shot of Morphine into her arm and after a few seconds she relaxed as the pain lessened.

"I'm going to have to put her under to set that arm and repair her shoulder. After that she's going to need a hospital." Doc Wozniac said.

"Who is above the chimney, waiting for you?" Jim asked in her Pinghua dialect.

"Our contact here in Brazil and six of his soldiers." Xun answered in a dreamy voice.

"I'll get them ready." Mark said quietly.

"Be careful climbing up that chimney!" Jim said.

"I don't think I'll have to climb up. She had a radio in her stuff.

I'll use that to contact them, tell them to lower a sling, and send her up." Mark replied.

"Oh! Good! That will make it easier." Jim replied.

Four hours later Xun was pulled up the chimney, and then her brother's body followed. As soon as the body began its journey up the chimney Jim moved everyone deeper into the corridor in the fear that the soldiers might toss down a grenade or two. He was wise. Six grenades bounced once on the floor and sent their shrapnel flying in a deadly spray.

"Thank God you moved us!" Alistair said to Jim, clamping a hand on his shoulder. Jim nodded, his face an angry mask.

Mark lifted the radio to his lips. "Leave now and you get to live. Follow us and every one of you will die." He said in Spanish. "Get Xun to a hospital. If she dies from her wounds all of you will suffer the consequences."

There was no answer.

CHAPTER 37

Four hours later they stopped to eat and to rest. Jim watched the two doctors, their wives, and Sean move through the crew making sure everyone was drinking enough water. As before no one had to be reprimanded for having too much water in his or her canteen. Any scrapes or cuts were treated immediately, but at the rest stops the medical team checked each treated wound with great care. It was obvious to anyone that they cared deeply for each person.

Dr. Gregg sat down next to Jim after setting up his chair carefully. As he broke open one of the packaged meals he talked.

"I've always thought that Chinese Martial arts were superior to all others. How is it that you so easily defeated that girl?" He asked.

"The martial arts I've been taught are not about looking good or making fancy motions. Her arts could produce deadly power, but that power came from a deadly darkness, from a worship of false gods, and all such knowledge and power is useless in the presence of light. My motions were all designed to stop her power and finally to show her how easily her art failed.

"What else did you want to ask?" Jim asked softly, noting that several people had listened to his answer with interest.

"You're right, of course. There is something else I don't like." He said softly. "We haven't encountered a single trap since those tiles and the rock. What are your thoughts?"

"I hear swift running water ahead. My thoughts are that we will find our answer there." Jim said after a moment of thought.

"That's what worries me. If we get things wrong, we could all be swept back to that abyss by a flood!" Alistair said, his hands busy making his Sloppy Joe sandwich. "This stuff may be messy, but it sure tastes good!" He added with a grin.

"I'll have to think on that. Maybe Wade can come up with something to protect us against being swept away." Jim replied. He was getting ready to enjoy his beef roast with vegetables meal. Cecilia, sitting next to him, was eating beef stew. Everyone had been permitted to choose his or her own favorite foods to pack and the tastes of his crew were amazingly diverse.

"I heard my name. What's up?" Wade asked, moving his chair to join their circle. JR and Pippi joined them as well.

"We may need to fabricate some type of emergency setup to keep us all from being swept into the abyss back there if we get crossing the water wrong." Jim answered, and shoveled a full fork of his beef into his mouth.

"Or from being swept anywhere else!" Alistair added.

After finishing their meals, and sealing the garbage in a vacuum-packed square, they left the refuse behind and moved on. Less than a hundred meters from where they paused to rest, they came to the underground river. On the other side of the river the corridor came to an end.

"Remember the waterfall we studied on the map?" Dr. Gregg suddenly asked aloud.

"Sure. The one with two openings!" Wade said quickly. "Are you thinking what I'm thinking?" Wade looked at him with wide eyes.

"There are steps in the water." Mark said. He'd been shining his light into the water.

"Yes. The next part of our trip will be in a lower corridor, presently submerged by this river. If we can figure out how to divert it into the next passage, we will be able to move down the steps and into the next corridor." Dr. Gregg said, shining his light along the walls.

For an hour he moved along the walls on either side of the corridor and finally he stopped at the stone jutting out of the downstream wall. It had been squared off, with the end like a puzzle piece, square and larger than the square shaft. At last he shook his head and looked at the expectant crew watching him.

"Clever blokes!" He said. "The mechanism to divert the river is under the water, and the person who shuts it off has to tie off here." He said, indicating the rock. "One can see, looking closely, that some sort of wear has taken place around this end block. My guess is they tied off their rope here, and then went beneath the surface to turn off the flow of water."

"That's a pretty strong current. How would they pull themselves back?" Wade asked, dipping his hand into the cool water.

"I'm guessing that they knew the exact length of rope necessary, and that the individual who went in to turn off the flow was pulled back by several men." Dr. Gregg said.

"It can't be far." Cecilia pointed out. "Whoever was on the other end of that rope would run out of air if it was very far."

"That's a good point. How did they measure distance?" Wade asked quickly.

"They used simple measurements." Dr. Gregg mused.

"So, two spans would give a man time to turn whatever mechanism is down there and get back before he ran out of air." Wade said.

"That would be my guess." Dr. Gregg said. "I also guess you will find a mechanism at one span. See if there's a second one further back. That will be the one to turn. Turning the first one would probably flood this corridor."

Wade stripped to the waist, his powerful physique rippled with strong sinews. Lisle Mirelle stood with some of the other girls and whistled appreciatively.

"I love it when he takes off his shirt!" She said with a wicked smile on her face. Wade blushed.

"Why Commander Adams! I believe your blushing!" FM spoke up.

"Just shut up!" Wade said, grinning in spite of the comment. He gladly stepped into the latrine enclosure Sturdy had quickly erected to change into his bathing suit. When he came out there were more whistles and more blushes. He really was a magnificent specimen of manhood.

"For all you soldier boys, that's a demonstration of what we ladies call power." Lisle said after the laughter died down. "Despite your muscles and military might, we can wrap you around our fingers easily." She laughed.

"Struth!" Lee said. "And we're willing, ladies!" He added.

Wade continued to prepare himself for being submerged. From his pack he pulled a small mouthpiece that held three minutes of compressed oxygen to give him a safety measure beneath the surface. He knotted a rope and stepped into a climbing harness, attached the rope to his harness, and taking some deep breaths he wrapped his rope once around the rock hook and handed the other end to Sturdy.

Sturdy nodded, hooking on. Should the rock hook break off, he would be the safety to keep Wade from being swept down and over the waterfall. Wade put on the underwater headlamp gear so that wherever he looked he would have light beneath the water, inserted the breathing device into his mouth, and leaped into the water.

The rope snapped taut instantly and they could see him moving further away as he moved down the knotted rope. Some kept their eyes on their watches, timing his submersion. From somewhere deep below them there was a rumbling sound. It went on for a long time, over a minute, and suddenly Wade's head broke the surface as he pulled himself to the ledge. C.G. and Vince grabbed his hands and hauled him out of the water. It had begun to drop.

"You were right, Doc!" Wade said as he pulled the breathing device out of his mouth. "There were two devices. You can't see the second from the first, so I had to travel two spans further to reach it. When those guys built this, they had to feel their way along the wall! It's dark in that corridor!"

"What kind of device was it?" Dr. Gregg asked as he looked first at Wade and then at the receding water.

"A stone lever, four feet long, with a block of rock to brace one's feet on to pull it." Wade said, drying himself off. Sturdy already had the latrine enclosure set up in which Wade had changed into his bathing suit. He went in and began to change, talking as he did so.

"That rumbling started as soon as I had the lever all the way forward. I heard something start turning inside, almost like stone gears meshing, and the rumble started." He said, his voice muffled as he struggled into his T-shirt.

"It's still rumbling." Angela said.

"Probably will for a while. I think this corridor is deep, and the rock has to drop several spans to seal it shut." Wade replied. He came out after he had tucked his shirt in and was doing up his belt. By the time he'd put all his other gear back on the rumbling had stopped, and with it the rest of the water seemed to rush out.

"These steps will be slick, so take care as we go down." Dr. Gregg said as he ventured out onto the platform. "There's another block of rock sticking out of the wall at the bottom. If we attach a rope to the top and bottom, we should have a handrail to keep us from slipping." He added.

Mark took the rope down the steps, planting his feet carefully, and tied it off taut at the bottom. Dr. Gregg followed carefully, slipping only once, but able to catch himself. One by one the rest followed to the bottom. Upstream, where the water had once flowed with a powerful current, a stone now kept it at bay.

Dr. Gregg went to the stone and put his ear against it. He smiled and nodded.

"This is at least three feet thick, so the water won't break through. Also, note how this little trench takes the water that leaks through the sides and runs it off somewhere? That's very clever!"

The floor of the corridor was bare rock. Dr. Gregg and Mark soon led off again until they came to a door set in the side of the wall. Dr. Gregg studied the two levers carefully. One was four feet long and set on the far side of the door. The other was only eighteen inches long and set on the other side of the door. Both were smoothed by the flow of water over the years. Critically studying them he finally spoke.

"This one opens the door, and this one reverts the river to its original corridor." He said after half an hour of peering through the crevice where the levers protruded. "They could open this door, and once everyone was through the last person would turn this lever, and as the doors began to close the main door of the river would begin to rise soon after. That's very clever! Whatever lies beyond this door must be amazing indeed!"

"Firefox volunteers to come last." Bill Dodge said in the silence that followed.

"Thanks." Jim said, nodding his head in approval. "The job is yours. Just make sure that you guys get through the door before the water takes you for a ride you don't want! My guess is it would wash you out at some point several hundred feet from another river below!" Jim added. Far down the corridor they could see the exit of the waterfalls, just a tiny speck of light.

"Done, boss!" Viper replied easily.

Dr. Gregg took a breath and motioned to the first shorter lever. Wade moved it slowly and everyone could hear the sound of rock gears meshing. Slowly, ponderously, the door began to lift. Years of collected grime from the river dribbled out of the sides as the door lifted. Dr. Gregg knelt down and looked inside and whistled.

"There's another door rising in there. This is like an airlock!" He said.

Soon the doors were high enough for people to duck beneath and move in. Mark and Dr. Gregg went first, carefully examining the floor and walls. Inside the second door the ceiling of the cave towered above them. Dr. Gregg motioned for everyone to move forward and they came through the double doors to stand in awe of the city they could dimly see a few yards in front of them. Once they were all inside Bill Dodge and RC activated the lever that would close the doors, and then the lever that would once again allow the water to rush past. They had time to go through both doors upright before they dropped into the slots. Perhaps forty minutes later they could hear the water rushing past.

"Well! We're all in!" Viper said.

"Listen everyone!" Dr. Gregg said loudly enough to be heard above the babble of voices. Silence settled. "Touch nothing! I mean it! We'll rest here for a bit, grab a snack to eat, and then we'll explore. Unless I give the okay, keep your hands to yourselves."

"Let's get the lights up and running." Jim said. Suiting his words, he began to assemble one of the lights.

Three small generators were produced, and a group of work lights plugged in. Soon the group was bathed in light as the lights were set outside their circle, pointing in. In that pleasant atmosphere they ate a meal and used the latrines that were quickly set in place. The tanks had been emptied earlier when they came to the river. New water and chemicals were in the tanks. By the time everyone had used them they had finished eating.

When Jim had everyone arranged properly the lights were shut off and the generators repacked. Everyone turned on their night vision glasses, having put fresh batteries in, and they began their exploration of the lost city of Z. With infrared lighting everything was cast in a greenish glow, but the cameraman could see clearly and film every step of the exploration.

First, they moved up nine steps to a terrace that surrounded the entire city. Dr. Gregg spent most of the next day measuring the city, discovering that it was built in a circle with a circumference of roughly 6,000 *thatkiys* or paces, a measurement popular with the Inca people. This was deducted by taking the diameter, and then using that to formulate the circumference or ($c = \pi \times d$). Round and square buildings were built with the temple dominating the structures at the center.

The temple was round, built on a terrace of nine levels, with steps set north, south, east, and west. To the north of the temple was the palace of the ruler. Each building had scorched walls from torches that were used for light, the blackened walls mute testimony of former torches, and several possessed lamps, with nine bowls in which oil would burn to provide light.

It was in the temple itself that Dr. Gregg discovered the entrance to the mines. Experimenting with a lever he found that seemed to have no purpose he turned it and a section of the floor dropped a full two feet, and then rolled back beneath the floor. A stairway led down.

"Everyone take out the flashlights for this exploration." Jim said, removing his night vision goggles. The cameraman attached powerful lights to his unit.

He estimated they traveled nearly two hundred meters beneath the temple floor when they came out in a series of caves. Exploration of the first cave filled everyone with wonder. It was full of opal that glittered a myriad of colors in their lights. Only a small portion of the mine had been worked. Above in the city they had seen the results of worked opal everywhere.

It was in a deeper cave that they discovered the skeletons of nearly a hundred people. Dr. Gregg had entered the cave when he suddenly turned and pushed everyone back. They climbed up the rough-hewn steps and out of the cave and he came last, gasping for air.

"Methane gas!" He said through his gasps.

"What were they after in that mine?" Jim asked, his own lungs feeling funny. "And are we safe out here?"

"We're good here, skipper." Neff said checking his meters.

"They were after a huge vein of gold." Dr. Gregg finally said as he regained his breath. "I feel sick!" He complained. Jim looked at him with concern, noting his pallor as he stood shakily, his hands clutched to his stomach.

Suddenly he bent over and lost his lunch. His wife knelt beside him and offered a wipe. Accepting it gratefully he wiped his mouth and face. Doc bent down and offered him two pills and a canteen. Smiling wanly at the doctor he took the pills and swallowed them. It was several moments before he returned the canteen and stood shakily to his feet.

"All those skeletons are facing this way. They must have realized something was wrong and begun heading back up." Doctor Penny said, looking down with his powerful searchlight. "Poor people never made it out of this mine!"

"They must have opened a source for the methane." Dr. Gregg nodded.

"It's a good thing none of us smoke!" Neff said with a grin.

"None of those people down there have torches." Dr. Penny stated.

"That's very probably why no one ever knew what happened to these people." Dr. Gregg said, allowing Jim to steady him on his feet. He drank some water from his canteen. "The rest of them are probably down further and dead also. My guess is that once they opened the fissure of gas it killed them all."

"How sad!" Cecilia said softly. "That explains all the children's skulls we found in the temple burial chamber."

"Yes, I suppose it does." Dr. Gregg said softly. "Although there was a very bad influenza that killed many. I'm thinking that most of the people that lived down here died from that. This was the final blow. I don't believe any survivors came out of this underground city."

"That explains why it remained hidden for so long." Jim said, nodding in agreement.

"People will be coming here in droves to study and preserve the city itself, and probably to mine the rest of the riches we've seen here." Dr. Mirelle said.

"Neff, will you come up with me and Mark, and keep us posted of any dangerous gasses?" Dr. Gregg said to the geologist.

"Sure thing, Dr. Museum." Neff said with a grin.

After that they found only one other cave, at a lower level, that had a high concentration of the methane gas. However, the richness of the gems and other stones would net a tidy sum for the company, and the government mining them. The notoriety of finding the lost city of Z after all these years would help with the company's reputation and further cement the bona fide cover they maintained. Jim was quite pleased.

Twenty-one days passed quickly, too quickly for some, while the teams studied, mapped, photographed, and uncovered the secrets of the lost city of Z. Each evening Dr. Gregg lectured in front of the camera with the help of Dr. Mirelle and Dr. Van Haaten, effectively demonstrating their theories on the civilization. None of them hesitated to describe both the good and the bad aspects of the politics and religion of the Inca people. Nor did the academics miss the opportunity to compare the civilization to modern civilizations that created horrendous injustice in sacrificing innocent blood.

After three weeks beneath the ground everyone was quite ready to leave the caves behind and travel back to their base camp. Knowing that Xun and her minions might be waiting above Jim took every precaution. Returning to the vent through which they'd gained access was impossible, and Jim didn't want to leave the underground river turned off so that anyone could have access to the caves. Instead they returned to the vent through which they'd extracted Xun and her brother.

Under cover of darkness Sniper climbed the vent in total silence, using infrared technology to mask their presence in the chimney. After nearly three hours of steady climbing Rock raised his head above the opening. Not far away six men camped, with only one on guard. Rock took a long time to study the camp and sleeping men, including the guard, before making hand motions to his three companions. In short order they knew how many men were above and where they were.

As silent as the grave they climbed from the chimney. Knowing that any man could cry out and raise the rest endangering everyone the men considered killing them, but then discarded that idea because they were in a foreign country and everyone knew they were there. Rock took the guard in a sleeper hold, keeping his hold for a full three minutes until he was sure his man was unconscious. When he released his hold, the man began to breathe again. He lowered him gently to the ground.

Norm struck the man on his left hard, just under the ear, and the man on his right equally hard on the bridge of the nose. Both men jerked, but made no sound as they slipped into unconsciousness. Earl and Lloyd were equally proficient and all six military men were out cold. That left the government official.

Using restraint ties they bound the soldiers, gagged them, and then dragged them away from each other and hogtied them. Through all of this the official remained asleep, his snores sounding loudly from his tent. Other less acceptable noises also traveled through the soft tent walls. Softly and quietly Norm unzipped the tent door. The noise, he knew, would draw any insects on the tent itself.

Nothing venomous appeared and he breathed a sigh of relief. Stepping into the tent he drew his pistol, flipped the safety off, and used it to rap on the official's nose. The man started awake, staring in surprise at the spectral figure standing over him. His eyes centered on the gun and he began to shake.

"Please! Do not kill me!" He cried out in Spanish.

Norm grabbed the man's wrist and dragged him from the cot, tipping it over as he did so, and out of the tent.

"Stretch him out and stake him down!" He ordered. Rock looked at him with one eyebrow raised but went about the task with Lord Lee without comment. When the official was stretched out, cursing and crying for mercy the whole time Norm found an empty cooking pot with a flat lid and wandered off where the official could watch him.

He made a great show of looking on the ground for something and finally found one. Carefully he put the pot over the spider, and slid the flat top beneath it, trapping the spider inside. Because the pan was aluminum the spider made a lot of noise as it moved over the lid, trying to escape.

Norm brought it back and put it on the official's large stomach. The man felt the movement and his eyes stretched wide. Holding the pan down Norm grabbed the edge of the lid.

"Now, my good friend. You're going to tell us everything we want to know, or I'm going to shake this pot, make this wandering spider very angry, and remove the lid and let it bite you several times. Do you understand me?" Norm said quietly in his cultured English voice.

"You would be guilty of murder!" The man sputtered in perfect English.

"Yeah, but my guys are the only ones who will ever know about that. To everyone else who finds you on your cot, in your tent, with the spider living off your blood, it will look like death by accident. You'll have no bruises or other marks on you, other than the marks from these ropes." Norm said conversationally. He shook the pot and the spider went berserk inside.

"I think that spider's angry enough to pump all its venom into this bloke!" Lee said with a low chuckle. "I wonder how long it will take him to die?" He looked up at Norm with a feral grin and Norm smiled in return, giving a single nod.

"What do you wish to know?" The man was weeping in fear now.

"Does your government know you're out here with six soldiers?" Norm asked. He watched the official's eyes and they told him the answer while the man spilled his story.

With a sigh he righted the pan, put it in the fire and put a rock on top. The spider actually screamed in the pan. It was a high pitched and hideous sound. Norm returned to the official.

"Let him up." He said. Rock cut the ropes and the official sat up and untied himself.

"You are in great trouble, senior!" The official said smugly. Something exploded against his face and the official hit the ground hard, his head bouncing twice.

"Not as much as you." Norm said quietly, shaking out his fist.

CHAPTER 38

Mid-morning came before the last person was hauled up the chimney. That was JR, and he tested himself as he climbed the ropes, reaching the top with a time just a second short of Rock's top score. Sweating and breathing hard he bent over at the top and took in the scene. Six guards were groaning from the cramps, hogtied and on the ground. The official was sitting on a stump and Doc Wozniac was working on his face. It looked like he'd been hit by a pile driver.

After a long drink from his canteen JR moved to his teammates and they compared times on the climb. Penelope wrinkled her nose at her husband's sweaty stench and punched his arm. He winked at her. She'd been only eight seconds slower, and that was a good score, putting her twelfth in the group.

"Where's Delta?" He asked as Jim came over to congratulate his brother. JR had beaten him by two tenths of a second.

"On the way for the chopper. Great climb!" Jim added, bumping shoulders with his brother.

"They were contesting against one another on the climb up?" Gwyneth asked her husband. He grinned at her.

"They contest in just about every physical activity. It helps them stay sharp." He answered.

Doc Wozniac finished patching up the official's face, fixing his broken nose. He put the final piece of tape over the man's damaged eye carefully.

"You need to be very careful to clean this eye with purified water. An infection could be very bad." He counseled the official. "What's your name?"

"I am Hefé Arturo Morales, Minister of Antiquities for the state of Mato Grosso!" He said haughtily.

"Arty! Don't get uppity with me!" FM said, stepping up to the official.

"That's Hefé Arturo Morales!" He spat. FM backhanded him hard enough to slam him to the ground. His ear began to bleed and Doc Wozniac helped him up and bandaged it, his face stoic.

"I'm afraid I'm going to spend a lot of time bandaging your wounds if you keep this up, friend." He said quietly. Arturo endured the bandaging and then stood before FM.

"You will be arrested!" He said.

FM's hand closed around his throat and he lifted the man from the ground with one hand. Arturo was struggling to breathe, with both hands on FM's wrist. When he looked into FM's eyes, he didn't like what he saw there. FM walked over to the chimney and held the man over the hole. Still struggling the man looked into the pit and paled. If FM dropped him, he would plunge to his death.

Then a giant was there, a huge man with huge muscles, who grabbed Arturo's wrist and lifted him higher, pushing FM away. FM let go with a grin and a wink at Sturdy. Sturdy looked at the struggling official and shook his head sadly.

"Release me!" Arturo demanded through clenched teeth.

Sturdy's arm dropped and the man screamed. The giant had never let go of him, simply dropped his arm. Now he lifted Arturo up again, his arm fully extended, and Arturo realized that he was dealing with a very strong man. He kept silent. Nodding Sturdy brought him to the very edge and set his feet on the ground.

"I'm not sure how strong this man's heart is, gentlemen. Let's not frighten him anymore. He's obviously a very foolish man. Just leave him alone." Dr. Penny said. Arturo noticed how small the good doctor looked next to the giant and swallowed hard.

"Let's see if I can get anywhere with the little turd." Pippi said. She grabbed the official and pulled him away from the edge of the chimney. When he resisted and tried to get away from her, she put him in a submission hold that had him screaming. After he had become hoarse from screaming, she leaned in and whispered in his ear.

"Behave, little man, or I will peel the skin from your scrotum and penis, pour salt and pepper juice on the exposed area, and watch you squirm and scream until you have no voice!" Her knife appeared in front of his face and Arturo went pale and silent. To his horror he felt his bladder give way through the fear and he closed his eyes as if to hide from the shame.

"Hey Doc! Let me borrow your scalpel!" Pen shouted. Doc Wozniac walked over and handed the scalpel to her without comment. Arturo fainted.

"Jeeze Louise! What did you threaten him with?" FM asked with a wide grin.

Will Penny put his stethoscope against the man's chest, moved it around, and then switched to his back. He shook his head.

"His heart is beating very fast. I suggest a rest period for our foolish little official." He said, looking sternly at everyone.

Without comment Pen handed the scalpel back to Doc Wozniac. He looked at it for a moment and put it back in his kit. As he did so he asked her in a conversational tone what she'd threatened the man with. When she told him he blanched.

"Remind me not to make you cranky, miss!" He said with a smile.

"If he starts blustering again, just hand me the scalpel." She replied.

Arturo, however, had reached his limit. He remained quiet, if irritable and cross, and kept his comments to himself. The huge helicopter came and carried the first group back toward their base camp. Twenty minutes later it returned and the rest of them were ready to go.

Jim nodded to the official once as he boarded the helicopter and the rear-loading platform began to rise. "You can release your men now. We alone know the secret of getting to the city and the mines. When you're ready to honor your agreement with my company you may have that secret. We'll even help you find the city and mines." Jim waved and disappeared into the aircraft.

After the dust cleared Arturo cut the men free. They rested in their camp for the day and all night before going down the chimney. Arturo, too fat to make such a climb, waited above for three days. His men did not return, and they were never heard from again. Alone and afraid he made the hike back to the camp, hungry and thirsty.

Arturo stumbled into the main building of the camp to discover the governor of his state, several state dignitaries, and other men he did not know, including the President of Brazil, whom he recognized. They were all seated and watching the film of the discovery of the lost city of Z. When the door opened, they all looked at him, and Don Patterson stopped the computer feed to the projector.

"My men went down, but they did not return." He said quietly.

"You sent unskilled men into that hellhole?" Dr. Gregg sputtered. "Are you mad?"

"You came back unharmed!" Arturo blustered.

"Yes! I am a trained archaeologist, with experience in this type of thing. Which of your soldiers was a trained archaeologist who could help the men discover the traps that were set by the Inca?" Alistair replied dryly.

"Let's get this gent a shower, a change of clothes, some fresh water, and a good meal before we go further." Abe said quietly.

"Yes. Do that Arturo. Shower, change, and eat. You will feel better." The governor of his state said commandingly. Arturo swallowed nervously, looking at his superior before nodding.

Arturo followed Norm out of the main building to the showers, and after a good shower, and clean clothes, he drank and ate to his heart's content. When he was finished, he felt much better. Before he rose from the table Norm sat down opposite.

"Arty, you'd better listen, and listen good. The President of your country has come down to personally see that the Governor honors our contract. No one gets to the city without that. If they find out you tried to arrest us, you might not have a job. Be smart for once." Norm nodded and stood, waiting for Arturo to get up.

With drooping shoulders, the official stood up and returned to the main room, where the film was drawing to a close. His eyes widened in wonder at the opal in the walls of the first mine. As the film drew to a close, he sighed with relief. There was no footage of his men trussed up and hogtied, and of him in his shame.

A new picture flashed on the wall, the waterfall roaring out of the opening in the side of the mountain. As Arturo watched he saw dark figures falling with the water, six of them, and he knew the fate of his men.

"I did not know, Excellency!" He said immediately, his hand spread in supplication.

"You didn't ask." Dr. Gregg said sadly. "Those six men made a terrible mistake in judgment. And now they are dead." He added.

"They were soldiers, trained men. Arturo did not know they could not accomplish the task of finding the city and guarding it against looters." The governor said softly. His eyes were on Arturo and the man nodded.

There were news people, national and international news people to record the event. Jim smiled to himself. He'd put the whole country over a barrel and they now had to honor their agreement. The governor of Mato Grosso looked at him bleakly and Jim winked and smiled.

Jim's team returned to the vent, erecting an elevator to take people down into the corridor that led to the city. The CH53 flew in a huge generator to provide lights. There was a water purification system added near the vent and pipe that led all the way into the city so that those camping there could drink pure water. Soon they had everything in place to allow for a revealing of the lost city.

Jim, Wade, and Dr. Gregg led the exploration team from Brazil into the lost city of Z, showing them how to find the mines. After cautioning them to be careful of the poisonous gasses Jim turned away from the mine entrance. One of the leaders of the explorers touched his arm.

"Do you not wish to see more?" The man asked.

"This is now your discovery and site. Dr. Gutierrez is an old friend of Dr. Gregg. He has assured us that he will copy us on everything he discovers in the mines and city. We wish you good fortune and safety." Jim replied. "I am a man of the sea, not of caves!" He added.

Walking back to their base camp the three men talked of what they had seen, and the amazing engineering skills of the Inca people. Jim listened to Wade and his father talk for nearly half the hike, thinking about what they were saying. At last Alistair realized that he and Wade had been monopolizing the conversation. He looked up at Jim.

"Add something to our scintillating conversation!" He offered.

"We were made in the image of God." Jim said quietly. "Look around you. God made all of this. Talk about creative design! Every multicolored bird, flower, tree, plant, insect, reptile, amphibian, arachnid, and mammal is His design! That we would be able to design simple and complex engineering is logical.

"But look what they did with the gifts He gave! They worshipped the creation, rather than the Creator. Every time they sacrificed a human being, they wasted a unique life, ended a unique DNA strand, totally unaware of how offensive to God that was. That culture was so steeped in darkness that light meant nothing to them. Didn't they have to see it, even as we see it? Sure! But they didn't appreciate it or understand it.

"As a result, they are now a defunct culture. Too many cultures we study have followed this path. Yet those who study the culture get so caught up in the cleverness and artistic design they miss the Master Designer, the one who gave us these amazing engineering abilities and building skills.

"Our ships are technological marvels. Designed by human beings, someone could study them, and be lost in the marvel of their making, and never see the brilliance behind the making of the mind that designed it! I find that sad." Jim said, surprised at his own intensity.

"Yes. Many will read about our exploration, and watch the film, but will miss the real genius behind it all. Every time we paused to pray before moving on will be overlooked or ridiculed by all but those who know the Lord. Even the riches our company gets from this endeavor will impress people more than the One who created those riches!" Alistair sighed. "We serve an amazing God who has willingly introduced Himself to us, but so many ignore Him.

"Yet for those of us who know the Lord, it is even more wonderful, and those things have no hold over us. They belong to Him and are to be used for His work. Every person on this crew is now independently wealthy, but I doubt if one will step away from this amazing work, son. In a way, you are a steward of the people He's given you. That's one of the things I admire about you."

Jim blushed deeply at the compliment and looked over his father at Wade who was grinning and nodding.

"I've always felt that God wanted me with you and JR, Shep." Wade said. "Now I know it. I'm doing what He wants me to do. That's what matters."

"Yes. That is what matters. It is only when we stop doing what we know He wants us to do that we make the mistake David made when he stayed behind instead of going off to war with his troops. We get side-tracked and that's when we get into trouble." Alistair said. He looked up at Wade and smiled. "I hope you don't mind when I call you one of my boys." He said.

"Jim's dad always did. I guess his second dad can do the same!" Wade replied. He clapped Alistair on the shoulder. "How you holdin' up, Pops?" He asked facetiously.

"You will remember, I'm sure with chagrin, that most of the women on the crew work with me, young man!" Alistair said with mischievous eyes. "I don't get even, I get ahead!" He added, shaking his finger.

"Gee, Dad! Does this mean I don't get the car tonight?" Wade said mockingly. All three men laughed.

That night, at dinner, Alistair indeed had his revenge and it was sweet. As soon as Wade sat down at his place at the table Lisle sat in his lap, running her hands over his face and snuggling into him. Carol Lowe came over and jerked her away and sat down in his lap and did the same. Angela Rysdale followed, and then Heidi Van Haaten. Rachel Hague, Stephanie Morris, and Lynn Ross were next, and then the Millstein sisters took over. The entire performance lasted through dinner and Wade was forced to look at his cold food, a congealing mess on his plate with a look of consternation on his face.

His face was beet red and he sat through all the laughter, looking at Dr. Gregg.

"I rue the day!" He finally said, bursting out laughing. "I rue the day!"

But the joke wasn't over. Abe came over, his muscles swelling and a scowl on his face. "You don't like my cooking?" He asked dangerously.

"I spent a long time working on that sauce!" JimJim said, crossing his arms in front of his chest. "You'd think you'd be more appreciative of our efforts in this primitive kitchen!"

Bob Hinkle just whisked the plate away while Wade was looking at JimJim and when he looked down, he puckered his lip and acted like he was going to cry. That was Barbara and Mary Anne's cue. They hugged and kissed him until his face was blotched red with lipstick. By the time the laughter died down, and tears of mirth were wiped away, Abe produced a fresh plate of food for Wade and everyone sat and watched him eat it, much to his dismay. It was a perfect ending to a great adventure.

Jim said so and Alistair put his finger up to his nose, as he often did when he was about to reveal a secret.

"Near perfect." He said, pulling a disk from inside his coat and holding it up. It was made of copper. "I hold in my hand a map I borrowed from the City of Z." He said, his eyes drifting around the now silent table.

"A map to what?" Gwyneth asked, excitement in her voice.

"That, I don't know . . . yet!" Dr. Gregg said with relish. "The language predates Quechua. I've never seen this writing before, but I believe it may lead us to a new discovery of an amazing civilization.

Then again, it may be a foreign coin traded by the Inca for something else." He grinned. "I'll study it though."

"I take it you didn't mention this little 'discovery' to anyone else." Jim said.

"Actually, I did!" Alistair surprised Jim. "I told Dr. Gutierrez but when I began patting all my pockets to find it, he waved me off and told me to tell him about it later."

"Just don't bring us back where there are poisonous caterpillars and wandering spiders and venomous snakes!" Lisle said with feeling.

"Amen!" The girls all chorused.

"Oh no!" FM quipped. "This will lead us to a place where there are giant man-eating sharks and angry whales that will attack our smaller boats!"

"Wow! That sounds cool!" Chief said, pretending to swoon with delight.

"I don't follow." FM said quizzically, smiling at Chief as he slowly rose from the floor and took his seat again.

"I've never heard of a Blackfoot Indian that was eaten by a shark." Chief said calmly. "But I have heard of some crazy pale faces that were eaten by sharks!"

"Let's put him in the shark cage next time we're around the reef, mates!" Ox quipped. "I'll bet great white's like dark meat as well as light!"

"Was that like a racial remark?" Loony asked, looking sternly at Ox.

"He doesn't like black folks." Lee Roy said with a straight face.

"But you're . . ." Loony broke off.

"I'm what?" Lee Roy asked.

"He was going to say that you're black." PU said with a grin.

"You are." Chance said.

"I am?" Lee Roy said plaintively.

"Yes, you are." Hammer said with a wide grin. "Bruddar!" He added in a mock Jamaican accent.

"I'm an Aussie. We don't speak Jamaican." Lee Roy replied, his face still a blank mask showing no humor.

"Jamaican's speak English!" Hammer exclaimed.

"We don't speak that either." PU replied with a straight face.

Jim listened to the continued banter and funny remarks and laughed long into the evening. Later, when he and Cecilia lay in their tiny cabin enjoying the cooler air stirred by the ceiling fan, he thanked the Lord for his creative and witty crew. Whatever lay ahead he knew that he had the best crew any man could lead. His heart was humble as he named each crewmember in his prayer, ending with his beloved Cecilia. She stretched and kissed him when he finished.

"I like the way you say my name." She said, snuggled into him, and fell asleep.